FIRST COMES LOVE

BOOK I OF THE SILVER SPOON TRILOGY

NICOLE FRENCH

R
raglan

To all the moms (single or otherwise):
You are beautiful. You are seen.

PROLOGUE I

Francesca

"I think you should wear the red one. You looked fantastic in red."

Standing in front of the over-the-door mirror in the bedroom I shared with my older sister Kate, I held up the little crimson slip dress against my body, then traded it for a green one on the other hanger. And then switched them back again.

"Sure, red looks good," I told Kate. "Just like it does on every other dark-haired Italian woman. Should I start singing 'Mambo Italiano'? Or maybe talk like one of the Mario Brothers wherever I go? Eat nothing but spaghetti and meatballs?"

"Classic is different from cliché," Kate replied from the other side of the door, where she was pawing through the meager options in our closet.

Her side mostly consisted of thrifted goods and vintage finds. My half was the wardrobe of a college student—nothing special, mostly knockoffs and fast fashion. The few dresses I owned were leftovers from high school dances and a few bits of cheap clubwear. Not that they had ever gotten much use. All four of my sisters and my older brother had called me a shut-in more than once. My friends said I cared more about books than having fun like a normal twenty-three-year-old.

Four weeks ago, they were right. Four weeks ago, I was still a virgin.

But that was before I met him.

I'd been with friends, enjoying a much-needed night out after finishing our midterm papers. I had a plan. Have a beer or two. Laugh at a few jokes, gossip, then go home for some much-needed sleep after a week of very late nights.

This plan did not involve a six-five, black-haired, devastatingly handsome British man named Xavier Sato. A half-Japanese aspiring chef looking for a job in the city, Xavier talked like Mr. Darcy, but looked more like a young John Wick. Seriously, you try staying a wall-flower when the twin of a young Keanu Reeves starts chatting you up with an English accent.

And once those clothes were off…well, let's just say he was singularly Xavier. No fictional hero would ever measure up again.

And so, while I was supposed to be studying and Xavier was supposed to be interviewing, we had instead spent the majority of the last twenty-some days in his hotel room. Naked.

"I can't get enough of you," he had murmured as his tongue tickled the crook of my neck just last night. *"You're a flavor I've never tasted. I must have more."*

It hadn't mattered that no man had ever looked at me, mousy wall-flower Frankie Zola, that way and there was no reason one should start now. Xavier's azure eyes had seared over my body like a crazy blue flame, and I flew straight into the fire like a moth.

"There's a reason why Sophia loved her red dresses," Kate said as she emerged from the closet empty-handed.

I snorted. "I don't look a thing like Sophia Loren. For one, I'm almost a foot shorter. And my tits are the size of apples, not melons."

Sophia Loren, otherwise known as my very Italian grandmother's favorite actress, was statuesque, buxom, and the definition of sex. At a few inches over five feet and the shortest of the six Zola kids, I was less statue, more doll. Admittedly, I'd developed a few more curves since high school, but my breasts were still small, my green eyes a bit too large for my face. My hair was the biggest thing about me, a thick, untamable mane of inky, almost black waves shared by the rest of my siblings.

"Look," Kate said as she came to stand behind me. "It's just like the dress Sophia wears in *Scandal in Sorrento*. The one where she dances around trying to make that guy jealous."

I shook my head. "Old movies are Mattie's obsession, not mine."

"Please. *Nonna's* watched that film so many times she wore out the DVD. I know you remember that scene."

That was true. We had all grown up with movies like that playing in the background.

"The dress is about the shoulders, not tits." Kate tugged the straps outward so they were just off my shoulders, then gathered my hair and twisted it up. "Remember how Sophia shimmies and drives everyone wild? You'll drive Xavier crazy too. Let him know for certain what he's leaving behind when he goes back to Merry Old England."

At the mention of exactly *why* I was looking for the perfect dress, I stiffened. After four perfect weeks, Xavier was leaving. Not permanently, he said, despite the fact that none of the positions he had applied for wanted to hire someone foreign. The obvious truth was that we lived in completely different countries. He was starting his life as a chef, and I was getting ready to begin graduate school. We were clearly traveling in different directions. For now, anyway.

The ping of my phone interrupted before I could reply. Kate grabbed it off my desk and started reading the message out loud.

"Hey!" I snapped. "Give me that."

"'Francesca,'" she intoned in an unnecessarily deep and truly terrible British accent. "'I can't wait to see you for my last night'—wait, wait, wait. This guy calls you *Francesca*? Who is he, Father Deflorio?"

I rolled my eyes at the mention of our local priest. "Ew, no. And for the record, I happen to like it." I grabbed my phone and read the rest of his brief message.

Xavier: Francesca, I can't wait to see you for my last night. Promise me I'll get the full 24 hours before I go.

"If it's his last night, then you're definitely wearing the dress. It's on the house. Just tell everyone you got it from the shop."

I glanced back at the mirror one last time. I definitely didn't look like a shut-in now. And Kate was right. I'd never forget Xavier. I wanted to make sure he didn't forget me either.

"Fine, fine. I'll wear the damn dress." I tapped out a quick response.

Me: I promise. In a fancy new dress too.

Then I flopped back onto my twin bed and sighed. "I can't believe you're abandoning me here with *Nonna* and the brats to sell used clothes."

After five years of scrimping and saving, Kate was finally living her dream, buying a vintage clothing shop in Riverdale. She was the third of the five Zola kids to fly the coop since we had come to live with our grandparents as kids.

I was happy for her. I really was. But right now, I could only think of one thing. "How am I going to survive without you?"

"Same way you survived when Mattie and Lea went." Kate sat down next to me and pushed her chin-length hair behind one ear. "It's time, Fran. We all have to leave the nest eventually. Mattie joined the Marines, and look at him now. Big shot with the Brooklyn DA. Lea and Mike are happy running the garage and making a zillion babies. Now it's my turn. I can't live in my grandmother's house forever."

I sniffed. Was it really so bad here? Okay, so maybe the shabby Bronx row house wasn't a Park Avenue mansion. And yeah, maybe it hadn't been the same since *Nonno* died. More than ten years later, my grandmother was still in widows' weeds. But it was still just a few blocks from the parish school where all of us had learned our letters, and from the bakeries and the fishmongers and market where everyone knew our names, even though we lived in a city of eight million.

I looked around at the smudged white walls, the battered wood furniture, and the faded lace bedspreads.

It was home. I couldn't imagine living anywhere else.

Before I could say as much, we were interrupted by a scream across the hall.

"Marie! I swear, if you don't give me back my phone, you're gonna wish you were never born!"

Joni, the youngest at nineteen, engaging in her fourth battle today with Marie, who was only ten months older. When our parents got busy back then, they really got busy.

Kate and I both rolled our eyes.

"I can't imagine why you would want to escape this sanctuary of peace and quiet," I said as Marie threatened to tear Joni's hair out by the roots.

The shouting descended down the stairs. My phone pinged again.

Xavier: You could wear a bin liner and still look good. But I can't wait to see it. And peel it off.

Kate's eyebrows practically touched the ceiling as she read the message over my shoulder. "Maybe you should finish school over there. I can't really imagine any place would be better than England at producing English Literature scholars."

"Oh my God, *privacy*!" I snapped as I turned away to hide my phone and my face.

I wasn't going to tell my sister that for a hot minute, I had thought about changing everything for someone I had met weeks ago. I was halfway through a master's in English Literature here at CUNY. This fall, I'd be applying for PhD programs all over the country, though the current plan was to attend Columbia or NYU if I could get in. I could slip Cambridge and Oxford in there, couldn't I? After all, I had the grades. There were scholarships for the fourth daughter of six who lived with her grandmother, weren't there?

But those plans I had? They didn't involve crossing the Atlantic and losing more than a year of credits, not to mention family and friends. Unlike my mother and my grandmother, I was *not* going to change the trajectory of my life for a man. No way. No how.

"It's just a fling, Katie," I said. "I'll enjoy it while it lasts, and then get back to work."

"A fling who popped your cherry?" She tipped her head knowingly.

I sat up a little straighter, willing myself not to succumb to my sister's X-ray gaze. She was the only one who knew about that.

"Well, fine," she said at last. "A fling is good for you anyway. You've been the perfect Catholic middle child for way too long. Finish your degree, then it will be *your* turn to fly the coop. And by then, you'll be ready." With a squeeze of my shoulder, she stood up. "I'm going downstairs to grab some food. I'll be up in a few to check your makeup."

I nodded, then got up and went back to our shared vanity, which was strewn with mostly Kate's makeup.

Ten minutes later, I'd done what I thought was a half-decent job at mimicking Sophia Loren's signature cat-eye.

"Not bad, professor," Kate said when she returned holding a bowl of pasta. "Did you use the Scotch tape trick I showed you?"

I turned from the vanity, still holding the tube of liquid liner. "I did. You're right. It was pretty easy. I—" Before I could finish the sentence, nausea seized my throat. "Jesus. What are you eating?"

Kate frowned at her bowl. "Just last night's Bolognese. Why? You want some?"

"*No*. It smells like a pig died in that bowl. Oh, *God*."

My stomach lurched. The black stilettos flew off as I sprinted out of the room and across the hall, barely making it to the bathroom in time to empty my stomach's contents into the toilet.

Kate appeared in the doorway, looking concerned.

"Kate," I breathed. "Get that thing out of here!"

She examined the offending pasta, then jogged it back downstairs to the kitchen. I retched again.

God. What was wrong with me? Two seconds ago I had been ready to fly across the city just to jump Xavier's bones—unusual, even if he *was* the hottest thing I'd ever known. Now I was ready to curl up and die on the faded linoleum. The only time I'd ever heard of someone getting sick like this was when women were—

I froze.

Oh, God. No. *No no no no no*. That wasn't possible. Was it?

I did a quick count in my head. In the whirlwind of the last weeks, I'd completely forgotten something that *should* have arrived about a week ago.

Eight days, to be exact. And the only reason I knew that was because other than this moment, I had never, ever been late.

I pushed myself up from the floor and flushed away the evidence of my state. My skin was clammy as I brushed my teeth, and all the blood felt like it had drained from my head. But the nausea was gone.

For now.

"Oh, God," I whispered, not sure if I was speaking to myself or the big man upstairs as I stumbled back to my room and plopped onto the bed again. "Oh, God. You have *got* to be kidding me."

"What's wrong?"

I sat up as Kate entered. One look at my face and she was on the bed in the less than a second.

"What's the matter? Are you sick?"

I swallowed weakly. There was no hiding anything from my sisters. There was no point. Not in this house.

"I think—I think I'm pregnant," I said in the smallest voice I could muster. "Oh my God, Katie. I'm pregnant."

"Stop." Kate set her hand over mine. She was preternaturally calm, though shock flared in the back of her cool green-eyed expression. "You don't know anything yet. I'll run to the bodega and get you a test. Don't freak out before you know anything for sure."

But I knew. Despite all the sense Kate was talking, I knew right then. I could feel my boobs getting sorer and bigger with every second, could sense my body slipping into a deep, intense fatigue. It was exactly like Sister Fatima, our high school health teacher, had told us it would be. Okay, yes, maybe it was too soon to be experiencing any of these symptoms. And sure, maybe I was imagining all of it, but *I knew.*

I was pregnant.

Then another thought occurred. "Xavier. Holy shit, Kate. He's only known me a month. He's going to freak!"

My sister bit her lip, clearly searching and struggling for some way to argue the point. Then her face relaxed. "Look, I've seen his messages.

And besides that, I've seen your face every day since you met him. Fling or not, the man is crazy about you, Frankie."

I swallowed. I couldn't pretend I hadn't wondered if there was more to this connection than sex. After all, a man who only wanted to screw you didn't take you to the best restaurants in town, did he? He didn't blow off all his meetings just to kiss you for an extra ten minutes. He didn't tell you he loved you two days earlier in a haze of champagne and confirm it with a bouquet of lilies the next morning.

But he was leaving. And so, despite everything we'd said, I'd decided, in the end, it was just the throes of first…well, if not love, then lust. The inevitable attachment that came from losing my virginity to someone as perfect as Xavier Sato.

But maybe I was wrong.

"You're right," I said. "I'll just be…I'll be straight with him."

"Silver lining?" Kate offered. "Maybe it's not your last night together after all."

I gave my sister a weak smile, then turned over to text Xavier. What, I didn't know. Just…something. I needed a connection. Make sure I really *would* see him for a conversation that was bound to change both of our lives.

Apparently, he had the same idea. When I picked my phone off my pillow, an icon alerted me to an email from the man himself.

Email? Why hadn't he just texted, like usual?

I pulled up the message. And immediately lost my breath.

"Frankie?" Kate asked. "Fran, what is it? What happened?"

Wordlessly, I handed her the phone. I couldn't say it. I couldn't speak at all.

Kate saved us both by reading the message out loud.

Francesca,

I'm so sorry to have to write to you this way.

I wasn't completely honest with you when we met. My trip to New York wasn't just for potential business. I was actually considering moving here permanently, something I wanted even more after meeting you.

Unfortunately, I just found out that my fiancée has been diagnosed with a brain tumor. I'm sure you can understand how impossible that makes it for me to break it off now. Regardless of what I might feel for you, I can't do this to her. Or you.

For now, the restaurant is on hold while I support someone who genuinely needs me. I'm all she has. I can't abandon her now.

I truly hope you have an amazing life, Francesca. I know I'll always wonder.

— Xavier

"Fiancée? That son of a bitch." Kate tossed the phone to the bed. "I'll kill him. Well, more precisely, I'm going to call Mattie and *he'll* kill him."

"No, you're not." When I found my voice, it sounded like stone. "You're not going to tell Mattie anything. Or anyone else. Not until I decide what I'm going to do."

"And what's that, Fran?" Kate asked, a little too sharply. "What are you going to do next with this two-timing asshole?"

I closed my eyes and focused on breathing. In. Out. In. Out.

Somewhere deep inside me, another being was going to have its first heartbeats. It was going to grow into a living, breathing person who would need more from me than I had ever thought I could give.

I knew myself. As terrified as I was, as worried, as completely blindsided, already I was attached to the baby growing inside me.

The popcorn texture of the ceiling blurred. But the crucifix on the wall next to the vanity still gleamed.

"The only thing I can do," I said. "Let him go."

PROLOGUE II
FIVE YEARS LATER

Xavier

Everything is better pickled.

All right, maybe not everything. But everything is better *with* something pickled, or at least something fermented.

Salty. Sweet. Savory. Bitter. Sour.

No meal is complete without all five components. It was one of the main principles of *washoku*, which I'd picked up during the summers I'd spent in Japan with my grandfather. The Sato family had worked at the oldest miso factory in Japan for nearly eight hundred years, through three shogunates and into the twenty-first century. They still made miso the old way, in huge cedar vats of mashed soybeans, koji, and salt, pressed with pyramids of hundred-pound river rocks for three years. The result was a dark brown fermented paste that could turn even a cup of hot water into something that stuck to your belly and satisfied even better than a plate of fish and chips. Umami gold.

More than that, it was exactly what I had needed to earn my first Michelin star. Ten years later, I owned an empire of fusion restaurants that spanned Western Europe. Not too shabby for the bastard son of an Englishman and a Japanese cook. Once, I looked forward to the day when my father would turn up in one of my restaurants. Then, after he died, I wondered if anyone else on his side of the family would take his place. My uncle, maybe. The grandmother I never knew. Maybe an odd cousin or two.

Not that I had any intention of recognizing their reservations either.

In my experience, it was the sour that ended up in European cuisine the least. Definitely here in England. Sure, you had gherkins, or maybe a bit of onion crisps or beetroot. And yeah, there was the national tendency to toss a little vinegar on a plate of chips.

The sour is supposed to add brightness to a dish. And famous English food, while comforting on a cold rainy day (for some, anyway), is anything but that.

I stood up from the pot of creamy parsnip soup and shook my head. "Why are you making me a traditional French soup in a fusion restaurant, chef?"

The broad, slippery mouth of Jean Le Ver, head chef of my newest restaurant, Chez Miso, fell open.

"It's classic," he argued immediately, vowels dripping with French disdain. "I have used variations of this soup on two other menus in London alone. It is my trademark."

I rolled my eyes. These arseholes were all the same. Had Le Ver come from another Michelin-starred restaurant in London? Yes. And had he single-handedly reinvented French cuisine on this side of the Channel? Absolutely. I understood that. It was why I poached him in the first place.

But like every other award-winning chef new to my payroll, he still had to learn one thing: there was only one boss. And that was me.

"Classic is boring," I informed him. "And you might have put it on two other menus, chef, but I've opened twelve other restaurants. This is lucky number thirteen. And I don't do knockoffs."

"But—but—" he sputtered.

"Try it with the hacho miso and mirin at the base instead of the Bordeaux," I said. "Finish it with a few of the *tsukemono* and some sesame oil." I nodded at the mason jar I'd brought from home. "Those'll do it."

Le Ver's face screwed up like he'd just sucked on a lemon, and I wanted to laugh. Sour. Yeah.

"Mr. Parker," he started—

"Xavier," I cut in with a cheeky grin at the sous-chef behind him. She flushed and ducked away, but not without glancing at me once more over her shoulder. "Sato, if you prefer. I only make people call me Mr. Parker when they owe me money."

I didn't like the name, to be honest, having spent most of my life as Sato, my mum's name. But it was the one thing he left me, and when the world found out I was Rupert Parker's son...well, let's just say Parker opens up a hell of a lot more English bankers' doors than

Sato. I was happy to accept their money to start new businesses. Still was.

Le Ver's voice only scrunched up that much more. "Monsieur. Parker. Please let me remind you. It is no more my custom to call my restaurant owners by their first names than it is to accept their advice on my menus."

I dropped the spoon with a clang in the stainless-steel sink. The entire kitchen was suddenly silent.

Slowly, I dragged my gaze down over Le Ver's body, and then back up, as if to emphasize the difference in our relative sizes. I eyed the chef's scrawny physique while he, no doubt, noticed the hard work at the gym my three-thousand-pound suits barely concealed. At six feet, five inches, I wasn't really the sort of bloke you could ignore.

"Mr. Le Ver," I said softly, in the voice I reserved for exactly moments like these. "Let me remind *you* of something. You may be head chef, but it's *my* taste that has made every restaurant in the Parker Group a raging success. Paris. London. Prague. Amsterdam. Oslo. Shall I keep going?"

I did anyway.

"Eighteen Michelin stars. Two top ten in San Pellegrino. Three James Beard winners. Call me Alexander the Great, because I've conquered them all."

"*Oui*, but—"

"Do you want that second star, chef? Then take my advice. Otherwise, there's the door."

Le Ver's bug eyes bounced between me and the swinging kitchen door at least four times before he tossed his spatula into a nearby sink, stripped off his white apron, and threw it at my feet.

"Good luck finding my replacement!" he hissed before swearing considerably in French on his way out the door.

I smirked. I didn't advertise that I was fluent in the language after a stint at the Cordon Bleu. Considering I employed a reasonably large number of French chefs, the ability to eavesdrop on their mutterings was an asset. The French are a vulgar people. But as my dad used to say, "The only thing the French can do is surrender." It was only a matter of time with Le Ver.

"He left again?" asked Ben, one of the sous-chefs. "Did you tell him his soup was bad?"

"No, he left because I made it better."

Ben snorted and turned back to where he was sautéing shallots. "He'll be back."

I nodded. "I give him thirty seconds."

Right on time, the door swung open, and Le Ver reentered the kitchen. The rest of the staff busied themselves as if nothing had occurred.

"*Fine*," he hissed at me. "I will try your abomination of a recipe. But I will not take credit for it. And when it fails, you cannot blame me."

"It won't," I said knowingly.

Just like I knew Le Ver would be more than happy to take credit when the restaurant got its first rave review. And gladly accept those Michelin stars. After which I'd just as gladly take the soup, the rest of the menu, and the three-year non-compete contract he had signed, and kick his arse to the curb for insubordination.

This was business. Nothing more.

I turned to where Elsie, one of my four assistants, stood in the corner chuckling next to Jagger Harrington, my COO and best friend, who was only shaking his head at her. I don't know why the old girl got so excited whenever she watched me tell off my chefs, but she wouldn't miss an upstaging.

"Can you stay on this?" I asked the two of them. "Make sure the menu turns out the way it's supposed to while I'm in New York?"

Glee spread across her wrinkled face. "Of course, sir. On it like a car bonnet."

Jagger just nodded. "No problem, so long as the French one behaves."

I slapped my hands together and rubbed them with delight. I'd tried to capture New York once before, not quite five years ago. Had toured a couple of decent locations before meeting a cute young student by the name of Francesca.

At first, I'd written it off to a few too many glasses of Barolo. The thrill of turning a good girl bad.

But then I'd gotten lost in those sweet curves. Had become consumed by the taste of those strawberry lips, the ripe softness of her perfect arse, the complete and utter perfection of that butter-smooth skin.

And so for a month, there had been no restaurants. No burgeoning Parker Group. Not even a Lucy, the girl I was supposed to marry. I might not have remembered I was in New York at all if it hadn't been for the Bronx accent that emerged whenever Francesca was close to coming. Good God, that husky shout of hers still woke me in my sleep from time to time. With my cock the size of a cricket bat too.

I'd considered getting back in touch over the years. Francesca was studying English Literature, after all. One well-placed phone call, I could have gotten her into Oxford or Cambridge. I could have gotten her anything she wanted.

But all good things come to an end.

I'd broken enough hearts, after all. I couldn't break another. Not Francesca's. Not Lucy's. Certainly not my own.

Though I was beginning to think I didn't have one at all.

I shook my head. It was better this way, the best sex of my life or not. Maybe, once, I'd been the sort of man who could give a girl like Francesca what she wanted, but that man was gone, along with my heart.

There would be no Francesca Zola this time around. This time I was the hottest entrepreneur under forty this side of the Atlantic, not a fledgling chef desperate to impress his daddy. My entire name was riding on this expansion. I wanted New York. I wanted it bad.

Women I could find anywhere.

But the perfect restaurant? The perfect meal?

That was the holy grail.

"Good," I said sharply. "Do I have time for the gym before my flight?"

Elsie shook her head. "No, but your trainer is on his way to your flat. He said he can fit in a quick spar before your car takes you to Heathrow."

I'd have to give Elsie another raise. No one was better at anticipating my needs. Not even me.

I turned to where Le Ver was scowling over the stockpot, looking a bit like a worm, as his last name indicated.

"I'll be back for the grand reopening in June," I said. "Elsie's my eyes and ears here. And Le Ver?"

My chef turned, trying, and failing, to wipe the sour look from his face. "*Mais, oui*, Monsieur Parker?"

I offered a smile. The signature one that I knew was more steely than sweet. The one that never failed to make any of my employees quake in their boots.

"You've got four days. If that soup isn't exactly as I imagine it, it's back to France for you. Because you'll be finished in London for good."

1

Francesca

"**M**s. Zola! Ms. Zola!"

Three. Two. One.

I took a deep breath as I counted down in my mind, then turned away from the sink at the back of my classroom toward the owner of the adorable, slightly too-shrill voice behind me, bracing myself for glue-covered fingers and some kind of complaint.

"Kyle," I said, summoning what my brother Mattie called my "too-nice teacher" voice. "Is there something you need?"

Look, it wasn't that I didn't like kids. I was the fourth of six Bronx-born Italian-Puerto Rican rug rats. I even had one of my own, whom I adored more than life itself.

But everyone has their limits. Seven hours a day, five days a week of sassy eight-year-olds for the last three and a half years, was apparently mine.

"Bryce tried to eat the glue, and I told him not to, but then he spilled it *everywhere*, and Ms. Zola, we didn't *mean* to, and—"

"Kyle," I interrupted with a soft voice that only he could hear. The round-faced boy was clearly as worried about the other students watching as he was about getting in trouble.

As it always did in situations like these, the mix of fear, shame, and anxious hope clouding the boy's face wiped all irritation from my mind. For a moment, I was Jane Eyre, faced with one of her many pupils. And this was just a child, after all. We were all just people, doing the best we could, even when we messed up. If the last several years had taught me anything, it was that everyone deserves a second chance.

"I am going to get some paper towels and cleaning supplies," I said calmly. "Can you please return to your table? And *don't* touch anything until I get there, all right?"

Kyle nodded happily, then scampered off to the other side of the small classroom at P.S. 058 that was my only true dominion.

When I first started graduate school to study English Literature, I hadn't exactly expected to Google "how to clean up glue" every other week. But beggars can't be choosers, and that's pretty much what I was at almost twenty-four, a new mom, and in need of a job that would somehow fit my credentials of "likes books a whole lot."

So long, Dr. Francesca Zola, PhD. Hello, Ms. Frankie Zola.

Thank God for family. Mine, in particular. Thank God for *Nonna*, who got up every night with me for months while I learned how to parent an infant. Thank God for Mattie, who had bought a house in Red Hook to share with me and Sofia, so we wouldn't have to smush into my old bedroom at my grandmother's house. I thanked God for my sister Lea, whose experience with her four kids provided enough knowledge and hand-me-downs to last the rest of my life; for Kate, who gave me a shoulder to cry on and made sure I got the occasional night out; even Marie and Joni, who, despite being selfish little brats sometimes, were good and loving aunties.

Sofia adored them all. It almost made up for the fact that she was growing up without a father.

Almost.

I was just cleaning up the final bit of glue when the bell rang, signaling the end of the school day. All twenty-seven of my charges made their mad dash for the exit while I oversaw the collections of backpacks, lunch boxes, and art to take home from their cubbies. Forty minutes later, I had cleaned up the classroom, shoved the final assignments I had to grade for the term into my messenger bag, and was off to the teacher's lounge to check my mailbox before leaving to pick up Sofia at daycare. She really hated when I was late. And today, when we had plans to visit Santa and buy Christmas gifts, my punctuality would be more important than usual.

"Doing anything fun for the holidays?"

I looked down. I wasn't sure what about a hand-me-down Yankees shirt and ten-year-old jeans said "check me out all day," but apparently they did it for this guy. Adam Klein, the school's art teacher, had been giving me that same leer almost every afternoon since I started at P.S. 058.

I turned with the same pasted-on smile I gave my students when I wanted to tear out my hair. No one ever tells teachers how much of their job is repressing their own emotions. Even around each other.

"Nothing special," I replied politely. "Christmas with my family. Teaching at the Y. The usual."

"You're still teaching those cardio dance classes, right?"

I gulped, trying to avoid the way his gaze slipped to curve of my hips before returning to my eyes. What did he think he was going to see under the layers of baggy denim? I worked hard to get my butt back after Sofia, but that didn't mean I put it on display for just anyone to see.

"That's right," I murmured as I paged through a few memos and kept my body language as closed as possible. No eye contact. Turned slightly away. Get the hint, dude. I'm not interested.

"I'm heading to Connecticut to see family," Adam said, even though I had not asked him about his plans. "Nephews are crazy about me. They just *love* their uncle."

His light brown eyebrows rose suggestively—suggesting what, I couldn't say. Maybe that if small boys loved their uncle, I should too?

I shrugged. "Sounds nice."

Adam was a nice enough guy. Reasonably good-looking too. Between the glasses, the consummate flannel shirts, and the scruffy brown hair and stubble, he was pretty much the consummate Brooklyn hipster doing good. More than one of my fellow teachers had a thing for him, though I'd only ever seen him hit on me. The one who wasn't interested.

Adam had asked me out at least once a term since I'd started working at P.S. 058 as a Teach For America recruit. Really, he was probably the best someone like me could do. A single-mom and third-grade teacher didn't exactly scream out "hot catch!" on the dating scene. But not once had I said yes.

The truth was, I hadn't had a serious boyfriend in, well, ever.

No, Sofia's dad didn't count. A four-week affair that ended in heartbreak and an illegitimate child doesn't count. A dashing lothario who had a secret fiancée the entire time he was making the moves on me doesn't count.

It didn't matter if his kisses lit my soul on fire or just *thinking* about his touch set the rest of me aflame. It didn't even matter if he was the one to take my long-overdue virginity and I hadn't managed to have a single satisfying sexual encounter in the five years since.

He. Doesn't. Count.

"You all right there, teach?"

Adam's voice pulled me out of the daze I always seemed to fall into whenever Xavier Sato came to mind.

I shook my head. "Sorry. Just lost in a daydream for a moment."

"Want to tell me more about it over dinner tonight?"

And…there it was. Right on schedule.

I cocked my head to the side and affixed the craft-paste smile. It wasn't any use pissing off a coworker. "I appreciate it, but I have the guppy to pick up."

You would think being reminded constantly that I was a single mom and not at all interested in dating would throw the man off his scent.

But Adam just smiled jocularly and held up his coffee mug like he was toasting a glass of champagne. "Next time, then."

I sighed as I swept the rest of my mail out of my box and turned toward the door. "Sure, we'll see. Have a good holiday."

"You too, honey. You too."

―――

I DROVE my brother's car through Carroll Gardens to the daycare center about ten blocks from the school. Matthew generally took the bus to his office in downtown Brooklyn, allowing me the freedom of his car to cart Sofia around on days like these when we had a lot to do. It was one of the many ways we patched together a life of incoherent pieces to make something almost whole.

It was annoying, really, how much I'd come to depend on my brother just to survive. Five years ago, I was on track to fly myself. My older sisters had done it. My brother had done it. Carved out their own careers, their own families. And just when I was about to do it too, Sofia came along.

Suddenly, there was a lot more to pay for than just my little self, and I couldn't ask my seventy-something-year-old grandmother to raise yet another child that wasn't hers. Nonna had brought up all six of us after our dad died in a car crash and our mother chose the bottle over her kids. She deserved a break.

But there were bedrooms needed. Daycare. Clothes. Diapers.

The list of things I couldn't afford as a poor grad student, then teacher, went on and on. It was either accept Matthew's help or find Sofia's dad. One of those things was absolutely out of the question.

"Mama!" Sofia squealed when I stepped into the daycare center. She beelined from the sensory table to launch herself around my legs.

"Hey, bean," I greeted her with a kiss atop her head. "Good day?"

"I thought you'd *never* get here," she informed me in her adorable way. She still couldn't quite pronounce Rs correctly when she was excited. And since she was just four, that was often. "Billy Hendrix wouldn't stop pulling my hair!"

"Well, you were also stealing his hat," pointed out her teacher as she handed me a clipboard to sign Sofia out.

I smirked and signed. "That sounds about right."

"That's different," Sofia said. "His hat was ugly. My hair was pretty!"

"Sof," I chided. "That's not for you to decide."

"Don't worry," said her teacher. "We had a long talk about it. Didn't we, Sofia?"

My daughter nodded, but I recognized that stubborn expression. It was the same one every other member of my family wore when they absolutely knew they were right and no one else would sway them. It would take nothing less than an act of God to convince Sofia anything other than her current logic.

I sighed. "Have a nice holiday, Dolores. We'll see you in the new year."

We walked out to the car and drove to the Y while Sofia babbled about her day (most of it involving Billy Hendrix, whom I suspected she liked more than she actually hated). Every now and then she would look sharply into the rearview mirror, and my heart thumped loudly in response.

Maybe I could have forgotten Xavier Sato's face if Sofia didn't look so much like him. She and I shared some features, of course. Her almost black hair was almost as unruly as mine. We had the same slightly bronzed skin and petite build, having both inherited Nonna's teeny tiny bird bones.

But that was where the similarities stopped. My nose could politely be called Roman while Sofia's was adorably button-like. My lips were curved and heart-shaped, but my daughter's were impossibly full. I loved pinching them to make her laugh. Her wide-set, slightly upturned eyes were a deep, dark blue, whereas mine were muddy green like the rest of my family. They twinkled when she laughed and flamed when she was angry, with all the passion of the man who had given them to her.

There was no getting around it. My little girl was the spitting image of her father. Who had no clue that she existed.

I had considered telling him over the years. The email he had used was no longer valid, apparently. I'd long since blocked, then deleted his cell phone number, so that was out of the question. I'd done a few cursory internet searches, but Xavier Sato seemed to go dark on social media and everywhere else just after we met. It was almost like he had never existed at all.

I could have tried harder. But honestly, it seemed cruel. Not to him, but to his fiancée—probably his wife by now. How could you fight something like cancer when you realized your husband fathered a love child in another country? I couldn't have cared less about Xavier's feelings at that point. But I couldn't do that to her. Whoever she was.

And then, as time passed, it just seemed more and more pathetic. Who shows up years after claiming to have had your baby? Xavier was rich. That much I remembered. His friends and family would call me a gold digger. And maybe that I could have taken. Sticks and stones, right?

But the idea of anyone calling Sofia names like bastard? That was out of the question.

Besides, Sofia was happy. She had a mother who loved her, aunts and an uncle who treated her like she was their own. We needed nothing more.

Or so I told myself. Most of the time.

————

"Mattie, we're back!"

Three hours later, Sofia and I arrived home, her dizzy with excitement after meeting Santa Claus, me still in my worn spandex after teaching cardio hip hop hours before. I desperately needed a shower. And dinner.

The little townhouse in Red Hook wasn't much. Twelve hundred square feet of crumbling brick that Matthew was slowly remodeling into something livable. Three small bedrooms (if you counted my blocked off area at the top of the stairs) upstairs, a kitchenette, living room, and half bath on the main floor, plus a basement apartment he rented out to help with the mortgage.

I was proud of my brother. Matthew had worked hard for a long time to have something of his own in the most expensive city in the world. And he was sharing it with us. I knew I should be grateful. And nearly every day, I was.

"Mattie, are you home?" I called as I dropped my bags in the foyer. "And by any chance, do you have dinner? We are starving."

There was a loud thump from upstairs, followed by a series of loud footsteps trampling down the stairs.

"Ouch, *shit*. I mean, shoot!"

"Zio!" shouted Sofia as she dropped my hand and made a beeline for her favorite guy on the planet.

As he was tackled on the landing, Matthew obediently swept her up and twirled her around. He looked a far cry from his usual polished self in a pair of old Marine Corps issue sweatpants, a ratty T-shirt, and three days of beard growth.

"Had a nice day?" I called from the kitchen. "Or should we say good morning?"

He gave me a dirty look, and I felt bad. For the last few months, Matthew had been on forced administrative leave and subsequently had to work nights as a bartender to make ends meet. It was only six p.m., but clearly, he was just getting up.

"Did you *just* wake up, Zio?" Sofia demanded. "It's almost nighttime!"

"Nighttime is my daytime, baby girl," he informed her before putting her down.

She scampered upstairs to say hello to her toys while Matthew and I walked into the kitchen. It was cold. No food or anything. My stomach grumbled.

"Stop," he said as I started rummaging around in the fridge. "I'll do it. You've been on your feet all day. Also, you need a shower."

"So do you," I said. "At least I have work to blame. You just stink of cigarettes and booze. What have you been doing all day?"

He shrugged as he pulled a few plates from the cupboard. "Sleeping. Hanging around."

"Chain smoking and drowning your sorrows with Oprah and a bottle of Jack?" I emerged from the fridge with a half a pan of ziti and things for a salad.

Matthew flinched, then took the pasta from me. "Let me warm that up. You always burn it."

I sighed. Really, I knew better than to mention his current predicament. My brother had been walking around like a ghost for months after his involvement with Nina de Vries had cost him his job.

I didn't know all the details since Matthew usually kept things like this close to his chest. The gist of it was that she was married to some jerk he was prosecuting, but Mattie couldn't stay away. My brother, good guy that he was, went to his boss hat in hand and fessed up to the relationship. And promptly lost his job.

You could say it was a sore subject.

Generally, Matthew was the most level-headed person on the planet, but from the moment he met Nina, he was in another dimension.

Guilt warmed my belly. Here I was giving him shit about his current predicament, and my big brother was still taking care of me, like he'd done all my life.

"Sorry," I mumbled. "I'm just hungry."

"No worries." He put the tray of pasta on the counter while he set the oven to preheat.

"I can do that," I said, pushing him out of the way. "And I'll set a timer so I don't burn it. Don't you have to leave for work soon anyway?"

Matthew shook his head. "Jamie gave me the night off. Going to a party instead."

"A party? Really?" That sounded promising. He hadn't been out in months except to bartend. I sort of missed the playboy version of my brother. "Whose?"

"My friends Eric and Jane. Early Christmas party."

"The fancy ones uptown?" I didn't bother to hide my frown.

The whole city knew who Eric and Jane de Vries were. Their wedding and family drama had been on the front page of every New York paper for more than a year.

They were also related to Nina.

"The same," Matthew admitted as he traced a finger over a crack in the Formica. "But I should go. Jane and Eric have been good to me."

"So good you're out of a job, right, big brother?" I asked as I returned to the fridge for something to drink.

It was after six on a Friday. A glass of wine would be nice. But pickings were slim this close to paychecks. I sighed and pulled out the Brita.

Matthew's face was dark when I turned around. "Nina has nothing to do with Jane and Eric."

"She's just his married cousin, right?"

"That's beside the fuc—" Matthew cut himself off as he glanced up toward where Sofia had gone, then back at me. "The freaking point. *She* didn't invite me. We haven't spoken for months."

"Since she got you fired?" I pushed, unable to help myself.

As soon as I said it, regret washed through me. None of this situation was his fault. I knew that. You couldn't help who you fell in love with. I knew that more than most.

But that fact that it obviously hurt so much? Maybe that was our fault. I couldn't help feeling like it every time I saw my brother coming home after a long night of bartending, I was a little bit responsible. His misery was for us, I knew. Sofia and me.

But I wasn't stupid. He was going to this party because there was a chance *she* might be there, whether he wanted to admit it or not.

"I'm going," Matthew said. "They're my friends, and I finally have a night off. And so do you, so you're coming too."

I looked up in surprise from the salad I was tossing. "What? No, I'm not."

"Yeah, you are. Kate's on her way with a suit for me, a dress for you, and free babysitting. You're coming."

"It's Friday night, and you bullied Kate into schlepping all the way to Brooklyn to play dress-up with me? She has a life, Mattie."

"Right now, we're more concerned about yours. Or the lack thereof."

I frowned. "I don't have a say in this? Who said I even want to go to a party full of snobby, rich people? I can just watch *Downton Abbey* for the wealth porn and turn it off when I'm sick of them."

Matthew leaned on the counter, giving me that knowing look that sometimes made me want to smack him. "It's either the party or I'm calling Derek to share this ziti with you. How long has it been since the Mets game?"

Now I really did scowl. The last date I'd had was over the summer when Matthew had set me up with his partner from work. Derek Kingston was…fine. Fine looking. Fine conversationalist. But an exciting afternoon to him was watching baseball and letting me make him sandwiches. Honestly, it wasn't that different from an average day at work.

"Besides," Matthew continued, "Eric was an English major like you. I happen to know the guy owns two first editions of W. B. Yeats's poetry."

I perked up. It was hard to say no to treasures like that.

"You can actually talk about iambic speedometer with him."

"It's iambic pentameter," I corrected him, unable to help myself though I knew he was just jerking my chain. Matthew was a lot more well-read than he let on.

"Whatever. It's someone else who actually likes all that English crap you're obsessed with. I thought you'd be down."

I could see these people now, swanning around in a big brownstone straight out of *The Age of Innocence*. It would be just like the books I had read in college, except in New York instead of London. Let's see, would that make me May Welland or Ellen Olenska? Ellen had the affair with a married man, but May was the mother. I was probably closer to May, the picture of innocence, until she married and had her kid. And then dies.

I frowned. Sometimes imagining myself as my favorite characters wasn't exactly the fresh escape I yearned for.

"Don't you think it's kind of weird, the way you want to pimp your sister out all the time?" I teased, trying to change the subject. "Should I come down to Envy? Maybe you can introduce me to some of the other bartenders."

But Matthew wasn't biting. "I'm serious. You're twenty-seven, Frankie. Kid or no kid, you shouldn't be living like somebody's spinster aunt."

I giggled. "But I am someone's spinster aunt. I'm an unmarried teacher with three nephews and a baby niece. Make me a governess and I'm a Jane Austen character. A regular bluestocking."

Yes, I liked that direction. Jane Fairfax *did* slip away with Frank Churchill in *Emma*, right?

Matthew was smart enough not to answer while I glanced over my shoulder at Sofia, who had snuck back downstairs, parked herself in front of the television, and already pulled up PBS cartoons. Without asking.

Smart girl.

Maybe he wants you gone.

The thought echoed through my mind before I could help it.

The truth was, Sofia and I were more of a burden than ever. Matthew would never say it, but it was true. The older she got, the more expensive her life was. And the meager raises I earned as a schoolteacher didn't come close to covering the life I wanted to give my daughter.

I smarted. The thing about Jane Austen was that her spinsters always found love, usually in the form of a rich bachelor who falls for the plucky, well-read young woman.

Well. I had never started a relationship for financial support before, and I wasn't about to start gold digging now. But a party full of rich, influential New Yorkers wasn't a bad place to look for other connections. People who could help me find a different job outside of teaching. Afford a different apartment outside of Matthew's generosity.

A different life outside of Brooklyn and P.S. 058.

"All right, big brother," I relented. "It's a date. Let's go to this party and see what's up."

2

I t wasn't a different life per se, but this one small corner felt like a
different universe from my own.

Four hours later, Matthew and I stood on one of the swankiest
blocks in New York City. Only a few houses down from Central Park
West, the lush brownstone belonging to Jane and Eric de Vries towered
several stories above the street, with a set of enormous double doors
that were probably solid mahogany. Through the open bay windows,
the sounds of music, clinking champagne glasses, and posh people's
laughter bounced into the night air.

And I felt like I was going to vomit.

Kate had arrived in time for ziti, bearing an armful of suits for
Matthew and a single dress for me sent with Nonna's blessing from her
actual closet. I'd waffled several times after being zipped up in the
slinky black dress. It wasn't until Kate had finally grabbed my shoulders and forced me to stare at myself in my full-length mirror that I'd
actually *seen* what she had.

"Damn," I had said. "I mean, I still kind of want to sleep. But I clean
up pretty nice."

I did, too. Nonna's dress fit like a second skin, accentuating the
hourglass figure that had gotten a little bit more so after Sofia. The
added height of heels made my ankles look dainty and small, and my
eyes glowed against the cat-eye makeup Kate had applied. My hair
wasn't even frizzing, spilling over my shoulders in sleek spirals.

From her place behind me, Kate smiled. "I told you so."

I continued to stare at my reflection. But the longer I did, the stranger I felt. The tiny hairs on my arms stood up, along with goose bumps. Nerves. The person in the mirror…she was pretty, yes. But she wasn't me. Not anymore.

She was a fraud.

"I know what you're thinking, Frankie. Stop it."

I bit my lip. "You don't know."

"Yes, I do. I know that look. It's the same one you gave Nonna when you said you were going to go to community college instead of interviewing for that scholarship at Columbia."

I scowled. "It is not."

"It is. You were scared then. And you're scared now." She tipped her head. "It's just a party."

"With all these fancy people. You're used to them. Matthew is too. But that's not me, Katie. These people are Cartier and personal trainers. I'm dollar store bracelets and the YMCA. It's a totally different world."

"It is," Kate agreed. "But that doesn't mean you're not good enough for them. If anything, they aren't good enough for you."

I snuffed and tried to turn away. "Please."

But my sister's hands kept me firmly in place.

"You're different than the rest of us," Kate informed me. "Smarter."

"Come on, Kate—"

"Just listen," she said, her fingers tightening above my collarbone. "The rest of us were so eager to grow up. To jump out there, get into trouble. But you were always reading your books. Because you knew what you wanted from day one. You were going to go to school. Become a professor, travel the world, live in London. Dedicate your life to that quiet passion."

I gulped and found myself blinking back a few stray tears. I tried not to think about the past. Those things that had almost been within reach. What's done was done, right? There wasn't any point of mourning what might have been.

"And then Sofia came," my sister continued. "I know you love her, Frankie. But it's not right that you have to give up all your dreams forever just because of one little girl."

"Kate, I didn't give up *all* my dreams," I said, blinking furiously to stave off the tears. I swung around to face her. "Matthew and this house. We have a nice life. I can't really complain."

Kate didn't argue, but she didn't agree either. Instead, my sister just squeezed my shoulders again, this time with more kindness.

"Go to this party. Meet some new, interesting people. Think about what's outside of P.S. 058 and Arthur Avenue and New York City, for crying out loud. There's still a whole world out there, waiting for you to grab it, Frankie. And after all these years, you deserve your chance."

Grab the world? Kate wanted me to grab this world? How in the hell was I going to grab anything if I puked all over Nonna's lovely dress?

I no longer felt like that beautiful woman in the mirror. I felt like my daughter playing dress-up.

I chewed on my lip, then stopped. God, the last thing I wanted was to have lipstick on my teeth in front of these people. This was the nicest house I had ever seen. The people in it were no doubt all rich, accomplished, beautiful, perfect.

I was nothing. A third-grade teacher whose entire life revolved around My Little Pony and nap time. A sad aerobics instructor whose biggest following was her Sunday morning Silver Sneakers class for seniors.

"Frances. *Francesca*."

I blinked, startled out of my daze, when I realized Matthew had probably been calling my name for the last few minutes.

So I did whatever any of the Zola kids did when we were caught: deflect, deflect, deflect.

"I know you're nervous when you use my full name," I said. "What is it?"

Unfortunately, my brother saw straight through me. "Nothing. You just look pretty tonight."

Suddenly I found myself blushing under Matthew's earnest gaze, and he swallowed thickly. We were both nervous, I realized, though I wasn't sure why he was. These were *his* friends, weren't they? And Matthew, with his fancy suits and slick lawyer's talk, always seemed more at ease with the finer things in life.

"Nonna let me borrow it," I mumbled. "She said it reminded her of Audrey Hepburn when she bought it." At least, that's what Kate had said.

Matthew nodded. "Yeah, you could be on the set of *Breakfast at Tiffany's*."

It was the best thing he could have said.

I smiled. "Thanks, big brother."

Both our spirits buoyed, Matthew knocked on the doors, which were immediately opened by one of the biggest men I'd ever seen. A security guard or bouncer, given the clipboard in his hand.

Security. These people were so rich they had security. We had a rusty deadbolt and a broken chain.

The man's face brightened when he saw Matthew. "Zola. Good to see you."

They shook hands and made some small talk while I peeked nervously through the doors. Big band music squealed off the hard-wood floors along with leather-soled shoes and countless stilettos. Jewelry, sequins, and bright white smiles flashed through the din.

Oh, God. Oh *God*. What was I doing here?

"My sister, Francesca Zola."

I snapped back to attention. The security guy and Matthew were both looking at me with knowing smiles.

"Got it." The guard winked as he checked both our names off a clip-board. "Have fun," he said and stepped aside to let us in.

I had grown up in the city, so obviously I understood the concept of the haves and have-nots. I'd seen treasures housed in every museum we had in New York while at the same time growing up in a neighbor-hood where my family home, with two grandparents and six kids crammed into three bedrooms and an attic, was considered a luxury by plenty. I saw that same disparity every day in my classroom, where half the kids lived in brownstones not unlike this one, and the others depended on the measly school lunches for part of their daily calorie count.

But it was one thing to know the numbers. It was another to see this kind of wealth up close.

I couldn't help but stare. The marble-lined foyer opened into an enormous living room centered around a house-sized fireplace. The room itself was actually three, flowing seamlessly into a dining room for twelve and the biggest kitchen I'd ever seen. The furniture was a mix of classic mid-century pieces combined with punches of color and textures, including several mural-sized pieces of modern art on the walls.

All around were tasteful holiday decorations—lighted garland hung from the ceiling, across the fireplace, and over the balustrade. In the living room window was the largest Christmas tree I'd ever seen outside of a mall or Rockefeller Center, lit with a vintage glass bulb and a gorgeous gold star practically jumping off its top to streak across the entire room.

And that was just the decor of the house. The people inside it looked like they had walked off the pages of *Vogue*.

"May I take your coats?"

Matthew helpfully handed both our coats to the attendant just inside the entry. Security *and* an attendant. And, if I was correct, those were uniformed catering waiters carrying crystal flutes of champagne and pastel-colored canapes all over the enormous living room. The only house parties I'd ever attended involved a keg or two and red plastic cups. Maybe a big bowl of Cheetos if the host really splurged.

"I feel like I just entered the Weasleys' tent at the Quidditch Cup," I muttered to myself.

Beside me, Matthew snorted. "Frankie, maybe cool it on the Harry Potter references tonight." When I looked hurt, he pointed across the room at a particularly beautiful painting. "Look. That's an original Gustav Klimt."

I swiveled, eyes bulging. "You're kidding."

"It's the most comfortable museum you'll ever visit," he confirmed. "But I promise, the de Vrieses are good people."

People? People didn't have priceless works of art just hanging on the wall like something they picked up at Target. People didn't throw parties where everyone seemed to gleam brighter than a lucky penny. The de Vrieses weren't people. They were Society. There was just no other word for it.

Which meant we were the penniless if well-intentioned relations, right? I was part of a quintet of sisters, just like the Bennets in *Pride and Prejudice*, my all-time favorite novel. So did that mean there was a Mr. Darcy floating around this room?

And back to Austenland I went.

"Drink, sir?"

We turned to find one of the waiters offering a tray of champagne.

"Please." Matthew took one for each of us. "Hold on a second, kid."

Both of us downed the glasses like they were shots, not delicate champagne. Immediately, Matthew handed me another. I didn't argue.

"I can't believe you hang out with these people all the time," I said as the champagne tickled my nose. My eyes were watering, but I wasn't feeling quite so terrified.

Matthew shrugged after tossing back a third glass. "I wouldn't say it's all the time. I see them occasionally. Not for months now."

I continued looking over the crowd. "You know, you fit in here."

"Pull the other one, why don't you."

"No, you do," I insisted. "We always make fun of you for your hats and your suits, but I'm looking at you. And in here, with all these fancy people. You blend right in, Mattie. You really do."

"Give or take a billion dollars."

"It's smaller than you think," I said.

For some reason, the idea that my big brother looked just as bright and shiny as any of these rich people gave me hope, even if I was a little jealous. We did share the same genetic code. Maybe I wasn't as much of a fraud as I thought.

"Is she here?" I wondered.

"Who?" Matthew asked.

I just gave him a look. "You know who. *Her*."

Nina was Eric's cousin, or so I understood. There was obviously a chance she would be here tonight, and Matthew came here fully knowing that.

"I don't think so," he mumbled.

"Good," I said, wanting to kick him. "You deserve a night off from the misery that woman brings you."

We both do, I wanted to add. Over the last year, my stylish, savvy brother had morphed into Eeyore.

Matthew frowned. See, a sad donkey. "What's that supposed to mean?"

But before I could tell him exactly what I thought about his personal version of Kryptonite, we were interrupted by someone who might have once been called mine.

"Francesca?"

I froze.

No. It couldn't be. Not after five years. Not after he had all but disappeared off the face of the earth.

Do you believe in ghosts? Because at that point, I did.

I knew that voice. Its owner had the same raven black hair and dark blue eyes I saw every day on my daughter, plus a pair of mile-wide shoulders and soul-searing lips I couldn't stop dreaming of no matter how hard I tried.

It was him. Xavier Sato.

Hotter than fire. Colder than ice. Father of my child.

And he had no idea.

3

Oh, God. Oh, *God*. I stared at my drink. The bubbles ran to the top of the glass with the same urgency I had to run out of this party.

But my feet didn't move.

When had my feet stopped moving?

When had my body stopped listening to me?

Maybe when I started hallucinating the father of my child suddenly appearing at a random party? Yes, that was it. I was cracking up from lack of sex and fun. Kate was right. I was too hard up to think straight, and celibacy had finally taken its toll.

"Francesca."

Oh. My. God.

Gradually, I looked up. And up. And up. I was five three plus heels, and just like before, he was a wall of lean muscle swathed in a black suit that perfectly fit a pair of impossibly broad shoulders, a tapered waist, and long legs that stretched for miles. His square jaw was dappled with stubble, shadowing full lips and high cheekbones topped with a shock of inky black hair that shone under the lights of the party.

He cleared his throat and tugged at a tie that matched his eyes. Oh, those *eyes*. Dark blue pools of charisma that I had wanted to dive into the moment I met him in a crowd thicker than this one, though much less formal. That was when I knew it was really him. They glimmered with promise and mischief, with the confidence of a man who knows he's attractive and knows the woman he wants thinks so too.

They glimmered like the last five years had never happened. Like he'd never sent the letter that broke my heart. And I'd never had his baby without telling him.

I swallowed. Opened my mouth.

Absolutely nothing came out.

"Frankie," Matthew was saying as he looked between Xavier and me with growing recognition. "Do you know him?"

Shit. Oh *shit*. Sofia might have been a secret from Xavier, but she wasn't from the rest of my family. Back then he was Xavi to me, but at home he was "the devil incarnate," "good for nothing shitstain," or "dickhead," depending on who you were talking to. You try keeping so much as your diary a secret when you share a room with at least two other women at any given time.

All I needed now was for my brother, already strung tight as a violin, to realize this was *the* Xavier who had knocked up his baby sister out of wedlock and given him two extra mouths to feed on his public servant's salary.

Xavier might have been a giant, but Matthew was a former Marine *and* he grew up in the Bronx. He knew how to fight dirty. In the mood he was in tonight, I doubted he would hesitate.

And so it was for that reason, more than any other, that my body somehow found its power of speech and movement again.

"Get lost!" I hissed as my hand flew out and shoved Matthew back a few steps.

His brow furrowed in surprise, but I gave him my best "don't cock block me" look. His expression morphed from confused to knowing.

"Going," he said, but not before he gave Xavier his patented big brother glare. "But my two cents? He's too tall for you anyway."

Before I could snap that my height or anyone else's was absolutely none of his business, Matthew disappeared into the crowd, sure-footed as a cat.

"Francesca? Is it really you?"

Trying not to shake, I turned. Around us, the party was launching into full swing. Champagne glasses were clinking, people were laughing a little too loudly. It should have been fun, like one of the balls Austen wrote about so much. But I couldn't hear anything other than Xavier's deep voice, Queen's English heavily overlaid by South London. Yes, I knew the difference. That's what twenty-five years of being an Anglophile gets you. *Way* too many Saturday nights binging BritBox. I don't even want to get into my obsession with Regency adaptations.

"Hello, Xavier." My voice was low, barely a whisper. Oh my God, Frankie, *talk*. He's a man, not a phantom.

And yet, was there a difference when it came to him?

He looked good. Edible, even. Somehow better than I had imagined over the last five years.

I shifted from one foot to the other. Suddenly, my dress was a bit too tight, and my skin tingled with anticipation. I felt drunk, despite only one glass of champagne.

"What—what are you doing here?" I managed to get out.

Stupid question. Xavier quirked a black brow and glanced around as if the answer was obvious. I suppose it was. It was a party. Why else would he be here if not to enjoy himself like everyone else?

Most of the guests were too absorbed with the free-flowing champagne, music, and well, themselves to take interest. A few, though, had definitely noticed him. More than one woman was eyeing Xavier over their flutes of Cristal.

"Business." Xavier pulled me back with a smile. It looked like he was trying to be nice, but something about his expression looked forced, like it didn't come naturally. It was distinctly…predatory.

What did that make me? His prey?

"I'm finally opening that restaurant in New York," he continued. "De Vries is one of my investors, and he invited me tonight."

"De Vries?" I frowned.

Xavier waved a casual hand toward the crowd. "Eric? The host? He and I were at university together when I did a semester abroad at Dartmouth. What did you do, sneak in with the caterers?"

I flushed. Did I stick out that much? I wasn't dripping in diamonds or couture, but I thought I looked respectable. Audrey, Matthew had said. But maybe he meant like in *My Fair Lady*. Before the makeover, when she was still the homely flower girl with the Cockney accent and rags for wear.

"I—no," I stumbled. "He—Eric—they're friends with my—"

I stopped, took a deep breath, then tried again. I could do this. Hold a conversation. I was a teacher, for goodness' sake. I basically herded cats for a living.

"I came with my brother, Matthew," I clarified. "The guy who was with me before. He's friends with the de Vrieses."

Translation: *I'm supposed to be here.*

Was it my imagination, or did Xavier's massive shoulders relax a little? That smile peeked out again, this time looking a bit more natural. Still an imitation of a shark, though.

I suppose that made me the minnow.

I swallowed the rest of my third glass of champagne immediately.

"Your brother? Do I get to meet him?"

He swung around, looking for Matthew. But thank God, he had disappeared into the sea of glitter and money.

I shrugged, then lunged for a glass of champagne on the tray of a passing caterer. "Hold on there, buddy," I said as he started to walk away. "One more for the road."

The waiter took my empty glass with a wry look and moved on.

I turned to find Xavier watching me intently. One side of his mouth twitched, like he was about to smile. But he didn't. I took another long draught of champagne. His gaze traveled with the glass to my lips and stayed there for several seconds until, again, he cleared his throat and pulled at his necktie.

"Too tight?" I asked.

He frowned. "What?"

I nodded. "Your tie. You keep adjusting it."

His hand dropped. "Eh. Well. Hate these things, if you want to know the truth. Like a bloody noose." He exhaled slowly through his nose. "Christ, what have you been up to? It's been, what, five years?"

I took another deep swig of champagne. Feeling lightheaded was better than feeling starstruck. And for some reason, every time the muscles of his neck tested his collar like that, I didn't quite feel steady on my feet. "Some-something like that."

"Did you finish school?" he pressed. "You were studying literature, correct?"

"Um, yes. That's right." I stifled a smile. "Good memory."

"You were writing your thesis on Austen. Something about Mr. Darcy and his evolution in the modern age, wasn't it?"

My mouth fell open. "You remember that?"

He took a step forward, closing the space between us enough that I caught a whiff of his scent: a touch of cologne atop something clean and slightly spicy. A chef's scent. Same as before.

"I have an excellent memory." His voice rumbled low.

"Like...for what?" I knew I shouldn't have asked. Or even cared. But his eyes were pulling me in—or up—and I couldn't look away.

"You have a London Fog every morning," he informed me. "Love peanuts, but hate peanut butter. Your favorite poem is 'Frost at Midnight.' In fact, you love all the Romantic poets except Wordsworth. Thought he was stodgy."

I gawked. "How in God's name do you remember all of that after five years?"

Again, that sharkish almost-smile appeared. "Oh, I remember everything about you, Ces."

Ces. Pronounced "Chess," a shortened version of my full name that no one had ever used but him.

My entire body shivered.

I was Frankie to everyone else in my life. Friends or coworkers, mostly. Frances sometimes (usually to a priest or my grandmother). Fran, maybe even Franny to Mattie or my sisters.

But with Xavier, there had been no in between. It was Francesca, my Christian name, when he wanted my attention. His eyes would glow, and his mouth would twist the word like it was wrapped around a ripe strawberry, luxuriating in each syllable with that wicked tongue.

And then there was this. When it was just us two, and he looked at me like he loved me, like I was the only one in the world. A nickname that belonged to him and only him, as intimate as anything else we had done together.

Ces.

As his gaze traveled up and down my body, it was quite clear just what *else* he was remembering.

I should have been appalled. But then again, I was remembering it too.

Xavier cleared his throat once more. Yanked the middle of his tie this time instead of the knot. "So. Are you a professor now? Should I call you Dr. Zola?"

I swallowed. Of course, it was *that* remark that made my cheeks flush again. With shame, not excitement. "Um, no. I, ah, actually left school to deal with some, um, family stuff. I teach third grade in Brooklyn."

"What's that, primary?"

I nodded. "Yeah."

My eyes darted around the room, looking at the splashy modern art hung on the walls. Toward the sound of breaking glass somewhere near the dining table. Anywhere but him.

When I finally found the courage to look back, his eyes bore down at me as intently as before. "Well, it's still teaching, isn't it? Do you read them any of your poetry? I seem to remember some rather racy bits in that journal of yours. Anything about me?"

Again, my mouth fell open. "You haven't changed either, have you? Just as arrogant as ever."

He was too. And I *hated* that it turned me on so much.

His sapphire eyes glinted, though suddenly, he turned away. "Well. I've earned it."

Before I could ask how, another caterer appeared.

"More champagne?" she asked, tittering up at Xavier.

"Sure."

I couldn't help feeling slightly jealous when an actual smile appeared for the stranger carrying drinks instead of me. It wasn't a real smile, at least. Xavier hadn't smiled much when I had known him before, and it seemed like he did it even less now. The shark made yet another appearance, without an iota of warmth or kindness.

If it had been directed at me, I would have been terrified. And maybe the waitress was too. But she was also clearly entranced as she handed Xavier the drinks, unable to look away.

"When you take those back to the kitchen, can you just bring us a bottle? Thanks, babe."

The waitress giggled and stuck out her considerable chest before turning away.

And just like that, his spell over me, at least, was broken.

Babe? Really? Sure, he had always used that term the way Americans say "man" and "dude." And once upon a time, I had liked it when he called me that too, among many other things. It was the familiar. Open.

Right now though? It made me sick listening to him flirt so openly with another woman, even if with the warmth of a brick wall.

Frankie, stop. You have no claim over this man. You don't want this man. You do not.

By the time I was done with my internal pep talk, I turned to find Xavier staring intently at my mouth. His smile had vanished, replaced now by a small indentation between his brows.

"What in God's name are you looking at?" I snapped a little too harshly.

Again, one side of his mouth twitched. "You still chew on your lower lip when you're thinking." He leaned down as he traded my empty champagne glass with a fourth serving—or was it my fifth? His scent, that intoxicatingly spicy blend, wrapped around me like a mist. "And it still makes your lips look like strawberries."

Another full-body shiver coursed through me. "I—you—what?"

His cheek brushed mine, and his voice dropped to a rumble only I could hear. "What do you say when that bottle returns, we find someplace a bit quieter? Somewhere we can catch up. Get…reacquainted."

He stood up straight, expression as stoic as ever. At first, I wondered if I'd imagined it. There was no emotion in his face. No sign he had actually proposed what I thought he had.

But he had. His blue eyes dilated with clear, hypnotic desire as he waited out my response. And I knew the same expression was echoed in mine but couldn't quite hate myself for it. Whatever pull he once had on me, it was still here. I was once again a moth drawn to a bright blue flame.

Slowly, as if to touch a wild animal, Xavier reached out a finger and hovered it over my jaw, above my chin, down my neck. I could feel goose bumps rising, despite the fact that he didn't touch me. Not yet. It was a tease, a preview of what he might do. A reminder of what he had once done.

But as soon as his finger made soft contact, just in the hollow above my clavicle, I remembered.

This wasn't a dream.

This was real.

Xavier was here and clearly as icy and dangerous as ever.

Touching me.

Wanting me.

And through this growing haze of champagne, there was absolutely no way I would be able to keep the secret I'd been holding for years if he did more than that.

I couldn't just think of myself here, I had someone else far more important to protect. I had to think of Sofia.

"No," I said clearly, jerking out of reach. "Oh, *no*. I—"

I cut myself off, looking around. Lord, where was my overprotective brother when I needed him? But all I saw were nameless faces, people awash in alcohol and laughter, riches and wealth and confidence that had absolutely nothing to do with me.

I turned back to find Xavier still watching me with a different kind of expression. Not one of patient waiting. But instead, like a victor. Like he had walked out of one of my beloved Austen novels. But he wasn't the hero. He was the villain who had just captured his prize.

"Shall we?" he asked as the waitress returned, giggling with the requested bottle.

I blinked between him and the girl, who looked like she would be more than happy to share the drink with him in my place. And he wasn't exactly correcting her either.

"No, I don't think so," I said.

And then I turned on my heel and left.

4

J ust go. Go, go, go, go, *go*.

It was the word that went through my mind the moment his finger touched my skin. Like a rabbit cornered by the fox, my reaction to Xavier's gaze had been visceral. Fight or flight.

So I fled.

Now, after snatching my coat from the attendant and sprinting across half the Upper West Side, I was genuinely lost. In New York City. Despite being born here and growing up here and literally only leaving maybe once or twice in my entire life.

If he was a shark, I was a guppy, drawn into his clutches like I was an idiot virgin all over again.

Frankie, you fool.

He didn't want anything from me but sex. Just like he had before. And look where that had gotten me.

I stopped beneath a streetlamp, on yet another block where May Welland might have lived. Good God, was there anything other than brownstones and perfect cast iron gates on the Upper West Side? The warmth of wealth glowed beyond gently curtained windows. Refined and elegant. A world I'd only really visited on class field trips and in books. So far from my real life of a crumbling Brooklyn row house and the peeling paint of my grandparents' home in the Bronx. Places where I belonged.

Dammit, where was the nearest subway stop? And the cabs, did they run uptown or downtown on Amsterdam? Which direction was

Broadway from this corner? Why couldn't I remember *anything* about this place?

"Francesca!"

My name echoed behind me, the voice deep and foreboding, hinting at the inevitable brewing storm.

My own personal tempest.

I heard his large footsteps pounding the pavement before I finally opened my eyes and looked up.

And there he was. Xavier.

"Ces," Xavier said as he came to a stop in front of me. "You ran out. Why?"

It was barely a question. A demand, really.

I gulped. Somehow, he was even more gorgeous out here, looming over me like a vampire, a bloodthirsty creature of the night. Our Austen novel had disappeared. Now I was in Bram Stoker's fever dream.

"I—I just have to go," I mumbled. "I can't do this. I forgot, I have to be somewhere else tonight."

Before I could leave, my hand was seized, and I was spun back around. Another thing just like before: that faint electricity, sizzling at a single touch.

I yanked my hand. He did not release it.

"What are you doing?" I demanded. "Let go."

"No." One of Xavier's black brow cocked in challenge. "You're lying, Ces. You think I can't tell?"

I pulled and pulled, but his grip was steel. "What? No, I'm not. I have to—"

"Go. Yeah, I know. But you're clenching your other fist like you want to punch me in the nose. I bet your nails left marks on your palm too."

At last I relaxed, but only because I realized he was right. My right hand was locked in his steel grip, but the other was, in fact, bunched so tightly that when I opened it, angry moon-shaped indentations lined my palm.

"Fine. I'm lying." I flexed my left hand. "I can't believe you remembered that."

Xavier looked me up and down, like he was measuring my flight risk. At last, he released me. "I told you, Francesca. I remember everything about you. Every. Single. Thing."

Another shiver traveled down my spine. Was that fear or anticipation? I couldn't tell. So I looked away, flexing my fingers to get the blood flowing again.

"So, why did you run?" he pressed. "Was it me? Did I scare you off?"

Yes. No.

I shook my head. "I—I didn't belong in there."

It wasn't what I had initially been thinking, but my hands remained loose as the truth settled in my bones like an anchor. I'd known it before I'd even gotten dressed, and I'd known it the moment we arrived in that fancy house with all those fancy people. My brother loved the finer things in life. But I was simple. A third-grade teacher and a single mom in her grandma's clothes.

I was a fake.

"I completely agree. You don't belong in there at all."

I looked up, feeling like I'd been slapped. It was one thing to think these things about myself. It was another to have them confirmed. I didn't even bother asking why his opinion would matter like this. It just did.

"What did you say?" I asked.

Again that brow rose knowingly. "That party was full of fools. Women with tits that could float them across the Atlantic, men with enough coke up their noses to power Times Square. You were the only real thing in there. Ten times more gorgeous. Ten times more interesting."

I frowned. His praise was the last thing I was expecting. Just like I wasn't expecting the sudden warmth that flowered in my chest with his compliments.

I shook the feeling away. "Then what were you doing there?"

Xavier just shrugged and took a step closer. His big shoulders blocked the light overhead. "I don't know. Maybe I was waiting for you."

I swallowed, cornered once more. But this time I didn't want to flee. Or fight. Because another memory, a deeper, more powerful one, was rising to the surface.

He remembered me? Well, I remembered him. I couldn't forget a man who could pick me up like I weighed nothing. Whose arms could shelter against any element in the world. He couldn't have known what that meant to a girl who hadn't known much in the way of safety in her life. My family, loud and loving as they were, weren't exactly stable.

For a few short weeks, Xavier had given me a break from all of that. He had given me a refuge against that broad, strong chest, in those massive arms. For a moment, he had been the safest place I could imagine, a refuge from the instability of my home life and the uncertainty of my future.

His fingers grazed my jaw again, just like they had at the party. I wanted to sink into the warm embrace that beckoned.

"You haven't changed, you know that?" he said, watching the path of his hand as it dropped down my neck, then toyed with the strap of my dress inside my coat. "So beautiful. Fucking exquisite."

I shivered yet again, this time, from pure anticipation.

Xavier leaned down farther like he was going to kiss me. And for a moment, I almost let him. God, it had been a long time, *so* long since anyone had seen me for something other than a teacher, a mother, a tired, weary woman. Or at least, since I'd wanted them to.

But then the truth—the other truth—hit me like a freight train.

"Wait," I said. "Stop."

"No," he growled, going in for the kill.

"*Yes.*" I smacked a hand on his chest and shoved.

He bounced back two steps onto his heels, then glared at me. "What the fuck?"

"Aren't you married?" I demanded.

Xavier recoiled like he'd tasted something horrible. "Married? Fuck, no. Why would you think that?"

"Oh, I don't know. Maybe because the last thing I heard from you was that you broke up with me to go back to your fiancée."

Another set of memories I usually kept firmly locked away flooded through me. The nights I'd spent staring at that email when I should have been combing Craigslist for a crib. Wondering what I'd done to deserve this. Realizing I was alone, *so alone* with the choices this man had left me.

I opened and closed my fingers, wishing I had something to punch. Preferably him.

Xavier just blinked, looking something like a disgruntled owl.

"Your email," I prodded. "'Dear Francesca, so sorry I can't see you anymore, blah blah, my fiancée is *dying*.' Or was that all more bullshit?"

There they were—anger and jealousy rearing their ugly heads. All the Zola kids had a bit of a temper. I could hold mine better than the others, but just like the rest of my siblings, when the cap came off the soda bottle, I exploded.

This man had played me. He had strung me along, made me believe I loved him when he was engaged to another woman. And then he had left me to raise our daughter by myself.

He doesn't know that, whispered some little voice inside me.

I didn't really care.

The anger had been wiped off Xavier's face, replaced with solemnity. And, if I wasn't mistaken…maybe grief? "Lucy. Fuck, that's right —that was just when you and I…"

I didn't know why, but the idea that he had forgotten a cancer patient he was supposed to have married enraged me even more. "You forgot? My God. You really are a sociopath, aren't you? Is Xavier Sato even your real name?"

His blue eyes bulged as Xavier cleared his throat. Then his expression flashed with something a bit more dangerous. "It's not what you think."

"Oh, it's not? Because from my perspective, you were engaged but decided to have a little fun on this side of the pond before the big day."

He growled. "I was a different person then. I can explain if you'll just—"

"Explain what?" I was on a roll now. No need to stop. "That you seduced me for a few weeks? Cheated on your sick fiancée? Fucked around on both of us and made me believe you lo—"

I smashed my lips together before the last word came out completely. But we both knew what I was going to say.

Love.

Because he had said it in the end, hadn't he? Just like I had. Cast under a spell of May jasmine floating through a window and eyes the color of a lagoon gazing down at me in a nest of clean white linens, clear with utter adoration.

In a few short weeks, Xavier Sato had made me believe that the stories I loved so much weren't just stories, and that I, Frankie Zola, unremarkable middle child from Nowhere Special, Bronx, could be a heroine too.

Now those eyes were scowling at me through the night. Fiery, but rimmed with sadness. Disdainful. Like the villain he was.

Xavier took a deep breath. Then another. Then another. His hand raked through his hair, causing a few shiny locks to stick up, then flop forward over his brow. It was disarming. Charming, even, the way I clearly disturbed his impeccable veneer.

It would be so easy to hate him if he didn't look like that.

Desire seared through me. And once more, *go*.

This time, I didn't let him grab me as I ran down the street.

"Francesca! Fucking—goddammit, will you just wait! FRANCESCA!"

I whirled around two steps from the curb. "Oh my *God*. It's Frankie. Absolutely no one calls me Francesca."

Xavier caught up to me with a few long strides. The streetlight above cast a halo around his looming form. How ironic.

He leaned down so I could see his face. And smirked. "I do. Remember?"

Francesca.

Francesca.

My Christian name, shouted by Xavier's utterly kissable lips as he grabbed my body, wound my hair around his wrists, held me down as we both shook in the throes of passion and lust.

Oh, yes. I remembered.

I gulped. "What—what do you want? Beyond tormenting me, that is?"

To my frustration, he checked his watch. His *watch*, which, if I wasn't mistaken, was a genuine Patek. Or something equally flashy.

"Right now?" he replied. "Dinner. It's late, but I came straight from the airport and didn't get much more than a drink at the party. There's got to be something decent in this city, and I couldn't possibly discuss something like a broken engagement on an empty stomach."

He tipped his head toward the busy street up ahead. Broadway, I registered vaguely.

Well, at least I wasn't lost anymore.

"Shall we?"

It was the closest to a formal invitation I was going to get.

Nope.

"That can't possibly be the best you've got," I said. "I deserve better."

The sudden nonchalance disappeared, replaced by his original glower. I wasn't sure which was harder, being on the receiving end of that nearly intolerable intensity or being totally ignored for a piece of jewelry.

Xavier extended his hand. "Please, Ces. Let me explain. And afterward, if you want to go, I'll let you. You have my word."

I should have said no. I should have caught the first cab back to Brooklyn, put on my sweatpants, and forgot that Xavier Sato ever existed.

But his eyes, so wide and blue, disarmed me even in the shadows.

Curiosity killed the cat. I wondered if it was going to kill me too.

"Fine," I said. "Dinner. Let's go."

5

W e walked in silence together for several blocks, the odd couple in our finery, Xavier standing more than a foot over me, blocking out the streetlamps as I gradually recalled where I was. I should have, considering I had planned to attend graduate school not twenty blocks from here. I had been obsessed with Columbia, even while finishing my degree about twenty blocks north at CUNY. Nearly every day, I took the B train down to 116th Street to study around the neighborhood.

There was the deli that made my favorite pastrami sandwich. And that was the brownstone where I dreamed of having my very own studio apartment. One of my classmates shared an apartment with two others in a building just four blocks west. We even passed Jewel, the bar where Xavier and I had met. Two blocks from the park, three south of the Columbia campus. The intersection of Kismet Street and Ruin My Life Avenue.

On and on I strode, like Ebenezer Scrooge, followed by my shadow and guided by my own personal Ghost of Christmas Past until I stopped at the base of a tall brownstone that at one point during the last century had been converted to an enormous bookstore and café that rivaled The Strand.

"What are you doing?" Xavier asked.

I turned. "You wanted dinner. It's my favorite place around here."

He looked through the windows with disdain. "It's a bookshop."

"Correct. It's called NovelTea. And they do, in fact, have novels. And excellent tea."

He looked horrified. "You want *tea* for dinner?"

"They have food too. I can order a salad, maybe. Or a sandwich. I like the avocado toast." I was definitely still feeling the effects of all that champagne. Avocado toast would probably be the perfect antidote.

"You want a piece of the overprocessed cardboard that passes as bread in this country smeared with overripe tropical fat for dinner?"

"That's right. Delicious."

Xavier rubbed a hand over his face, muttering something that sounded an awful lot like "Good fucking God" before looking back at me. "I don't think so."

I huffed. "Where were you thinking?"

He shrugged, then pulled out his phone and scanned it for a moment. "There's a kaiseki restaurant near Lincoln Center I planned to try during my visit. Doro." He wrinkled his long nose like he had just smelled something bad.

"What now?" I asked.

"I was just thinking *I* wouldn't name my restaurant after the Japanese word for dirt." He smirked, but in a blink, his steely expression was back in place. "Just one more competitor to put out of business and poach their staff. Anyway, they're known for their Miyazaki beef-wrapped oysters. The chef has a Michelin star."

I blinked. "Is that supposed to mean something to me?"

Xavier blinked right back like I had just morphed into a cockroach. "You don't know what a Michelin star is?"

I glared. "I'm not a complete moron. I live in New York. Of course, I am aware of the world's preeminent restaurant rating system. My point is rather, why should I care?"

"Because—because—" he stumbled, almost as though the words were caught in his mouth. "Because it's the best!"

I tipped my head. "There's a lot of the best here in New York, you know. Some of it only costs two dollars a slice. Or, you know, per pot of tea."

His neck muscles bulged, but the only other sign of his annoyance was the ticking at the corner of his jaw. It would have been funny if I hadn't found his stern glare attractive. Too attractive, really.

I rolled my eyes. Apparently, champagne made me particularly flippant. "Anyway, some of us don't care about fancy schmancy oysters. Some of us just want something familiar to put a horrible night to rest."

Irritatingly, he rolled his eyes right back. "Obviously, I would pay. I am a gentleman. Some of the time, anyway."

"Are you saying I can't afford to buy my own dinner?" I demanded.

Xavier coughed. "What? No, of course not. Only that Doro is fairly expensive, and—"

"And I couldn't possibly afford it on a teacher's salary, right?"

"Well, er—"

I couldn't help arguing. I was enjoying being the one with the upper hand now. He'd had me so flustered I'd literally run out of a party, and now just a slight overreaction had this ice sculpture of a man stumbling himself.

Petty?

Maybe.

Satisfying?

Absolutely.

"You can just say it," I continued. "My tastes are plebeian, and you'd literally rather eat dirt than subject yourself to something as basic as avocados on sourdough. I'm too poor for good food."

He straightened, and the change was immediate. "Actually, yes. Probably."

My jaw dropped. "Excuse me?"

That careless shrug made another appearance. "I need to go, though. Scope out the competition, if you will. I'm inviting you along because I want to catch up. Mix a bit of business and pleasure. If there is any pleasure to be had in this conversation. Honestly, I'm not convinced."

Upper hand traded back. In the form of a slap across the face. Xavier Sato: Two. Frankie Zola: One. Or maybe just one-half.

Dammit.

I crossed my arms tightly. "I don't think I'm interested. For one, I don't like fish."

He stared at me like I had just grown three heads. "You don't like fish? Who doesn't like fish?"

I waved my hand. "Plenty of people. I had some bad clams when I was a kid. Put me off them for life."

He shook his head, muttering something like "bloody woman" under his breath. "Fine. You can have chicken teriyaki on a skewer. Maybe they'll have some day-old rice you'd prefer."

"No, I'm good with some tea and a book. Enjoy, though."

We stood there for a moment, bristling at each other outside of the bookshop without even moving out of the way of three separate people that left the place, forcing them to walk through our matched scowls.

At last, Xavier exhaled visibly through his long nose as he peered into the shop. "Fine. We'll go where you like."

"Even if it's a bookstore?"

"I love bookshops," he pronounced with the same enthusiasm people talk about the dentist. "Books are...excellent. Great...stories. Lots of...words."

"Oh, really? What's your favorite?"

"*Pride and Prejudice*," Xavier replied automatically.

No. There was no way.

"Your favorite book is a domestic romance about a bookish second daughter and a grumpy gentleman who reluctantly falls in love with her?" I snorted, pulling my coat closer. "Please. What's your favorite part?"

He gave me a look that said he wasn't playing this game anymore. "Right, then. *Harry Potter*. The Bible. Pick whatever you think is most believable."

"How about Machiavelli's *The Prince*?" I suggested coyly.

His eyes glimmered with something that approximated humor.

But before he could reply, his stomach emitted a loud growl that could be heard even over the passing traffic. I stifled a grin. The twitch in his mouth was more pronounced.

"Let's hurry," he said. "I've got to eat something, or else it's you for dinner, babe. And I don't think you'd like to know what I'd make of that."

————

TEN MINUTES LATER, I was seated in the back of NovelTea at a tiny table for two while Xavier waited near the bar for our respective orders. Tea and toast for me, beer and salad for him. After learning that the majority of the food served here was delivered premade, the salad was the only thing he was willing to eat.

I inhaled, enjoying the distinct smell of books that surrounded us on built-in shelves that reached all the way to the twelve-foot ceilings. Even at nearly eleven o'clock at night, the shop was full of students and faculty from the university who loved spending their Friday nights literally with their noses buried in books.

Envy snaked through my bliss. I tried not to think this way most of the time, but a part of me still wished I could be one of them. I'd written more than one paper in this exact cafe, had wracked my brains over countless pots of tea, trying to figure out new and exciting ways to argue against Ian Watt's novel theory. I had only just started learning all the ways that academic writing was actually like going on a treasure hunt using the very best questions and creative blends of philosophy and interpretation. I missed that challenge. I missed it a lot.

Well, even if I couldn't be a scholar, I could still read, I thought as I pulled a copy of one of my favorites off the shelf behind me. After all, that's what Elizabeth Bennett would do.

"So, who are you now?"

I looked up to find him carrying a tray bearing food. Just a hint of a humor flitted over his stern face.

"What?" I asked.

Xavier set down the tray, then proceeded to fold his long legs under the little table. It was funny, really. Like watching an extremely serious grizzly bear smash himself into a thimble.

"Before, anytime I saw that look on your face, it was because you were imagining yourself into one of your stories. So, who was it this time?"

I frowned at the book I was holding. How in God's name did he remember something like that? Then I looked up from my book and offered the sweetest smile I could muster. "'It is a truth universally acknowledged, that a single man in possession of a good fortune must be in want of a wife.'"

Xavier nearly spat out his drink. "Excuse me?"

"I was answering your question. I was thinking of one of the many Miss Bennetts. I usually am about half the time." I flipped my book so he could read the title. *Pride and Prejudice.* "You mean you don't recognize the famous opening line of your very favorite book?"

Xavier looked like he wanted to pound his chest. "Ah. No, of course I did. Great stuff. Really wonderful."

There was something about the way his voice wobbled slightly that made me peer at him for a moment. Xavier just picked at his own food, looking distinctly irritated with the state of the cucumber. Well, it was his fault for choosing something that couldn't possibly be enough for a man his size, the big silly snob.

"It was my mum's favorite, actually," he muttered just when I thought to give up the conversation.

I perked up. I could only recall bits and pieces about Xavier's mother. She was originally from Japan and fairly young when he was born. She had died when he was just a teenager after being hit by a car. They were close, but that was about all I knew.

He had never been particularly forthcoming about his family life. Or anything, really. Not when we were too busy tearing each other's clothes off.

Not for the first time, I wondered just what I had been doing all those years ago thinking I was in love with a man that really, I had barely known.

"What was her name?" I wondered.

He looked at me for a long time. "Masumi," he said quietly.

"Masumi," I repeated. "What does it mean?"

Xavier pulled at his tie again. "It, ah, can mean a few things. But the characters she used meant 'true purity.'"

"Lovely," I said honestly. "Was she a big reader?"

"Sometimes. She learned a lot of her English that way. Reading at the restaurant during the slow hours. Stealing some time at night when she should have been sleeping."

I chuckled to myself. I understood that better than he could know. How many nights had I chosen books over bed over the last four years just to have one solitary moment of pleasure for just myself? Sometimes as a mother, sleep was just overrated.

"She came to London before you were born, right?" Vaguely, I remembered some story about how his mother originally went to England as a student but had left school to have Xavier.

Now her story sounded familiar in more ways than one.

He nodded. "Yeah. She opened the restaurant in Croydon after I was born."

"Sushi?" I joked, thinking of his love of fish.

"*Izakaya*."

He tipped his head when I just blinked at the word.

"Think Japanese comfort food. Tempura, *karaage*, *yakisoba*. That sort of thing."

"Yum." I wasn't that familiar with Japanese cuisine, but I had tried a few of those. "So she must be who taught you to cook."

He gave me a queer look, something that was both terribly dangerous and terribly vulnerable. Then he stabbed a piece of lettuce, took a large bite, and nodded shortly.

We sat in awkward silence for a minute, and I pretended to read while an avalanche of questions crashed through my brain. I was tempted to press for more information, if only for Sofia's sake. It was always a little awkward when pediatricians, for instance, requested a family health history only to find I could give them just one side. But also, I knew one day she'd want to know who her father was, who his family was, and so forth. And while she was willing to be put off now, that wouldn't always be the case.

Which probably meant that I needed to tell her father that she existed too.

Shit.

"So, I've got to know."

I looked up, startled. "I'm reading." And lying, apparently.

He raised a brow. *Pride and Prejudice* was open, yes, but we both knew the pages hadn't turned once in ten minutes.

"And being quite rude to your date," he replied. "You think I'd have this rabbit food without repayment? You owe me some answers, Ces."

I swallowed. He didn't know, did he? No, he couldn't. Right?

"All right," I said. "What do you want to know?"

"Well, what've you been doing the last five years? Where do you live? Why did you leave school and become a primary teacher? Back then, all you talked about was becoming a professor." He took a sip of his beer and didn't even bother to hide his grimace.

I sighed and set down my book. "I…life got in the way. Grad school just didn't work out."

"Didn't work out how?"

Tell him. This is where you tell him.

In my lap, my palms started to sweat. Suddenly, the avocado toast looked about as appetizing as marsh goo.

But before I could answer, one of the bar girls approached the table. I frowned. This wasn't the sort of place that offered table service.

"Hi." She elongated the word in that flirty way that gave a single-syllable greeting six extra beats. "I just wanted to check in and see how everything's going. Can I get you anything else?"

Her words were pointedly not for me. Normally, I would have found it kind of funny. After all, I did have a stupidly good-looking brother who fended off his fair share of come-ons in front of me. It had become a game my sisters and I all played over who could make Matthew the most uncomfortable by pretending to be his jealous girlfriend.

But right now, I was actually annoyed. Though I couldn't have quite said why.

Xavier turned stiffly as if the girl were an irritating fly he wanted to swat, then offered that same broad, rapacious smile I'd seen at the party. "Not unless you've anything off-menu I must try."

The girl trembled and flushed bright red. I might have felt sorry for her if I didn't want to dump my tea all over her cleavage. Just how many buttons had she undone before prancing over here?

"Um, no, I'm sorry," she said. "I can ask the kitchen, though. Sometimes they experiment. Maybe they would for you…"

But Xavier's smile disappeared once he realized he couldn't get what he wanted.

"No, thank you," he said stiffly and turned away.

"Sorry. *Sorry*," the girl babbled before giving Xavier an awkward half-curtsy and stumbled away. I had to give her some credit. Hard to do in combat boots.

"Bit jealous, are we?"

I turned back to Xavier. "What?"

"Your eyes are especially green. You look like you want to murder the poor girl."

Caught out, I just snorted and snapped my book open again. "More like dumbfounded. I don't know how anyone could listen to you and not collapse under the weight of your bullshit. Unless they're young and stupid, I suppose."

"You liked my bullshit all right, once upon a time."

I swallowed, focusing a bit too hard on my book, despite the fact that Austen's words had completely blurred together. "Young," I repeated through my teeth. "And *very* stupid."

Xavier sighed and stabbed again at his salad. "So, you were telling me about your postgrad…"

I dropped my book and eyed him. Suddenly, the willingness to make small talk had left me. I wasn't the only one who had explaining to do. "No, I don't think so."

His black brow rose. "Don't think what?"

"I don't think we're going to talk about that. You owe *me* some answers, Xavi."

The familiar name fell out before I could help it. He'd been alternating between Francesca and Ces all evening, each of them stopping my heart a little in their own small ways. But I'd carefully maintained his given name, unwilling to use the endearment that he had asked me for once, long ago, when we were locked in post-coital bliss.

Call me Xavi, he had whispered between warm, deep kisses. *My mother called me Xavi.*

At the sound of it now, he froze, then carefully placed his fork on his plate. When he looked up, his blue eyes had deepened, slightly warmed, yet mirrors of the same longing I knew had to be in my own.

"So I do," he admitted.

My heart thrilled.

6

"Um. Is that it?" I said.

Xavier's sharp gaze darted up. "As it happens, I'm not used to having to tell this story."

"Oh? And why is that?"

"Because most people in London have already read about it in the bloody papers."

His tone cut across the table like a knife. Clearly it was a sensitive subject, and I had the good sense to let him breathe a bit while I processed the fact that at some point since the last time I'd Googled him, Xavier had gained enough notoriety to make the British tabloids. His restaurants must have been more successful than I realized.

I cleared my throat. "All right. Why don't you start with her name?"

"I—her name was Lucy." His throat tightened. "Lucy Douglas. Our, ah, fathers were close. Neighbors, actually."

"Fathers?" I repeated.

This I knew nothing about. Even back then, Xavier had been completely mum about his dad. Had said at the time he never knew him.

Apparently, that was a lie too.

Xavier swallowed. "Er, yeah. They were both involved in, ah, local politics."

"Councillors, were they?" I wondered. "Which district?"

"Er—" He polished off about half of his beer in one go, then set down his glass. "Forgot you knew a bit about British politics."

"Enough to understand what I read." I tapped the cover of my book. "So what happened?"

He exhaled heavily. "Lucy and I were mates, is all. Said we were engaged to get her parents off her back, but we never actually planned to marry. She died shortly after I returned home. She was sick. Cancer."

Another silence lay heavily over the table, dulling the casual clinks and slurps of the café. First his mother, then his fiancée? How much grief had Xavier had to suffer as a young man? Even worse, had the girl known about his betrayal?

That feeling in my chest dropped like a stone, lodging itself in my stomach the way it always did when I thought of those days.

"Poor girl," I said unsympathetically. "And I suppose she died thinking you loved her too? While you were off sleeping with me."

His head snapped up. "Not that it's really any of your business, but I'll have you know I never cheated on her with our little fling."

"Not my business? That's right, I forgot, I was just some piece of ass you were hitting on your way back to England, right?" I shook my head, fighting the urge to get up and run away from him again. I didn't want to have this conversation. It was just like I had thought. "You really haven't changed. Still a heartless bastard."

"We were never more than friends. We only said we were engaged to get her parents off her back. It's just when I found out she was sick, I couldn't leave her. Not for a piece of ass, as you put it. Not when she was dying."

I gripped the rim of the teacup, wishing to God I could throw the thing against the wall. Suddenly, I wanted to be anywhere but here. The walls filled with books seemed to be closing in on me. Like every one of the volumes was about to topple off and bury me under their words. Not out of anger. Out of shame.

"I'm sorry," I said quietly. "I'm being unfair."

"Yeah, you bloody are," Xavier agreed. "But I was unfair to you too back then. So there's that."

I looked up. "You were?"

He nodded. "I was. The email. It wasn't the right way to end things, Ces. Not after—not after what we had together."

So it wasn't just me.

Somehow, it was a small comfort. But other questions emerged out of it.

What was it you thought we had?

Was it as special for you as it was for me?

Did you really mean it when you said you loved me?

I settled for more logistics. "How did you meet? You and Lucy, I mean. You've never mentioned anything about your dad."

Xavier sighed. "You really want to know all this? She's dead. It's long gone. Can't we just leave it there?"

I drummed my fingertips on my book for a few seconds. "I don't think so. I think I need to know."

Xavier sighed again, forked his lettuce some more, then finally just pushed the plate aside, seemingly resigned to the fact that he wasn't going to enjoy any of it. "Luce and I met after Mum died."

I nodded. I just wanted him to keep talking.

"I never told you who my father was, did I?"

I shook my head. "I gather someone important. Would I know him?"

Xavier looked like he had a bad taste in his mouth. "In England you would. Rupert Parker. Proprietor of half the farmlands in the Cumbria. Though my uncle Henry is actually the steward."

My jaw dropped. Proprietor? Steward? "I'm sorry, what? Are you some kind of gentry?"

Xavier shook his head vehemently. "Fuck, *no*. My father—if you could even call him that—could have qualified, I suppose. I'm just the bastard he got on an exchange student during his university days. His family paid off Mum to keep me a secret—that's how she started the restaurant, you know. So for most of my life, I had no idea who he was beyond the money Mum got to put me through school."

"So, what happened?"

"Mum died when I was in secondary. Car accident."

I nodded. "I remember. I'm so sorry."

My chest tightened like it did whenever I thought of anyone losing their parents. My own father had died when I was little, and my mother had been less than present. I understood parental absence well, particularly since I'd lost my father to a car wreck too.

Xavier was quiet for a long moment. "Right. Well. After that, my dad popped me into boarding school. Maybe it was guilt. I don't really know. But it was certainly the easiest way to be done with the brat he'd never wanted to begin with, right? Shut up the restaurant, put the proceeds in an account for when I graduated. Done."

"You couldn't go back to Japan?" I wondered. "Where was your mother's family?"

His broad mouth twisted. "They were estranged. Because of me, of course. Mum had shamed her family, right? Caused a lot of strife." He drilled his long fingers onto the table. "I did go back, though. Took

Mum's ashes home to Aichi and scattered them in the Yahagi River like she wanted. I ended up staying two more years in Okazaki after I finished school. Lived with my granddad, working at the miso factory. But when I returned to England, expecting to get work as a cook or something else like my mum, another life was waiting for me."

I frowned. "What do you mean?"

He sighed. "Rupert Parker had a heart attack, apparently grew a mediocre conscience, and decided to be a father, after all." He chuckled, almost as if he thought it was absurd. "I'll never forget the day the old man showed up at my shitty flat, saying he wanted to name me his heir and offering twenty percent of his estate up front if I'd leave culinary school and come live with him, learn the running of it, and attend proper university."

"Let me guess. You took the money and started your restaurants?"

Xavier recoiled like I slapped him. "I did fucking not. Is that what you think of me?"

Unable to meet his sharp gaze, I rotated my teacup round and round on its saucer. "Right now, I'm not sure what I think of you."

It wasn't a compliment. But it wasn't exactly an insult either.

Progress, I supposed.

Xavier grunted. "As it happens, Mum had been squirreling away his blood payments for years. When she died, the money from the restaurant, plus what she left, was more than enough to get started. So, initially, I said I'd go to uni, but then I went to Dartmouth just to get away from him. Dropped out after a semester and told him to fuck off."

His broad form leaned back, getting into the story now. I waited somewhat impatiently for him to continue.

"I did exactly what he didn't want. Finished culinary school. Opened my first restaurant, then another, and another. I wanted to blend what I'd learned in Japan with what I knew about European food. I was just starting to expand when I met you. Was thinking about coming to New York then, actually. That's what I was doing when we met."

I gulped. When we met, he had said nothing about his burgeoning restaurant empire. No, he was simply "looking for work," like he was an errant traveler hopping between jobs as a kitchen grunt to pay for hostels.

Looking for work. Sure, it was the truth. Maybe. But scouring a city for your next restaurant wasn't exactly washing dishes and chopping onions.

"Anyway, almost ten years later, and here I am, CEO of the Parker

Group and the most successful restauranteur under forty in Western Europe."

Xavier's mouth quirked again into something resembling a hint of a smile. But it wasn't the fake predatory grin he served. This was real satisfaction. Pride. And then back to annoyance.

"But I underestimated my father," he continued. "The old ass was even more stubborn than I was. Started showing up at my restaurants. Hired someone to tail me, know where I was going to be on any given night."

"He sounds very controlling," I remarked.

"Obsessive was more like it. I must get it from him. And I knew what he wanted. It wasn't a son—he'd never cared about me enough for that, you know? He wanted an heir to secure his legacy. But little by little, he wore me down."

"What do you mean, he wore you down?"

Xavier glanced toward the exit, as if now he was the one who wanted to escape. "I suppose it was curiosity, really. When I was a kid, I used to wonder who my father was. Dream he'd come find me one day. Rescue me and Mum from our life over the restaurant, have some good reason for staying away. Finally, he did show up. Maybe I was a grown man, but there was a part of me that wanted to know what he was all about."

I didn't like the way this conversation made me feel. Guilt swept through me, partly hearing the echoes not only of my own childhood wishes from my mother, but from the questions I was fielding from Sofia more and more often. Wishing to God it was something much stronger, I tossed back the rest of my tea like a shot, then swallowed the rest of my pride.

"Can you imagine what it's like?" Xavier asked. "To have a parent who ignores you, treats you like you're nothing, and yet there's still a part of you that loves them, wants them to love you back?"

I stared into my teacup. For a few long moments, it was my mother's face I saw in muddy brown liquid. Her muddied expression when she came home from work after sneaking shots behind the counter of the Dollar Store. I could see the way she'd bat me and Marie and Joni away when we cried for attention, only to fall down on the sofa and pass out, leaving Matthew, Lea, and Kate to do the work of parenting for her. I could hear Joni's unanswered whimpers when we slept together on the bed.

"Yes," I finally managed. "I can imagine that exactly."

Xavier looked like he wanted to ask why. Just like he hadn't divulged much about his upbringing back then, I had never told him much more than the fact that I was raised by my grandparents instead of the mother who was still living. Neither of us had wanted to discuss the past. The present had been much more alluring.

But instead of pressing me in the exact way I'd been pressing him, Xavier had the good sense to finish his story.

"Anyway," he said. "After my second restaurant opened, I finally accepted his invitation to dinner. And then to spend the Season with him and his family."

"The London Season? Like in the books? The Royal Ascot, the Jubilee, all of that?"

Xavier looked uneasy. "Er, yeah. A bit. Most of the events are sponsored by large companies, so all sorts get invited. But yeah, the Ascot is part of it." He snorted, clearly with some strange memory. "Dad acted like I was a fucking debutante. I wasn't received at court—they don't do that anymore—but I did meet the queen at one of her garden parties. Can you believe that? Me, his half-breed bastard, in front of Her Majesty. He was lucky I even showed up."

It was hard to imagine. He was dropping words like "Royal Ascot" and the "Season" in his South London drawl, and all I could imagine was the Prince of Wales and the cast of *Downton Abbey*. It was a world I could only understand through books and television, maybe the occasional tabloid story. Nothing about it seemed real.

"You can imagine what that lot thought of me," Xavier said. "Slant-eyed bastard of the—of Rupert Parker. Treated me like I was no better than the dirt on their shoes. Except for Lucy."

"Your…fiancée?"

"My friend," Xavier corrected me. "She was nice, Ces. Not much of a looker, to the point where the others made fun of her. She was sick a lot of the time, you see. Something called mast cell activation disorder. It was why her cancer spread so fast."

I nodded. I had a student last year with the same issue. He had a tendency toward sudden anaphylaxis and a whole host of seemingly random medical issues that made it very hard for him to thrive.

Xavier continued. "I didn't care. She talked to me like a normal person, which was more than I could say for anyone else. Explained the rules of games I didn't know, helped me learn the people worth talking to, and those who weren't. Lucy kept me from making a total arse of myself. Turned out to be my best friend."

The vise around my chest squeezed even tighter, and I had to put my hands in my lap to hide the fists they were making. Pity mixed with complete and utter jealousy. It was pathetic. This woman—this dead woman—he was describing sounded perfectly delightful. Kind and generous. All the things I wasn't. Not right now.

Right now, I hated her. So. Much.

"So you fell in love with her."

It wasn't a question. There was dread in the statement as I grabbed my fork and knife and started sawing at my cold toast with bitter regret.

Xavier looked up from his pint glass, his gaze straight and true. "No."

I still wasn't sure I believed him. But before I could say so, he reached across the table and grabbed my hand. The sudden contact sizzled like I'd touched a live wire. But he wasn't letting go.

"*No*," he repeated when my eyes, prickling with irritating tears, met his. "Ces, I was not in love with her. Nor was she with me. We were friends. Best friends. And so when her parents kept trying to marry her off to any idiot who'd take her hand—and her inheritance—I offered to fill the role. At least until she met someone she actually wanted."

"Better than you?" I scoffed.

I tried to tug my hand away, but the gesture was half-hearted. I allowed him to keep it firmly in his, enjoying the feel of his long fingers threaded between mine.

"I'm glad you still think something good of me, Ces," Xavier said bitterly. "It's probably the only nice thing I ever did anyway, agreeing to marry her. Got my father off my back, too. Turns out the only thing Rupert Parker liked more than forcing his errant heir to heel was that heir marrying a rich heiress. Suddenly, everything was about the wedding. And I could do what I damn well pleased."

"Like screwing me?"

The tears pricked harder. This wasn't making me feel better. It was making me feel like the other woman. The slut who ruined everything.

"Like falling in love." Xavier's soft, deep words floated across the table. "Or so I thought."

My tongue just choked in the back of my throat while I tried to blink back my tears. I would *not* cry here. I absolutely would *not*.

By the time I was able to look up at him, he allowed me to pull my hand away so I could pick up my tea. You couldn't cry while drinking, Nonna had told me once. I polished off the entire cup in one go.

"Look," Xavier said, once I'd finally set down my cup.

His large blue eyes glimmered with hunger. Pain. The desire for me to know the truth.

"I should've told you about Lucy from the beginning," he said. "She knew all about you. She did. It's why she wouldn't let me marry her. We were going to call off the engagement when I got back. But the day I was supposed to see you last, Luce called me with the news. She'd been tired, thought it was because of the wedding preparations. But turns out it was a brain tumor. Cancer. Stage four. Terminal, of course, but made worse by her syndrome."

I swallowed thickly. It was hard to hate a dead woman, especially one who clearly had been such a saint. It was even harder when, with every revelation, I could imagine her in my head. I could see her last days, shriveled up like a prune, unable to get out of bed. Ruined by chemo, medicine, surgeries, whatever the doctors told her.

"How—how long?" I wondered.

"The doctors gave her nine months," Xavier replied. "She lasted six."

"Jesus," I whispered.

"I had to go back, Ces. I couldn't leave her to go through all that on her own. I told her I'd marry her too. I'd stick with her, through thick and thin, just like she did with me. But she wouldn't let me. And then when she died…a part of me died too. For a while, anyway."

We sat there in silence, both of us digesting the end. It was hard to hear a story like this without feeling my own pangs of grief. My father's funeral was one of my first memories, a cold, rainy day at the St. Raymond Cemetery. And then later, echoed again when my grandfather died maybe six years later. But despite longing for a mother who was absent after her part in her husband's accident, I'd still spent most of my life around people who loved me in their own way. Between Nonna's old-fashioned child-rearing, Matthew's overprotectiveness, and my sisters' chaos, I had never wanted for love. Not like Xavier.

Now was the time to tell him. Explain that he wasn't alone in the world. Not now. That in Brooklyn, there was a little girl who looked just like him. Who was dying to know who her daddy was. Who would give him all the love in the world if he would just let her.

But the problem was, I wasn't sure he would.

"Fucking hell," Xavier snapped bitterly. "What's a man gotta do to get a real drink around here?" He turned, looking around for the chittering bar girl. "Oi, girl! Got any vodka back there?"

My chair leg screeched across the worn wood floors as I stood up. Xavier turned back, looking up at me warily.

"Leaving?" he asked. "Did I scare you off, then?"

But to my surprise, I shook my head as I pulled my coat back on.

"Let's walk," I said. "We can go to that restaurant if you want. Or there's a good ramen place down the street, if you'd rather. They make cocktails, and I could use a drink too. And you need more to eat."

Xavier tipped his head, examining me for some other revelation. "I could do with some noodles."

I nodded, then pulled my purse over my shoulder. "Then let's go. I have more questions. But I'm...willing to talk too. If you want."

7

I didn't know what to think about the story he'd just told me. It seemed crazy, fantastical. But every bone in my body knew he wasn't lying. It was his eyes that did it. They flashed bright blue fury when he talked about his father and their relationship that seemed to be alternately positive and adversarial. They glowed with mirth and warmth when he mentioned his mother. And they welled slightly, pools of sorrow, whenever Lucy came up. She had obviously meant a great deal to him.

I tried to ignore the pangs of jealousy when I thought of that. Not because they were lovers. They clearly weren't. But even if he wasn't *in* love with her, he certainly loved her in his own way. They were friends. And she had known him better than almost anyone.

Which also meant that I hadn't really known him at all.

I led the way up Amsterdam toward the ramen restaurant where I used to slurp down noodles and broth while I worked out my next paper or tore through a new Victorian novel. Another life, another time. I hoped the noodles were still good.

"Cat got your tongue?" Xavier's brooding timbre yanked me out of my thoughts.

My gaze jumped and landed on a pair of planters bookending an apartment entrance, both brimming with uncharacteristic winter blooms. "I was…thinking it's nice to see flowers in December," I fibbed. "Most of the time, the city is covered with snow and slush. There's no color."

"This is a camellia," Xavier said, bending down to pluck one of the pink blossoms off the tree. "They were my mum's favorite flower, actually. She used to keep pots of them on the fire escape." He twirled the bloom from side to side. "They symbolize types of love. Red for passion. White for waiting. Pink is for…longing."

It took every ounce of control not to check his face when he said that.

Instead, I accepted the flower and became inordinately interested in its rounded petals. "Are flowers important to your, um, people?"

Xavier snorted. "My people? I grew up in Croydon, Ces, not a hut in the Sahara."

"I didn't mean it like that. Just that—Xavi, when I met you, you said your name was Sato, not Parker. Clearly, you identify with your mom's heritage. And isn't there a whole thing about flowers and symbolism and all that in Japan?"

"*Hanakotoba*, yeah. But I don't know much about it. Just what Mum told me. Like about these."

He took the camellia out of my hand and tucked it behind my ear, his finger grazing my jaw, trailing to my chin, then dropping reluctantly. I shivered, but not from the cold.

"When did you start using Parker?" I asked. "Why not the Sato Group?"

The pride faded, replaced by annoyance again. "Ah, well. See, to expand the way I wanted, I needed investors. Turns out Parker—my dad's name—opens a lot more English bankers' doors than Sato." He shrugged. "It's nothing more than that."

I wasn't sure I believed him. "So you used your father's name to get your business started?"

Xavier's jaw clicked like he was grinding his teeth. "You really didn't look me up at all after I left, did you?"

My cheeks colored, but I shook my head. "Once or twice. But Sato was a dead end. And after that…I was mad."

"Mad?"

"Furious, actually."

"Furious."

I looked up. He was so tall; I had to crane my neck. "What do you want me to say? I understand what happened now, but at the time, all I knew was that you were engaged. You broke my heart. When someone does something like that, I generally don't look back, if you know what I mean."

His suspicion morphed into something approaching respect. "Yes, I do."

"So what do I call you, then?" I wondered. "Sato or Parker?"

His lips pressed into a thin line. "Parker's fine. I've made my peace with it." Then he asked, "What about looking forward?"

I opened my mouth, but nothing came out. Looking forward to what? Another week or two of sex? A life's worth of one-night stands?

And then what?

Tell him.

My subconscious was a professor, tapping her nails on her arm, waiting for me to come up with the correct answer.

He's her father. He deserves to know. You'll have to tell him, and then this will all be over. Again.

I swallowed. "The only thing I can look forward to right now is ramen. Come on, the shop is two more blocks that way. And I'm guessing if you don't eat something other than rabbit food, that big body of yours is going to combust."

———

TEN MINUTES LATER, Xavier and I sat at a bar looking toward the Museum of Natural History Museum across Columbus Avenue, two steaming bowls of noodles and broth in front of us as onlookers passed, looking somewhat envious.

"I don't know if it was the four glasses of champagne or the pint of horrible ale, but I'll admit—this is damn good," he said as he used his chopsticks to shove a large bite of noodles into his mouth, then slurped them loudly.

I stifled a laugh. "Has anyone ever said you have terrible table manners?"

He offered me his sharkish grin again, this time with a trail of noodles cascading toward the bowl. He slurped up the rest even more loudly, then smacked his lips. "I'll have *you* know that it's considered rude in Japan *not* to slurp noodles. If you don't, your host will think you hate the food."

"I thought that was just a stereotype. Something they made up for the movies."

But he shook his head while he slurped even louder, mouth too full to answer.

"Ew," I said. "That's revolting."

Before I knew it, his bowl was half empty. "Maybe. But it's still good manners."

We sat companionably. I even slurped audibly, just to try to make him smile again. I got a few twitches, but nothing more. Still, there was a sparkle in those eyes I recognized from years past. I couldn't help it. I wanted more.

"I used to come to this place after class," I said when our bowls were nearly empty. Well, his was. I couldn't eat more than half, myself. "It was the only place within walking distance of Columbia I could afford. A bowl of ramen would keep me for the day, and they were open late. I'd get some tea and study until I couldn't keep my eyes open."

"Why didn't you just go home?"

I shrugged. "I couldn't study there. I don't know if you remember, but I lived at my grandmother's house when I was in school. It was nice not having to pay rent, but two of my sisters were still there. And they are…well, if you met them, you'd understand why I needed space."

"How many sisters do you have again?" he wondered, picking up a piece of soft-boiled egg with his chopsticks.

"Four, plus a brother."

"Six in all, then?"

I nodded.

"Let me guess—you're the baby."

I looked up to find Xavier peering at me with knowing eyes. It was infuriating.

"I am not," I said. "Middle child, actually. Kate and I share that. She's the youngest of the first bunch. I'm the oldest of the second." I held out my hands to count us off. "It goes Matthew, Lea, Kate. Then our parents split up for a bit. But when they got back together, it was me, Marie, and Joni. Marie and Joni are less than a year apart, and I'm almost eighteen months older than Marie. Both of them are still living with Nonna, freaking leeches. And they are *such* pains in the ass."

Xavier chuckled.

"What?" I asked. "That makes you smile, of all things?"

"It's funny, is all. The way siblings talk like they love and hate each other at the same time."

I nodded. "Sounds about right."

"I always wondered what it was like to have brothers and sisters. It was just me and my mum growing up, you know? Sharing a one-bedroom flat."

"I doubt our family squabbles were very idyllic," I replied. "Or any less crowded. There were six of us stuffed into that house with our grandparents. For a while, Marie, Joni, and I were all in the attic."

"Why were you there?" Xavier asked. "After your dad died, you didn't live with your mum?"

I shook my head. "No. Mom was…is…a bit of a mess."

"What do you mean?"

I bit my lip. It was hard talking about Mama. The older three's bitterness toward her was much more palpable given the fact that they had all been asked, to varying degrees, to step in when she failed. At fourteen, Matthew had essentially raised all of us with our grandparents. I didn't think he would ever forgive her for that. Lea and Kate were trying more these days to mend things, but it was slow going.

For us youngers, it was the life without a mother, despite knowing she was alive, that tended to hurt more than the loss of my father. I was only five when the accident happened, so I still remembered my dad. I could see him a lot like Matthew—tall and slim, with dark hair and a daring grin when he was sober and a mean frown and a loud shout when he wasn't. Joni and Marie didn't remember him at all, though they did recall begging Mama to stay if and when she visited Nonna's. We all did. But she always left.

It was even harder to understand that now that I had a child of my own. Leaving Sofia…I couldn't fathom it.

"She left," I said shortly. "Right after the accident."

"Car wreck, right?"

I nodded. "Good memory. Yeah, um. They were both drunk. But Mama was the one driving."

"And so, what? Your mum just up and leaves her babies after they lose their dad?"

I shrugged. "That's about the gist of it. Kind of harsh, though."

A low, long mumble slipped out of Xavier's throat.

"What's that?" I asked.

"I said not as harsh as abandoning your kids." He shook his head. "You were better off without her."

I didn't know why, but his quick judgment bothered me more than the story itself.

"You don't know her," I said. "You have no idea."

"I know if you're not prepared to do the hard work of parenting, you shouldn't become one in the first place," he said flatly. "Nothing fucks a kid up more than an absent parent. Tell me that's not true."

I thought about it and found I couldn't. I still remembered the confusion. Wondering why she left us with our grandparents. Why she hardly ever visited.

Why we weren't enough for her to try. To stay. To be better.

Xavier and I stared at each other for a long time, his blue eyes glimmering at my green.

"And you," he said in a way that made my heart thump above the traffic rushing by the window. "How could anyone in her right mind leave someone like you?"

I swallowed, tears pricking my eyes.

"You did," I said, though I knew it was unfair. "Maybe you should ask yourself."

"I was a fucking idiot," he said solemnly, no sign of jest in his voice or expression.

His lashes dropped, gaze pinned to my mouth. I knew what he wanted. And I couldn't lie. I wanted it too. I remembered all too well what magic that mouth could create.

But before he could make a move, we were interrupted by the distinct clip-clop of horse hooves coming down the side of the road. A white horse-drawn carriage with red velvet bench seating, the kind that looked like it had rolled right out of a fairy tale.

Xavier examined it with curiosity. "Ahh. I wondered if one of those might show up. You want to go?"

I snorted. "Only tourists use those."

"I am a tourist. For now, anyway."

Before I could ask exactly what he meant by that, he slapped a few bills onto the bar, jumped up, and pulled me along with him out of the restaurant. He whistled toward the carriage driver while I pulled my coat back on.

"Oi! Mate! Can we get a lift?"

The carriage stopped, and the driver turned around, wearing a dour expression. "I have to stay in the park limits, south only. I'm on my way home."

"Perfect. I'm at The Plaza. Hundred do it to take us there?"

The driver looked considerably cheerier. "Hop in."

"I cannot believe I am doing this," I said as I followed Xavier to the curb. "I feel like I have to turn in my New Yorker card by default."

"Then you might as well shut up and enjoy it," Xavier said.

Before I could offer a retort, he slipped his hands around my waist and lifted me into the carriage like I weighed nothing, then hopped in and settled his big body onto the plush red seat next to me.

"All right?" he asked.

Breathless, I nodded, allowing him to tuck the thick blanket provided in the back around my legs and waist. It felt good, maybe too good, to have someone take care of me like this. Lord, when even was the last time anyone had tucked me into anything?

"All right?" he murmured again once I was settled, though his hands lingered at either side of my waist. Once again, his gaze dropped to my mouth.

My lip caught between my teeth. He had such a nice mouth. Full, but not too full. Wide, but sensitive. Curved to one side with the promise of perfect mischief.

Suddenly I was twenty-three again, begging for a taste. Lord, and it was easy to remember just how delicious he was.

If he kissed me now, I would let him, five years gone or not. Broken heart or not. It had been long, so, so long since I'd last felt anything close to what I'd had with this man. My body ached for it.

Still, a tiny voice inside held me back. The same voice that had appeared the moment I was responsible for the love and care of another human being in the world.

Careful, she said. *Don't move too fast.*

As if sensing my reticence, Xavier sat back, sending a waft of his fresh, sharp scent through the air.

He wrapped an arm around my shoulders and pulled me into a crook that my body seemed to fit perfectly, then called to the driver.

"All set, mate. Help me take my girl for a ride."

8

S omehow, in the space of just a few minutes, or maybe the last
hour, something had changed.

He still wasn't the Xavier I had met five years ago in a bar.
That man had still been in his twenties. His uniform had been jeans,
thick black boots, and a concert tee stained with some sort of kitchen
concoction. Instead of a sleek crop, his shoulder-length black hair,
coupled with the smattering of tattoos down his left forearm, had made
him look more like a warrior than an aspiring young chef.

That man, too, had been more carefree. Still buttoned-up, guarded,
but vulnerable just the same, with the slight gangliness of a man who
hadn't quite hit his prime, with the final flashes of youthful naivety.

I remembered that naivety in my own face. It disappeared when I
had to raise a child on my own.

A child. My daughter. *His* daughter.

Tell him. Tell him.

The thoughts repeated with every clip-clop of the horse's hooves.
But still I couldn't, although now it was for an entirely different reason.
Now my biggest fear wasn't what would happen *if* he discovered Sofia.
It was what he would do *when* that happened. Whether or not he
would love her. Care for her. Treat her well.

As selfish as it was, I was terrified that once he did find out, he
wouldn't look at me the same way. I wouldn't be the girl he'd once
loved anymore. I wouldn't be his Ces, a beauty. Someone he *wanted*.
Even if it was just for the evening.

And it had been so, so long since I had felt this wanted.

Xavier wrapped his big arm around me, hugging me into his side as the carriage made its way through the park. Ahead, the gold-lit buildings of midtown peeked over the silhouetted trees, but the city's heart still seemed far away. Xavier's body was warm and solid. So much larger than mine. A true shelter.

"I've never ridden in a horse-drawn carriage," he remarked, almost more to himself than to me. "Makes me feel a bit like Prince Charming." When he looked down, that almost smile made another appearance. "What a laugh, right?"

I might have smiled back if I hadn't been so busy fighting back terror. Instead, I cleared my throat a little too loudly. "Actually, I haven't either."

"Nice, though, isn't it?"

I nodded, unsure where this was going. I wasn't really in the best state of mind for small talk, and Xavier wasn't particularly good at that anyway.

"You know," he said. "I didn't say it before. But I really am sorry, Ces, about the way things ended, back then. I should have come back to tell you face-to-face what was happening. With Lucy. With all of it."

I swallowed. I couldn't deny how hurt I had been by his sudden goodbye. But now that I knew the story behind it, all the anger had dissipated.

"It's okay," I replied. "No, really, it is. I was hurt, yes. But I understand. You—you were going through a lot. I can't blame you for not putting a meaningless fling ahead of real-life issues."

A pair of warm fingers slipped under my chin, turning my face up toward his.

God, he was beautiful. The passing streetlamps lit the sharp planes of his face like a statue, casting shadows at all the right angles. His intensity was otherworldly. I couldn't look away if I wanted.

"You were *never* a meaningless fling," he said solemnly. "I'm sorry if you ever felt that way."

His eyes dropped again to my mouth, and my breath caught in my belly. We both knew what was going to happen. He was going to kiss me. And what's more, I *wanted* him to kiss me. I wanted it more than I had wanted anything or anyone in years.

I closed my eyes.

Felt his breath on my cheek.

And then my face smashed directly into his as the carriage pulled to a stop.

"Gah!"

Xavier pulled me back upright and glared at the driver. "Nice stop."

The driver just pulled off his top hat and waved it toward the end of the block, beyond which the lights of Fifty-Seventh Street clearly shone. "We're here. I can't leave the park, though."

I followed his gesture. The hallmark green roof of The Plaza peeked over the trees from across The Pond.

Xavier gave me a look that was half cross, half embarrassed, then tossed a bill at the driver before hopping out himself. Before I knew it, he was lifting me out after him as easily as he had helped me in.

"All right?" he asked as he set me on the ground.

I nodded as the driver left us standing there at the edge of the park. Xavier was still holding my waist, large hands splayed around my hips even after the clip-clop of the horse had faded into the trees.

"You're so small," he murmured. "My hands almost touch, even with this coat you've got on."

I gulped. Even through the layers, I could feel the warmth of his fingers. Wanted more of them. All over me.

Lord, *how* had I gotten here tonight?

Tell him.

"Xavi," I whispered.

The right side of his mouth twitched with what I thought was pleasure. "Mmm?"

"What are we doing?"

The Plaza wasn't a castle, and Xavier wasn't a prince. But right now, he was making me feel like a princess being escorted to her tower.

He pushed a stray lock of hair from my face. "Is it unclear?"

I bit my lip. "No. But I want to hear you say it anyway."

And I did. I wanted him to open up. I wanted to know he was feeling all the things I was. Confusion. Yearning. Frustration.

Sudden, unexpected desire.

Xavier smirked. "Well, if I'm being quite honest, I was hoping you'd continue the night in my suite. In my bed, preferably. Though I'll settle for a nightcap to start."

He traced his thumb over the curve of my bottom lip. As if mirroring the action, his tongue slipped out and traced the edge of his own lip. God, I wanted to bite it.

"You haven't changed, have you?" he murmured. "Still just as exquisite as ever. Perfect."

Guilt dropped in my stomach. "Xavier, I'm really not—"

"Yes, you are," he interrupted gently—or as gently as someone like him could. "Right now, to me, you are."

He took my hand, then carefully turned it palm up and pressed his lips to its center. Such a seemingly innocent gesture. But I shivered anyway, and my thighs squeezed together.

Tell him. You have to tell him now.

"Xavi," I started again.

"My God, Ces, *don't.*"

I blinked at his sudden vitriol. "Don't what?" I asked, just as sharply.

Lord, the man was as mercurial as a thermometer.

"Don't say it," he retorted. "Whatever it was you were about to say to ruin the night. 'I'm really not that kind of girl.' 'I'm not sure we should do this.' Blah, blah, blah. Whatever it is, it doesn't matter."

My jaw didn't drop this time. Maybe in some odd way, I was growing accustomed to his sudden outbursts. But that didn't mean they didn't make me angry.

"Excuse me?" I demanded. "You don't know what I was about to say. Maybe I was going to say yes. Maybe I was going to ask you to keep saying all these nice things to me."

Maybe I was going to tell you you have a daughter.

"You don't know," I finished emphatically.

He took a deep breath as he looked up at the sky. Then exhaled long and low before turning back to me.

"Then how's this?" he asked with slightly less bite. "I can't think of anything I want more than to have you, Francesca Zola, alone, naked, and willing, in my bed. It might have been five years since I last saw you, but I haven't forgotten a single second of those four weeks. And now you're here, and I'm here, and I literally cannot think of a single fucking thing that could be more important than stripping your clothes off and worshipping you until the sun rises."

By the time he was done speaking, his voice had dropped to a low growl. Once more, he brushed his thumb over my lips, his gaze following, searing across my skin.

"Fireworks," he whispered, and the word echoed through my very soul. "Tell me I'm wrong."

I couldn't. Every part of my body ached for him, right on the street. Every cell set alight by his tender touch. My lower lip trembled. I didn't understand it until now what it meant to want something—some*one*—so much I wanted to cry.

"Look." His hand slipped down my arm to take mine again. "If all you want is to sit upstairs and drink subpar tea and talk for another few hours, I'll take that too. I just don't want to miss out on *you*, Ces. It feels like the restaurants, the business, everything brought me here. Just for this night. This moment. It was all leading me back to you."

I'd wished for his thoughts, and by God, now I had them. Every overwhelming one.

"So." He stood up fully, his height demanding a response. "Do you really have to go?"

I swallowed thickly. But I didn't pull my hand away.

"No," I said. "I don't."

9

Without talking, we made our way out of the park and across the street to the Plaza entrance. He didn't ask if I'd ever been here before. He didn't have to. Xavier knew I'd grown up in a distinctly different part of the city, one without golden towers and gilded lobbies. I was accustomed to Nonna's stained crochet work, not satin upholstery, grubby bannisters instead of marble columns.

"You're in the penthouse?" I asked after Xavier pressed the button marked PH in the elevator.

The doors closed. "It's the best. Or so my assistant says."

"Do you always have to have the best?"

He looked me over, a slow, lazy progression that seemed to touch every inch of my body before his mouth pressed together in mild anticipation. "I do now."

Robbed of my words, I couldn't help staring at his mouth. At the hint of a smirk playing over its soft fullness.

He leaned down. I sucked in a breath. Big mistake. That sweet scent of his was absolutely overpowering in such a small space. I mean, it made my bosoms heave. Like *heave*, like an actual eighteenth-century heroine begging for her chemise to be torn apart. Screw Jane Austen and give me Julia Quinn. Right now I was smack in the middle of a bodice ripper, which made *me* the lustful virgin.

Well, not quite a virgin.

But before he could do what we were both clearly dying for, we were interrupted yet again when the elevator doors opened into the biggest hotel room I'd ever seen. A short, portly gentleman decked in pin-striped trousers, a gray waistcoat, and a jacket that reached his knees stood just inside carrying a gold tray that matched the nameplate affixed to his lapel.

"Your—" greeted the man with an awkward sort of half-bow as we walked in.

"Mr. Parker's fine," Xavier barked before he could finish. Then he sighed, almost apologetically. "Thank you, Martin."

The butler only nodded, unperturbed by his outburst. Xavier accepted one of the cloths on the tray and walked inside, wiping his hands as he went. Nervously, I followed suit. The cloth was damp and warm, scented lightly with lavender. A rich man's way of washing his hands when he came home from the day.

"Miss?"

I turned to find Martin waiting with his tray outstretched. Xavier's cloth was already crumpled on one side.

"Oh, um, all right." I dropped the cloth back on the tray, then turned to Xavier, who was removing his coat.

"Can I get you anything, sir?" asked Martin as I took the moment to walk around the room and examine the gilt rococo designs and velvet curtains. It reminded me a bit of the Met. Some of the fancy picture frames had similar looks to them.

"A bottle of champagne," Xavier was saying. "What's the top shelf downstairs?"

"The Palm Court offers the NV Ruinart Blanc de Blancs, sir, at two fifty-five a bottle."

"Which vintage?"

"I believe they are serving the 2015, sir. If that doesn't serve, perhaps the sommelier at Daniel's can provide something adequate."

Xavier wrinkled his long nose. "Better get a bottle from Daniel's then. And a filet mignon, while you're there. Done rare."

Apparently, the ramen hadn't been enough either.

I turned and looked out the window toward the vast, dark expanse of the park, not wanting to listen anymore to their conversation. Hearing a man sniff at a bottle of champagne that cost more than two hundred dollars was surreal. To say the least. I was back in that space again. The one where I distinctly felt like I didn't belong.

Xavier had always been particular, of course. As a chef, he had very specific tastes. But five years ago, they were tastes that could be met just as easily at a hot dog stand in the park as in a five-star restaurant. For the weeks we had seen each other, most of the places we'd eaten had been five dollars a plate. Two-dollar slices. Four-dollar falafel. Cheap, food fit for students, but oh-so-good.

That denim-clad hustler who had sunk his teeth into a gyro had been replaced by this stranger in a three-piece suit. It was clear the world he'd once inhabited wasn't good enough for him anymore.

The world *I* lived in. The world our daughter lived in.

I was so lost in my thoughts, I didn't even notice the pair of hands slipping around my waist until I was pulled against Xavier's broad body.

"He's gone," he informed me as his fingers brushed over the silk and he pressed his nose into my hair. "What are you so absorbed with over here?"

I shuddered as the tip of his nose touched my neck. "I—it's a different world up here, isn't it?"

"I suppose."

His big hands pushed my coat off my shoulders, and I let it slip away, then allowed myself to lean back into him, accepting the simple contact of bodies through a few thin layers. I wasn't sure what I was doing here. But his touch felt good. Too good.

"This isn't really where I'd have expected you to be," I said quietly, waving my hand around the vast suite. "Before…"

"Before, when I was a pauper, you mean? I suppose a bit's changed since then."

I chuckled, then considered his story about his father. Even then, he hadn't been a poor student, but had already started his business. "But you weren't really a pauper back then, were you?"

There was a brief pause in his ministrations. "Not quite, no."

He didn't elaborate anymore, instead taking the opportunity to nuzzle into my neck. I couldn't help but arch into it. His lips were soft, and the way his large form arched around me, I wanted more. So much more.

"What is that you're wearing?" Xavier wondered after a long inhale just below my ear.

"It's called C-covet." I could barely get the word out.

"Of course it is," he purred as his teeth ran over my pulse. "How fitting."

I shuddered as fear and desire warred with every heartbeat under his lips. Only one of them won.

"Xavier, wait."

He sighed, but stopped, as good as his word. "Whatever you say, Ces."

He didn't move but stood straight and pulled me back against him while we both focused on the city. Or tried to.

I looked down to where his arms now encircled my ribs completely. My fingers drifted over one of his knuckles, stroking the edge gently.

"We really hardly know each other at all, do we?" I asked quietly.

There was a long silence. For a moment, I thought he might have had enough of all my doubts.

But then he gently rotated me in his arms so that I was facing him, back to the window, trapped against the glass. But I didn't feel trapped. I felt precious.

"What do you want to know, then?" he asked gently.

I couldn't quite meet that deep blue gaze. "I don't know. Anything. Everything."

"Come on, Ces. Don't be shy."

I sighed. "Fine. What's…your favorite color?"

I looked back to find him staring directly at my mouth.

"The kind that's almost dark pink. Like a lip that's been bitten."

Gently, he tugged at the bottom lip I didn't know I'd been biting.

"Xavi," I murmured.

One side of his mouth curved into a delicious half-smile. "I like it when you call me that."

I tipped my face up without even realizing it, and delicately, he clasped it between his hands. His thumb again drifted over my bottom lip. He bent down.

And the damn elevator door opened again.

Xavier growled, face suddenly full of thunder. "Fucking hell." Then, as he released me to sag backward against the glass, he called with slightly less vitriol, "Come in, Martin."

I took several beats to catch my breath while Xavier left to direct the butler where to put our drinks and two steaks that had been rushed over from the nearby restaurant.

"That'll be fine, Martin," Xavier was saying as he passed the man a tip.

The butler gave another funny bow-nod, then left. Then Xavier poured us both flutes of champagne before taking a seat on the sofa, food on the coffee table in front of him.

"Are you coming?" he asked when he realized I hadn't moved from the window.

It was only because I still couldn't *quite* feel my legs.

"Um. Yes." I made my way to the sofa and eyed the meat there. "I didn't order that, though."

"No, I did. You don't have to have it now. Steak is actually better at room temperature anyway. Most people don't know that."

I murmured something along the lines of "Nor did I" while I watched, fascinated, as I took a bite of his own filet. For such a large man, he was almost dainty with his fork. He sliced his bite off perfectly, then examined it for a few seconds, smelled it, then placed it in his mouth, where he held it still and then, at last, started to chew. Only after he had swallowed did he realize I was staring.

"Something interesting?"

I took a sip of the champagne. It *was* admittedly the best drink I'd probably ever had. "I, um, just haven't ever seen anyone eat like that before."

"This is a Wagyu filet, dry-aged a hundred and twenty days. The finest cut you can get." He eyed me carefully, as if he were measuring me up the same way. "I take my time with things worth savoring." He cocked his head, causing a spare black lock to fall over his forehead. "Or don't you remember?"

I shivered and sat back farther into the couch as he cut another piece. And another. The way his eyes closed and mouth moved over each bite was almost erotic. Actually, no. It *was* erotic.

"All right," he said once he had finished. He reached over to refill my champagne glass, which was empty. "I've answered some questions. And you've just watched me eat the rest of my dinner—quite uncomfortable being stared at. So now it's my turn to ask a few more things."

My stomach clenched, and I could feel my cheeks redden. "What, um, do you want to know?"

"Let's see…" He drummed his fingers on his knee. "Something interesting. Something no one else knows."

I swallowed. How about that I have a daughter? Oh, and that's she's yours.

"My favorite fruit is kiwi," I offered lamely.

Xavier gave me a look that told me he thought it was an idiotic answer. "Come on. You can do better than that."

You have no idea.

"I know. How about your number?"

"My phone number?"

He chuckled. "No, I already have that, thanks. I meant your *number*. You know. How many suitors has Francesca Zola had to chase out of her bed since last we met?"

I nearly choked. "You don't think that's kind of personal?"

Xavier snorted. "There's nothing to be embarrassed about. I'm just curious, is all. Isn't that the point of this little game we started? To really get to know each other?"

"Maybe. But asking me about my sexual history isn't really the same as you telling me your favorite color."

This time, he laughed outright. It was more of a bark than a laugh, but it was still there.

"It's not funny!" I screeched.

"Yes, it is." But he stopped laughing anyway. I was almost willing to be the butt of a joke again if he would keep doing it. "Fine. You can go again. Something equally intrusive. If we're doing this, we're doing it right. No more favorite fruits."

I tapped my lips for a moment, enjoying the way his eyes dilated slightly at the gesture. At least I wasn't the only one feeling things. "All right. You want sex? I want love. Who is the greatest love of your life?"

Xavier shrugged. "That's easy. No one."

Immediately, I deflated. *No one*? "Come—come on. I thought we were being honest."

"I am being honest. I've never been in love."

I balked. "Never?"

"Never. And since we're telling the truth, I don't even know if I'm capable of it. Love, I mean."

"What about Lucy?" I pressed. "You were willing to marry her, after all. Didn't you love her at least a little?"

But again, he just shrugged. "I cared for her. I wanted to do right by her. But love? No, I don't think so."

I mulled for a long moment. It didn't make sense. He was willing to throw his life away for a woman, but he didn't love her? Not even as a friend?

There it was. The memory I'd always tried to forget, all those years ago. Clearly, he had forgotten the way the early morning light had flowed into his hotel room when we had lain together in the bed, tossed in the white sheets, red-faced from sex and heartsickness.

"You said you loved me," I whispered, more to myself than to him.

But Xavier heard me anyway. He tipped back the rest of his champagne, then set the glass next to his empty plate with a clink. "I guess I did. I'm sorry for that."

I reared back as if stung. "You're *sorry*?"

His eyes were so dark a blue, they almost seemed black. "Yes. I am sorry."

"Because, what?" I asked. "Because you didn't mean it? Because you were just trying to get me into bed?"

"Well, I'd already gotten you into bed, Ces," he pointed out.

My palm twitched where it lay on my thigh, and I pressed my knuckles into my leg, forcing myself not to slap him. I almost left right then and there. But he kept talking.

"We were young, if you remember. And I liked you, Ces, I really did. Maybe even thought I did love you at the time. But now that I'm older, I know that you can't feel that after just a few weeks. If you ever feel it at all."

I remained silent, just stared at him, daring him to say more.

Really, though, I was gobsmacked. Because honestly, he wasn't wrong. How did we know that we actually loved anyone? Sofia? I loved her without a doubt. Mattie? Kate? The rest of my sisters, my grandmother. Sure. But that was family.

This was something different.

"See, I think we're all lying when we say it," Xavier broke through my thoughts.

"Lying." I repeated it deadpan, hating the taste of it in my mouth. And the way it echoed through my belly. "You think everyone in the world who has ever said 'I love you' is lying? All, I don't know, six billion of us?"

He just shrugged in that carefree way I was starting to loathe. "Maybe not lying, per se. But I don't know, maybe fooling themselves a bit. Saying what they want to feel instead of what they actually feel?"

I grimaced. "Maybe. Some people do, certainly. But—"

"Most," he interrupted. "Because real love…it's supposed to be unconditional, yeah? And whether we want to admit it or not, there's always something another person can do to ruin things. Even parents will walk away from their children if they fuck up enough."

I opened my mouth to argue that not all parents were like that. But then, what did I know?

Wasn't that the same thing my mother had done to me?

"And so," Xavier concluded, "if that love can be broken, I don't really think it was love in the first place. Infatuation, maybe. But not love. I've only ever known one person I loved that way. My mum. And now she's dead, so…"

As he trailed off, a shadow swept across his hardened face. I didn't press, lost as I was in my own thoughts.

It was good to hear him say it. Some mothers left their children, but not all. It was my deepest fear that I'd end up like mine, careless and hurtful to my own blood and soul.

But no, I'd never do that to Sofia. I loved my daughter beyond measure. And I'd protect her at all costs.

"You might be right," I admitted as I swirled the champagne around in my glass. "There's nothing like a mother's love. Maybe nothing more we can ever expect."

Xavier nodded, like he completely understood.

But he didn't. I knew he didn't.

And at that moment, I knew I'd made the right decision all those years ago.

It took him a few moments as I rose from the couch to realize I wasn't using the bathroom.

"Where are you going?"

I retrieved my coat from where he had laid it over a dining chair, then turned as I put it on. "Home."

Xavier frowned. "What? Why? I thought we were getting somewhere."

"We were." I pulled my hair over my collar, then located my clutch, which had been placed on the sideboard near the elevator. It wasn't until I pressed the call button that Xavier finally sprang up from the couch.

"Francesca. Don't do this."

I sighed and pushed the button again. "Xavi, I can't. I'm sorry."

"Can't what? Talk? Get to know each other again? I don't understand."

I didn't respond, just stared at the doors of the elevator, *willing* them to open before I changed my mind. I squeezed my eyes shut, trying to pull my daughter's face before me. It was for her I was walking away. Because this cold, brooding creature had no place in our life.

Sofia was bright, affectionate. Mercurial and stubborn, yes, but incredibly loving. She was open with her heart and wanted nothing more than for others to do the same with her. So how, in good faith, could I offer her a father who had just admitted he could never love her?

I turned around to tell him exactly that.

But before I could, he kissed me.

His mouth was softer than I remembered. Warm and demanding, with the taste of steak and good champagne swirled through a flavor that was uniquely his. His hands were back around my waist, pulling me flush against his broad body before they slipped down, down to take a firm hold of my backside and lift me up so we were face-to-face.

The second he touched me, some current of energy deep inside me sprang to life. My fingers entwined through his silky black hair. As his hands slipped under the hem of my dress to take lush handfuls of flesh, I groaned into his mouth. He sucked my lower lip between his teeth and growled again before devouring me once more. And I opened like a parched flower to a rainstorm, soaking up every bit of it.

Something crashed to the marble floors of the suite. I had no clue what it was. The lights flickered on and off. I didn't know if it was because I was backed against a light switch or if it was the pure energy flowing between this man and me.

It didn't matter that he had changed so thoroughly from a lonely, if brooding young man to this jaded, ice-cold stranger. Some things apparently never change. Like the wanting—oh, *God*, the wanting—a deep chord of yearning that cut straight to the quick.

Five years ago, I'd been a naive virgin with no qualms about giving myself to someone I'd thought loved me. Now I knew exactly what he could offer, the heights of pleasure he would provide.

And I knew the price of falling after he brought me there.

"Stop," I muttered, hoarse and out of breath.

My fingers stayed where they were, my legs wrapped completely around his waist, dress hiked up around my hips while he kneaded my thighs mercilessly.

"Fuck, Francesca," he muttered before kissing me again. "*Fuck*. This mouth. I've been dreaming of this mouth for *five fucking years*."

"You—I—we—"

I could barely get words out between kisses. So much for savoring. He was eating me whole.

But I was giving as good as I got. I wanted nothing more than to tear his shirt off, rip the tie from his neck, and feel every inch of hard muscle under this finery. Feel its heat pulse under my fingers.

Except.

Sofia.

"Xavi—*oomph*—STOP!"

It was halfway between a shriek and a moan, but his lips paused, teeth poised over my collarbone. He leaned back to examine me as if I were a wild animal he'd caught in a trap. Like he knew if he made a wrong move, I'd chew my own leg off trying to escape.

"What is it?" he purred. "Tell me. I'll fix it."

Behind him, the elevator door opened. I seized my chance, wriggling out of his arms and hurtling toward the carriage.

"Francesca, wait—fucking hell—where are you going?"

I pressed the button for the lobby, not caring about the wrinkles in my dress, the state of my hair, streaked makeup, or my undoubtedly swollen lips.

"I'm sorry," I said as the doors began to close. "I'm sorry. I can't do this. I'm sorry."

"Ces—stop—just—"

He was clearly flustered trying simultaneously to put his clothes back into order, calm the obvious evidence of his arousal, and somehow stop the elevator doors from closing too.

He failed.

I should have been relieved. I know I should have.

But when the doors had finally shut on his shocked, disoriented face, the pit that had opened in my stomach earlier that evening widened even more. I pressed my face into my hands and, for no reason I could fathom, began to cry.

10

"**M**amamamamommymomMOMMEEEEEEEEE!"

I squinted in the sunlight streaming through my window. One day I'd invest in blackout curtains. It would be the same day I could afford an actual bedroom, or at least double-paned windows to mute the squeaky breaks of the B61 bus or better ventilation so I wouldn't smell the exact moment Mattie's tenant decided to cook his favorite pork sausage. Basically, when I didn't have to spend all my extra money on things like preschool and underwear and snack packs and all the other things small children need.

Sofia yanked at my arm like it was a water pump, jumping up and down in excitement. "Guess *what*? Aunt Kate said she would stay for breakfast, and she let me watch *Daniel Tiger* all morning, and you've been asleep forever, and we're going to the park now, so *get up*!"

"Okay, okay, peanut. But first, Mommy needs to remember she's human."

Hand pressed to my temple, I forced myself out of bed while Sofia pounded back downstairs, leaving me to get dressed and find my way to the bathroom to splash water on my face. When I returned, Nonna's dress was hanging over the back of my wardrobe door like a black ghost of last night's fiasco. I stood before the wardrobe mirror, looking between the LBD and the pajamas covered with pizza-eating unicorns gifted from Sofia (meaning Matthew) last Christmas.

I snarled at my reflection. I'd scrubbed off my makeup so hard last night my cheeks were still red. Pillow marks streaked across the left side of my face, and my hair had frizzed up beyond belief.

I turned away, then hastily stuffed my hair into a messy bun. A shower could wait. I needed some tea.

Downstairs, I found Kate in the kitchen, already pouring me a cup.

"Oh, you saint." I slid onto one of the counter stools as she slid the mug across the stained brown tile. "What are you still doing here?"

She shrugged. "You seemed a little worse for wear last night, and Mattie didn't get home until God knows when. I thought it would be best if I stuck around when Sof got up."

A glance at the microwave clock told me it was just after nine a.m. Which meant Kate had dutifully risen with my four-year-old at approximately five thirty in order to let me sleep in.

"You're amazing," I told her.

"I know." She glanced back at the TV, where Sofia had plopped herself back on the sofa to watch the next episode of her beloved cartoon tiger, then leaned across the counter toward me. "All right. You going to tell me what the hell happened last night?"

I stared at my reflection in the deep brown liquid, pretending I hadn't heard her.

Last night...hadn't been pretty. Specifically, *I* hadn't been very pretty. Not while I ran in Nonna's wrinkled dress all the way to the Fifty-Seventh Street station. Not while I had felt lonelier than the rats gathered on the subway tracks while I waited for what seemed like hours for the F-train to rumble down the tunnel. And not while I had ruined my best black pumps jog-walking the mile across the Hamilton Heights footbridge from Carroll Gardens to Red Hook at close to two in the morning, praying I wouldn't get mugged on my way there.

When I'd finally gotten home, Kate had popped up from the couch, half asleep in a pair of Matthew's pajamas, informed me that Matthew had decided to stay at his friend's uptown, then asked me blearily how the night had gone.

I'd lied, then run upstairs behind the privacy screen so I could cry alone.

But sisters know. They *always* know.

I sighed and stirred my tea. "I ran into Xavier."

"Who's—oh! You mean..." Recognition dawned on Kate's face as she did a series of rapid takes between me and Sofia.

I nodded. "That's right. In the middle of that stupid party. Apparently, he's this big-time restaurant owner or something. Friends with all these rich people. He changed his last name, which is why I could never find him."

Something twisted in my gut. Based on what I'd seen last night, he was *one* of those rich people.

"Holy shit." Kate shook her head. "So, Jesus, what happened?"

I cringed. I really didn't want to go into this. "We talked some…and then he followed me out of the party…and I sort of went back to his hotel room."

"You *what*?"

A squeak from the TV told me Sofia was now half-paying attention. "Aunt Kate, can you please be quiet? I'm trying to watch my program."

Kate and I both bit back giggles. When she was irritated, Sofia tended to talk like Nonna.

I motioned for Kate to button her lip, then called to Sofia. "Sorry, Sof. We'll keep it down."

"Thank you!"

When I looked back at Kate, she was drumming her nails on the counter.

"What?" I asked.

"Don't 'what' me. You know what. Give it."

I sighed. There was no getting out of this. "Fine."

And so, in hushed tones my daughter wouldn't hear, I proceeded to tell her everything that happened. All about seeing Xavier at the party. The way he had followed me around the Upper West Side. About the carriage ride in the park and just how close I'd come to spending the night with him in the Plaza.

"Holy shit," she said again once I was finished. "No wonder you were upset."

"Yeah." I took a long drink of my tea. Nothing was better than tea.

"So, what happens now?"

I glanced at Sofia, then back at her. "What do you mean, what happens now? Did you not hear my story? He's a sociopath, Katie. He doesn't believe in *love*, of all things."

She shook her head and looked at Sofia for a long time. "I don't know. I seem to remember him saying it to you…you know…back then. More than once."

I didn't reply. Yeah, I remembered that too. Just like I remembered the feeling of having my heart torn out of my chest.

Kate shrugged. "His best friend dies. His mom dies. His dad's a jerk. Seems like the guy has been through a lot. That kind of trauma can take a while to come back from. We should know."

Something squeezed deep in my chest when I remembered the look on Xavier's face as he had told me about Lucy. Or mentioned his mother. On the outside, that wasn't the expression of a man who couldn't love.

So maybe it wasn't that he couldn't. Maybe he just wouldn't.

But really, wasn't that worse?

"Also, and I hate to bring this up…if he's loaded, couldn't you sort of use the money?"

"Oh my God, thanks! I'm not a gold digger."

She rolled her eyes. "I didn't say you were. But hello, you're bringing up that one by yourself, and dude owes you five years of child support. Make the rich bastard pay up."

I bit my lip. I couldn't pretend the thought hadn't occurred to me, particularly when the B61 woke me up for the third time in the night. But even then, the thought of Sofia's face upon learning she had a dad only to have him break her heart killed any instinct to pad our savings or her college fund. It wasn't worth it if he couldn't be the father she really needed.

"No," I said. "I can't. It's better I didn't tell him. And it's going to stay that way."

This time, Kate remained silent, lips pressed together. She clearly didn't agree, but unlike the rest of my family, she knew when not to press an argument.

Which reminded me of something else.

"One more thing. Katie, you cannot tell anyone in the family. Especially not Matthew."

She gaped. "You can't be serious. Frankie, you live together. He's basically Sofia's surrogate dad."

"So? You know how everyone gets. Joni and Marie will gossip with everyone, Lea will come over here to tell me what to do, and Matthew is so bored and depressed right now over that woman uptown. He'd probably hunt Xavier down with his Beretta just for fun." I sighed. "I don't want him sticking his nose into my business. Especially when I'm not even sure what's going on."

Kate looked doubtful. "Still. This is huge. You can't expect me to keep your secret indefinitely."

"Why not?" I countered stubbornly. "I keep yours. Did I ever tell Nonna that you spent that week in Paris with your boyfriend, not on a class trip? Or have I ever told anyone about that girl you dated last year?"

Kate just scowled. Her somewhat fluid sexuality wasn't something she was particularly open about inside our grandmother's extremely

Catholic purview. She wasn't in the closet, per se. But like me, she wasn't interested in inviting our nosy family into her personal life.

"Fine. Your secrets are your secrets, just like mine belong to me. But that doesn't mean I agree with them." Her dark eyes gleamed. "Is he a good kisser, though?"

I blew a raspberry. "Um. Yes." Good didn't even cover it.

"Better than Jeff Lopez in the tenth grade?"

I closed my eyes. "So much better."

Kate just watched me with something amounting to regret. "Damn."

I nodded. "I know."

But before I could agree with her, the doorbell chimed through the house.

"I'LL GET IT!"

Sofia catapulted off the sofa and flew past us down the hallway.

"Nothing is more exciting to a four-year-old than answering the front door," I told Kate. "It's probably just Pete, the downstairs tenant. I think his rent is due tomorrow." I pushed up from the stool. "I should probably put on something other than pajamas. Like a bra so Pete doesn't have to stare at my headlights."

"He'd probably love it," Kate said.

I trudged down the hallway, calling as I went toward the front door. "Hold on, Pete. I'm still in my pjs. I'll be right there after I grab a sweater."

"Mommy, it's a man!"

I frowned, suddenly alerted to the long shadow splayed over Sofia's tiny form where she stood in the middle of the hall, looking at the door. Every hair on the back of my neck stood up.

I knew that height. The span of those shoulders. The haughty cock of that head.

"Shit," I whispered as I grabbed a sweater off the coat rack and made a beeline for the front door.

"Mama," Sofia called behind me, still watching the silhouette through the translucent windows. "I don't think it's Pete."

It was *definitely* not Pete. For one, this silhouette had about eight inches on our downstairs tenant.

"Sofia, *don't*," I snapped, much sharper than I would ever normally.

Guilt flashed through me, but she stopped just before opening the door and turned, lip quivering.

"I'm sorry, baby. Just…you shouldn't answer the door for strangers," I told her, more gently this time, at odds with the thump of my heart in my chest. "Please go back to the kitchen with Aunt Kate, okay?"

Her blue eyes narrowed suspiciously at me, but she nodded. "Okay."

"Thanks, peanut."

She shuffled down the hall.

Then thunder sounded on the other side of the door.

"Francesca!"

I didn't move. I knew exactly who it was, but I couldn't answer the door. It was like asking me to open a fireplace and jump right in.

"Francesca!" he shouted, followed by another thunderclap of knocks.

"Mama?" Sofia called from the kitchen.

"Stay—stay there, please," I called back. "I'll be right there, honey."

Then I took a deep breath and opened the door.

Xavier stood with his fist raised, ready to launch another onslaught of knocks. He was dressed down from last night in a pair of tailored jeans and a black Smiths T-shirt that revealed a bit of a tattoo peeking up from the collar, plus an Army green puffed jacket that made him look like a street fighter. The one bit of color other than his eyes was the pair of explosive orange and blue Adidas high tops. He looked utterly gorgeous, much closer to the carefree boy I had met five years ago.

But that storm in his eyes was miles away.

"Where is he?" he demanded, looking over my shoulder.

I backed up. "What are you talking about? What are you even doing here?"

"I'm not fucking around, Francesca. Where the fuck is he?"

"Where's *who*?" I demanded.

"It. Him. He. That fucking prick you have in there—don't fuck with me, Ces. No one runs out the way you did last night unless they have something—or some*one* to hide. So tell him to come out here and face me like a man."

My jaw dropped. "Are we in the middle of a Regency novel? Did you bring pistols or swords?" I made a show of looking around him toward Van Brunt Street in one direction, toward Coffey Park in the other. "This is Brooklyn, Xavi, not Grosvenor Square. You can't duel someone just because he's my significant other, even if I had one, which I do not."

"Then what's with all the stupid excuses?" he rattled on, suddenly jumping between the balls of his feet, hands flexing open and closed like a boxer ready to take an opening jab. "You ran away last night faster than a train. I didn't get a wink of sleep thinking about it. One minute you've got your tongue down my throat, the next you're bolting for the lift like a scared fucking rabbit!"

"Keep your voice down!" I hissed. "I have neighbors."

"Oh *really*. 'Neighbors' are we calling him? I don't buy it. Who is he, Ces? I want to know his name before I punch his fucking face in."

"Mama, who is that? He said a *bad* word!"

With the slipperiness of an eel, Sofia slid in front of me to examine the perpetrator. I might as well have been made of stone.

"Who are you? Why are you yelling at my mama?" she demanded, staring straight up at the man who suddenly looked about as inanimate as I was.

The reasons were obvious.

Xavier's stare was fixed on the little girl whose face looked so much like his. Whose deep blue eyes tilted in the same way. Whose cheek-bones were evident even under her chubby, rose-hued cheeks. Whose long nose snubbed in the same way and whose lips mirrored his scowl when she was angry.

The daughter he never knew he had.

His eyes widened as if he had seen a ghost.

I supposed in a way he had.

"Xavier," I whispered.

The sound of his name jerked him out of his daze. It was strange to see him like that. The Xavier I knew was laser-focused to the point of suffocation. Utterly vigilant and totally single-minded.

But the stupor was short-lived, because when his eyes met mine, there was no sign of distraction, no lack of focus. Once again, his gaze was as sharp as a blade.

And I knew at that moment my secret was out.

11

I t's hard maintaining one's dignity in pajama pants covered with pizza-scarfing unicorns. It's even harder when you have six feet five inches of fury tailing you, looking like a supermodel. An extremely pissed-off supermodel.

Kate had wisely shuffled Sofia away from the door as soon as she glimpsed who was there, leaving me to step outside. Now that I had to have this conversation, I wasn't doing it within the supersonic hearing of my four-year-old. Nor was I about to leave her alone with her unbeknownst daddy while I put on something that wasn't covered in cartoon characters.

And so, I left the house in my fantasy wear, an old pink sweater, plus a ratty parka to guard against the wind while Xavier used the sidewalk as his own personal runway.

You have to pick your battles, is what I'm saying.

Xavier made it exactly two blocks before he picked his.

"Francesca, stop."

I shook my head. "I need breakfast. Pioneer Works actually has a decent café in the back. They make a really good matcha latte."

"I don't give a fuck about matcha lattes, Ces. Who the hell was that? Did I imagine I was talking to my own baby picture back there?"

I sighed and finally stopped on the corner, ignoring the looks of a few passersby walking their dogs or likely on their way to Fairview Market at the end of the pier.

"Xavi, I will explain everything, I promise. But first, can I get some breakfast? And maybe take us somewhere so we aren't discussing the fact that my daughter has your eyes in the middle of the street?"

Maybe it was the simple admission or the fact that I was acknowledging out loud what we both knew, but Xavier opened his mouth and nothing came out. Much like last night, when he was telling me about Lucy, he looked vulnerable. Scared, even.

Welcome to parenthood, buster. Terror had been my constant companion since that second line appeared on the pregnancy test five years ago. She was a persistent bitch too.

"Come on," I said gently. "It's cold. I'll buy you a hot drink, and then we can talk."

I was stalling, but it appeared to work. He followed me another few blocks to the café inside the local art gallery I had mentioned, then waited silently while I chitchatted with the baristas. I ordered us both matcha lattes and a couple of the locally made scones, then guided Xavier back out to Van Brunt and on toward the river's edge.

We sipped our drinks and ate our pastries while we walked. Even Xavier couldn't sniff at their buttery goodness. But the second we arrived at the tiny park on the Hudson, populated by only a few dog walkers braving the frigid December drizzle, he exploded.

"How could you fucking do this to me?"

I finished my latte and tossed it in a nearby trashcan, focusing on anything but him. "You're going to need to be more specific than that."

His glare was machete-sharp when I finally looked up.

"Now is not the time to play games. That little girl—"

"Sofia," I interrupted. "She has a name. It's Sofia Elizabeth Zola, after her great-grandmother and then my favorite book character."

"Sofia."

He said the word slowly, like he was tasting each syllable. I tried and failed to ignore the tension gripping every inch of my body. God, we were only at her name, and I was already about to implode.

"It's pretty," he said.

Well, it was something.

Xavier swallowed thickly and pulled at his scarf. "So…*Sofia*. She's…how old?"

"She just turned four."

"And she was born…"

"December third."

"Which means she was conceived…"

His eyes flickered as he was clearly counting back approximately nine months from December third. Hope crossed his face, and I wanted to slap him for it.

"According to my doctor, approximately May third," I said sharply. "I'm sure you can remember what exactly we were doing on May third."

His mouth opened, then closed, and his eyes dilated slightly. Yes, he remembered. So did I.

"She was almost two months early," I added, if only not to imagine the way Xavier's big body looked over mine naked. "Spent two weeks in the NICU before they sent us home. She was a fighter."

I didn't elaborate more, though I could have. You can't really explain the trauma of birth to someone who hasn't been there, and you really can't explain the terror that comes when your new daughter weighs less than three pounds, can't eat or even breathe on her own, and has to live in a plastic box for the first two weeks of her life. It was touch-and-go there for a few days.

Xavier stared at me while he processed everything, those blue bullets tunneling through me. I resisted the urge to avoid his gaze and toe my sneaker into the sand. This was *my* daughter. I wasn't ashamed of her when I arrived at the hospital alone to a bunch of pitying looks from the nurses and doctors. I wasn't going to be ashamed of her now. I'd take whatever was coming for my choices about raising her the best I could.

"So she's…she's mine?" he asked finally.

He asked like he felt he had to. I supposed he did, but it still felt like a slap in the face.

"Of *course* she's yours," I snapped. "I wasn't the one who was engaged to another woman while we were sleeping together. *I* was a virgin when we met, in case you forgot. Did you think I was lying about that?"

He blinked repeatedly, looking rather like a fierce, oversized owl. Clearly, he didn't remember that minor detail. Or else he was still in shock from the previous disclosure.

Yes, Xavier, she's your daughter.

Yes, that means you're a father.

Yes, yes, yes.

"How could you keep my own—my own daughter—from me?" He started out shouting, but by the end, his deep voice cracked.

My hands folded into a tight fist over my heart. For some reason, all the heartache, the frustration, the isolation of becoming a lonely single mom at twenty-three—all of it throbbed anew.

So, while I felt for him, I was also angry all over again.

"It's not like you're that easy to reach," I said lamely.

Xavier's head snapped up like it was pulled on a string. "Oh, really? What, with my massive public profile, five email addresses, multiple assistants, social media accounts, and so on?"

"I think you're forgetting that you weren't using the same name, you asshole," I retorted. "You may be Xavier Parker now, but back then, to me, you were Xavier Sato. Not that I would have cared any more than I do now, but on top of not telling me about being engaged, you also neglected to tell me who you *actually* were."

"Sato was my mum's name," he sputtered. "I only took on Parker for the business. I told you that last night."

"Yes, you told me. The point is, I didn't know then, did I? So how could I have reached you, huh? I didn't really have loads of energy to track you down as a new mom. You know, between recovering from birth, learning to breastfeed, trying to find a job, and taking care of an infant *by myself*."

"Fuck that. You had my number. You don't think it would have been so hard to drop a quick message? 'Hey, Xavi, great shag last month. Those eight inches really did it for me. In other news, you're gonna be a dad.'"

"You know what? Fuck you," I snapped, surprising even myself. Four years of being a mother and then an elementary school teacher had rendered my language G-rated most of the time. If this was an indication of what Xavier brought out in me, my instincts were right from the beginning.

"Fuck *me*?" he repeated, dumbfounded.

"That's right! Fuck *you*. That heartlessness right there? *That's* why I didn't contact you. Because what child needs a father who thinks about women like that? Who shows up at their door the morning after they make out just to ruin their lives and threaten their family!" I grabbed at my hair hard enough that the elastic band holding it back snapped, tossing my sleep-tangled curls all over my face. God, I had barely even begun to process the things he had been yelling once I opened the door. "Fuck!"

"That's horseshit, and you know it," Xavier retorted right back. "I have a right to know about my own daughter, Francesca."

"And I have a duty to protect my baby girl from anyone who could hurt her!" I threw back at him.

"What?" He looked absolutely flabbergasted. "Why in the fuck would you think I would hurt her? My own flesh and blood?"

"Because you hurt *me*!" I fairly shrieked, startling a flock of pigeons and a few people walking their dogs by the waterfront.

"Everything all right?"

We both turned to find a man and his boxer stopped nearby.

"Fuck off," Xavier snarled.

"Calm down," I said. Then, to the man, "I'm sorry. We're fine, thank you."

"You sure?" he asked, looking suspiciously at Xavier. Not exactly like he wanted to fight him or anything. But like he wasn't above calling the police.

I couldn't really blame him. Last night, Xavier had looked refined and distinguished in his three-piece suit. Today, in his street clothes, combined with his overall size and obvious anger, he looked more like a criminal than a respected businessman. Downright dangerous.

"I'm sure," I said. "I'm just fine. Aren't I?"

We both turned to Xavier, who had folded his arms across his broad chest and continued to stare daggers at the guy while he mouthed "fuck off" again at him.

I sighed. Not helping.

Our interloper looked like he didn't believe me, but slowly backed away under the force of Xavier's glare. When he turned back to me, his eyes were ice cold. But he also looked like he was about to crumble. Just like me.

"You broke my heart, Xavi," I said, unable to keep my voice from cracking. I swiped at the tears leaking out, one by one. "I was in love with you, and I thought you loved me too. I would have done anything for you. I would have married you if you'd asked—yes, even after just a few weeks. But then you just…well, you know what you did."

I shook my head, wiping again at a few more insistent tears. I sounded insane. Stupid and naive. But of course, that's what I had been, once. Didn't he understand how fragile that kind of naivety really was? Hadn't he *ever* felt so breakable?

Xavier exhaled forcefully through his teeth. "I—I know. But it's not the same thing. This is—this is my daughter, Ces. Not some tawdry love affair. She's more important than a broken heart."

I couldn't help but wince at the word "tawdry," but he didn't seem to notice.

"You know what I went through as a child, not knowing my dad." He pressed his hands hard into his temples, then shoved them back through his hair. "How could you think it would ever be okay to let her believe her father abandoned her?"

"Because I've been on the other side of that," I replied. "I was part of a family whose parents kept coming back again and again, but also kept hurting us every single time. How was I supposed to trust you when you hid an engagement and ended things so callously? Over a freaking email! Like I didn't matter at all."

For a moment, I was five years old again, standing at my parents' bedside, trying to wake my mother up as a bad thunderstorm rocked the city. She had been passed out cold after another bender, too far under to even register her daughter's needs. It had taken my fourteen-year-old brother to get me back into bed. Matthew had sat with me through the storm until I'd finally gone to sleep, supporting me just like he supported his niece now when I wasn't around.

But I'd still wanted my mother. As any child would. As I always would, time and time again, until finally she left for good.

"You said it yourself," I said quietly. "You don't believe in love. But Sofia deserves to be loved. Every child deserves to be loved by their parents. And when they just get scraps, it hurts more, I think, than not having that parent at all."

I squeezed my hands together, then shoved them deep into the pockets of my parka and stared at the ground. I didn't really have anything more to say about the matter. I probably wouldn't know for many years if I had been right or wrong to keep Sofia a secret. But I had done my best to protect her, which was a lot more than my parents had ever done for my siblings or me. And I couldn't be sorry for that.

Xavier stared out at the water for a long time. At least two Staten Island ferries passed the Statue of Liberty, one in each direction, before he spoke again.

"I want to see her." He looked back in the direction of the house. "I'd like to meet her. Properly, this time. I think we can both agree you at least owe me that."

The slight glimmer of hope and vulnerability almost had me.

But I had also noticed that he hadn't refuted anything I'd said about him. About my reservations, and the reasons behind them.

"I—I can't do that. Not yet."

His eyes flickered back at me, twin pools of icy heat, with something dangerous lurking below the surface. "Why not?"

I forced myself to tip my chin up and met his gaze. *Stand your ground, Frankie. If not for yourself, for Sofia.*

It always had to come down to Sofia.

"I am *very* careful about who Sofia meets and when," I said. "Something like this? Introducing her to her father? It's going to affect her a lot." I shook my head. "I'm sorry, but I have to think about this. How, when. If."

The muscles in Xavier's jaw clenched on that last word. "If."

Keep going, Frankie. Don't move.

"Yes, if." I inhaled, then breathed out. "I don't know you anymore, Xavi, last night notwithstanding."

"That's absurd. You just said you loved me."

"And *you* said it was nothing but a tawdry affair." I shook my head. That one had really stung. "No, you're going to have to wait. I need to see what's best for Sofia. Get to know you better. See what your life is. Find out who you *really* are. Then, and only then, if I believe you won't hurt her…then you can meet your daughter."

He examined me for what seemed like hours. Now would have been a great time to make my exit, to sweep away on the last word like the heroines of my favorite books. It's what Elizabeth Bennett would have done, for sure.

But the intensity of his gaze kept me rooted to the spot like I had been completely turned to stone. A statue to his Medusa's glare.

Did that make him a snake?

After what seemed like an eternity, Xavier shoved his hands deep into the pockets of his jacket and took a few steps so we were less than six inches apart. Slowly, he bent down, and even in the winter wind, his salty-sweet scent of cologne, soap, and brine washed over me, causing a different kind of tension to ripple over my skin, a different kind of knot to twist in my stomach.

I closed my eyes. How could anyone bear this kind of torture? How could anyone fight it at all?

His breath was warm on my ear as he spoke.

"You'll be hearing from my lawyer."

The deliciously twisted knot turned to an anvil. When I finally opened my eyes, he was gone, swept away like a phantom, but leaving the ghost of his unspoken threats behind.

INTERLUDE I

Xavier

It was close to eleven p.m. by the time I made it to Miss Flanders, a pub just a few streets from my office west of Camden. It was my last meeting of the day, and since it was with Jagger, I insisted on going over the weekend numbers from the opening of Chez Miso with a pint and the best beef Wellington in London. Normally, I preferred to eat cleaner food like I was brought up on, but tonight I just needed a drink and something heavy to calm the knots in my gut that hadn't loosened since I'd left New York two days earlier.

"Fuck me, that's it," I greeted Jagger when I saw he'd already taken the liberty of ordering my drink.

"Cheers," he replied, accepting a fist bump before we both settled down to our sides of the booth. "Thought you might need that."

"You've no fucking clue." I polished off about half of it before setting the glass back on the coaster. "Did you order for me too, like I asked?"

"The waitress said they were out of the Wellington, but special tonight is steak and kidney pie, so I got that. Work for you?"

I nodded. I would have eaten grass at this point in the day.

"So." Jagger leaned back in his seat and stroked the goatee he'd grown after some girl had told him he looked like Tony Stark. He didn't, and it was ridiculous, but he was still my mate and really good with numbers. At least one of us finished our degree. "You want the good or the bad?"

I finished my ale and waved my hand at the server for another. "The good. The bad is always the longer conversation."

"Raves from the *Guardian*, the *Mail*, the *Observer*, and ten others. You're booked out for six months. I think it's fairly certain you've got another hit."

I nodded. It was what I expected. "And the bad?"

He shrugged. "Just Louise Fernsby."

I scowled. "That witch? Let me guess—another rant?"

Jagger nodded. "Fucking brutal, man. Wish you hadn't dumped her after one night, eh?"

I scowled. "A one-night stand by definition is for *one night*. I thought she was just a girl looking for a good time, not the newest food critic for the *Times*. Or daughter of its bloody owner. She told me her name was Lulu, for fuck's sake."

Jagger just grinned good-naturedly. My mistakes with women—this one in particular—were legendary, but he only ever laughed with me, not at me. This was why I had hired him when I started the Parker Group. As much for his affability, which I lacked, as for his business sense.

"Well, for what it's worth, I think she'd give you another shot," he said. "Every time I run into her at a party or what, she's always asking after you. Calls you 'that horrible lord,' like you were a character from *Downton Abbey*."

"You've watched *Downton Abbey*?" I wondered, thinking of Francesca. She'd know exactly what he was talking about.

Jagger just snorted. "'Course I have. Women fucking love it. All I have to do to get laid is invite a girl over to Netflix and chill, put that show on, open a bottle of wine, and my night is made."

I shook my head. "You're an idiot."

"An idiot who gets some anytime he wants. Not that you have that problem."

I remained quiet as the waitress set down our plates.

"Cheers," I said to her when she smiled at me, but I didn't give her more than that.

"Right," Jagger said. "So the opening was a smash, other than Lulu's shit review, which means we can focus next on Paris, yeah?"

"Actually, I'm going to be heading back to New York," I said in between bites of pie.

Jagger frowned. "What? That wasn't the plan. You said you were there to check out the competition, not to start a new restaurant. We already leased the space in St. Germain, and you're supposed to be interviewing designers and head chefs next week."

I shook my head. "Change of plans. New York is the next destination. Paris is too saturated."

"And New York's not? There are more restaurants per capita there than any other major city." Jagger squinted and rubbed his goatee. "What aren't you telling me?"

I stared at my plate. The pie was delicious, filled with aromatic beef and kidney, the delicate gravy Miss Flanders was known for, the flaky pastry crust that melted in the mouth. Suddenly, though, it tasted like sawdust.

I set down my fork. "Something came up."

"Something came up? Xav, if I have to cancel all our carefully-laid plans to take over France, you're going to have to give me more than that."

I heaved a sigh. "I—you remember that girl I met when I was there looking for my first expansion? Right before Lucy got her diagnosis and Kori finally took off?"

Jagger's face darkened, both at the memory of Lucy and the difficulty with our first joint venture. He had been friends with her too—mostly through me. "Ah…sort of? Wait, the one from Brooklyn?"

"The Bronx," I corrected. "She's Italian. Or her family is."

"Is? So you saw her again this last trip? You dirty dog."

"It was a bit more than that." I pushed my plate forward, unable to eat anymore. My stomach was growling, but every time I thought about what Francesca had done, I wanted to be sick. "Turns out she had a kid just after I left. And, well…it's mine. I have a daughter, Jag."

It was the first time I'd said it out loud. Not even at home in the mirror. The words stuck in my throat, choking me one by one.

"Bloody hell," Jagger said after a few long seconds.

That's when I knew it was a real mess. Nothing shook my best friend.

"So, what happened?" he asked. "How did you find out?"

With some difficulty, I told him the entire story, beginning to end, when Francesca and I shouted at each other in the middle of the street and I threatened her with the courts. Jagger listened through it all, taking pensive bites of his fish and chips with the occasional forkful of mushy peas. In the end, his response wasn't exactly what I expected.

"So, how'd she look?"

I glared at him. "After all that, *that's* your first question?"

He shrugged. "Well, yeah. If I recall correctly, you wanted to marry this girl. You came home from New York that year looking like a Disney character, all starry-eyed and twitterpated. Like, you actually told me you loved her. And, mate, *I* know you don't have a heart of stone, but it's what everyone else says about you."

My scowl hardened even more. I was perfectly aware of my reputation. Sometimes I was even proud of it. People don't fuck with someone they think has no conscience.

"Francesca looked good," I admitted, then bent to my food.

Jagger's brows rose about an inch.

"Really good," I conceded.

"Yeah?"

"Yeah." When he waited even longer, I elaborated. "All right. She's a fucking snack."

Jagger chuckled. My friend knew me well enough to understand that I barely gave compliments to anyone. And when I compared Francesca to food, what I was really saying was that she was a five-star, ten-course meal at the best restaurant in the world.

Shit. Did I really think that?

"It can't be all that bad, then," he said. "Don't you worry about Paris. I'll delay the frogs, and you go back to New York, win back your girl and your daughter, then bring them home when you're ready." For some reason I couldn't fathom, he grinned like he wanted to break open a couple of cigars or some shit like that. "Congratulations, Xav. You deserve a bit of happiness."

At that, I just shoved my head in my hands and groaned. "Happy isn't really the word for it. She lied to me. About my own kid. There's no coming back from that."

"Right, but—"

"You don't understand. I found out about Sofia, and I swear to God, I've never gone from wanting to fuck someone to wanting to kill them so fast in my entire life."

Jagger munched a bit of fish meditatively while he examined me. "Well, this is you we're talking about."

I scowled. "What's that supposed to mean?"

"Well, I'm sure you know the story of Dr. Jekyll and Mr. Hyde?"

I rolled my eyes. "Fuck off."

He shrugged, like I'd suggested he have some more black pepper. "If it's really as bad as all that, maybe it is for the best you keep things platonic. If this girl brings out Hyde in you that fast, you don't want anything to do with her. Best let her go, for her sake as well as yours. Just focus on the kid."

He was right. I knew he was right. But I didn't like the churning in my gut when he said, "let her go."

"What'd you say her name was again?"

"Francesca," I said immediately.

He shook his head. "You already said that. I meant your kid."

"Oh." I swallowed. "Sofia."

Again, that feeling like my stomach was turning inside out. I'd only seen her for a few seconds, really. Long enough for the blue eyes that matched mine to laser straight through me. Long enough for every cell in my body to register some odd kind of belonging. Kinship.

"So, what'd the lawyer say? I assume you saw one."

"Three, actually, and they all said the same thing. Most I can expect right now is joint custody."

Jagger cocked his head. "You actually want custody. *You*?"

"What's that supposed to mean?"

"I mean, it's not like you have a lot of experience with kids. Do you even like them?"

I frowned. "I could like kids."

Jagger just gave me a long look.

"I could like my own kid," I amended.

His expression didn't move.

I finished my ale and sighed. "Anyway, it's a long shot, and that's only after I sue for a paternity test and spend the earth proving Francesca's a poor parent."

"Well, you can afford it. And she wouldn't be the first you conquered to get what you want."

Another stomach flip. When it came to my business, if there was something I wanted, whether it was a particular chef or a property, I'd bulldoze through any obstacle until I got it. But this was different. Jagger was right. I could take Francesca to court for years if I wanted. Bury her in legal this and motion that. Play really dirty and twist her life around.

But then what? I'd have a little girl who didn't know me from Adam wanting to know what the fuck happened to the mother she loved. And for some reason, I didn't doubt for one second that Francesca was loved by our kid. Something told me she was an excellent mum. Maybe even the best.

And who knew what kind of dad I'd be?

As much as I hated it, Jagger was right about that too.

Fuck.

"Speaking of estranged fathers, have you heard from yours lately?"

I frowned and looked up. Jagger might have been my best friend, but he wasn't given to asking after the man he knew I hated most. "Henry Parker is *not* my dad."

"Well, since yours passed, your uncle's the next best thing, no?"

I grimaced and forked a big bite of pie to avoid answering. Jagger knew exactly how I felt about my uncle and steward of my father's estate. Henry Parker had moved right in after his brother's untimely death. At first, I'd been happy to let him do it. I didn't belong there, no matter how hard my father tried in the end. And the rest of the estate's denizens always let me know it.

"Anyway, there's news from Kendal, my friend."

I rolled my eyes. "How much do they want now?"

"Didn't say. Just that he's been trying to reach you, and you're giving him the cold shoulder."

"My uncle actually called? Not his secretary or that idiot who wants to be his fourth wife?"

Jagger just shook his head. "The man himself. Didn't say what about, but I can see you know."

I huffed and swirled my pint glass around, watching the amber liquid slip down the sides. "He's been trying to bring me in for a while."

At that, Jagger nearly fell out of his seat. "In? As in back to Kendal and parliament and—"

"I don't know," I cut him off. "And honestly, I don't give a fuck. Just like I didn't give a fuck four years ago. Maybe he's getting old and wants to make up for being a complete arse when Dad died. I don't really care anymore."

"Yeah, but…" Jagger trailed off, like he was trying to figure things out. "He's still family, yeah?"

I swallowed guiltily. Jagger was an orphan, raised in a series of group homes in Croydon. We'd met when he was staying with a couple living across the street from Mum and had kept in touch even after he'd been moved again.

I wouldn't have wished my friend's life on anyone, but I wasn't sure having a bloodsucking uncle constantly after you was any better. My dad's people had proven time and time again they weren't better than the end of a cigarette butt. Whatever soul-searching Henry Parker was doing these days, I wasn't interested. He wanted a blessing before he died? He could visit a minister. I had more important things to do.

"He calls again, you tell him to fuck off," I said. "Just like that."

"Errrr…" Jagger looked like that was the very last thing he wanted to do, especially to someone like Henry Parker.

"Just do it," I said. "I'm unavailable for the next six months, at least. I've got a new restaurant to open. And a daughter to meet."

12

"Bye, Ms. Zola! Thanks for the sticker!"

"Bye, hon. Have a good weekend."

I waved to my last student, a round little guy named Aiden, who had a sweet tendency to return to the classroom at least three times every day for things he forgot. Some days, like today, I was able to round up the items and leave them on my desk. If he got them all in one go, I gave him a sticker. Today's featured Snoopy.

I waited for the door to my classroom to close completely so I could slump behind my desk like a deflating balloon. The first week back after vacation was always difficult, but this one had been harder than most. I felt like I'd been through a tornado, with a headache that was pounding like hailstones.

Maybe it was because the holidays hadn't really been a vacation at all. Two weeks of checking my phone while pretending to my family that Sofia's father hadn't stormed back into my life like a rain cloud, threatened legal action, and been completely silent since—yeah, not so relaxing. I couldn't even remember what I'd gotten for Christmas.

The only one who knew anything was Kate, who still texted at least five times daily, telling me to clue Matthew in.

"You're being an idiot," she had told me three days ago, when we were walking back to Nonna's from New Year's Mass. "Our brother is a lawyer. And right now, he's an unemployed lawyer and part-time bartender, which means he has more time than ever to save your ass."

"Did it ever occur to you that I don't always want Mattie—or any of you—to save me?" I countered stubbornly, kicking aside an ice-covered rock. "Other people shouldn't have to clean up my messes."

"It's not a mess, Frankie. It's your life. And we're not just people. We're family."

I huffed and focused on Sofia, who was skipping ahead with her cousins, Matthew a shadow just beyond them. "Well, I can't tell him now. He's leaving for Italy tomorrow."

Matthew had informed the family at Christmas that he'd gotten a job as an interpreter for a few weeks in January. A bit more prodding at home revealed it was for *her*—one Nina de Vries, of whom I'd heard exactly nothing since the Christmas party almost a month earlier. None of my sisters made a secret of the fact that they thought she was nothing but trouble, but his face when he told us said otherwise.

"You haven't been living with his glum mug since he got put on leave," I added. "Maybe we don't approve of her, but he's been looking forward to this trip for a month. It's the first time in months he hasn't started drinking before noon. And he's stopped chain-smoking too."

Kate had just grumbled something about a blonde bimbo and too much wine but had the sense not to argue. We both knew Matthew needed a change of pace. Whatever was going to happen with Xavier would have to wait another few weeks.

A knock on the door of my classroom pulled me out of my thoughts.

"You look like you need a drink."

Adam Klein, the art teacher, stood casually in my doorway, one thumb hooked onto a belt loop of his slightly too-skinny jeans, the other braced against the frame.

"Oh, hey," I said, summoning a bit more energy to be civil, despite just wanting to take a quick nap before picking up Sofia. "Just a little tired, I suppose."

"A few of us are going to Dave and Buster's for happy hour…"

I scowled. Dave and Buster's really didn't seem like a great antidote for a headache.

"But," he pivoted, "I happen to know a fantastic place that does killer margaritas a few blocks north. What do you say?"

"I mean, I need to—"

"I know you don't pick up your kid until five on Fridays, Frankie," Adam cut in with a toothy grin.

I frowned. "How did you know that?"

He shrugged. "Heard you tell Jenna at lunch a few days ago."

I breathed a little easier. It was too easy living with my brother to get suspicious about every little thing.

"Right, yeah. I usually give myself an hour on Fridays."

"Sounds good."

Adam sauntered into the classroom, grabbed one of the extra chairs sitting next to my desk, then flipped it around so he could sit on it backward, exuding that easy confidence of a man who knew he was good-looking, at least in his immediate milieu.

Once again, I wondered if I should consider taking him up on one of his offers. I happened to know at least three teachers who had already made it their life's goal to bang him before the year's end. I always figured that when you're surrounded by mostly other exhausted women and tiny children for the majority of the day, you'll take just about anything. But maybe I was wrong.

I looked at him again, trying to see what the others did. Most male teachers I knew were attractive in that mussed, homey sort of way academics and graduate students have about them. Sort of like a worn-in couch. Not exactly stylish or sexy, but not altogether an unwelcome place to be.

Adam definitely fell into that category. Average height, floppy brown hair, tortoise-shell glasses, and friendly brown eyes. His legs did fill out his jeans nicely, even if they were stained with paint. His smile was bright and non-threatening. Patient, despite the fact that he was the definition of persistent.

"So tell me," he said. "How are *you* doing these days? I feel like we barely get to talk."

I tried not to point out that I didn't really talk to anyone. It was hard to be close to your coworkers when you were leaving as soon as possible every day to avoid daycare overage fees. Twenty dollars a minute was no joke.

I shrugged. "I have a kid." *And a baby daddy. And maybe a pending lawsuit.* "I'm busy."

Adam clicked his tongue knowingly. "I get that. Your daughter— what's her name again?"

"Sofia."

"Right, right. And she's how old?"

"Four." I busied myself with rearranging my pencils. Where was this conversation going?

"Frankie."

I looked up. "Yeah?"

Adam's eyes were wide and guileless. Bright. Light. "I'm kind of fumbling this, but it can't be that surprising that I'm kind of into you. Have been for a while now."

I blinked. It wasn't. I knew it. But I also wasn't used to anyone being that direct.

"Like, since you started teaching here," Adam rattled on, apparently unaware of my sudden discomfort. "You always seem too busy with your kid and everything, but I figured why not, you know? No one can be a nun forever. And no time like the present. So, maybe we can get a drink or something. Nothing major. Just a drink."

I still didn't say anything. I wasn't sure how to respond to any of this. Honestly, I'd never even thought about Adam like this.

Maybe because he isn't blue-eyed, British, and out for blood? Kate's voice rang loud and clear.

I smarted. What did she know?

Adam didn't seem to notice my internal dialogue. "Come on. You look like you need a break from this place. I'll walk you out."

He didn't wait for an answer, just stood up and tucked the chair back under the desk. The rest of the room was pretty much in order, so I grabbed my messenger bag, pulled on my parka, and followed him out.

He chattered as we walked through the halls, waving to the remaining teachers we passed, commenting on the occasional student's artwork, until we had crossed the playground and left school grounds. I offered the occasional "sure" and "yeah," but just like every day of the past month or so, I could barely focus.

I turned in the direction of Sofia's school with every intention of stopping for a cup of tea and some quality time with the newest romance on my Kindle before picking her up. But before I could, Adam threw a casual arm around my shoulder and grinned down at me.

"So, what do you say?" he asked. "Sound good?"

I blinked. I was horrible. So rude, and to someone who had been nothing but nice to me for years.

"I'm so sorry," I replied, straining a little under the weight of his arm. "I totally spaced out there. Does what sound good?"

Adam just tipped his head good-naturedly. "Margaritas?"

I was going to say no. I was going to say I didn't even like margaritas that much. That I didn't like being touched without my consent, or that it was kind of inappropriate for him to be doing this to a coworker on school property. I was going to say a lot of things, namely that I had no interest in happy hour with Adam Klein now or ever.

But before any of those things could be said, I caught sight of a shadow hovering underneath a barren maple on the corner.

Xavier Parker stood wrapped in a black overcoat, hands shoved deep into his pockets, stone-still despite the chilly breeze floating off the nearby East River. His dark hair was combed back, waving softly in the wind, but that gentleness was erased by the way his dark blue eyes, with the precision of a dagger, were trained not on me, but on Adam.

I should have been terrified. It had been a month. I had taken him at his word that he was as successful as he seemed—if only because I was too scared to learn exactly *how* powerful Xavier really was. How easily he could ruin my life.

So yes, there was unfinished business between us, not to mention a threat he had yet to make good on. And now that business that needed to be resolved as soon as possible, if not for my sake, for my daughter's.

But there was also something about Xavier that made me do a lot of things I shouldn't.

Instead of doing what I knew was rational and sensible, I looked up at Adam with my sweetest smile. "Sure. A drink sounds fine."

———

FOR A MINUTE, I thought maybe I'd imagined him. Adam led me a few blocks up Court Street, gabbing the entire way about some portrait series he was working on at home, preferably something that could be featured in a new gallery in Fort Greene. He'd learned to paint during a short course at St. Martin's in England, apparently, when he lived there briefly with his family. On any other day, I might have found the story interesting. I would have peppered him with questions about the place I'd always wanted to go.

Unfortunately, I was too distracted to listen as I kept looking over my shoulder for my big black shadow.

I had imagined him. I must have. There was no one there when I'd looked back again, nor had there been for the past four blocks. This was my fear playing tricks on me. Another sign I needed to take care of my business before it took care of me.

By the time we reached the pub Adam had suggested, I was satisfied that Xavier's scowl had in fact been a product of my imagination. I smiled to myself as I found a seat at the bar while Adam left to use the bathroom. And then shrieked at the sound of my name in a familiar brooding British voice.

"Francesca."

I spun around and nearly fell off my barstool. "Oh my God, *what* are you doing here?"

Xavier slid onto the stool next to me and rolled his eyes. "Well, I didn't come all the way to Brooklyn for the views, Ces. You saw me outside the school."

Catching my breath, I gingerly sat back down. "You mean when you were stalking me at my place of work? Yes, I caught that. Just like *you* clearly saw me leave with my coworker."

"Yeah, I think we all know what your *coworker* wants from you."

Xavier glanced with a skeptical brow toward Adam, who was now at the other end of the bar, presumably ordering drinks. He was laughing and grinning at the bartender, who was batting a pair of fake-looking eyelashes at him.

"And the barmaid, it seems," Xavier remarked. "And probably anything in a skirt." He turned back to me, his dark gaze taking more than a few moments to drink me in. "You can do better."

I swallowed, feeling slightly uncomfortable in my favorite corduroy overalls, a Blondie T-shirt, and one of the many wool sweaters I picked up at the Goodwill. My fingernails were unpainted, with a few remnants of glitter from today's art project stuck to my palms. My hair was tossed up in a floppy bun, and the only attempt was my favorite gold hoops. Xavier, on the other hand, was wearing a cashmere coat, sleek leather gloves, and yet another black suit. I looked like one of my students, while he looked like Bruce Wayne. I was dressed for going toe-to-toe with eight-year-olds, not a tycoon.

No, no, no. He was not getting the upper hand. Not this time. This was Brooklyn. My school. *My* turf.

"Everything all right?"

We both turned to find Adam standing in front of us with two glasses, one with his drink of choice, the other wine.

He held the latter out to me. "I took the liberty of ordering you a Chardonnay, since you didn't want a margarita."

"She doesn't like white wine," Xavier cut in. "Only red."

"Oh, shit." Adam glanced between the two of us and the wine. "I can get you another glass—"

"No, that's fine." I accepted the wine and took a sip. "That was very thoughtful, Adam. Thank you."

Xavier was right—I didn't typically like white wine. But I'd gulp this entire thing down like water if it wiped that smug look off his face.

"Hey, man, I'm Adam." Adam held out his now free hand to Xavier.

"Oh, sorry," I said. "I'm rude. This is—"

"Xavier Parker," Xavier interrupted. He did not put out his hand.

"Nice to meet you," Adam said, squinting slightly as he took back his hand and examined Xavier. "You look familiar, actually. Have we met before?"

Xavier just snorted. "Unlikely. Unless you read the *Mail* or the *Mirror*."

I resisted the urge to flick him on the temple like I would do to Marie and Joni when they were being brats. "Stop being a snob," I murmured before turning back to Adam. "Xavier is…an old family friend."

Adam looked between us dubiously. I did my best not to twirl my hair and whistle. I knew what he was thinking. Between Xavier's fancy duds and my red sweater that had been pulled out of shape by too many little hands, we didn't exactly look like friends. Or people who would even exist within the same universe together.

"That's right," Xavier said smoothly. "A *very* good friend. Who, I'm afraid, is going to have to steal her away."

"I don't think that's necessary right now…" I started.

Xavier arched a sleek black brow. "But we have important matters to discuss. Or did you forget?"

I sniffed. "Adam was nice enough to buy me a drink. I'm going to finish it. *You* will have to wait."

"Francesca. I mean it."

"Francesca?" Adam snorted. "You mean Frankie?"

Wrong. Move.

Xavier turned that deadly blue glare onto my companion, who visibly shrank under its force. "Yes, Francesca. As in, her name. What's it to you?"

I sighed and set down my wine. A brawl over my given name was the last thing I needed.

"Adam, I'm so sorry, but Xavier is, unfortunately, correct. We have some personal things to talk over. I'm afraid I'll have to take a rain check." I fished a ten-dollar bill out of my purse. "Will this do?"

"I've got it."

Xavier smacked a twenty down on the bar top. "Least I can do for ruining your little date."

Adam stared at the bill, then Xavier, like he wanted to punch them both. I closed my eyes, exhaled, then picked up the bill and tucked it back in Xavier's jacket pocket, just below the pocket square that matched his charcoal-gray tie.

"Thanks, but that won't be necessary," I said. "If you'll just wait for me outside, I'll finish up here."

When he didn't move, I gave him the same look I practiced on Sofia when she refused to clean up her toys. The same one my grandmother had given me for years every time I bitched about doing the dishes or folding laundry. And probably the same one her mother had given her back in Italy, and on and on for who knew how many generations.

Xavier shuddered, as if he had just been shot through with an arrow. "Christ," he muttered, but stood just the same.

"I'll see you outside," I said sweetly and turned to pay for my drink and make amends with Adam.

"I'm sorry about that," I said once Xavier had exited the building.

"Interesting guy," Adam replied before taking "You sure you're all right?"

I nodded. I felt anything but sure, but I didn't really have a choice, did I?

"He really does look familiar," Adam was saying. "Where is he from again?"

"South London." Dammit, where was my other glove?

"Curious. I'll have to look him up. He didn't go to Eton, did he?"

I opened my mouth to say no, but then realized I didn't know. "I'm not sure. I know he moved schools a bit when he was a teenager. I'm not sure where he ended up, though." I frowned, having located my glove on the floor. Gross. "Why?"

Adam gazed at the exit contemplatively while I finished putting on my coat and scarf. "Oh, that's where my parents stuck me when we lived there for a couple of years." He caught me watching him curiously and grinned. "Diplomat's kid. Like being an army brat, but with better perks. You need help there?"

I blinked, shocked. Uber-hipster, tortoise-shell glasses-wearing, slightly scruffy *Adam* attended Eton College? Along with my ex-boyfriend and father of my child?

Without waiting for my answer, he got up and helped me with the other arm of my coat, which was inside out, while I slung my messenger bag over my shoulder.

"Well, at least I got a few minutes this time," Adam said as he leaned down to press a brief kiss on my cheek.

I wanted to step out of reach but was too tied up between my things and the bar top to duck him. We were at the kissing stage now?

"Rain check," he said kindly as he stood back up, despite the fact that I was the one leaving.

"Sure," I murmured. "See you Monday."

"Have a good weekend."

———

I REEMERGED from the bar to find Xavier pacing outside like a dog waiting for its master. I couldn't help the satisfaction pooling in my belly. Yes, I'd taken a little longer than was strictly necessary to come out. Yes, I was hoping for this exact effect.

I'd been sweating for a month. He could sweat for ten more minutes.

When he saw me, he stopped, masked the irritation, and offered a cool half-smile. "I hope he wasn't too heartbroken you had to ditch him."

That did it. All the stress, annoyance, frustration, and fear that had been piling up for the last ten minutes, not to mention the last month, came flying out of me.

"Yes, I came out here, but only to prevent you from causing an immature scene with someone I work with." The more I thought about it, the more upset I grew, getting to the point where I was stripping off my gloves and shoving my hands into my pockets for want of something to do. "I know we have things to settle, but, Xavi? I am not at your beck and call anytime you want to show up and play the caveman. What are you doing here, anyway? It's been a month, and I haven't heard from you once."

Xavier's smug expression vanished. "Do you know, you are terrifying for someone so small. How do you manage it?"

I just folded my arms and stared up at him. I wasn't in the mood for games.

He sighed. "Fine. *Fine*. It seemed more appropriate to come in person. Given, you know, the circumstances."

"I think it would have been more appropriate to pick up the damn phone. Given, you know, the threat you made. Where have you been, if not consulting your giant team of lawyers on how best to screw me over?"

He exhaled through his teeth. "I was calming the fuck down," he said through his teeth. "Seemed necessary after I was told I had a *daughter* I never knew about."

I just rolled my eyes. "I wish I could take a month to cool down every time someone pissed me off. But since I live with a four-year-old, it doesn't really work like that."

Xavier's entire body tensed at the mention of Sofia, and a finger of fear slipped right down my neck.

"Right," he said. "Well, about that—"

"If you're going to serve me with papers or a lawsuit or whatever, you could have just sent a process server or some delinquent to do it," I rambled on, suddenly unable to keep my hands still. "You didn't have to fly across the big blue ocean to scare me and Sofia again."

"I—no, I didn't." He dragged the ball of one foot across the sidewalk, then the other, like a slow motion tap dance. "Look, can we go somewhere and talk? Just you and me. About everything."

"No lawyers?" I meant to sneer, but it came out more like a whimper. I didn't want to admit how much he had scared me with that.

He gave me a hard look, but one that softened after a few seconds. "Not today," he said finally.

My stomach twisted. I supposed it was better than the alternative.

"I have some time," I said. "Maybe I'll get a glass of wine after all. Red, of course. Not white."

I turned around before that wicked, knowing smile crossed his face again. I had to. I was afraid I would smile back.

13

"So, are you really here just for me and Sofia?" I asked as we started back up Court, this time heading past the school where I worked and up toward Cobble Hill and more restaurants.

I liked Carroll Gardens. It was a little nicer than Red Hook and close enough that I could walk home on nice days. I also liked the fact that there were still traces of its original Italian roots in a few remaining shops and fire escapes. It felt a little like Belmont too, the neighborhood in the Bronx where I'd grown up. Close to home, and yet far enough that I'd gotten away.

"I—for the most part," Xavier said. "I was supposed to be opening a new restaurant in Paris, but I pushed that date. I'm prioritizing New York for the time being."

"So it's a work trip."

I wasn't sure why that bothered me so much. Obviously, he was a busy man, but I didn't like the idea of Sofia as an afterthought.

Or yourself, my subconscious sneered.

Oh, shut up.

He sighed, looking up at the cloudy sky, then back at me. "It's a reason to be here until I know what's going on with the *real* reason to be here. If you get my reasoning."

I laughed. "Um, not really."

To my surprise, he chuckled back. Not quite a laugh. But it was in the neighborhood.

"Look, when I left before, I was angry. Justifiably, I might add. But I thought about it, and now I'm mostly..." He shook his head, like he was trying to sort out the words. "Curious, I suppose. Still gutted about all of it, of course. But, right. Yeah. I guess now I'm mostly curious."

Curious. Well, that wasn't exactly what I was expecting.

"About what?" I asked.

"I want to know everything there is to know about her," he continued as we walked. "I assume that will take time. So I made some. I'm a busy man, Francesca. But I won't be too busy for my own blood. You see?"

I swallowed. What did that mean for me? Was he planning to hire some big-shot city lawyer to take custody away? Was he planning some kind of revenge that would undo the life I'd built for me and Sofia?

Looking up at him, the way he glowered at nearly everything we passed, I wondered if he was the kind of person for whom revenge was an everyday practice. Which made me wonder if he had any of the softness required to love a child.

"So, let's start at the beginning," he said.

"Which one?"

"You find out you're pregnant. And you think I'm in London, engaged. So...what next?"

I closed my eyes for a moment, inhaling the scents of Brooklyn in the winter. Car exhaust, a few hints of wood burning fireplaces, and the thick overlay of ice and snow. It was a tactic I generally used to keep me in the here and now. Those weren't really days I liked to think about. Most of them had been blocked out.

But I couldn't be scared of them anymore. It was the past.

"Fear," I admitted. "I was scared to death."

Xavier was quiet for once, waiting for me to continue.

"I finished that semester—I only had a few weeks left, you see. And I intended to continue graduate school that fall. But by September, I was showing. A lot. My family knew, of course, and I needed to make some real plans. But then all that went to hell too."

"Because she came early, right?"

"Almost two months," I confirmed. "She was tiny. Two pounds, four ounces. Like a pack of chicken breasts, no bigger."

He held his hands out in front of him, clearly imagining something that size cradled between them.

"She was in the NICU for another two weeks. I spent the first few sleeping there with her, but then they made me go home." I sighed, resisting the urge to stop. The terror and confusion and fatigue of those days were rushing back with every word. "I cried every night until she came home with me. I was so, *so* scared. You can't understand—"

"Unless I was there," he said quietly. "Yeah."

I couldn't argue with him. Guilt sprouted in my belly. But what would he have done?

"And after that?" he wondered.

"She came home eventually. We lived with my grandmother, holed up in the attic for about six months while she grew and got healthy. It was all right. Nonna fed me a lot and sometimes got up with me when she woke in the night. My sisters watched her sometimes so I could sleep. But it was clear I wasn't going back to school or anywhere else for a long time. And so mostly it was just…us."

It was hard not to tear up at those memories. Matthew had worked tirelessly to convert the old attic into a room where Sofia and I could convalesce apart from everyone else, hanging drywall, painting the subfloor and covering it with old rugs, laying a huge king mattress directly on the ground so we could sleep together safely since she hated the crib. Sometimes I had felt a little like Rapunzel, locked in a tower— especially when Sofia had colic. But mostly it was a safe space. A place I felt loved. A place where I could figure out what would happen next.

"When she was six months old, that's when I applied to teach. I knew I couldn't go afford to go back to graduate school on my own. Not with a premature newborn, and not as a master's student without funding. And New York City schools have this program where you finish your degree while you work because they need staff so badly. And so, when I got the job in Carroll Gardens, Mattie—that's my brother—got an apartment for the three of us. And then his house in Red Hook, where we live now. I got my master's—in teaching, not English. But still, it's something. And Sofia gets a home and a family."

Xavier was quiet for a long time, digesting my story. I couldn't imagine what he was thinking, especially with his unreadable, stony expression.

"You never thought of…"

I turned at the corner of Court and Union, outside an Italian restaurant named after Marco Polo. "Of what?"

Xavier looked queasy, like he didn't want to say it. Immediately I knew.

"Oh," I said. "Of getting rid of her, you mean?"

He nodded slowly.

I shrugged. "Well, no. I didn't, to be honest. I mean, I could have. But…no."

It was hard to explain. Yes, we were Catholic. So, nominally, we didn't believe in abortion—though to be honest, I didn't know anyone, my family members or otherwise, who weren't pro-choice. This was New York, after all. And I could also understand fully—maybe even more now than before I had Sofia—why a woman would choose not to sacrifice her own body, life, and essential wellbeing for a pregnancy. Motherhood was unbelievably difficult, and I was only four years into it. I loved my daughter more than my own life, but raising her was the hardest thing I would ever do.

The truth was, at any other time, with any another man, if I'd gotten pregnant by literally anyone else…yes, I would have done it just to save my own life and protect my future. Even then, sitting in the bathroom, staring at that damn test, the thought flickered through my mind quicker than lightning. But it was expelled just as fast.

Because she was his. Maybe Xavier had never felt that way, but at the time, I believed he loved me like I loved him. An all-encompassing, life-consuming, once-in-a-lifetime kind of love that I might never see again but had been blessed to find in the first place. Yes, he'd broken my heart, but even then, what we had felt sacrosanct. And in Sofia, something of that love had survived.

But how do you tell someone who doesn't believe in love that that is exactly what saved his child?

"I loved her," I said simply. "Even then. Even before she was hardly…anything. I loved her. And I wanted her. And so that was my choice."

"Even though it cost you so much? School, career, independence. I don't suppose most twenty-seven-year-olds in this city are more worried about changing nappies than nightclub entry."

Again, I shrugged, then crossed the street without answering, Xavier close behind. At this point, there was no use worrying about what might have been. This was my life now. You couldn't go back.

As we passed a bookstore, I stopped and gazed inside at the shelves and shelves of beauties. My first loves, really.

"I used to take Sofia here when she was a baby," I said. "They had a story hour. She had no idea what was going on, really, but it was a reason to get out of the house. And it was a place where, I don't know…I guess it was a place where I still felt like myself."

He looked hard through the window like it would reveal something important to him. I was tempted to go in, but my watch informed me I had maybe twenty minutes before I had to pick up Sofia. Then, poof, back to pumpkin land. I'd have to save the red wine for home.

"Who knows about me?" Xavier asked as I turned down a quieter street toward Cobble Hill.

I glanced at him, then back toward the beautiful brownstones that lined this particular street. So quintessentially Brooklyn.

"My family," I admitted. "Meaning, my grandmother, my sisters, and my brother."

"But not Sofia?"

I shook my head. "No. We all agreed it would be better to wait until she was old enough to handle it."

"Handle what?"

I shot him a glance. "Do I really need to explain it again?"

Something like guilt crossed his fine features. "No, I don't suppose you do. So, your family hates me, then?"

I tipped my head back and forth. "I suppose it depends on who you ask. My younger sisters don't really think of you at all, to be honest. They're too absorbed in their own lives. But Lea—that's my oldest sister—probably thinks you're the devil incarnate, and she's a bully. She'd be able to corral the others to her side in a jiffy."

"That's three. What about the fourth? And your brother?"

I twisted my mouth around. "The fourth is my second oldest sister, Kate. We're close. And lucky for you, she has a more nuanced view of things. She isn't likely to judge you until she actually meets you. Mattie, though…"

"He was the dark-haired bloke with you at the party?"

I nodded. "That's right."

"The one who looked like he wanted to tear me a new one?"

I bared my teeth guiltily. "I'm afraid so. He's the oldest, and on top of raising me and my sisters after our dad passed, he took Sofia and me in. He's probably the one you have to worry about the most if you really want my family to like you."

The idea of Xavier and Mattie meeting face-to-face made me kind of queasy. I couldn't put my finger on why, exactly, I wanted my brother to like Xavier. I wasn't even sure I liked Xavier anymore.

Sofia. It must have been for Sofia.

Xavier whistled. "So what you're saying is, I can't exactly pop by for tea."

I chuckled. The idea of Xavier popping anywhere was just plain funny.

"It's not your fault completely. I have some explaining to do. But they're all very…" I sighed, trying to come up with the correct word. Pushy didn't even cover it.

"Protective?"

"I would say controlling. Nosy. And completely unaware of bound-
aries. There's a reason I had to leave my grandmother's house."

It was true. I loved my family. Sofia and I trudged uptown every
Sunday so she could grow up with her cousins, eat her great-grandmother's food, attend Mass, and know her people. But that didn't mean
I wanted to go back to five different people busting into my room (or
landing) at any given moment. I only had one now who did that. And
she had the excuse of being four. What was theirs?

"Kate knows everything, but she keeps to herself," I told him. "My
brother knows you were involved with someone else. The rest of my
family knows I had a fling, and like an irresponsible college girl, got
knocked up. But that's it."

Xavier frowned. "You don't think they should know I'm here now?
Maybe I should meet them all. Get it over with."

The idea of Xavier crammed into Nonna's kitchen for Sunday
dinner, peppered by questions from all five of my siblings, plus any of
the cousins, aunts, uncles, and neighborhood friends who would probably show up once word that "Frankie's man" was back on the scene
was too much to bear.

I grimaced. "Believe me, that's all you want them to know for now.
Unless you'd like about a hundred Italians and Puerto Ricans to show
up at your restaurant every day to henpeck you, critique your food,
and demand why the hell you haven't married me, that is."

That got him. The abject horror on his face made me laugh out loud.

"Perhaps a bit later," he agreed. "After I've met…her."

I didn't have to ask who he meant. It was telling enough that he
struggled even to say her name. Still, he was trying.

"Right. Well. Perhaps." I stopped outside a large brick building and
turned to Xavier. "This is where I leave you today, I'm afraid."

He frowned in confusion. "What? Why? I thought you had more
time to talk."

"I did. About twenty minutes, which I spent walking here with you
and talking. And now, if I don't get in there within the next ten, Sofia's
preschool will fine me a small fortune per minute I'm late."

He started, like a cat who had just seen a bird, then swiveled his
head back and forth between me and the door next to us, which was
clearly marked "Happy Faces Preschool" between two picture
windows mostly covered by closed white curtains.

"She's—she's in there?"

"She is. Xavi, I trusted you enough to walk here, but now you need
to go. It's not the time. We have other things to discuss. A timeline, for

instance. What is expected of you if you really want to be a father. What it means. You understand?"

He looked suspicious. "So you still want to keep me away. Francesca, I already told you. I'm not going to be kept from my own daughter. It's not happening."

I frowned, resisting the urge to argue with him. I didn't like being dictated to any more than my four-year-old. But this was no place for an argument, and I didn't want to escalate things further.

So I tried a different tack.

"Look. That's her."

I pointed to a break in the curtain, through which Sofia's capable little form was extremely busy packing plastic fruit into a play refrigerator.

Xavier bent down next to me, then watched a long time, completely rapt until she finished her task, then trotted off, waving some sort of stuffed banana at another child.

"I forgot," he said.

I smiled. "That she looks like you? Yeah, spitting image, I'm afraid. No DNA test needed."

"No, it's not that." He stood straight and seemed to take a long time to adjust his scarf while he continued watching the shadows of children still evident through the curtains. "It's only, well—I only saw her the one time. And…she's quite beautiful, isn't she?"

I softened. I couldn't help it.

"Xavi." I touched his arm, which was currently trembling at his side.

When he turned back to face me, his eyes were as wide as the river just beyond us.

"What you said…about the lawyer…" I glanced toward the preschool, then back at him. "If you send someone to tear Sofia's family apart, it will kill her. Ruin her sweet innocence. You can understand that, can't you?"

Slowly, and with a few more glances back toward the covered window, he nodded.

I reached out and squeezed his gloved hand, pulling his attention back toward me. And then I took a deep breath and did something I never thought I would do again.

I begged.

"Xavi, please. Leave the lawyers out of it. For her sake, if no one else's. I know I should have told you about her. I know that. But if you can take things slowly, let things come naturally…if you can give us that, I'll make it right. I promise."

Again, that blue-eyed gaze darted back and forth between me and Sofia's shadow, now dancing behind the curtain. I didn't like the idea of using my daughter as a bargaining chip, but here we were. Here I was. Doing what needed to be done for her safety and security.

Or was it for mine?

"All right," he said. "On one condition."

I gulped. "What—what's that?"

"You come to dinner this weekend. We'll sort out the details of the future then. No running off. No games. Just the truth. Can you do that?"

Solemnly, I nodded. "I need to check on childcare, but I think so."

Relief flooded through me, followed by a different kind of tension. One that was curiously like…excitement. Kate would have to babysit. I wasn't giving her an option.

"And, Ces?" he asked as I was about to enter the preschool.

I turned back. "What?"

A sly black brow lifted. "Wear something nice. This time I pick the place."

I had a hard time catching my breath, and it had nothing to do with nerves. "As—as you like."

A hint of a smile rose to those full lips. "I do. I will."

14

"**O**h my God," Joni yowled for what had to be the fourth time since we had gotten out of Mass that morning. "Nonna, that was too much food. How am I supposed to wear my new crop top tonight when I have this pasta belly? I look freaking preggers!"

Because my youngest sister was always good for a bit of whining, the rest of us tended to ignore her. That included my grandmother, who was busy cleaning out the manicotti pan on the other side of the kitchen counter.

It was another Sunday meal at the ramshackle house off Arthur Avenue that my grandparents, Mattias and Sofia Zola, had bought in the spring of 1959, when they had barely been married two years. The paint was peeling on the front steps, the oak floors needed to be refinished, and the old fireplace needed its crumbling masonry repaired, but this would always be Grand Central to the Zola clan in more ways than one, particularly since the six of us had come to live here permanently when we were fourteen, eleven, eight, four, one, and six months old. Only Joni and Marie still remained with Nonna as the rest of us had gradually moved out, but we still came most Sundays to enjoy our grandmother's homestyle cooking after Mass at Our Redeemer.

Today was different only because Nonna was leaving shortly for a friend's birthday party. Matthew was also gone on his expedition to Italy with the Ice Queen, as Lea had christened her, leaving the rest of us to gossip while Sofia played with her cousins upstairs.

I smiled when someone screamed "READY OR NOT, HERE I

COME!" from what sounded like the second floor, reminding me of similar games I played with my sisters when we were about the same age.

"No one said you have to eat four servings of manicotti, Joni," Marie said, prompting Joni to stick out her tongue. "Just like no one said you had to quit school again. Do you know how embarrassing it is to tell people my sister is a stripper?"

Marie, only ten months older than Joni, could never resist the opportunity to cut her down a notch. It didn't help that despite being practically twins and sharing a room until just a few years ago, the two of them were about as opposite as it got. Joni was loud, bright, and spoiled with her big gold earrings and long red nails, but a born flirt who could charm a snake out of its skin. Marie, on the other hand, was about as sharp as a thumbtack when she chose to be, but otherwise tended to fade into the background in her glasses and series of floor-length skirts.

The older two of the Zola sisters just rolled their eyes and went back to looking above the mess, the way older sisters do, as Lea nursed her youngest, Baby Lupe, and Kate just swirled her wine around in her glass.

And then there was me, stuck in the middle, both proverbially and geographically. At least at this table.

"No one said you have to be such a horrible shrew," Joni retorted. "And it's go-go dancing at a bar, not stripping."

"Is there even a difference?" Marie haughtily pushed up her glasses, preparing for Joni's revenge.

"Mind your own business, Mimi. Just because I don't dress like I'm Amish, you think I'm a slut."

"If the shoe fits…"

"Can you two stop for one damn second?" I stood and started collecting plates to bring to Kate, who had gotten up to help Nonna clean up. I'd only helped myself to one small serving since dinner with Xavier loomed that night.

"I don't know why you have to wear these half-shirts anyway," our grandmother commented wryly in her thick Neapolitan accent as she emerged from the kitchen, patting her well-sprayed helmet of black hair, and adjusting the cuffs of her tracksuit. "Show your belly all over the city, what does it get you? A trail of men to follow you home?"

"Only if I'm lucky," Joni snarked with a grin my way. "Didn't I tell you I got a callback for that audition for *Chicago*, Nonna? They need to see a little body."

"Did you really?" I asked as I collected her plate. "Joni, that's amazing!"

My baby sister preened, flipping her tousled waves over her shoulder and making her feather-shaped earrings twirl. She'd been dancing since she was in diapers, and between all the times she'd failed at school, it was the one thing she had ever been really good at. She had wanted to dance on Broadway since I could remember. I was genuinely proud of her.

"Don't fall," Marie sneered.

"Don't be a shut-in," Joni cut back.

"Don't be children," Lea snapped as she lifted Lupe to her shoulder for a burp.

Kate popped over the kitchen counter. "Nonna, the dishes are almost done. We'll finish up if you need to get to Paulina's birthday party."

Nonna nodded. "Sorry I have to leave, but I promised her I would help with the sardines. She never makes them crispy enough."

"It's fine, Nonna," I said, giving her a kiss on the cheek on my way to the kitchen with the plates. "Enjoy yourself. Tell Paulina I said hello."

She smiled kindly at me. "My sweetheart. Maybe you should come with me to the party. Paulina has a very handsome grandson, you know."

I shook my head. "Nonna…"

She shrugged. "I have to try." Then she leaned in conspiratorially. "You're the kindest of all my granddaughters, Frances. You deserve a good man to take care of you and my sweet *nipote* upstairs, eh?"

I swallowed. It was hardly the first time Nonna had tried to set me up—it had been a regular thing since I turned sixteen, though her efforts really jumpstarted once I was pregnant. But this time, it felt different. This time, a glowering pair of blue eyes watched from the back of my mind while she said it. Demanding that I tell her no.

Shoo, I thought, batting the image away. *No one has time for you.*

"Maybe next time, Nonna," I said.

"Okay, okay, I'm going," Nonna said. "I'll be back in time for dinner for Sofia, okay?"

"And you'll drop her off at school tomorrow?" I pressed, depositing the plates on the counter.

"Don't worry about a thing." Nonna dropped a kiss on my forehead. "Yes, Joni will take her to school before her audition, won't you, *cara*?"

Joni's face squirreled up into a scowl. "Seriously? Nonna, Brooklyn is all the way on the other side of the city. I'll have to leave super early to get her there on time."

"What else do you have to do? Curl your hair?" Marie asked, earning a shove.

"She can be late," I offered. "It's preschool, not the bar exam. Just drop her off before and take your time."

"You can borrow my car if you don't scratch it," Nonna said. "That's that. Ciao, my girls!"

And then, with a wave of her hand and the clink of her bracelets, she was gone.

"Okay, good. She's gone." Marie watched the door for a few more minutes before turning back to the table. "I have news."

Immediately, the water at the sink was turned off. Lea looked up from where she was rocking the baby.

"What, did you finally get a life?" Joni cracked.

"Joni, give it a rest!" I snapped as I retook my place at the table. "My kid has better manners than you." I turned back to Marie. "What's going on, babe?"

"And why didn't you want to tell Nonna?" Lea asked as she started to rock Lupe.

Kate wandered back in and sat down, silent but curious.

Marie pushed her glasses up her nose and fidgeted with her napkins. "Well, I got a promotion."

"Marie, that's great!" I exclaimed, patting her on the shoulder. "What is it?"

"Thanks, Frankie." She nodded, flushing slightly in the cheeks. "Yeah. Chelsea—that's the head cook at Lyon House, the estate where I work—is planning to retire soon. And she told Mrs. Lyon she wants me to train to take her place."

Lea, Kate, and I all rained congratulations on our wallflower of a sister. Marie had never been one to step out of her comfort zone, more interested in watching and learning than actually taking part in things. She had gotten her current job at the Westchester estate as a maid and kitchen assistant right out of high school only because Nonna insisted that if she wasn't going to college, she had to work full time and contribute. But other than that, Marie had stayed in her same room, at this same house, essentially doing the same things since she was barely two.

"I didn't know you were interested in cooking professionally," I said. "Nonna said she taught you some stuff, but this is a whole new level."

"Yeah," she admitted. "It is. It's kind of scary, actually. And I didn't say anything because, well, it's going to be a lot. They want me to move up there when I become assistant cook. Sort of permanently."

"You're abandoning us?" Joni joked. "Nonna is going to freak!"

"Hush," Kate chided her. "It's going to be fine, babe. She'll understand. She understood when Lea and Fran and I all moved out. She'll be all right when you leave too."

"It's not just that," Marie said. "They want—" She gulped. "After I'm done training with Chelsea, if it works out, in a year or two, they want to send me to Paris. To culinary school at the Cordon Bleu."

By the time she was done speaking, her face had turned completely red, like she was overcome herself by the idea. The room turned into a frenzy.

"Paris!" Lea whisper-shrieked, if only to avoid rousing her nearly sleepy daughter. "That's amazing, Marie!"

"Oh. My. God," Joni uttered, envy dripping from every syllable.

Kate shook her head with a long whistle. "You lucky bitch. Can I come too?"

I just sat there, smiling at my sister while trying and failing to untie the jealous knot in my gut.

Paris. London. Europe. At one point, it had been everything I'd wanted, to see the places that had inspired my favorite pieces of literature. I'd wanted to jump into traveling like Alice down the rabbit hole.

Marie looked absolutely terrified at the idea. Could she not see how blessed she was?

"Culinary school," I murmured. "Wow. Oh, man, you should talk to Xa—" I cut myself off, realizing what I had almost said.

"Talk to who?" Joni pressed curiously, her hoop earrings swinging as she turned.

"Ah, no one," I replied, all the while ducking Kate's sharp gaze. "A friend, but he's not around anymore."

"Oh, bummer," Marie said. "I could have used a friend in France."

"Well, it's not for two years, you dork," Joni said. "You have a bit of time to figure out how to make some new ones. Or at least one."

"Shush!" Marie hissed back.

"What about you?" Lea turned to me, clearly eager to change the course of the conversation. "Tell me something is happening to shake up that boring life of yours, Frankie."

"Yeah, Frankie," Joni chimed in. "With Mattie out of the house, are you finally gonna get some action? Have a little party? Let the mice play while the cat's away?"

"Everyone else shared," Marie said pointedly.

Four faces quite like mine turned to me expectantly. One of them—Kate's—bore a knowingly arched brow.

Tell them. I could feel her mentally lecture. *We're your sisters. They should know too.*

Maybe it would have been safe. Maybe they wouldn't have immediately run to Matthew, told our overprotective brother what was going on at his house without him around.

But I knew I couldn't trust them all to do that.

"Nothing much," I squeaked, suddenly very interested in mopping up the rest of my sauce with a bit of bread.

"Well, you're going out tonight," Joni pointed out. "Otherwise I wouldn't have to schlep Sof all the way back to Brooklyn in the morning."

"It's just a girls' night," I fibbed. "Some colleagues from work. I haven't had a night off in a while, and Nonna said she would babysit, and—"

I was babbling. I knew it. And every green-eyed woman at the table knew it too. Which meant they knew I was lying. Which meant that unless something else came to my rescue, I wasn't getting out of this house without an explanation.

But before they could press me more, the loud chimes of Nonna's doorbell warbled down the hall.

"I'll get it," Lea said, jumping up from the table, sleeping baby in one arm.

"It's probably Tino's new waiter," Joni said as she picked at a piece of bread. "He won't stop asking me out. Like, he's kind of obsessed."

Marie muttered something under her breath that sounded like "because you gave him the milk for free," but I couldn't quite make it out.

"Well, maybe I'll leave you to it," I said, getting ready to stand up.

But then I turned, and we all saw the last person any of us expected.

"Mama?" I said. "Is that you?"

"It's me," said my mother as she walked into the room.

———

"Surprise," Lea said weakly as she guided the stranger who happened to be our mother into the room. "With both Matthew and Nonna out of the way, I thought I'd take a chance. *Mami* wanted to see us, so I invited her over."

"Holy crap," Kate murmured on my right so only I could hear her.

My heart sank heavy in my chest. What were we supposed to say now?

She was shorter than I remembered. Closer to my size, whereas the rest of my sisters were a bit taller, pulling from our dad's side of the family. Her nose was wider than mine, but looked a lot like Marie's, and her hair, which had always been lighter than ours, was almost blond now, pulled back into a practical ponytail at the base of her neck.

Her eyes, though, were what we all shared—every single person at the table had the same bright green emeralds that twinkled when we were happy and seared when we were mad. Hers were just as expressive, if somewhat dulled with time. And maybe substance abuse.

These were all the things I studied and thought about while she explained to us where exactly she had been since we'd seen her last at a party thrown on her family's side, where she'd fallen off the wagon for what had to be the last time.

That was two years ago. Apparently, she'd gone back to rehab, made it through some kind of transitional living program, and had gotten herself a job at a convenience store in Hunt's Point. She was living with two other women she'd met in rehab in the same area—a less than ideal part of the Bronx, but one that she could afford.

"So that's that," she finished. "I'm sober two full years now. I'm ready to be in my girls' lives again. Can you ever forgive me?"

She held up her hands and lay them flat on the table. Two fingers were adorned with immense turquoise rings. The others were bare, but all her nails were perfectly done, long, with broad white tips. Vaguely, I wondered how she could afford such a beautiful manicure on a clerk's wages.

"Oh, *Mami*," Joni said as she got up and warmly embraced our mother. "Of course we forgive you. Everyone deserves second chances, don't they, girls?"

Or third, I thought. *Fourth, fifth, six…*

"Absolutely," Lea said warmly, but she would, considering she was the one who had reconnected with Mom in the first place last year. When she had gotten pregnant with Lupe, she'd started taking the boys to the odd Ortiz family gathering. The rest of us hadn't had much interest in knowing that side of the family, but I knew things had gone well. Really well, considering she had named Guadalupe after the woman standing here.

"Yeah, they do," Marie said, for once agreeing with Joni as her eyes shone through her smudged lenses.

Kate, though, remained quiet. I didn't know what to say either.

Maybe the difference was that we were both old enough to remember what happened, whereas Joni and Marie didn't. I remembered the look on Nonna's face when she found out her son was dead, and the blurry-eyed expression on Mom's mug shot when she was arrested for a DWI and two counts of vehicular manslaughter—one for the other driver, and one for her husband.

I was only Sofia's age, but I also remembered clearly what it felt like to be told my mother wouldn't be coming home because she had to serve a five-year sentence at Riker's. That was when this house became my home. When Nonna and my older sisters became my mother, Matthew and *Nonno,* my father. When I learned exactly whom in my life I could trust.

And that did not include Guadalupe Ortiz.

"I need to get going," I told Kate more than anyone. "I'm sorry. I wish I could stay, but I really have to leave. Sofia! Mama's got to go, babe! Come down and give me a hug."

I left the dining room to meet Sofia as she tramped down the stairs, her cousins following closely behind.

"Bye, munchkin. Remember, Nonna's putting you to bed tonight, and Aunt Joni is bringing you to school in the morning, okay?"

"Okay, bye, Mama. Oh, who's that?"

Sofia pointed a chubby finger over my shoulder. I turned to find my mother following me into the foyer, looking up at where Sofia stood on the fourth stair from the bottom.

"Oh. Oh *my,*" she whispered. "Is this my baby Sofia?"

Great. She might have asked.

I picked Sofia up and settled her on my hip. At four, she was almost too big for this, but since she was so small, I was able to get away with it for a scant few more months, maybe.

"Sof, this is your grandmother. My mother. Her name is Guadalupe. Mom, this is my daughter, Sofia. You actually met her at that party a few years back. But, um, maybe you don't remember." *Because you were drunk as a skunk.*

Sofia's blue eyes grew wide. "Guadalupe like Baby Lupe?"

Guadalupe nodded and offered a bright smile, though several of her teeth were stained from years of neglect. "That's right, baby girl. I'm your *abuela.* What do you think of that?"

Sofia cocked her head. "What does *abuela* mean?"

"It means grandma, *linda*. That's Spanish too, for 'pretty.' My mother was from Puerto Rico, so she taught me Spanish. That means you're part *boricua* too, you know? So maybe I can teach you."

Guadalupe reached out to touch Sofia's cheek, but my daughter shied into my shoulder.

"Come on," she said. "Give your *abuela* a hug, *mamita*."

She looked as if she expected me to hand over my child. But I kept her to my side and shook my head. "I'm sorry, Mom. I don't force her to hug people if she doesn't want to."

"Oh come on. I'm not just people. I'm her grandmother. I deserve to hug my granddaughter. Come here, *mami*."

Sofia recoiled, wrapping her arms tightly around my neck. I turned her away, putting my body between her and Guadalupe.

"I'm sorry," I said firmly. "Maybe another time."

"So there will be another time?" My mother brightened just as I realized how I'd backed myself into a corner.

"Um."

"Please, baby."

"Mama." Sofia started to squirm.

I set her down and let her scamper back upstairs to join her cousins, then turned to my mother with a sigh.

"I just miss you," she said. "I missed a whole life with you. In rehab, we have to take accountability for these things. We say sorry to the people we wronged. Joni and Marie came that day. Lea came later. But you and Matthew and Katie…and sweet little Sofia…I never saw any of you."

I bit my lip. I wanted to tell her that was because we'd shown up countless times before. That she had already missed the parts of our lives when we needed or wanted her. Now we had to be even more careful because we'd been burned too many times.

A squeal rang out from the top of the stairs, where Sofia was happily playing hide-and-seek with the "hooligan boys," as Matthew had taught her to call her cousins. She played tough, but I knew on the inside she was just as fragile as anyone. Maybe even more because it was just her and me.

"I'll think about it," was all I said. "But right now, I really do have to leave. Enjoy your lunch, Mom."

"I'll see you soon, *mami*!" she called.

But I shut the door without answering. Once again, I didn't know what to say.

15

"So, who's this Adam bloke?"

Four hours after I had been blindsided by my mother, I was blindsided again by the first question out of Xavier Parker's mouth once we were seated at Doro, the restaurant Xavi had wanted to try the first night we ran into each other.

Honestly, I sort of felt blindsided every time I saw Xavier. He just seemed to have that effect on me.

Texts from Kate assured me that our mother left soon after I did, but I couldn't shake the icky feeling in my stomach when I thought of her insistence on hugging Sofia. Everything about it felt wrong.

Maybe that was why I had spent close to three hours at home getting ready for this little dinner of ours after teaching a particularly vicious dance class. Whatever good that did me. A long soak in the bathtub didn't do a whole lot for my anxiety either. Neither did taking the extra time to shave every inch of my body, giving myself a full manicure *and* pedicure, nor setting my wayward hair into hot curlers so they would tumble over my shoulders in silky spirals.

Still, I was determined to face Xavier with my best foot forward, and that meant not looking like a mop. And so, when I reached the restaurant in my favorite Ralph Lauren cigarette pants that I'd snagged at Century 21, a green blouse that made my eyes pop, and the black stilettos I saved for special occasions, I thought I looked pretty good. Not like a date, but something stronger. Something that would make me look and feel like I was supposed to be at a table with a restaurant tycoon bargaining for my child's wellbeing.

It made me feel like I couldn't fail. Or at least that I might have a chance.

That was before I saw him, dressed as impeccably as always in black pants and a burnt-orange V-neck sweater that, even under his wool coat, emphasized the flat muscles of his chest in ways that should have been illegal. He was pacing outside the restaurant like a tiger instead of sitting at a table like I had expected. He didn't see me—probably because he was intently shouting into his phone.

"I told him to stop calling me, Jag," he snapped. "Again and again. What in the bloody hell doesn't he understand about 'I don't want anything the fuck to do with you,' eh? Tell me that!"

Another pace or two led him away from the restaurant, where he stopped at the curb, looking like he wanted to throw his phone directly into oncoming traffic.

"No, I don't. I said I *don't*...well, tell Henry Parker again if he wanted that so badly, maybe he should have sniffed around more than my dad's money during the past thirty-two fucking years. I've got my own life to worry about. And it doesn't involve him!"

He appeared to end the call, then shoved his phone into his jacket pocket before staring up at the awning over the restaurant and yelling "FUCK!" loud enough to startle several passersby.

Nervously, I inched closer. "Xavier? Are—are you all right?"

He swung around as if startled and stared at me like I was a ghost. "How long have you been standing there?"

I looked around, as if the street corner might help answer that question. "I, um. A few moments. Not long."

He frowned, then closed his eyes and expelled a long sigh through his nose. When he opened his eyes again, they managed to glimmer blue even through the night air.

"I'm all right," he said, more to himself than to me, and then strode abruptly to the restaurant door and opened it without another word, waiting impatiently for me to walk through.

Was I supposed to be grateful he had even opened the door for me at all?

Honestly, I would have taken a basic "hello" instead.

We were escorted to a small table in the center of the bustling restaurant and handed two menus containing a short list of a la carte items and a few other things in Japanese I didn't understand.

That was when Xavier asked the question.

I looked up from the menu. It didn't matter. I didn't know what to order anyway. "Adam—oh, you mean my coworker?"

"Humph," he grunted.

"He's just a friend. Actually, he thinks he knows you. You didn't go to Eton, did you?"

Xavier frowned and stiffened. But before he could answer, a waiter appeared carrying a small clipboard. "Hi, all. Welcome to Doro. Have you been in before?"

"No, we haven't," I started with a kind smile. I tried to be nice to service workers.

Xavier clearly did not.

"We'll start with the tofu foie gras," he said without even looking at the server. "And then the kaiseki menu. For two."

I glanced back at the menu and immediately balked. "Um, Xavi, the kaiseki menu is six courses."

For that, I received a dark blue glare. "And?"

My gaze ping-ponged between him and the waiter, who was trying not to look curious.

"And…it's a hundred and fifty a pop," I whispered, though I couldn't have said why. Our audience of one could hear me just fine.

"You also have the choice of an optional wine or sake pairing," the waiter added most unhelpfully.

"One of each," Xavier said as he handed his menu back to the waiter. "You don't mind sharing, Ces."

It wasn't a question.

"Um, I do, actually," I said. "Nothing for me, please. And I'll just have, um, the *agedashi* tofu. It looks good."

I didn't actually have the slightest idea what *agedashi* meant, and the menu didn't elaborate. I also didn't particularly care for tofu, foie gras-style (whatever that meant) or otherwise.

"That's an appetizer," Xavier put in irritably.

"It's also the only thing on the menu less than twenty dollars," I replied. "Sounds good to me."

The muscle at his neck began to twitch, and the tips of his ears pinked under the fringe of black.

"Well, actually, we can only do the tasting menu if the whole table orders it," said the waiter, looking nervously between the two of us.

Both of their gazes turned to me. Xavier's was basically an icicle, it was so cold.

I will not look away first. I will not look away first.

I looked away first.

Xavier took the opportunity to snatch away my menu and hand it back to the waiter. "We'll have the foie gras, the kaiseki, and both of the drink pairings, like I said. That will be all."

"Sir."

The waiter left, leaving us each with the tiniest porcelain spoon of caviar balanced delicately on a saucer no bigger than my thumb.

"I actually prefer to order my own food," I said. "And in case you forgot, I can read a menu as well. Xavier, I can't afford a two-hundred-and-fifty-dollar meal. I just can't."

"And I didn't expect you could," he said, almost impatiently. "After all that blather about your salary and whatnot…"

"Blather?" I repeated. "That's my life I was talking about. How I take care of my—our—daughter. It's not *blather*."

Xavier opened his mouth like he wanted to argue back, but then our eyes met. Something in his gaze softened. Slightly.

"Of course it isn't," he said. "I shouldn't have said that. I apologize."

His big shoulders relaxed. Mine mirrored the action.

"Thank you," I said stiffly. "But, Xavier—"

"Xavi." He stopped me, his hand covering mine once more. "I—I like it when you call me that, Ces. It makes things easier, I think."

I stared at his hand for a long time, trying not to notice its solid warmth and long-fingered grace. Trying not to remember what it felt like when those fingers played over my body like it was an instrument he invented. Or maybe some delicious dish.

Xavier cleared his throat, then took his hand back to his lap.

"Besides," he said in a slightly strained voice, "I told you, it's research. I intend to put this restaurant out of business by the end of next year. I can't do that if I don't know what I need to do better. Their kaiseki menu is what earned them a Michelin star. I need to know why."

"So you can ruin them?"

He bared a set of bright white teeth. I wasn't sure I liked it. "It's what I do."

"So you're like Caesar or Alexander the Great. Just with food instead of war."

"You'd be surprised how warlike the restaurant industry is. We do have very sharp knives." He did another excellent imitation of a feline predator. A panther, maybe.

I laughed. He looked like he almost wanted to smile that time.

And with that, he picked up the tiny spoon of caviar and popped it into his mouth, taking his time to pull it back out. It was hard not to stare.

Slowly, I followed suit and had to fight not to spit it out. I had never been much for fish, and now that included their eggs.

"Like it?"

"It's…salty," I said.

"It's a delicacy," he corrected me. "But a bit boring, I think. Any twat can purchase a jar of beluga at Harrod's, you know. They've got to do better."

"Mmm."

I didn't have much to say to that. Honestly, I had a feeling that was how much of this dinner was going to go. We were supposed to be here to talk about Sofia and make plans for him to see her. But instead I was watching him lick caviar off a spoon like it was ice cream and wishing I were back home watching *Sense and Sensibility* for the thousandth time, imagining myself waiting for my own Edward Ferrars.

That feeling was back again. The one that told me I didn't belong.

"Who is it now?"

I blinked, pulled out of my daydream. "What?"

Xavier smirked. "You have that look again. Lost in a character. Who was it this time?"

I shook my head, cheeks reddening. How *did* he know that?

"Come on, Ces. You might as well tell me."

"Elinor Dashwood," I muttered down at my plate.

"More Austen?"

Silently, I nodded. This was mortifying.

"Guess I'm going to have to get round to reading England's national treasure," he said. "Otherwise I'll never understand you."

I opened my mouth to argue but found I couldn't. Honestly, there is no better way of knowing a woman than reading her favorite books. If that was what he really wanted.

"So, you were telling me about your man."

I blinked. "Huh?"

"The *Where's Wally*-looking arsehole who wants to get in your pants."

I snorted. "You mean *Where's Waldo*?"

"It's Wally in the UK, babe. They just changed it for the Americans. Anyway, you know who I mean."

I had to chuckle. With his glasses and the red and white shirt he'd been wearing on Friday, Adam did sort of resemble the cartoon character.

"Adam is just a friend." I decided not to tell him about the many times Adam had tried to make it more. "Anyway, why do you even care? Are you jealous or something?"

That black scowl made another appearance. But this time, I *really* wanted to laugh.

"It's not funny," Xavier said.

"Oh, so you *are* jealous?"

"Not in the slightest."

At that, I could only arch a brow. Maybe I didn't have a lot of experience with men, but I did have an older brother.

Then Xavier's big hand covered mine again, and every bit of my smug amusement died under its heavy weight.

"I'm not jealous," he said again. "But even if I was, it wouldn't matter."

This time I was the one to frown. "What does that mean?"

"We have a child. Getting involved again wouldn't be particularly smart, would it?"

"I…" For some reason, I couldn't immediately agree.

We stared at each other for another few seconds. I swallowed. He swallowed.

Shit. What was happening?

"All right, I've got your tofu foie gras in a ginger-soy-mirin bath, topped with house-pickled ginger and shaved endive," interrupted the waiter.

We both withdrew our hands so he could set a small bowl in front of us containing a gelatinous white cube sitting in a pool of thin brown liquid.

"Enjoy!" said the server, leaving us to stare at the appetizer.

"How can tofu be foie gras?" I asked, eyeing the white cube suspiciously. It looked more like Jell-O than something that could pass as meat. "I thought foie gras was made of duck or something."

"It is," Xavier said, picking up his spoon. "But Doro mimics it with tofu. It's their other claim to fame, and I'm curious if they really pull it off."

I watched pensively as Xavier spooned a bit of the tofu and broth. He took his time to enjoy the flavor, tongue slipping over the side of the white porcelain, lapping up the broth before tucking everything into his mouth and pulling the spoon back out, slowly, between his lips.

I was unabashedly transfixed.

He looked up to find me watching him. "Try some."

I looked down. "Is it good?"

"You'll have to try it to find out."

I rolled my eyes. He wasn't giving anything away.

Not to be outdone, though, I picked up my spoon and took a small bite of the gelatinous blob, which jiggled in its broth while I put it in my mouth.

My disgust was immediately quashed.

"Holy shit." My eyes widened. "That is insanely good."

Xavier's blue eyes sparkled from across the table. "Like it, do you?"

"My God." I took another bite, closing my eyes in bliss. "I could eat that every day for the rest of my life. *How* do they do that to the most tasteless food in the world?"

"My guess—a fuckton of cream and really good salt." He smiled. "It makes all the difference. In Japan, there are places you go where they put salt on ice cream."

"Ice cream?" I grimaced. "That sounds horrible."

"Nah, it's fantastic. Really makes the sweetness stand out."

I considered. "That makes sense, I guess. Like how Italians like to eat their prosciutto with melon."

Xavier nodded, pleased. "Exactly."

I took another bite of the tofu, then looked up to find him watching me intently, his bottom lip pulled between his teeth like he was trying to hide a smile. *Oh, Xavi, just let it out*, I wanted to tell him. Suddenly, I wanted to see that smile more than anything else in the world.

"Well, whatever they do, it's amazing," I said. "You've got your work cut out for you."

He leaned across the table, conspiracy and mischief blazing merrily across his honed features. "I could do better."

I swallowed, frozen in his intensity, my next bite poised, but unmoving.

Then he winked. Xavier Parker actually winked.

Joy—and maybe a little hope—sprang in my belly along with the delicious tastes on my tongue.

And then we both settled down to enjoy the rest of the dish.

———

WE TALKED our way through four more courses, and several glasses of wine and sake, while Xavier listened to stories about Sofia growing up. It was strange being with someone who actually wanted to know everything about the little creature who was the center of my life. I spent so much of my time trying not to be that parent who couldn't stop talking about their kid, but also envious of the people who had a partner to share the interest. My sisters and brother dealt with it, but they were her aunts and uncle, not her parents. They cared, but not enough to want the lowdown on her last playdate or to reminisce about playground politics.

Xavier, on the other hand, was absolutely rapt.

"That Melinda sounds like a piece of work," he said after I'd described an instance the week before where Sofia had come home angry at one of her classmates for taking her grapes at lunch.

"Well, to be fair, she told Melinda her fruit was poisonous," I said. "And I can't really blame the other kid for taking some of hers. They are only four."

"It's just bad manners," Xavier said, already on his daughter's side. "I don't care how old you are. You don't touch someone else's food."

I laughed. "You would say that."

"I certainly fucking would," he agreed before finishing his glass of wine.

The server appeared with another, as well as a tray bearing our final course.

"Dessert," he said. "Tempura-fried taro mochi with a green tea gelato. Enjoy."

Xavier and I both leaned eagerly over our dishes. I was stuffed to the gills, despite already having had a few to-go boxes set aside. But I had to admit it—this had probably been one of the best meals of my life. The idea that Xavier could somehow top this was unbelievable. And yet, he remained confident that he could.

"What about when she was born?" he asked after a few bites of the chewy cake. "You said it was hard, the actual birth. Why was she so early?"

I sighed and pushed my dessert away. It was delicious, but this story always made me feel a bit queasy with anxiety. Besides, I'd already eaten too much. "Well, there was a placenta rupture—do you really want to hear about this? It's kind of graphic."

Again, it was one of those stories I could only share with a very select few. Lea and I sometimes swapped war stories about the birthing room the way former soldiers talked about war. But even she wasn't as invested in the gory details as I was. After all, I had been the only one there.

Xavier just nodded, unperturbed. "Tell me."

I sighed. "Well, I woke up in the middle of the night with this horrible pain in my belly, and my sheets were soaked with blood. Like a lot of it." I covered my mouth, wincing with the memory. "Honestly, I thought I'd lost her. Seven months in, after everything I'd already been through, and I was losing her."

I exhaled slowly. It was still a fear that returned, often in the middle of the night, just like when I'd been woken. Sometimes I had to get up and check on her, just to make sure she was still alive.

I wasn't sure I'd ever get over it.

"Anyway, I went to the hospital, and they had to induce labor. That means they give you this drug, and it gets things going. I was—it was a lot of pain. But it worked, thank God. My body knew she needed to come out."

Xavier didn't say anything, just took a sip of his wine and then started running his finger around the rim of the glass while he listened as intently as ever.

"When she arrived, she was blue," I continued quietly, fingering the edge of my sake cup in an action that mirrored his. The ceramic cup was patterned with white and blue flowers. The exact shade of Sofia's eyelids when they had placed her in the oxygen chamber. "She couldn't breathe on her own, and she'd been at critically low oxygen levels for a while because of the rupture. She was so helpless. She couldn't do anything. She had to stay at the NICU while they helped her breathe and fed her through a tube. She couldn't even breastfeed until she was almost two months old."

I swallowed hard at the memories. How terrified I'd been every time I'd left my newborn baby in a plastic box. How I'd barely slept for fear they would call to let me know she hadn't survived the night.

She had been so fragile. So unbelievably precious.

"I wish I'd have been there," Xavier said in a low voice that shook slightly. "I wish I could have seen her."

"Well, you can," I said. "I just mean...I do have pictures."

He looked up sharply. "Show me."

"Do you really want to?" I asked, already pulling out my phone. "It's not—I mean, I always thought she was beautiful. But it's not really what people expect a newborn to look like. Sometimes it freaks them out."

Xavier held out his hand wordlessly, brooking no argument.

I pulled up the series of pictures I looked at sometimes late at night, when I wanted to remind myself of how far my girl and I had really come. Sofia on the day she was born, hardly bigger than a hand's width, tinged with blue, skin so delicate you could almost see it. Sofia wrapped in a gauzy cloth, but still on the ventilator, a bit pinker but with a thick tube spilling out of her mouth, helping her breathe the air she couldn't quite take in by herself. And finally, Sofia on my chest, still with the tube, but skin to skin at last while my dark hair tumbled around us in a messy halo of new motherhood.

Xavier gazed at the last one the longest. "She's so small. She looks like she could just be snuffed out. Like a candle."

"She almost was."

He glanced between the picture and me. "And you had to go through that alone."

I shrugged and focused on reorganizing my chopsticks again and again. "I wasn't really alone. I was still living at my grandmother's house. Two other sisters with me, and my older ones just a few blocks away. When I was finally able to bring her home, it could have been worse."

"Ces."

I looked up. His eyes were large and full of some unnamable emotion.

"All right," I admitted, trying not to cry and failing, as I did any time I remembered that horrible period. I swiped at a few tears as they emerged, determined not to have a complete scene in the middle of the restaurant. "I was alone. My family was around, and yes, they helped, and I'll be forever grateful for it. But honestly, it's just not the same when the baby isn't—"

"Your own?" Xavier finished for me.

Our eyes met, and I couldn't look away.

"Yes," I whispered.

They loved her. Nonna, Mattie, my sisters. They all loved Sofia deeply in their own ways. But those days in the hospital and afterward, when I brought her home, they were more worried for me than for her. But I didn't care at all what was happening to me. Right from the beginning, something inside me knew Sofia was *mine*. That my entire mission on this earth was to keep her safe. And from the beginning, I was so afraid I couldn't.

Xavier looked back at the photos, scrolling through them a few more times.

"And now?" he asked. "Is she safe now?"

"Well, she's with my grandmother and her aunts, so she's pretty damn happy at the moment, yeah."

"That's not what I meant." He pushed the phone back across the table and held my eyes. "I meant her home. With you."

I didn't like what he was insinuating. I straightened up in my chair so I could look at him eye to eye without blinking. Without cowering under that ice-blue gaze.

"For the last four years, I have done nothing but keep that girl safe and healthy," I informed him. "I have given everything I could to provide her with the best life I can. She is safe in her home, Xavi. I can promise you that."

I waited for him to break away first, but he didn't. That penetrating blue gaze, so unearthly, seemed like it was trying to tease something else out of me.

Finally, he pulled out his wallet and set several hundred-dollar bills on the table. I didn't have time to gape before he had pushed back in his chair and stood, then offered his hand to mine.

"Then show me that too," he said. "Please."

16

The house was dark when we got out of the car—a plush Mercedes Xavier had rented while he was staying in the city. He loomed behind me, and suddenly I felt so small and my house felt so small in comparison to everything I knew this man had. I wondered again why I'd let him talk me into taking him back here, even if it was empty and Sofia wasn't here to see him.

By New York standards, it was actually a fairly big place. A three-story townhouse half a block from a park, consisting of a basement apartment and the two bedrooms up top (and a half, if you included my little area). Sure, it was maybe a quarter of the size of the grandiose brownstone where I'd run into Xavier, but still nothing to laugh about. Red Hook was an up-and-coming area too, known more now for its restaurants and galleries than for its previous life as a stronghold of crime and poverty. My brother had done well for himself.

"The basement's rented," I told Xavier as I unlocked the door. "My brother, Sofia, and I have the rest."

He followed me inside, peering over the foyer toward the staircase, then down the skinny hall. At first, I felt shy by its shabbiness—the cracked plaster here and there, too many coats hung on the rack, the pile of shoes near the doorway. I thought of the kitchen still stuck in the 1970s, the dining nook that barely fit a table for four, and the living room with the TV awkwardly mounted over the fireplace. None of this would come anywhere close to the finery Xavier was accustomed to now.

But I pulled my shoulders back and forced myself to stand up straight. It took every penny Matthew had and countless weekends of working on the place to make it livable. But he had, and then he had shared it with me and Sofia.

I'd never be able to make it up to him.

"Can I get you anything?" I asked as I led Xavier into the kitchen. "Wine? Tea? I think Mattie has some beer in here somewhere."

"Water's fine."

I pulled the Brita out of the fridge and poured him a glass, then set the kettle on to boil. Xavier wandered about the living room, taking in the tiny deck overlooking the yard Matthew wanted to turn into a garden someday, then turning back to peruse the black-and-white photos of Florence Matthew had hung in one corner. I tried not to over-whelm this place with photos of Sofia, saving most of them for my small space upstairs. While we were a family unit of sorts, my brother was still a bachelor. A single thirty-something man didn't need to define himself via his four-year-old niece.

Her father, however. That was a different story.

"It's all right," Xavier said, returning to the counter while I started steeping tea for myself. He accepted the water and glanced around the kitchen with open curiosity.

I looked around, imagining his disgust. "It's fine. Not what you're used to, I'm sure. But it's safe, like I said, and in a good neighborhood. Bigger than I could get on my own, that's for sure."

"It reminds me of my mum's flat in Croyden. The one above her restaurant where I grew up. This kitchen, though."

I offered a sheepish smile. "It's old, I know. I don't think it's been updated in about forty years. My brother's been remodeling the rest of the place first, little by little."

Xavier looked surprised. "This place has been remodeled?"

"Yes, it has! It was basically studs when he bought it. Mattie had to rip out most of the lath and plaster and redo the wiring. He did the basement first so he could take on a tenant, and then spent the better part of a summer getting the rest of the house habitable. The kitchen is the last step."

That summer had been hard on both of us. We were still living in Matthew's old apartment in Sheepshead Bay, where Sofia and I shared a bedroom while she was going through the terrible twos times about twenty. The summer had turned the city into a sauna. Money had been so tight we couldn't afford to run the air conditioner more than an hour a day or so.

I ran a hand over the yellowed Formica counter. It wasn't pretty, but it worked.

"Where does she sleep?"

I didn't have to ask who he meant. He had asked to come here to see her space, after all. To see who his daughter was.

"Follow me," I said and led the way back toward the foyer and up the stairs.

Xavier followed step by step, taking in the family photographs lining the staircase, glancing into Matthew's sparsely decorated room to the left, the bathroom at the center, and then slowing as we entered Sofia's room at the other end of the hall.

It was a typical little girl's room. I'd done my best with limited funds, painted it gray with lilac-colored drapes I'd found at the Goodwill and a matching lilac-sprigged quilt rumpled on her little white daybed. In one corner, a dollhouse sat atop a child's table, strewn with little people, their clothes, and other bits and bobs she liked to insert into their world. Next to that was a vintage chest open on its side. I'd found it on the street, cleaned it up, and painted it white, then installed a bar across one side where Sofia could hang the few princess costumes she had collected from family and friends. The rest of the room consisted of a small closet, a knee-high shelf with a variety of picture books, and a purple shag rug from Ikea.

Unlike the rest of the house, however, the walls were almost completely filled with images. Sofia wanted nearly every bit of art she made at school hung up for people to see, every picture we printed right along with it. After more than two full years at her current center, almost every space in the room was covered with construction paper, finger paintings, scribbled sketches, and grainy photographs. It was messy and chaotic, and I loved her all the more for it.

"She likes princesses?" Xavier pointed at the open chest, where a particular sparkly gown had fallen off its hanger.

I snorted. "Try obsessed. It's a four-year-old thing. I read her *Cinderella* once, and she has demanded a weekly recitation ever since. She wants to be a princess when she grows up."

"She'll love England, then," he said with a funny, unreadable face. "I'll take her to Buckingham Palace."

I tried to smile, though a certain tightness in my chest arose at the idea of Sofia going anywhere without me.

"It's small," Xavier noted as he strode around the rest of the room, which took him exactly four seconds.

"She doesn't need much space."

"I don't mean it like that. It's lovely, Ces. Really nice."

I smiled. "Got a thing for lilacs and fairy dresses too?"

His mouth twitched. "I only meant that if I were a little girl, I imagine I'd like this very much. Well done."

We stared at each other across the room for an odd moment. Then Xavier turned toward the exit and cleared his throat.

"The other room's your brother's. So where do you sleep?"

I gestured out the door. "Around the corner."

He followed me toward the landing at the opposite end of the hall, a glorified storage area between the other side of the bathroom. On it, I managed to fit a twin bed against one wall, a rack for my clothes on the other, and a small bookshelf under the windows looking out toward the street. Against the wall lay a folded screen, which I took out at night for a bit of extra privacy. We called it my "room," but it wasn't quite that.

Xavier looked around at the little space with a deep frown. "There's no door."

I shrugged. "I felt guilty taking the other bedroom since my brother is the one who pays most of the mortgage. I have a place to sleep. I'm fine with it."

He gave me a long, unreadable look. "I don't understand. Do teachers really make such poor wages you can't even afford your own room?"

I sighed. "Most of the teachers I know either have roommates or are married. After taxes, I take home maybe thirty-nine thousand a year, most of which goes to childcare. Most landlords require leaseholders to earn at least three times the rent, and I have student loan payments too. You try finding a two-bedroom anywhere in New York for thirteen hundred dollars a month. I promise you, it can't be done—not for another seven years, anyway, until I get a real salary increase. Either Sofia and I live comfortably with my brother or hole up in a crappy studio in East New York. I'm good with our choice. She's been happy."

"And you?" he pressed. "Have you been happy sleeping on a landing? No walls, no doors, no bloody privacy?"

I sighed again and placed my hands on his lapels, urging him to calm down.

"It's good enough for *her*," I said. "And for the next fourteen years or so, that's all I care about."

He was quiet for a long time, worry etched between his eyebrows. Then, as if moved by marionette strings, his hands rose to cover mine, pressing them harder into his muscled chest. I could feel the beat of his heart even through the layers of cotton and wool.

Gradually, it slowed. Until I looked up.

"And what of the men you bring home?" he asked, voice low and foreboding. "Where do they sleep?"

"Xavi…"

"No, really." He released my hands and took a few steps back. "You're only twenty-seven. I know there's been a bloke or two up here, hasn't there?"

I couldn't lie. I'd tried to date a few times over the years. Once, a guy I'd met at the library. Another had been a friend of Matthew's. But nothing had lasted more than a few weeks. Nothing more than a few make-out sessions. Maybe some heavy petting on my bed. All it ever took was a bad dream or a call for "Mama" to erase what romance there was in my little corner of the house.

"My personal life hasn't been my priority," was all I said.

He didn't need to know every detail.

Xavier watched me intently. And then, ever so subtly, his gaze dropped. "Do you remember the last time I kissed you?"

I smirked. "You mean about a month ago?"

He rolled his eyes. "No. I mean, before I left for London. Before…Sofia."

I bit my lip. I couldn't help it. Did I remember the most soul-searing kiss of my life? Oh, just a smidge.

"You came with me to the hotel to drop me off on your way home."

I nodded. "Traffic was a disaster that day."

"We took the train back from downtown. It was so busy that you had to sit in my lap. I didn't care a bit, though. I just wanted to hold you in my arms for as long as I could."

I smiled. The subway had been particularly crowded that day. And the A train had been running very late. Neither of us cared at all, though.

"Then you walked me all the way to the door instead of transferring. Do you remember what I asked you?"

I nodded. My skin prickled with the memory. "You said—" I cleared my throat. I had to. My tongue felt too thick for it. "You told me to kiss you."

He took another step forward, prompting me to back against the mattress edge. "And did you?"

I closed my eyes. In a second, I was there again. Standing outside his hotel near campus while throngs of other travelers funneled in and out of the building. I had thought I would see him again that night. It was our last night before he was going back to London. And so all day there had been an air of desperation about him. About us. As we tracked through the Guggenheim together. Played in Central Park. Acted like tourists at the planetarium.

We couldn't keep our hands off each other, but that had been something different.

"Kiss me like your life depends on it," he'd commanded.

And so I'd jumped up, wrapped my arms and legs completely around him while he held me there on the street, crushed my lips to his, and I'd kissed and kissed and kissed him while he spun us around in circles. We had devoured each other right there on Amsterdam Avenue until we were dizzy and out of breath. Until the city, the streets, the noise—all of it disappeared. But him.

"Yes," I whispered. "I did."

"You did."

He was now only a few inches away. Slowly, slowly, he leaned down, slipping a hand around my back to rest on the bed's headboard. Trapping me with his dark gaze. His clear intent.

"Xavi, stop," I breathed when his lips were less than an inch from mine. His salty-sweet scent consumed me. *Oh*, this was hard.

"Christ," he muttered, his low voice growling over my collar. "I'm not going anywhere, Ces. I thought we established that tonight."

But that was just it.

I tipped my head, leaning back to look him in the eye. "Did we? You live on the other side of an ocean. And, as you pointed out earlier, this isn't really the time, is it?"

With a long sigh, he stood up straight and shook his head. "The restaurant is going ahead. I'll be here for the next few months at least while it opens, and even after…well, London's only a few hours away, really. My life isn't the same as it was four years ago. I'm not going to disappear again. Ever."

I took a deep breath. My heart was pounding so hard I was surprised he couldn't hear it. His proximity wasn't helping. Everything about him—even the parts that were cold and harsh—wasn't helping. I wanted them all.

I slid out from between him and the bed, taking a safer place near the window looking out to the backyard. "All right. You can meet her."

Xavier jerked. Immediately, the lust clouding his eyes disappeared. They were bright blue again and crystal clear. "When?"

I swallowed thickly, running over a brief timeline in my head. Mattie was in Italy. I had the house to myself. Maybe that was a bit more dangerous, considering it would open me up to more moments like these with Xavier. But it was better than having my family sticking their noses where they weren't wanted. Not now.

"Later this week. On one condition."

Xavier tipped his head, looking a lot like a skeptical raven. "What's that?"

"I don't want her to know who you are yet."

Xavier frowned. "Why the fuck not?"

I took a deep breath. I was pressing my luck. A month ago, I'd been convinced I was going to be destroyed in court by this man. Instead, he had reneged on that particular promise and agreed to do things my way for the sake of Sofia.

But this was for her. I had to stick to my guns.

"In case—in case you don't like her. Or something."

His black brows nearly smashed together. "What does that mean—'or something'?"

I sighed. "Do I really have to spell it out to you?"

He stared at me so hard I honestly thought two holes might appear in my forehead. "Are you suggesting I might be a poor father?"

"Well, I don't actually know, do I?"

He looked completely bewildered. "Are we really back to that? Just because a few men out there are shitty fathers doesn't mean I'm going to be one of them, Ces. It's unfair to blame me for their sins."

I scowled. Men always made this excuse. If I had to hear one more sentence start with "not all men," whether it had to do with domestic violence, catcalling, or even just doing the dishes, I was going to scream.

"I'm sorry, but no," I replied stoutly. "It's no different than getting a vaccine. Or STD testing. Or putting on a seat belt, for crying out loud. We don't do it because every single driver out there is a maniac. But enough of them are that we prepare for the possibility. And just like some people shouldn't be drivers, there are also *many* who shouldn't be parents."

Xavier rubbed his chin, looking like he wanted to argue back.

"There's another reason, too," I added.

"Oh?" He didn't sound particularly thrilled.

"My family."

"I thought you loved your family."

"I do. But like I told you, they consist of four extremely nosy sisters, my very protective big brother, and a pushy grandma who would like nothing more than to see me married and Sofia have a dad. If they catch wind you're back in my life, they will be on you like white on rice, my friend. I'm okay with that. But I'm not sure you're quite prepared."

For the first time all night, Xavier actually looked unsure. I sort of hated him for it, but I'd been banking on it.

"I see," he said. "And I'm guessing Sofia can't keep a secret."

"Well, she's four."

If he needed more explanation than that, then he *really* had a lot to learn about children.

He was quiet for another minute.

"It will just be until she gets used to you. And until you…" I almost said "love her," but caught myself in time. He had already made it clear that was too much to ask. "Until you get used to her too. If you can do that, you can meet her this week."

He looked up like an alerted animal. "This week?"

I tipped my head. "Too soon?"

"No, it's just—I was thinking—fuck."

I chuckled. It was nice to know he didn't have *everything* under control.

"How about Friday?" I asked. "It's movie night. My brother is out of town. If it's nice, I'll pick her up early and meet you at to the park. Next time you can come over and watch *Moana*. That's her favorite. If you learn how to sing 'You're Welcome' like The Rock, she'll adore you."

He looked at me like I was speaking a foreign language but gave a short nod. "Friday, then."

"Meet me outside my school again at three thirty," I said. "And this time, stay put."

17

A t three thirty the following Friday, I kept my word to Xavier. I can't lie. I thought about canceling. That's what happens when the cute sweater dress you wear to work for once gets stained in three separate places with acrylic paints and coffee, so you have to change into your spare jeans and a Care Bears sweatshirt fished out of the lost and found. Xavier would be dressed like he walked out of *Esquire*, while I looked like I was made out of Play-Doh. Fantastic.

But this wasn't about me, I kept reminding myself. And everything else about the day seemed to be lining up perfectly. Sofia was in great spirits when I picked her up from preschool, and New York was blessed with unseasonably warm weather for the end of January. Most of the snow had melted off the sidewalks, and the slides would actually be dry. I couldn't begrudge Sofia an afternoon outdoors. Just like I couldn't begrudge her a chance to meet her dad. Not anymore.

"The park is that way, Mama," Sofia said as we walked past the entrance and continued back toward P.S. 058.

"I know, bean. But my friend is meeting us outside my school. We'll pick him up and walk back."

"Why do you keep calling him 'my friend,' Mommy?"

I squeezed Sofia's little hand. "Why wouldn't I?"

"You call everyone else by their names. Aunt Kate is Aunt Kate. Zio is Uncle Mattie or just Mattie. Kim. Adam. Derek. Fatima."

I had to chuckle as she continued to rattle off every friend, coworker, or acquaintance of mine she'd ever met. My girl never missed a beat.

"You're too quick, kid," I told her. "This friend's name is Xavier."

Her button nose wrinkled into a raisin. "He's a boy? I don't really like boys as much as girls."

"You like Mattie."

"That's different. He's family."

My heart thrilled slightly at the word. She had no idea.

"Well, give him a chance, bean," I told her. "You never know."

"If you say so."

We turned the corner back toward the school. The playground was empty but for a few stragglers left with their parents or nannies. But standing smack in the center of the foursquare courts stood Xavier, clad in his customary black suit along with a beautifully tailored wool coat that reached his knees. It occurred to me that he probably had most of his clothes custom made—otherwise, I couldn't imagine how he fit into them.

"Xavi," I called.

He turned immediately, clearly jerked out of a daze, but didn't blink once as we approached, flattening one empty hand against the lapel of his coat while the other clenched a nosegay of pink camellias so hard his knuckles turned white.

He was nervous, I realized. Really nervous.

Somehow, that made him more attractive. For a moment, he reminded me of the budding chef standing on the precipice of launching a dynasty. A healthy dose of fear had been in his eyes then too. But I had also known then that he was the kind of man who could conquer it. And it had only made me want him more.

"Good, you're here," he said with relief as we stopped in front of him. "I was starting to feel like a paedo, strange man at a children's playground all by himself."

"What's a paedo?" Sofia piped up.

Xavier's eyes shot open. "Fuck. I mean, shit. I mean—ah, bollocks."

I couldn't help but laugh.

"Those were bad words, Mama, not funny ones," Sofia said, looking suspiciously at Xavier. "I remember you. You shouted the bad words at my mama at our house too."

"I—uh—yes," Xavier agreed awkwardly. "I did. Caught by surprise."

Sofia was not impressed.

"Everyone makes mistakes, bean," I reminded her. "Like when you kept taking home those Calico Critters from school, remember?"

Sofia nodded solemnly, looking like she might cry. The sticky fingers phase had been a particularly hard one.

"But I got better," she whispered shakily. "I stopped."

I squeezed her hand. "Yes, you did, babe. And Xavi will too if we help him. He's just excited to meet you."

I turned to Xavier with a warm smile. He seemed to relax. Slightly.

"Xavi," I said. "This is Sofia, my daughter. Sof, this is my friend Xavi."

Sofia drew her little gaze from Xavier's shiny black shoes slowly up his long legs, then up his tall body until her neck was craned completely back. They stared at each other for a long time, reminding me somewhat of dogs of the same breed who instantly recognized each other at the park. Not always friendly, but somehow noting a kinship.

Terror washed through me. What if she knew? Sofia was at the age where she liked nothing better than to prance in front of the mirror in one of her princess costumes, cooing at her reflection. What if she looked at the face peering down at her and recognized the deep, sloping blue eyes, the full, broad lips, and onyx hair?

What if she never forgave me for it?

"You're really tall," she told him, then turned back to me, possibly just to rest her neck. "He's really tall, Mommy. He looks like a skyscraper."

Xavier's black brows formed a deep frown, then slowly, he squatted down until he was closer to her level, only a few inches taller instead of several feet.

"Better?" he asked, one side of his mouth quirking, blue eyes twinkling. "These are for you. Camellias. My mum told me never to meet a new girl empty-handed."

Sofia's eyes popped open as she accepted the flowers. For a second, I could imagine myself in her shoes—a tall, handsome man, bending down almost to one knee, presenting flowers, speaking with a dashing accent. It was like one of her fairytales had come to life.

Lord, my daughter was a goner.

"What?" Xavier asked, clearly dumbfounded as he looked up at me. "Did I do something wrong again? I didn't say 'fuck,' did I?"

I looked back at Sofia, who didn't seem to have noticed the second curse.

"You sound like a prince," she said, which came out solemnly as *pwince* while she accepted the flowers. Then to me, "Mommy, he sounds like a prince. He looks like one too."

Xavier frowned up at me questioningly. But I understood immediately.

"It's the accent," I told him. "She watches a lot of Disney."

"Mommy *loves* princes," Sofia told him. "She watches movies about them all the time."

"Sofia, I do not," I scolded her a little too harshly. "You're the one who loves all the Disney princess movies."

She shook her head vigorously. "No, not those, Mama. Like the movies *you* watch when you think I'm asleep. Like Downtown Cabby and Sense and Spaghetti."

"Ooh," I said, managing not to laugh at Sof's creative titles.

Xavier wasn't quite so good at hiding his own dismay. But he didn't laugh. In fact, he almost looked concerned.

"Those are period dramas," I corrected her. "Most of the characters are gentry, not royalty. None of them are princes."

"Well, they all look like princes," Sofia assured herself. "And they sound just like *him*."

Ergo, it was clear, Xavier was a prince.

"No wonder you like him, Mommy. I heard you tell Aunt Kate that you wanted to marry Mr. Darcy because of his voice."

My cheeks immediately flushed.

"Is that so?" Xavier murmured warily.

"Oh my God," I muttered, studiously avoiding his gaze.

"Are you going to marry Xavier because of his voice, Mommy? He sounds just like Mr. Darcy." She turned to Xavier. "Are you a lord or a duke? Because that's okay too."

Xavier's face flushed the color of the flowers in Sofia's little hands, and he looked like he wanted to jump into his fancy black car and drive all the way back to England. I closed my eyes, willing the question away. So much for an easy meeting. This. Was. Mortifying.

"Er—" Xavier mumbled, pulling Sofia's attention back his way. "I think your mummy can do better than me."

"I don't know…" Sofia was saying. "You're pretty handsome."

I looked down just in time to see the left side of Xavier's mouth curl upward. He peeked up at me and allowed his gaze to drag down the rest of my body—my sweatshirt-clad, paint-stained, frump-fest of a body—before returning to Sofia.

"You're very kind," he told her. "Now, I have a secret. I've never been to this park your mum told me about. And I was wondering if you might show me the best places to play."

He stood back up, and Sofia looked him over doubtfully.

"You're kind of big for the park," she told him.

"I am," he confirmed. "But I'd love to see it anyway. I want to see how it's different from the parks in England. Would you show me?"

There was a long pause. Then Sofia nodded. "Sure. The best is the swings. You can push me if you want."

———

"Mama, what's for dinner?"

Thirty minutes at the park turned into ninety, which turned into an invitation to dinner on Sofia's part, which brought me back to my house sometime past five, trying to decide what the hell I was going to prepare for a world-famous chef with my own meager cooking skills.

So far, Xavier had been the perfect gentleman. A little awkward at first, maybe, with a tendency to drop the F-word when he made a mistake. But as long as he was willing to follow her around and "talk like a pwince," Sofia happily allowed him to push her on the swings and merry-go-round for as long as they both wanted.

Now, as I watched him remove his coat in our foyer and allow her to take his hand and guide him down the hall to the living room for a quick tour of the house, I wasn't sure how much of this I could take. I had expected that it would be difficult to see him try to melt Sofia's heart, and maybe his own. I hadn't expected the process to melt mine too.

"I'll think about it upstairs," I said. "You good with her? I just need to change."

Xavier gave a brief nod, too busy listening to Sofia introduce him to her set of My Little Ponies to care about me.

I took the opportunity to race up to my little portion of the second floor and furiously yank through my clothes. The jeans could stay. They were old, but still made my ass look good. The Care Bears had to go, though.

Ten minutes later, I was flying back down the stairs wearing a cropped red sweater, my hair down, my favorite silver hoops dangling from my ears, and a swipe of red lipstick for good luck. What can I say? Single moms learn to work fast.

Xavier and Sofia were on their way up to her room for part two of the tour. Xavier looked up and stilled when he caught me coming down, then paused when our shoulders touched.

Sofia slithered out behind me, babbling about needing to set up her costumes or something. I honestly didn't know. Xavier's eyes had pinned me in place.

"I remember this shirt," he murmured, touching the red knit material lightly with one finger. "You wore it the day we met."

"D-did I?"

Oh lord, he was right. For a moment, I could see us both at that bar, a place in Morningside Heights where my grad school friends and I liked to pretend we went to Columbia. I'd ordered a cheap beer, which the bartender gave me before informing me that it had been paid for by the guy at the other end of the bar.

I'd turned, and there was Xavier, looking every inch the rogue in distressed jeans, combat boots, and a black T-shirt that showed every outline of his chest and the tattoos that slithered over his left arm and licked his neck.

He'd approached with a single boring line that came to life with the spark in his deep blue eyes: "I like your shirt."

It had taken exactly ten seconds for me to like his too. Twenty more for us to make it to the dance floor. Another hour after that, he kissed me for the first time, and I didn't leave his arms for a month.

Now he wore a suit and polished shoes, though he looked no less the rogue. But it was very clear he still liked my shirt.

I looked down at the sweater, then back at him. His blue eyes darkened as he took in the cropped hemline, revealing just a sliver of the stomach I had fought long and hard to get back after Sofia was born.

In direct response, my nipples tingled. I knew if he looked at them, he would see them clearly through the thin fabric. Remembering his deft touch. Dying for it, in fact.

"Xavi! Are you coming?"

Xavier jerked, then turned. "Er, on my way." He cleared his throat and disappeared up the stairs without a second look toward me.

I remained where I was, taking a few more minutes to catch my breath after having it stolen by the intensity of his gaze.

18

A few minutes later, after I'd fetched myself an extremely cold glass of water, I was joined in the kitchen by Xavier and Sofia while I stood in front of the fridge trying to figure out what the hell to make. Sofia had changed into a purple princess costume with aquamarine sequins, while Xavier had long since shucked his suit jacket and tie, looking considerably more casual with his shirtsleeves rolled up to his elbows, revealing the tattoos twisting around one forearm. The effect, however, was balanced by a bright pink boa tied around his neck.

"Mama, I'm hungry," Sofia complained as she climbed onto one of the barstools on the other side of the counter.

I looked up from the fridge and grinned when I caught sight of the two of them. "Well, don't you two look dashing."

Xavier reddened, but to his credit, made no move to remove the boa.

"How about spaghetti, Betty?" I asked, turning back to the fridge. "I can whip it up while you introduce Xavi to the wonders of *Moana*."

"My name's not Betty," Sofia screwed her face up adorably like she always did when I made that terrible joke. "And we had that yesterday. We have that *all* the time. Can't we have something else?"

I grimaced and looked back into the fridge. I wasn't very good at improvising—had never had to be a good cook when we had several much better ones in my family. Nonna was a force, of course. Marie was getting there, and Matthew and Lea both knew their way around a stove. The best I could usually do was boxed pasta or some sandwiches —otherwise I was happy enough heating up my brother's leftovers.

Except when I had a professional freaking chef to dinner.

Crap.

"Grilled cheese?" I suggested feebly.

"Let me."

I turned to find Xavier at my elbow, one hand taking the top of the door so he could open it wider, essentially caging me against the opening. His broad chest just barely brushed my shoulder blades. Despite being caged against the cold, I was suddenly very hot.

"Sorry. We don't have much. I, um, wasn't expecting you to come over today." Again, that salty-sweet scent of his made it very hard to think.

"I know," he said gruffly, apparently oblivious to my sudden stupor. He reached around me to grab several items off the door, then started pawing through the crispers. "Excuse me."

Obediently, I stepped back, as much to find my bearings again as to allow him to forage. At least I'd cleaned it out before Matthew had left. Still, this was getting absurd. I had invited him here to meet his daughter, not put me in a tizzy. I needed to get a hold of myself.

"This was my favorite meal when I was about your age," Xavier said as he turned around and set out a bunch of different ingredients on the counter beside the stove. "We're going to do it a bit funny, but I think it will taste all right."

He started to turn on the stove, but before he did, he tipped his head at me, clearly indicating that I needed to be on the *other* side of the counter with Sofia. "Off you go."

"Oh!" Happily, I scurried around and took the other stool.

Together, Sofia and I watched as Xavier removed his boa and gave it to Sofia. She and I both watched eagerly as he found one of the aprons Matthew stashed in the pantry and quickly tied it around his trim waist. This was clearly his comfort zone. Every movement he made was efficient and graceful.

"Anchovies?" I said as I looked over the assembled ingredients while Xavier located a mixing bowl from one of the cabinets. "I promise she won't like those, and neither do I. Fish, remember?"

Xavier tossed the small jar onto the counter next to a bag of coleslaw mix I'd grabbed on sale, a bunch of green onions, plus mayonnaise, ketchup, and soy sauce I didn't even know we had.

"You'll like what I do with them," he informed me.

"What's anchovies?" Sofia wondered.

"Zio sometimes puts them in sauces," I told her. "They're a really salty fish."

Sofia wrinkled her nose and looked like she was about to shout "Yuck!" and sprint out of the room. But then she turned to find Xavier watching her carefully. Her mouth dropped open, then closed again.

"I shall try it," she announced formally and, if I wasn't mistaken, using some odd accent that was intended to sound British. Then she folded her tiny hands neatly on the countertop and laid her chin on top of them like a prim poodle.

My eyebrows almost hit the roof. Boys of all ages were usually deemed "bozos" before she adjourned herself to find her dolls and lecture them all about the shortcomings of men. But right now, she was trying her hardest to impress our guest.

Well, I supposed it was fair. I was pretty sure he was trying to impress her too.

We watched intently as Xavier combined a few anchovies with pieces of onion, salt, and water in a saucepan, then set them on a hot burner before turning back.

"Flour?" he asked. "Sugar? Vinegar?"

"Pantry. What are you making?"

He didn't reply, just found the things he needed. Then suddenly he was a rush of neat, precise work with the knife as he chopped, minced, and diced everything in sight, most of which went into a large mixing bowl, followed by the salty fish broth (that he had just brewed on the stove using the anchovies) and a fair amount of egg.

"Mama," Sofia whispered. "He just put the lettuce and the flour in the *same thing*."

"It's cabbage, babe. But, yeah." I shrugged. I was as mystified as she was by what was going on.

"*Okonomiyaki*," Xavier said as he spooned out some of the concoction onto a hot cast iron pan on another burner. "It's a sort of pancake with dashi—that's like the fish broth—flour, egg, veg, whatnot. My mum used to make it for me when I was a boy. Excellent way to use up food."

The batter hissed in the oil, and suddenly the scents of sizzling flour and fresh vegetables filled the air.

I raised my nose appreciatively. "It smells good."

Sofia nodded, though she was still watching his process somewhat suspiciously.

"*Okonomi* means 'as you like it' and *yaki* means 'grilled.'" Xavier started viciously whisking some sort of ketchup-based sauce into submission. "You get to put what you like on top and hang the rest."

With a triumphant flourish, he grabbed the cast iron pan and flipped the pancake with a quick jerk of his wrist that made every tendon in his tattooed forearm stand out in high relief.

Then he turned around and winked at Sofia over his shoulder. My heart gave an extra hard thump. Her cheeks reddened as she mouthed "hang the rest" to herself. I was pretty sure my face was equally flushed, though if pressed, I would have sworn up and down it was because of the rising heat in the kitchen, not the look of Xavier with his shirtsleeves rolled up, apron on, moving about my kitchen with the ease of a ballroom dancer.

A few minutes later, he flipped the first pancake onto a small plate and topped it with a drizzle of thinned mayonnaise, the sauce he had made, and freshly chopped green onions, then set it in front of Sofia with a fork and a knife.

She looked at it for a long time, then turned back to me.

"Try it, Sof," I urged her as I picked up the utensils and cut her a few pieces. "Tell me what you think."

Tentatively, she speared a piece of the pancake, avoiding the green onions, but keeping a bit of the sauce on it. I didn't have to look to know Xavier was watching intently.

She touched the tip of her tongue to the slice. Then, gingerly, as if she was sticking a wriggling creature into her mouth, she nibbled a tiny corner off the square. A glance at Xavier revealed a vein pulsing dramatically over his temple, but other than that, he betrayed no sign of impatience. *Good luck with that*, I wanted to tell him. *Try four years of this crap and then tell me how you fare.*

It took nearly ten minutes, but eventually, the bite did make it into Sofia's mouth completely. Then her eyes popped open in delight.

"Oh, Mama!" she cooed. "It's *good*! You have to try it!"

I smiled. "Definitely."

I turned to check on my serving but immediately stopped. For the first time since I'd seen him last December, there in my homely kitchen, watching his daughter eat a bit of his homecooked food, Xavier Parker was smiling. It wasn't just any smile, either. It was a full-on grin from ear to ear that revealed a deep dimple off to the left side of his mouth, cast his jawline in full relief, and made his blue eyes twinkle like they were each separate stars. It was blinding, shining across the stove, the counter, Sofia, and probably myself.

My mouth dropped. His pleasure was instantaneous and utterly infectious. His gaze traveled to me, and I couldn't help but grin back. For a long moment we just stood, two grinning idiots, while Sofia squealed like a piglet over her food.

"Xavi, get Mama's," she ordered him through a mouthful of *okonomiyaki*. "She needs some too."

Xavier looked around at the skillet and jumped like a rabbit.

"Ah! Fuck!" he cried, though now he was laughing as he flipped the second pancake, revealing a slightly scorched bottom, though nothing I would call inedible.

All of us were laughing now, watching this big, generally staid man hop around the kitchen while he cooked, giggling like a hyena, all of us having the best time ever.

"Here, Ces," he said, finally handing a plate to me before starting on his own pancake. "Bon appétit."

I accepted it gratefully. Sofia was right. It *was* good. A hell of a lot better than canned sauce and boxed pasta.

"I had all of this in the fridge?" I asked through a bite.

Xavier smirked. It wasn't quite the grin he had given Sofia, but that dimple was still present. "I had to make some last-minute substitutions, but it should taste all right."

"You're going to have to teach me to make it," I said. "She doesn't like anything but noodles and toast, this one."

"Can't. It's a family secret." He winked at Sofia, making her burst into another round of giggles.

The doorbell rang, and I slid off my stool, too caught up in the mood to worry that he had just hinted at the whole damn secret.

"I'll be right back," I said. "Don't laugh so much you choke, you two."

I left them while Xavier was listening to Sofia do some impression of her cousins, then mimicking her himself, causing another avalanche of giggles.

I opened the door thinking I'd find Pete asking for some quiet, but instead discovered Derek Kingston, my brother's investigative partner and a man I'd gone out with for about a month, standing on my porch in his street clothes.

Dressed in a Mets T-shirt and wearing an open smile, Derek looked about the same as any other thirty-something guy in the neighborhood and liked most of the same things too. Baseball games, pizza, cheesecakes, good barbecue. It might have worked out between us if I had shared his interests. Or at least hadn't dreamed of something, I don't know, *more* outside of Brooklyn.

That didn't mean we couldn't be friends, though.

"Hey, stranger," I greeted him with a brief hug. "What are you doing here?"

"I was in the neighborhood. Zola asked me to check in on you guys while he was gone." Derek had the decency to look a bit sheepish at the request.

"Did he now?" I rolled my eyes. Once a big brother, always a big brother.

"Sorry. Yeah." Derek glanced around me. "Sof around, or is she in bed? I brought her a black and white from Weiss."

He held up a paper bag presumably containing one of the classic bakery cookies.

"Ooh, she'll love that, thank you," I said. "She's, ah, a little busy right now, though. Getting ready for bed and all. Can I give it to her tomorrow and let her know you stopped by?"

"Sure, that's fine. I was just going to—oh, hey, man."

My stomach dropped. He didn't. He wouldn't.

"All right?" Xavier's deep voice rumbled behind me, but without any of the humor I'd just experienced moments earlier.

I turned just in time to watch the geniality of the evening erased as soon as he set eyes on our visitor.

He glared at me. Then Derek. Then me again. "Who's this?"

On the porch, Derek straightened. "Ah, Derek Kingston. Frankie, I didn't know you had company. You, um, could have just said."

"This is only a friend from school," I lied a little too quickly. "He stopped by for dinner."

"I *made* dinner," Xavier corrected me through his teeth. His blue gaze darted between me and Derek with the speed of a cheetah. "How do you know Francesca?"

"Francesca?" Derek snorted at the name. "Ah, *Frankie* and I used to—"

"He's my brother's old partner," I cut in, eager to avoid the conflict I saw coming.

Xavier was quiet for a long minute. "Well, don't let me stop the reunion," he said, then stomped back down the hallway without another word.

"Nice guy," Derek remarked. "Bet he's a real peach at work, you said?" He couldn't quite hide his resentment. Or skepticism.

I felt horrible, especially since I had been the one to break things off between us. This wasn't fair to him, especially considering how it looked.

"It's not—we're not—" I sighed. "It's complicated." I didn't know how to explain it without telling him everything.

"Sure. Yeah." Derek thrust the cookie toward me but didn't meet my eyes. "I'll, ah, see you."

I sighed. "Wait. Derek?"

He turned, looking slightly hopeful. "Yeah?"

"Do me a favor? Um, don't mention this to Mattie?"

Derek glanced over my shoulder in the direction Xavier had gone, then back at me questioningly.

"It's new," I admitted. "Not—not me and him. It's not like that, really. The truth is…"

I paused for a moment to close the door behind me and sighed. I'd known Derek for years. Yes, he was one of Matthew's best friends. But he'd also dated me. He looked out for me and Sofia too. On some level, he had to care.

"Derek, that's Sofia's dad. None of my family knows yet that he's, um, back in New York. I'm trying to see how things go. Give them a chance to get to know each other before I bring my whole family in. Before I actually tell Sofia who he is. You know?"

His dark eyes widened as I spoke. Derek knew enough about my family and my situation with Sofia to know why I would want to keep things quiet for a bit.

"All right," he said slowly. "I get it. But even Zola doesn't know? Come on, Frankie, you gotta tell your brother."

"I will," I promised a little too quickly. "I will. I just need some time, all right?"

Slowly, Derek nodded. "All right. But is he—you sure he's all right around her?"

I glanced over my shoulder, like I could see the two of them right through the door. The truth is, I didn't know. I hoped he was. But that flash I'd just seen in his eyes had been alarming. Not toward her. Toward me.

"We'll be fine," I said.

"All right," Derek replied doubtfully. "But you need something, I don't care if homeboy in there is a saint or not. You got a cop on your side, Frankie. Remember that, okay?"

I nodded. Derek and I hadn't worked out, but I appreciated his loyalty to Matthew and this family.

"Thanks, Derek." I leaned in and pressed a quick kiss to his cheek. "I'll see you."

I reentered the house to find Sofia sitting on the sofa happily watching *Daniel Tiger* instead of *Moana* while Xavier was back in the kitchen, this time doing dishes with a thundercloud for a face.

"You little minx," I scolded her politely before dropping a kiss on the top of her head. "You're supposed to ask first before you watch."

"I asked Xavi," she replied. "He said okay."

"Xavier's not your mom," I informed her, despite the fact that, by all rights, he should have the same authority. "We're getting a little too close to bedtime. One episode, all right?"

She was already turned back around while I went into the kitchen.

"Sorry about the interruption," I said. "Let me do that. Cooks don't clean in this house."

Xavier said nothing, just surrendered the sponge and pan with a splash of soapy water, then stomped out of the kitchen to join Sofia on the couch. She was too entranced by her cartoon to notice the way a scowl had replace Xavier's grin.

"Fuck," he muttered to himself as he got a look at the wet stains on his shirt. "Fucking mess."

I huffed. It wasn't like Sofia didn't hear her fair share of profanity. Matthew had many excellent qualities, but censorship wasn't one of them. Still, Xavier was going to have to work on his mouth if he was going to take on more parental duties with this one.

Sofia took things into her own hands.

"You say the F-word a lot, Xavi," she told him matter-of-factly.

Xavier blinked down at her. "Yes, I do."

Sofia nodded, still watching the TV. "So does my zio. But when he says bad words, he has to put money in the swear jar." She pointed at the canning jar stuffed with one- and five-dollar bills, sitting on the end table next to Xavier. "When it's full, we go to Coney Island and ride the Ferris wheel. We go a lot."

Xavier examined the jar for a moment, then pulled his wallet out of his back pocket and extracted two bills.

"Consider it an advance," he told her dryly.

I chuckled as I scrubbed the skillet.

But Sofia shook her head. "Um, you have to put in real money."

Xavier frowned at the bills. "This is a hundred quid. It's as real as it gets."

"Let me see that." Sofia yanked one of the fifty-pound notes out of his hand and examined it between her chubby fingers. After a moment, she handed it back to him. "Yup, it's fake. I can't do nothing with this."

"What are you talking about? You can do more with that than a hundred dollars."

"No, you can't," Sofia insisted. "It has a lady on it."

"That's because it's the bloody queen of England!" Xavier sputtered.

Sofia frowned. "Um, that's not a real place."

"Yes, it is."

"No, it isn't."

"Yes, it is."

"No, it isn't!" Sofia threw me an expression that basically asked, "Who is this bozo?" without actually saying it. "This is a real place. New York City. Where *I* live. England is made up."

Xavier looked like he was about ready to tear his hair out. "And why in the hell would you think that?"

"Because queens and princesses only exist in fairy tales. And *fairy tales aren't real life*. Right, Mama?"

Two pairs of bright blue eyes turned over the back of the couch and lasered onto me. Lord, they were intense.

It didn't help that she was quoting me. I did my best to counter the cultural programming she received as a little girl growing up in a world intent on teaching women to be saved rather than saving themselves. It would do her good later on, I hoped. But it certainly wasn't helping me right now.

"Is she always this stubborn about her own idiocy?" Xavier demanded irritably.

That did it. I turned off the faucet, marched around the counter, then grabbed Xavier by the shirt collar and proceeded to haul him out of the room.

"Ooh, he's gonna get it," I heard Sofia telling one of her stuffed animals as we left.

"Sof, just keep watching *Daniel Tiger*, all right?" I called but didn't bother to wait for a response as I towed Xavier down the hall, out to the front porch, and slammed the door shut.

"Let's get one thing clear," I said, ignoring his glare, yanking him down so I could look him in the eye. "She's four. You're thirty-two. She barely knows the difference between green and red, much less England and America. She might act like she knows everything, but only because that is all completely normal for a tiny person who is just figuring out how to *be* a person."

"So, what then?" Xavier retorted through his teeth. "That means I just have to let her say the wrong fucking thing and make a fool out of herself?"

"No, it means that you, a fully grown man, don't get to make her feel like shit about it," I snapped right back. "Especially when you're actually just taking out your frustration with me on her!"

Xavier had opened his mouth like he wanted to shout back, but now couldn't seem to say anything. That was all fine by me. I had plenty more to say.

"I know this whole parenting thing is new to you, so let me spell a few things out," I told him in a low, insidious tone that Matthew jokingly called my "Ms. Zola" voice. "As her parents, it's our responsibility to teach her right from wrong. But only about five percent of that is what we say—the other ninety-five is what we do. If you insult her, talk down to her, or show her she is deserving of anything but respect, then that is all she will do to other people, and it's all she will expect for herself. And Xavier? I will. Not. Have it. You treat her like that again, it will be the last time you see her. Do you understand?"

We stared at each other for a long time, playing some strange game of owl right there on my front porch. It didn't matter that we were getting odd looks from a few of the neighbors out walking their dogs. I was going to force him to look at me until every word I said got through his thick head.

Finally, he nodded slowly, and eventually, I released his collar, allowing him to stand fully and shake out his craned neck.

And then he did the last thing I expected.

He kissed me.

It wasn't a kiss full of passion. Well, maybe a little, bundled up with frustration and annoyance and anger and anything else he was feeling. His fingers gripped the sides of my face, fitting over my cheeks and jaw while his thumbs latched over my chin, giving me no more ability to leave than I had given him when gripping his shirt. His lips forced mine open, supple, and insistent, but only long enough for our tongues to touch.

It was brief, more of a stamp than anything else. But I still felt its intensity tingle from the top of my head all the way down to my toes.

And then, just as quickly, it was over.

"Sorry," he said after he released me. "I didn't mean—I just thought —it's only—"

He shook his head abruptly, like a dog shaking out it coat. Then he blinked, like he wasn't quite sure *what* he was trying to say. Or think.

"You're a good mum," he finished at last. "I had no idea."

"Oh, um. Thanks."

I frowned, still touching my lips. I had stumbled backward into the door and had essentially forgotten everything I had just said. The flavors of ginger, soy sauce, and something immeasurably savory were ripe on my lips.

What was I saying?

Oh, right. Sofia.

Xavier swallowed, still looking befuddled by my earlier reaction. Or maybe by his.

"And you're right," he said. "I'm a complete wanker." He glanced back toward the closed door. "I don't even know that I can go back in there."

"Oh, you're going back in," I told him. "We also teach her to apologize. That means we have to do it too when we mess up."

"You mess up too?"

I nodded. "Of course. We're only human."

He raised a brow. "Does that mean you're going to apologize for dragging me out here like a dog?"

"No," I said. "You deserved that completely."

He sighed. "I suppose I did." Then he yanked at his collar like he was about to tug himself somewhere. "All right. I'll apologize. And I think it's time to go back to my hotel. Take a shower and watch that stupid tiger too. Maybe learn something."

I nodded, still feeling shaky. Great. Now I was imagining Xavier naked. In the shower. Completely wet.

I fought the need to fan myself despite the fact that it was probably twenty-two degrees outside. "Okay, yeah. That's probably best."

"I have to go back to London tomorrow night, though. Can I see her in the morning? Take her to breakfast?"

I snorted. "Breakfast is pretty early when you're a four-year-old."

"Why?" Xavier pressed. "What time does she wake up?"

"Believe me. You don't want to know."

"Try me."

I shrugged. "Five, five thirty most days. Sometimes earlier if she has a bad dream. We go to bed in about an hour."

Xavier thought for a moment. Then a sly smile hovered just behind his stubbornness. "Breakfast it is. I'll take her to the fish market. I need to meet the vendors anyway."

I scoffed. "Xavi, the last thing she's going to want to do is be dragged around your business crap at five in the morning."

"She'll like it, I promise. You will too. Please, Ces. Let me make it up to you both. Second chances, right?"

I eyed him for a long moment. He seemed completely in earnest.

"All right," I said. "Five. But you better bring breakfast."

He tipped his head, looking for a moment like the perfect gentleman. Even so, his eyes gleamed with mischief. "How do they say it in those posh shows you like? 'It would be my pleasure'?"

I flushed brightly but nodded anyway. He was making fun, and so couldn't possibly know how much hearing exactly that phrase turned me on. My ovaries had had enough torture tonight. I didn't need to hear Xavier acting like a gentleman of all things to top it off.

Xavier gave a curt nod, then turned just as he was about to open the door. "And Ces?"

"Hmm?"

"Tell me again when I'm being an ass with her. Anything else, I want to know."

Again, I nodded. "Sure. Yeah."

He nodded. "I'll learn. I promise."

19

A t approximately five the next morning, after Sofia had gotten up even earlier than normal to put on her favorite purple tulip-printed dress and ladybug rain boots for the excursion, we were on our way north. The three of us were lined up in the back of Xavier's plush rented Mercedes after Sofia had insisted that Xavier and I sit on either side of her.

I had to give it to him. Last night's outburst aside, he was charming the heck out of my kid, and that was not easy to do. Sofia was taking to him like a duck in water. I couldn't help but wonder if some part of that was genetic.

The car was ironically making its way back to my home borough— the Bronx. We were going to the Fulton Fish Market, which, despite its fame as the second largest market in the world and a veritable New York institution, I had never visited. I didn't really have much need for fish. Nor did I particularly want to go to one of the most dangerous parts of the city just to see other people buy them.

Xavier, however, had insisted it would be fun for Sofia and was clearly trying to bribe me with a large London Fog, made with a particularly strong Earl Grey. So there I sat, slightly squished and sipping my tea while Xavier and Sofia entertained themselves with the other item he had brought: origami paper.

"It's nothing," he said with slightly reddened cheeks when I asked how he got it. "Saw it when I was in Chinatown last night."

I didn't reply. Why had he gone to Chinatown last night, after we'd all enjoyed his dinner? Was he there for the nightlife? Was he meeting up with someone else while he was in New York?

Why did I even care?

I ignored all the questions and sipped my tea, which was as irritatingly perfect as he was this early morning. What a jerk.

"Where did you learn that?" Sofia asked as she watched Xavier swiftly fold a square of paper decorated with ducks.

"Ah, my mum taught me," he answered, carefully avoiding her gaze as he worked. "Sort of like the pancake I made for you last night."

"Mum? You mean your mama?"

He nodded as he licked one side of the paper and made a final fold, large hands impressively dexterous. "That's right. In England, we call her Mum. Or maybe Mummy when we're little like you."

"I'm not so little."

Xavier held back a clear smile at the pronunciation of little as *wittle*. I couldn't help mine. It also hadn't escaped me that Xavier's showstopping grin was likely to make another appearance, again in response to Sofia. Was it possible she was charming him as much as he was her? Was that smile back to stay?

"No, you're not." He offered her another square decorated with sparkly socks. "Which is why I know you can do this. Now look, first you fold it in half diagonally. That's it. Then open it up and do it again on the other side."

I watched curiously as he gently but firmly guided Sofia through the short folding process. It took a few missteps, but Sofia didn't complain. Both of their brows furrowed identically as they focused on the tiny squares in their hands, and when they were finished, I was presented with two twin expressions of triumph that were so similar, it took my breath away.

"Mama, look! I made a fishy!" Sofia squealed as she offered me a paper fish.

I swallowed, trying to find my voice. "You—you sure did, baby. I love it."

"Just like Nemo!" Then she turned back to Xavier, who was smiling with her in a way that made my heart jump in my chest. "Actually, yours is Nemo because he's the boy. Mine's Dory."

He looked over her to me, blue eyes dancing, but adorably confused.

"Cartoon characters," I managed to say. "Keep up."

For that, I received a delicious eye roll, but he wisely didn't respond as Sofia pulled on his sleeve.

"Come on, let's make another."

They bent to their work, but I turned toward my window only to be faced with a still mostly black sky, the horizon only just starting to lighten through the buildings at the horizon. If I was getting such strong reactions to tiny scenes like this, maybe Kate and Matthew were both right. I needed a man, pronto. Because Xavier was definitely the wrong one for me.

———

Twenty minutes later, we followed Xavier into an enormous warehouse at the end of a pier on Hunt's Point. It wasn't an area of the city I would have typically gone, particularly with Sofia, given its status as a haven for addiction and crime. But the car took us directly to the enormous wharf at the end of the neighborhood that was lined with the city's notorious culinary supply markets. Even I, who hadn't so much as served coffee for work, knew about this place.

"It's closing already?" I wondered as we entered a hangar still full of vendors. "At five thirty in the morning?"

Many of their stations seemed bare, with maybe a few items still on ice, if at all. Some were already starting to pack everything up.

"Yeah, most of their business is done by now," Xavier told me. "If I were actually here to buy, I'd come at midnight, when it opens. But I'm here to meet vendors."

"Ooh, look at that *huge* fish!" Sofia crowed, immediately scampering a few feet away to examine a tuna approximately her size.

Xavier surveyed the market, looking more like one of the men working the stalls than a rich businessman they should be courting. The boy from South London was back in jeans, a black hoodie, an insulated vest that pulled across his chest, and a backward cap with Arsenal printed across the front. Lord, he looked good in denim. It made his long legs look even longer, and the material encased his taut backside to perfection.

Yeah, I *definitely* needed a man. And definitely not this one, no matter how good he looked in jeans.

He turned, catching me mid-perusal. I reddened as one side of his mouth lifted.

"I like that tracksuit," he told me, openly looking me up and down as I'd just been doing to him.

I followed his gaze. "It's just sweats."

I was totally lying. Most Saturdays saw me in old T-shirts and yoga pants while I cleaned the house, not my favorite matching red Adidas pants and jacket that Kate had found for me on consignment. Nor did I usually wear the big silver hoops dangling from my ears. Or put on eyeliner and mascara. Or curl my hair and pile it into a high ponytail that bounced around my shoulders.

Okay, so maybe I had gotten up even earlier than Sofia. So maybe I'd barely slept last night remembering the sudden pressure of those lips on mine last night. Or the way his blue eyes darted hungrily over my body before letting me go.

"Well, whatever it is, it makes your arse look great," Xavier rumbled into my ear, causing goose bumps to rise where his warm breath touched my skin.

His fresh scent briefly overpowered the smell of brine and fish that filled the room. I shivered. When he stood straight again, he was so clearly pleased with himself that I offered my best scowl, which admittedly wasn't particularly good at the moment.

"You should not be saying things like that to me," I told him, quietly enough that Sofia wouldn't hear.

I know, I know. I couldn't even convince myself.

"Probably not," he agreed. "But I never do what I'm told."

He offered half a cheeky grin, and again, I found it hard not to smile back. Gradually, his grin disappeared. Then neither of us seemed to be able to look away.

"Mama!" Sofia shouted, breaking the trance. "*Look* at this fishy!" She turned to the seller. "How much?"

"Wow!" I called back to her, then looked back at Xavier. "Do we have an agenda here? Or are the fishmongers good with Sofia interrogating all of them?"

Xavier cleared his throat. "Ah, yeah. Elsie sent me a list, and there are a few more," he replied, pulling out his phone.

"Elsie?" I wondered as we started walking.

He smirked but didn't look down at me. Almost like he was avoiding me now. "My assistant. Keep your knickers on."

I smarted. "I wasn't the one throwing another fit last night, Xavi."

All humor vanished from his face. But instead of answering, he scanned the fishmonger stalls, then offered his hand to Sofia when she returned.

"There's one. Come on, girlie. Let's go meet some swimmers."

———

FOR THE NEXT hour or so, I followed Xavier and Sofia from stall to stall while he interviewed vendors for his new restaurant, and she interviewed them for *her* new restaurant. Her menu apparently included "fish, but only the mean ones" and "yummy things." To his credit, Xavier maintained a completely straight face while he and the vendors entertained her questions ("Did this fish ever hit anyone?" and "Do you like princesses?"). The vendors themselves just answered in that jovial, direct way that only men in New York really have.

The jokes, however, ended when Xavier handed them his card with a stern expression. It was obvious that every seller in the market wanted the Parker Group's business. Word got around quickly as we walked through. Some of the stalls that had been closed when we entered were miraculously open again. Samples appeared of sushi-grade fish along with other creatures I couldn't identify. Massive smiles appeared on the faces of previously wearied men.

"Yum," Sofia purred around a mouthful of something yellow that looked like brains.

I gaped. *My* picky daughter was eating something raw, mysterious, and vaguely gelatinous…and liking it?

"Mama, you have to try that," she said. "It tastes like butter."

I frowned at the questionable pile of goo nestled in some sort of spiky shell.

"It's *uni*," Xavier told me, spooning out a piece of it and holding it up to my mouth. "Sea urchin. It's a delicacy."

"I don't like—"

"Ces, just try it. Have I ever steered you wrong?"

I examined the blob, then him, then Sofia. She was watching with glee, Xavier with more of a smirk.

"Fine," I said.

Not to be outdone, I opened my mouth and allowed him to feed me the urchin.

It was…

"Delicious," I admitted with surprise after I'd gotten over the chilled, wobbly texture. I didn't love that part, but Sofia was indeed right. It wasn't the least bit fishy and had a slightly buttery flavor.

"It melts into an incredible sauce," Xavier said with a satisfied grin —one that was finally directed at me. "I'll make it for you sometime."

For me, or for us both?

I hated that I even wondered.

Before I could stop him, he reached out and drew his thumb slowly over my bottom lip, eyes pinned to the trail left by his finger.

"Mama, I'm hungry. But not for any more fish."

Xavier jerked, then pulled his hand away. "Er, you had a bit on your face."

Immediately, I wiped again at the spot. His fingerprint seared.

Xavier exchanged cards with the urchin vendor, then offered Sofia his hand. "Come on, kid. Let's get you a sandwich at the café. Then if your mum's up to it, we can find a park and run around."

We followed him out of the hangar and around the corner into a grubby bodega on the corner that appeared to have a grill in the back. There was a small line clearly serving the workers who were already done for their "day." The smell of frying eggs, ham, and toasted bread filled the air alongside the familiar scents of cafe con leche, newspapers, and all the other odd little things common to shops like these all over the city.

"I'm shocked you're willing to eat here," I murmured to Xavier, who just shot me a look of faux outrage. "You do know it's not organic, right? And I'm sure the eggs aren't free range."

For that, I received a playful nudge.

"I've not completely grown out of my roots, you know," he said as we stepped to the counter. "Besides, one of the fishmongers told me they get everything fresh around the corner. Bread from Il Forno, eggs from Hunt's Point Produce. You get the picture. So what'll it be?"

"I could do with a fried egg sandwich on a kaiser roll," I said. "Sofia'll have a bagel and maybe an orange—Mom?"

I blinked when the cashier turned around and I was faced with the same surprise twice in one week.

She looked the same as she had on Sunday, except this morning her blond hair was pulled back, revealing some graying roots, the circles under her eyes were a little more pronounced, and the clothes she wore were a bit grubby around the wrists and collar.

"Frankie?"

Guadalupe Ortiz's large green eyes immediately brightened when she caught sight of me and Sofia. Then they shifted to Xavier and stayed there a beat or two longer, full of sharp curiosity and something else I couldn't quite name. She turned and barked something in Spanish toward one of her coworkers, then stripped off her apron and scurried around the counter.

"Hi, baby!" she cried a little too loudly. "Come say hello to your abuela!"

We shifted to the side to allow the line to pass us, and my mother squatted down right there in the shop and spread her arms expectantly for Sofia, who looked up at me with questions in her eyes.

I shrugged, as if to tell her *it's your choice*.

She turned back shyly back and then tentatively allowed her a hug, tapping her shoulders lightly until she was finally released.

Xavier watched with his stern resting face. Skepticism played over his features, and I didn't miss the way he took a step in front of Sofia after my mother released her.

"I thought you worked at a convenience store," I said.

"Bodega, cafe, convenience store. Same thing, isn't it?" Mom replied as she stood back up. She turned to Xavier, clearly unable to stifle her curiosity any longer. "And who is this tall drink of water?"

"Er, Mom," I said. "This is my, ah, friend. Xavi."

I explicitly did not use Xavier's full name on the off chance she was going to see Lea or one of the others anytime soon.

"He's *my* friend too!" Sofia put in with a stiff upper lip.

Xavier smiled down at her. "'Course I am."

"Pleased to meet you," Mom said as she held out a hand to shake Xavier's. "Do I hear an English accent there? Where are you from?"

"Cheers," Xavier replied. "I'm from South London, originally."

"Ooh, London. That sounds so glamorous! And *look* at that beautiful watch," she fawned, pulling him closer to examine the Patek. "How does someone so young afford something like *that*?"

"Mom!" I chided. "Please."

I was almost afraid to check Xavier's expression. He allowed her to look for approximately five seconds before gently extricating his hand from her clasp.

"It's a family heirloom," he said evenly.

"Heirloom!" my mother crowed. "My, my, what are you, some kind of lord or duke or something like that?"

She chuckled to herself like it was the funniest thing in the world. Meanwhile, a line appeared between Xavier's brows, and his lips flattened into a tight line.

"Mom," I snapped. "Stop embarrassing yourself."

It was just like her to make completely inappropriate comments about someone's money while at the same time ignoring her own kin. Two days ago, she made all sorts of noise about wanting to know Sofia, but now she was more interested in the first shiny thing in front of her.

"Xavi makes food!" Sofia chirped, taking his hand for herself almost proprietarily. This time, Xavier did not reclaim it, but allowed her to shake it all she liked. "That's why we're here. To see the fishes for his new restaurant."

"Restaurant?" She perked up like a sparrow looking for spare crumbs. "What sort of restaurant?"

"Japanese fusion," Xavier replied shortly.

"Oh, *fusion*! That sounds incredible. I don't really know what it means, but I'm sure it's great!"

"Mom, don't you have to get back to work?" I said irritably, noticing the replacement cashier watching us with very little amusement. I didn't know what she was up to—I never did—but I was more than ready to get out of this shop.

"Oh, sure. Yes, I do. What do you all want, hmm? I can get you ten percent off."

"It's not necessary—" I started but was waved away almost immediately as my mother jogged back around the counter and started punching numbers into the register.

"Nope, I got it," she said. "On me." She glanced at me, then looked meaningfully back at Xavier. "It's the very least I can do."

I frowned. What was that supposed to mean?

"Fine," I said. "Xavi, can you take Sofia outside? I'll get our food."

"Oh, it's all right," he said. "I've got it—"

"Please," I interrupted. I didn't like the way my mother was looking at him and Sofia like they were worms and she was the robin ready to eat them.

Xavier blinked, glanced between us, then nodded. "Right. Sure."

I watched them leave, then turned back to my mom. "What are you doing?"

She frowned. "What are you talking about? I'm being perfectly nice! I never get to see you, and then you walk into this little store. It's fate, baby, you know it is."

"It's not fate," I said. "It's coincidence. And you know what I'm talking about. You barely said hello to me and Sofia before you were drooling all over a man you hardly know. And for what?"

Her lower lip started to tremble, and her eyes grew into wide green pools of sadness. "Oh—I—I'm so sorry. I didn't think…I was only being friendly…"

I rolled my eyes. "You must think I was born yesterday. I've seen you do this before."

"What do you mean?"

I scoffed. "Mom, come on! How about when you stole half of

Nonna's jewelry to pay your dealer? Or how about when you blew all of Dad's life insurance money on booze, huh?"

"Shh!" Her posture stiffened with each statement I made. "I've changed. People can change."

"That might have worked with Lea, but it's not going to work on me. Xavi is just a friend, all right? He has a nice watch, but he's not here to pay for your next score or whatever else it is that you're looking for."

Her face fell even further. "Frankie, that was cruel."

Guilt blossomed in my belly. Shit, maybe I *had* gone overboard.

"I—" I shook my head. It was hard to separate her inappropriate behavior now from years past. Maybe Matthew was right. Maybe some things were too hard to forgive.

"I'm sorry," she said softly, coming closer so her coworkers couldn't hear. "For today and all those years and all the mistakes I ever made. I'll tell you every day if I have to. But *amor*, forgiveness is divine, remember? It's not fair for you to hold a grudge against me forever and keep me from my granddaughter. She's making…new friends…isn't she? Why not with her abuela too?"

She glanced out the window of the shop, where Xavier and Sofia were playing some sort of game that consisted of her standing on his shoes while he twirled around.

I rubbed my face. This was too confusing. I had too much to nego- tiate right now without my mother complicating all of it.

"I just need our sandwiches," I said. "Beyond that…" I shook my head. "I'll think about it, all right?"

My mother smiled and gave me another hug—without asking, but I couldn't deny that it felt nice.

"Perfect," she said. "Just perfect."

20

"So," I said. "Are we ever going to talk about it?"

I'd had it with the waiting. After two hours of fish shopping, feeding Sofia breakfast, and now watching her give day old bread from the café to the ducks across the river in Soundview Park, Xavier still hadn't said a word about yesterday's outburst. Meanwhile, I could still feel the imprint of his lips on mine.

I had been putting it off too, but it had to be discussed. I wasn't an idiot—he was noticing me just as much as I was noticing him. Feeding me food. Flirting constantly. It was like we couldn't help it.

And yes, I could admit, it also felt kind of good. But it still wasn't a good idea.

His blue eyes narrowed at me, then darted away as we sank onto a bench overlooking the water and Sofia's exploits with the ducks. His knee rubbed against mine, but he didn't move it away.

"You mean the fact that your mum works in a bodega and every time she spoke you looked like you'd drunk bad milk?"

I frowned. "I told you she worked somewhere up here. And that we don't talk much. Running into her outside a fish market isn't going to change that."

Xavier just gave me a long, blue look.

I grimaced. "I know you understand what it's like to have family who don't know what the word means. She's making another move back into our lives again. I haven't decided how I feel about it."

Xavier continued staring at me.

"What?" I asked.

He mumbled something like, "Glad I'm not the only one," then stretched his long legs out in front of him. "Then I assume you mean my behavior last night. I already apologized for snapping at you and Sofia. I said I won't do it again, and I meant it."

"I'm not talking about that. You're doing fine making up for *that*." I checked that Sofia wasn't listening, then continued in a lower voice. "I'm talking about the part when you got jealous about another guy—again, I might add—and then kissed me. Also again."

"Oh. That." Xavier reached back and tugged at the bill of his cap before dropping his arm across the back of the bench. "And you want me to apologize for that too?"

I noticed he did not.

I sighed. "It is what it is. But don't you think we need to talk about the fact that you have thrown two tantrums now when you thought another man was present in my life?"

Another tug at his hat. Another chew of his very full lower lip.

"Well, in my defense, the first one was right after you'd practically let me into your knickers, then left me cold," he pointed out.

I reddened, unable to help myself. Yeah, I'd been about to let him do a lot more than that.

"I was crazed with lust," he continued with a smirk. "Not accountable for my actions."

"Fine," I said. "We'll let that one go. But last night? What was that about?"

He shrugged. "Nothing."

I huffed. "Xavi, spare me the studied nonchalance. You were pissed. And then you bit our heads off because of it. I've accepted your apology, but we haven't exactly addressed the root cause."

His face went through a surprisingly wide number of expressions before it settled on a frown. "Fine. I didn't like it."

"Didn't like what?"

His eyes narrowed. "You know what."

"So you *were* jealous." I felt a small thrill at the idea, though I knew I shouldn't. Things were complicated enough with this man. I didn't need him to throw jealousy into the mix.

Xavier shrugged, but still couldn't meet my eyes. "I wouldn't call it that, exactly."

"Then what would you call it? Envious? Possessive? Controlling?"

I shouldn't have liked the way any of those words sounded. I really, really shouldn't have.

"I'd say…particular."

I snorted. "Oh, really? Particular about what, pray tell?"

"Well, how about the men introduced to my—er—little one over there."

A quick glance at Sofia informed us both she was still happily oblivious to our conversation, tossing breadcrumbs into the water like fairy dust.

"Yeah, I don't think so," I said. "Using Sofia as a way to control who I see isn't going to fly, buddy. I could have a date this weekend if I wanted to, and you couldn't say anything about it."

His head whipped around like it was attached to a pair of reins. "A date?"

I shrugged. "Why not? You remember Adam. He likes me."

I didn't mention the fact that I had absolutely no interest in Adam or the many other times he had asked me out. I was tired of being made to feel that someone like me didn't deserve anyone else's love and affection. My sisters wanted me to get laid, but the rest of my family wanted me to settle, mostly for Sofia's sake. There was no in between. There was nothing that was just for me.

"Do you have a problem with that?" I asked Xavier.

His blue eyes narrowed in an expression that was harrowingly similar to Sofia's when I turned off her favorite show in the mornings. "Not at all." Each word was delivered through a nearly closed mouth.

"Delighted to hear it. Now try again. What was the real problem with Derek showing up?"

I didn't know why I was pushing this so hard. Maybe it was because I wanted to hear that I wasn't alone in this irritating push and pull. Maybe I wanted to hear him admit that I affected him too. Then we could at least manage it together, couldn't we?

Xavier just sighed. "Does it really matter? He wasn't any good in the long run. No big loss for you."

I frowned. "How could you possibly know that? Derek is a perfectly nice guy."

"You said you were with him for a month. He's obviously an upstanding fellow, likes Sof, friends with your brother. If he was even a half-decent shag, you'd not only be with him, but you'd also have a perfectly tiny diamond on that finger by now, wouldn't you?"

My jaw dropped. "You," I said as evenly as my shaking voice could handle, "are an asshole."

"True. But I'm also right," he said with satisfaction that I wanted to slap off his face. "Unless I'm missing something, of course."

"Not that it's any of your business, but you definitely are," I sputtered. "Particularly since Derek and I didn't actually get that far."

I had no idea why I'd just told him that. I wasn't exactly a prude, but the idea that sex would be the deciding factor for marriage really irritated me. Or maybe it was just Xavier saying it that irritated me. I honestly couldn't say.

All signs of joking disappeared from Xavier's face. "You didn't what?"

I frowned. "I'm not repeating myself."

"I—you—well, you just proved my point, didn't you? Of course you couldn't marry him. You don't even know if he's good in bed, do you?"

"Oh my *God*, you brought up marrying him, not me!" I hissed, struggling now to keep my cool. "We didn't do anything because *I* didn't want to. Just like I haven't wanted to do more than make out with anyone for about five freaking years now!"

I was speaking in relatively veiled terms, but my voice shot up several decibels, high enough to scare a nearby pigeon into flying away.

"Mama?" Sofia called from the water's edge. "Are you okay?"

Slowly, my heartbeat returned to its normal rhythm. I had to keep it together for her.

"I'm fine, peanut," I replied, though I couldn't for the life of me keep my voice even. "Keep feeding the ducks." Then I turned to Xavier. "You can forget I said that."

"I don't think so." There was not one iota of humor in his voice.

I looked up. "I wish you would."

He was quiet for a long time. I focused on Sofia, who had abandoned the breadcrumbs and was now doing her level best to skip rocks. The best she had gotten was one.

"So, have I got this right?" Xavier asked after what must have been about a million seconds. "You were a virgin when we met."

I flushed. That's right. He knew. Hell, I had only just reminded him about it myself.

"You haven't been with anyone since me? As in, it's been *five years* since you've…"

"Oh my God, you don't need to announce my involuntary celibacy to the world." Frantically, I looked around.

We were alone but for Sofia.

"I'm just—it's just—Christ, *how* is that possible?"

I scowled. "Don't get too excited. Not a lot of men are in the market for a single mom and a date with her four-year-old."

"A lot of men are fucking idiots." His voice was still low, but so intense, it was almost threatening.

I shivered, and not because of the wind coming off the river.

"I'm not waiting for marriage or anything," I said. "Obviously. And it's not a religious thing, so don't ask."

Xavier didn't respond, just waiting in that patented way of his. He always seemed to know when there was a whole other story waiting on the tip of my tongue.

I sighed. It's funny how you go from sexy to sexless in the span of nine months. Even funnier how easy it is to stay there. No one ever pushed me on this anymore. Not my sisters, who had mostly resigned themselves to the idea of me as a spinster. My friends in college had pretty much floated away when the word "baby" came into play. Even Nonna had stopped trying to set me up *every* weekend with some neighbor's son or nephew.

"I just want it to be special." I didn't know how else to put it. "I don't need to be completely in love with the guy or anything. But I need to care. And he needs to care about me. Doing *that* with my body…I just think it's basically the most intimate, vulnerable thing people can ever do. I know not everyone feels that way, but I do. So I need more than just a spark."

Xavier studied me for a long time.

"What?" I demanded. "You think I'm nuts, don't you? You think I should just 'get out there' and throw myself around like a cheap toy. Preferably with you, right?"

My voice was shaking. I hadn't realized how important this was to me. But clearly it was.

Xavier raised a hand, then placed it lightly on my shoulder. It was heavy. Solid. Almost comforting.

"I wasn't thinking that at all," he said quietly.

"Then what?" I demanded, suddenly feeling a rush of tears. This man really did turn me into an emotional mess.

"I was thinking that a woman as beautiful as you ought to have men trailing out the door," he said carefully. "That it's a bloody miracle you're not married or at least taken. But I was also thinking it makes sense that you're waiting for the right one."

His voice was so low I almost couldn't hear it. But somehow more powerful than if he had shouted.

I turned. "And I suppose that's you? Because that would be totally inappr—"

"No," he cut me off quickly. "It's definitely not me."

I tried to ignore the way something in my chest dropped about a foot at his immediate refusal. I shrugged, and the hand on my shoulder fell away.

One black brow quirked. But his eyes dropped to my mouth. And stayed there.

"I just know more than anyone, don't I? Because you're right, Ces. You definitely need more than just a spark. *You* deserve a fucking bonfire."

His eyes returned to mine, and there they stayed. We stared at each other for a long time, the sounds of the park muddying together. The rush of wind in the trees, Sofia's babble with the ducks. All of it blended together, leaving us in a bubble, a world for just me and him, where all I wanted to do was tackle him to the ground and—

"Mommy, mommy, momeeeeee, I saw a fish, but this one was alive!" Sofia came running up to the bench, popping the bubble as soon as it had appeared. "The duckies scared it away, but maybe it will come back! Come see!"

She yanked on my arm, pulling me literally and figuratively out of my trance. Somewhat reluctantly, I stood, though I managed to free my arm.

"All right, peanut, we're coming, we're coming," I told her as she scampered back to the water.

"Ces."

Xavier's low voice pulled me back as he stood.

I turned. "What?"

"You deserve that fire." He took a deep breath, then stood next to me. "Take that date. I'll take care of the kid. If you're all right with it, I mean."

I balked. "*You* want to babysit?"

His blue gaze drilled right through me. "It's not babysitting if she's my"—he lowered his voice—"if she's *my* daughter."

I opened and closed my mouth, probably looking a lot like the fish we'd gone to see. He had me there.

"We'll be all right," he said, though maybe not as sure as he wanted.

"You want to do dinner? Bedtime? The whole nine yards?" I joked. "I'm only kidding a little, Xavi. She can be a little terror at bedtime."

But Xavier just nodded, completely unfazed.

"It's been five years," he said. "I'll call you if anything goes wrong. I've had a life, and you deserve one too. I just want to know her, Ces. Let me try."

21

E verything about the date was perfect.
        The restaurant.
        The food.
The weather.
The music.
Everything was perfect. Except my actual date.

I sat primly at the tiny table at Rio Blanco, the romantic tapas restaurant in Gowanus that Xavier of all people had recommended. I wasn't sure he had actually meant his bizarre and frankly shocking offer to babysit Sofia so I could see Adam. But when he had texted halfway through Monday asking which night that weekend he should make himself available, I decided the hell with it.

After I'd asked Adam if he'd like to go to dinner that Monday, I'd considered canceling at least five separate times. But the days ticked by with Xavier confirming again and again that he was looking forward to his night with Sofia. His excitement was palpable, as was hers. I couldn't disappoint either of them. Plus, if he really wanted a taste of legitimate parenthood, trying to put Sofia to bed was a great way to get it.

He had arrived an hour early, allowing Sofia to show him her doll collection while also allowing for a particularly awkward moment when I stepped out of the shower in only a towel on my way to my "room." His hot gaze seared my damp skin. Then he blinked and went right back to inquiring after Sofia's dollhouse while I stood there like an idiot, dripping all over the hardwoods and wondering what the hell I was doing.

Other than the exchange in the hallway, Xavier continued to be magnanimous toward the date. He had something to say about everything I was doing, and Sofia was happy to jump right in with him to critique my wardrobe, hair, makeup, jewelry, all of it. My initial choice of jeans had to be swapped out for a black miniskirt that showed off my legs. My hair had to be down, not pulled back into a practical bun. Smoky eye instead of simple mascara. I drew the line when they suggested a red lip. I already felt like a lady of the night, and not in a good way.

And so that unease continued, from the moment I left my house to when I arrived at the restaurant, through accepting Adam's awkward compliments and kiss to the cheek, sitting through a delicious meal, and now waiting for him to return from the men's room.

I should have been enjoying myself. But instead, I was yet again wondering what the hell I was doing here. Or why in the world Xavier had been so adamant I go.

Wrong, wrong, wrong, wrong, *wrong*.

My phone buzzed on the tabletop. I turned it over, revealing yet another new message from Xavier, who had been taking full advantage of the fact that I had to answer any texts from him in case something happened to Sofia. I honestly couldn't tell if he was goading me or genuinely interested. Or why the latter bothered me so much.

Xavier: Still eating?

I rolled my eyes. I didn't *have* to answer. Not really.

Me: Almost done.

His reply was almost instantaneous.

Xavier: Where to next? There's a new club in Williamsburg that's supposed to be great.

I scoffed. He had been back in the city for all of what, a week? And suddenly he was divulging advice to a born-and-bred local?

Me: I'm not really a club kind of girl.

Xavier: That's not what I remember ;)

Something deep in my chest squeezed as a memory floated to the front of my mind. A dark basement lounge somewhere on the Lower East Side. Sultry trip hop, occasional whiffs of vanilla-scented hookah smoke, bodies swaying while I pressed mine to six feet, five inches of muscle in time to the beats. A pair of large hands sliding around my waist, then down, down, down…

Xavier: Has he put the moves on you yet?

I started, then stared at the message for a long moment. Good lord, could he read my mind from there? Irritably, I punched out a reply.

Me: omg that is NONE of your business.

His own reply buzzed while I was still trying to rid myself of his ghost.

Xavier: Just saying. If it were me in his shoes, I wouldn't be wasting time with a cute bird like you.

I giggled. I honestly couldn't help it.

Me: I'm a "cute bird" now?

Xavier: You know you're gorgeous. Especially in that skirt.

It was a game, obviously. He was toying with me little better than a cat playing with a mouse.

Even so, my heart thrilled a little at the compliment.

"You brat," I murmured, trying to come up with something pithy in response.

"Everything all right?"

I startled, hastily stowed my phone in my purse, and pasted on a bright smile. "Fine, thanks. Just a text from one of my sisters."

"Are they all as gorgeous as you?" Adam took his seat across from me and adjusted the driver's cap he had not removed for the meal.

I wasn't sure why that bothered me so much. Maybe because I grew up in a house where no one, not even my grandfather, was allowed to wear anything on their heads during mealtimes. Some things just stick with you.

"We look alike," I conceded, frowning to myself.

How was it that the same essential compliment from Adam felt like a wet finger down the back of my neck? He was supposed to be the nice one in this situation.

He was nervous. I could see it in the way he kept pulling at his goatee while he talked and fidgeted with his glasses whenever he listened. I wanted to tell him to stop, that he had nothing to worry about. But I couldn't, because honestly, it wasn't true. I already knew the moment I walked into the restaurant that we wouldn't be doing this again.

It didn't have anything to do with the glower on Xavier's face just before I'd closed my front door. Or the constant texts. Or even the fact that he would still be there when I got back.

Nothing at all.

"I really had no idea," Adam continued. "Like, wow. At school, you're always so—"

He cut himself off, like he had just realized he was about to say something that *wasn't* particularly complimentary for once.

Well, at least it would be the truth.

"Dowdy?" I finished for him. "It's okay. You can say it."

He almost looked relieved.

"Well, yeah. I mean, I always thought you were cute, obviously. But the baggy clothes and T-shirts. And, oh my God, those black sneakers you always wear! I think my grandma has the same—"

"I get it," I cut him off sharply. "My work clothes suck."

"I'm not blaming you or anything," he rattled on, oblivious to my irritation. "We work with kids. But, yeah, not exactly the sexiest stuff in the world. This, though…"

His eyes perused me openly, probably with the help of the bottle of wine he had swallowed over the past two hours.

I'd had half a glass.

I shifted uncomfortably in my seat. This guy was everything I should want. Elementary school art teacher. Indie rock aficionado. Self-proclaimed literature lover. Everything a nerdy bookworm like me should want. But everything out of his mouth either made me feel on display for his overeager gaze or slightly put down. Sure, I'd helped him along his train of thought, but it didn't exactly feel great to have your worst fears about yourself confirmed. That I was, in fact, an unattractive lump of clay when I didn't take all the extra time to make myself look like this.

The problem was, this wasn't me any more than the bargain bin crap I wore to work. Both were reactions to my environment, to the expectations of me in those places.

It occurred to me then that was the problem with the entire night. Maybe it had nothing to do with Xavier. Maybe it was more because from the second I'd agreed to this, I was playing dress-up yet again. There were times I mourned the girl I had been before Sofia—the one who had the extra hours every day to do my hair or go to the gym or put on makeup. The one who could wear short skirts because she didn't have to squat down to help a small child at a moment's notice. The one who could actually have casual relationships.

Well, not that one. That girl had never existed in the first place.

"Well, hopefully dowdy is more your style," I said. "I probably dress like this once a year."

"And I got the benefit? Lucky me."

Ew.

"So, who's watching your kid tonight?" Adam asked after he started back into his tacos.

I forked up a bit of my arroz *con pescado*, wishing I had more of an appetite. I still couldn't believe I'd ordered fish of all things—on Xavier's insistence, of course. "Ah, that would be her dad."

"Her dad? I didn't realize he was in the picture."

I froze, realizing what I'd just done. Lord, I hadn't told my family about Xavier yet. I hadn't even told *Sofia* who he was. And now I'd just let the cat out of the bag with someone completely random.

"Er, they're sort of getting to know each other," I said. "Adam, I'd appreciate if you could keep that to yourself, please."

Adam smiled kindly like I hadn't said a thing wrong. "Is he from here?"

I shook my head. "No, he's from London, actually. But he's back in New York on business, so I'm giving him a chance to get to know Sofia."

"Makes sense. What kind of business is he in?"

I swallowed a tasteless bit of rice. "Restaurants, actually."

"No kidding. That's cool. I'm a bit of a foodie myself."

I looked down at his plain chicken tacos, ordered *without* hot sauce or really any interesting condiment, and back up at him. He didn't seem to notice the irony.

"You know, he looked familiar when I met him," he prodded

through a mouthful of poultry. "I kept trying to figure out where I'd seen him before. He said his name was Xavier. What's his last name? Maybe I've heard of him."

"I doubt it," I replied. "Xavier Parker?"

Adam froze mid bite, revealing a mouthful of chewed chicken. He swallowed. "Ah, of the Parker Group?"

So he *had* recognized the name.

"Yes," I said slowly. "Everything okay?"

He coughed slightly, then offered a wry smile. "I—holy crap. Small world, I guess. I went to school with the guy. Christ, he's changed a lot."

I frowned. "Really? He didn't attend college for more than a year."

Adam just shook his head, shoved another bit of taco into his mouth, then continued talking through his food. "Actually, it was in high school. Or secondary, in England. He looked a lot different back then. Tall still, but really skinny. And his hair was down to here." He gestured about six inches below his shoulder.

I blinked, trying to imagine Xavier like that. The man I'd met five years ago had been somewhere in between. That muscle had obviously grown in between his teen years and twenty-seven, but the hair had been the same. Now, though, I could imagine someone who probably looked like a rock star wannabe in his teens was almost unrecognizable as the suave, besuited CEO Adam had met.

"England..." I mumbled for want of something else. I realized guiltily that I hadn't actually asked Adam a question about himself the entire night. I'd been too busy wondering about Xavier. "Are you from there originally?"

Adam shook his head. "No, I kind of grew up all over the place. My dad was sort of a diplomat. We spent some time in London, so I went to Eton for a bit, if you remember."

My jaw dropped. I did remember. Xavier had mentioned being carted off to prep school after his mother died, but I didn't realize it was the most famous boarding school in the world. Good lord, he was probably there at the same time as Prince Harry. Or maybe even William.

It was, to say the least, a strange coincidence.

"That *is* a small world," I agreed after another unsteady bite of my rice. "That must have been amazing, growing up abroad."

Adam just shrugged and didn't quite meet my eyes.

"So, when did you move back to the States?" I wondered.

He swallowed his food. "After about a year. My parents split up, so my mom and I moved home to Connecticut. I liked it a lot better there."

It was an interesting story. It really was. But I couldn't make myself ask anything more. Or at least, I didn't want to ask *him* the rest of the story.

My phone buzzed in my purse. I didn't answer it, but I knew exactly who it was.

Yeah, it was time to call it.

"Can I interest you in some dessert?"

We turned to find the waiter approaching us with a small paper menu fluttering in his hand.

"Sure," Adam started, only to be cut off by me.

"Actually, do you mind if I cut the evening short? I'm not really feeling that well. I think the fish is bothering my stomach."

His surprise morphed into one of immediate concern. Once again, guilt stabbed.

"Yeah, of course. Let me just get the check."

———

CONTINUING to be the present (and irritating) gentleman that he had been all evening, Adam insisted on accompanying me all the way home. And that was after the dinner he insisted on paying for, even going so far as to yank my credit card out of the server's hands and shove it toward me.

I let him pay. At that point, it seemed like the safest thing to do.

"It's fine," he said several times as we climbed into a Lyft together. "I don't live that far from here, really."

"I thought you lived in Park Slope," I protested even as the car started off down Third Avenue. "That's in the opposite direction."

But Adam just offered me a grin. "I can't let a lady go home by herself."

He leaned in a little closer, smudged lenses full of intent.

"You, um, have a bit of spinach on your tooth." I indicated just above my own right incisor.

He flushed and started prodding at it with his tongue. I turned away.

"Feeling better?" he asked once he was finished.

"I am," I said truthfully. I didn't want to lie *too* much. "Maybe the atmosphere of the restaurant was getting to me."

He smiled. To my surprise, however, when the car stopped in front of my house, Adam followed me out onto the curb and right onto my front stoop. The car remained, clearly waiting for him. Good. He wasn't expecting an invitation inside.

"I had a really good time tonight," he told me, pulling at his goatee again.

I masked a cringe. He'd been doing that all night, and I could practically feel the tug of skin on my own face.

"You did?"

The question flew out before I could stop it. I wanted to ask why he was lying. I hadn't been a particularly engaging date. Honestly, I hadn't even been trying. And no, I wasn't ready to ask myself exactly why that was.

Adam leaned closer, a knowing smirk framed by his facial hair and creased skin under his eyes. If I looked hard enough, there were still some crumbs in his chin hairs.

He slid a hand around my waist. I backed away, my shoulder finding the door, but he followed, unwilling to let go.

"Adam," I tried, no longer willing to make eye contact. "I should really be getting inside."

"I know," he said. "But, Frankie, I was hoping for at least a good night kiss."

I swallowed. There was something distinctly transactional about it all. The car still running behind him was another reminder of everything he had paid for that evening. And now he was expecting his returns.

"Hey," I said. "Let me give you some cash for dinner, all right? It's not fair for you to treat me on our pittance."

But Adam didn't seem to hear me as he stepped even closer, trapped against the door and the porch railing.

"Frankie," he crooned. "You don't need to play hard to get."

His lips landed on mine, prodding and insistent. I felt like I was being mauled by a rubber chicken.

I pulled away, repulsed. This was more than wrong. This was horrifying.

"Adam, no." I put my hands on his chest, trying to push him away. "I'm really not—"

"Come on, Frankie," Adam continued, pressing his mouth up and down my ear with all the energy of a wet stamp. "You've been giving me fuck-me eyes all night. You can't expect me to take anything less than a kiss. Give me something here."

Fuck-me eyes? Was he serious? I had barely paid attention to the man all evening.

"Adam, seriously. Please stop."

"We don't need to play games," he cooed, his lips pulling over the edge of my jaw like one of my kids' rubber erasers.

But before I could answer, the door opened. I stumbled backward, out of Adam's insistent arms and into a quivering wall of muscle.

Adam and I both turned to find Xavier looming in the entry, staring at us both with a face full of murder. Even with his white shirt wrinkled and untucked, feet shoeless, hair mussed from lying on the couch, he was ten times the specimen of the other man standing beside me. With his arms crossed like that, every line of his biceps, his tattooed forearm, and even his shoulders were cast in high relief through the white cotton; buttons pulled across the wide expanse of chest. With the posture of a warrior and the sharpness of a chief, he was the very definition of what my nonna would have affectionately dubbed "a real man."

A real man who wanted to tear the other one apart.

There was no recognition in his blue eyes as he looked Adam over. Only cool acknowledgment of someone he clearly regarded as no better than a bug on his shoe. And fire. The dark blue kind at the center of a flame. The kind that can burn anything it wants.

"Good night?" he asked but didn't wait for an answer before turning to me. "Your daughter needs you."

Without waiting for an answer, he took me by the wrist and yanked me inside, behind his big body and completely out of Adam's reach.

"Good ni—" Adam started to say just before Xavier slammed the door in his face.

"Fuck off," he snarled over his shoulder.

And then he turned that fire on to me.

22

"What are you doing?" I yelped just after the door closed. "Let me go!"

"Frankie?" We could hear Adam's voice calling through the door, but neither of us replied.

Xavier's hand was still locked around my wrist. To my surprise, he obeyed my command, though he certainly looked like he didn't want to.

"What the hell, Xavi? You had no right to drag me inside like an overbearing caveman." I shucked my scarf and gloves, practically throwing them into the basket at the base of the coat rack. None of them made it, but I couldn't even bother to retrieve them.

"No right—no *right*?" he demanded. "He was all fucking over you!"

"So what if he was? I was on a date for crying out loud! That *you* encouraged me to go on, I might add. That's what happens. People make their moves, right? Just like your text said."

"Don't give me that shit, Ces," Xavier snapped, storming down the hallway toward the kitchen, me hot on his tail. "This is the type you go for? The kind that won't take no for an answer? He deserved a fuck lot more than a door slammed in his face. Like my fists, for a start." He shoved both hands into his hair, tugged, and groaned. "Christ, I could *hear* the bastard on the other side of the door, just like I could hear you telling him to get the fuck off!"

I recoiled. "You were listening in on us? What else were you doing, spying through the peephole?"

"*Yes!*" he hissed, whirling around so fast I was forced to take a step backward, essentially caging myself in one corner of the kitchen. "Is that what you want to hear? That I've been sitting on this fucking couch for the last three hours, playing it cool and driving myself crazy? Thinking of you out with some four-eyed twat, smiling at his pat compliments, laughing at his jokes, twirling your hair, and making doe-eyes at him while he's thinking of all the ways he wants to reenact his favorite pornos. Yeah, he's really hot for teacher, right?"

My jaw dropped, and before I could stop it, it started to quiver. "I can't believe you just said that."

"You can believe it and a whole lot more. This isn't you. I know it's not you. I knew it the second you left. You're not meant to be dressed up in some fancy clothes for some arsehole, painted and primped so he can untie you like a fucking package."

"Oh my God, *you* made me dress like this." I poked a finger into his chest with every word.

"Well, I had to get something out of this fucking night, didn't I?"

"That makes zero sense."

He leaned down so our noses were practically touching while he spoke through his teeth. "I. *Know.*"

The quiver of my lip turned into a sob. With sudden force, I shoved him away, then darted around him as quickly as I could, back down the hall and into the half bathroom, where I didn't *quite* slam the door. Bracing myself on the sink, I took several deep breaths, begging myself to calm the hell down.

It didn't matter. His words didn't matter. Adam's words didn't matter. None of them mattered.

Then I looked at myself in the mirror, took in the reddened cheeks, the mussed hair, the smudged mascara. And promptly burst into tears.

Rationally, I understood that Xavier couldn't have known the way his words zeroed in like sniper bullets on the very things I'd been thinking all evening. That no one, including Adam, was really interested in me. That to him or anyone else, I was nothing more than a mousy little teacher, good for a quick piece of ass and nothing else. That I was a fake in my makeup and finery and whatever else I did to put lipstick on a pig.

I sobbed hard and silent, watching the remnants of my makeup melting down my face. I hated all of it. I wanted my hair back in its messy knot, my eyelids plain and mascara-free, my skin mottled and pink. I wanted to be back to normal. Safe, if essentially undesirable.

"Ces?"

There was a light knock on the door. But I couldn't answer. I couldn't stop. He was right. Adam was right. What was I thinking, dressing up like this, trying to impress a man, whether it was the one I'd gone to dinner with or the one who had waited for me at home?

Romance wasn't for me anymore. This was a joke. *I* was a joke.

"Ces?"

I took a deep breath. Then another.

"Ces." There was a note of irritation in his voice now. "Ces, open the door."

I swallowed. "I just need a moment."

"Ces, I swear to God. If you don't open the door right now, I'll break it down. Don't do this."

I shook my head silently. He probably would, too. If Xavier's temper so far was any indication, patience was not his strong suit.

And so I obeyed, grasping the knob, and slowly opening up to find the tower of man standing with his hands braced on the frame, head bowed in shame.

Then he took one look at me, and the scowl returned. "I knew it." A vicious shake of his head caused a few locks of tousled black hair to fall over his forehead. "I fucking knew it. What else did that motherfucker do? I'll break his fucking neck, I swear I will."

"Nothing!" I gasped, finally able to swallow back my tears. "Oh my God, calm down. He tried to kiss me, and then you stopped it, all right? Nothing else happened."

"Then what is it?" He turned from side to side in the doorway, as if the beige walls would somehow reveal the answer. He crowded the tiny space, filling it—and my world—with his larger-than-life presence. "Why are you crying in here?"

"Because I'm—I'm—Gah!" I groaned with frustration, both with my own issues and my inability to say them out loud. "Because you're right, okay? The both of you."

"Right?" he asked. "About fucking what?"

"Stop swearing so much," I hissed. "And can you let me out of the bathroom, please? All I really want is a cup of hot tea and a book and my bed."

I shoved past him and made my way back into the kitchen, ignoring the six-foot-five wildcat on my tail.

"Right about what?" he persisted. "You can tell me while the water boils. I'm a lot more stubborn than you, Ces, so you might as well be out with it. We were right about what?"

"About the fact that this entire night was a big waste of time." I grabbed the kettle and made for the sink. "That someone like me has no business in this kind of getup, trying to be someone I'm not."

"Someone like you? What exactly does that mean?"

"Don't play dumb, Xavi. You know. Someone like this." I gestured up and down my body emphatically. I was still bound in the short skirt he'd picked, but he had to know what I meant.

His clear befuddlement, however, had drawn a deep line over his brows. "Can you stop talking in gibberish and say it in plain speech? What the fuck are you talking about?"

I sighed impatiently. He really did love to humiliate me, didn't he?

"I'm a frumpy, bookworm teacher and single mom who's about as sexy as a mop. Adam as much as said it at dinner, and now you just did too. Good for a lay and maybe a quick bite. A stopover while men like you wait for the real deal to come along. I'm playing dress-up, just like I did at that party. I'm a fool."

Tears pricked once again, and I turned around quickly to avoid sharing them, focusing on putting the kettle on the stove to heat.

Behind me, Xavier was silent for once. I took that to mean I was correct. Of course I was. How could I have ever thought that someone like Adam, much less the Adonis standing behind me, would ever think I was worth more than a quick fling, whether it was after dinner or on holiday?

"Is that what you really think?" When he finally spoke, his voice was hoarse, incredulous. "That I don't think you're *worth* more than a quick fuck?"

I swallowed, another sob stuck in my throat. "I—well, it's true, isn't it? You basically dressed me like one, didn't you? Look at me."

"I am looking at you. Ces, turn around so you can see me too."

As if pulled by a string, I obeyed, turning slowly until I was facing him, my back against the counter once more. I pulled at my skirt and gestured at my ruined makeup. "I'm a joke."

Xavier stepped forward until he had caged me against the counter, looming over me, tall and imperious.

"Look at me," he commanded, though the finger under my chin was gentle as he pulled my face upward. "Open your eyes."

Powerless, I obeyed again, finding his deep blue pools brimming with promise and something else I couldn't identify.

"You," he pronounced slowly, drawing out the word like he was reciting a poem, "are the sexiest thing I have ever seen in my entire life. That was true when I met you in that club five years ago. It was true when I saw you at that Christmas party. And when I found you at your school last week. And it's true now, when your face is covered in tears and whatever that black shit is under your eyes. Fucking gorgeous, inside and out. You're not a one-night stand, Francesca. You are the kind of woman men wait their whole lives to find, Francesca. *That's* what you are."

My breath deserted me. My legs deserted me. My hands on the counter held me up, and then quickly, it was him. Xavier lifted me onto the Formica and stepped between my knees, crowding into me until our faces were even. Eye to eye. Nose to nose. Mouth to mouth.

"Ces," he whispered, eyes zeroed in on my lips.

I was staring at his too. They looked soft and supple. Inviting and utterly delicious.

"Xavi," I whispered back.

He slipped a finger under the collar of my coat, and I shivered when he found my skin and pushed the heavy fabric from my shoulders. Less from the cold and more from the sudden electricity of his touch.

"Your skin," he murmured as he slid his hand down my neck. "So smooth. Like silk…"

I couldn't help but close my eyes as he turned his finger over and drew it down, finding where the curve of my neck met my shoulder, slowly exploring that delicate skin no one had touched in years. His hands dropped to the hem of my sweater, and then, even more slowly, drew it over my head, leaving me in nothing but my bra. Then his fingers danced back up my arms, then made quick work behind my back so he could push the straps over my shoulders too, baring me to him.

I sat there, topless, as his hands cupped my breasts. He didn't move, just held me, kneading ever-so-slightly as his thumbs brushed over my nipples.

While gentle, his movements weren't tentative. I wasn't sure that Xavier Parker had ever made a tentative move in his life. It was more than just his size, although that certainly didn't hurt anything. Every-thing about him spoke of power, assurance, the knowledge that what-ever he planned would happen exactly as he wanted.

And there I was, apparently part of the plan. Nearly naked in the middle of my brother's kitchen. A world-famous chef staring at me like I was the most delicious meal he'd ever seen.

He arched over me, bending his head to brush his lips across mine. Once. Twice. Taking his time. Sipping me. Savoring me.

"Francesca."

The sound of my full name, hypnotic though it was in his sonorous baritone, lifted me out of my trance. He leaned in, and I didn't shy away. Instead, I leaned right back and allowed his lips to guide us in a slow, tangled kiss. Remnants of tears were still slipping down my cheeks, but the sadness was being banished by a fire warming my belly.

Before I could stop myself, my hands were undoing the buttons of his shirt. One, two, three, until his shirt lay open, revealing the smooth plane of his chest and the flat, chiseled contours of his abdomen, triangulated into a delicious path of muscle that disappeared below his belt.

His hands slid down my sides to take a full grip of my ass and pull me flush against him. He was tall enough that the counter brought me to exactly the right level. His length, so evident behind his trousers, pressed into my inner thigh. The sudden feel of him *right there*, separated from me by only a few scant layers of clothing, made me gasp.

"Xavi," I whispered just before his lips found mine again, accompanied by his hot, slick tongue. He sucked on my lip, hard enough now to elicit a moan. In response, he kept going, alternatively licking, sucking, and biting until I started to squeal—right along with the tea kettle.

We broke apart, breathing heavily, but only long enough for Xavier to move the kettle off the burner, then pick me up and turn me around to sit on the opposite counter—the one that wasn't next to a burning hot stove.

"Oh, no you don't," he murmured as I shifted under his hands. "Not this time. You're not stopping this now."

I had absolutely no intention of doing that.

His large hand pressed between my breasts, pushing me back gently. My skirt was quickly removed, followed by my tights and underwear until I lay flat and spread on the kitchen counter.

I looked up to find Xavier gazing down at me, hunger alight in his dark blue eyes. He trailed a finger up my thigh until it rested just at my center, hovering over my opening.

"You look fucking delicious," he said.

His finger dipped inside me, then back out. He raised it to his mouth and set it delicately to the tip of his tongue, like a cat might lick its paw.

I shivered.

And then, before I could stop him, he bent and placed his mouth where his finger had been. His tongue slipped inside me, exploring, tasting, savoring every bit of my most private and deep spaces. Spaces no one had ever explored but him.

I arched against him as a breathy moan escaped my throat. His hands grabbed my thighs and lifted me higher so he could feast. He found my clit with his tongue, and soon I was thrashing on the counter, thighs clenched around his head as two fingers, then three, slipped inside me.

He sucked hard. I came even harder with a shout.

But he didn't move, only continued claiming me with his mouth and dexterous fingers, pulling out every drop of my orgasm until I lay limply in front of him.

For a few seconds, anyway.

"I'm not done with you yet, woman."

Vaguely, I registered his hands slipping under my back, pulling me to sit up, sliding to tip my chin up. And then a kiss—that mouth-watering, body-twisting kiss of his that brought me to a whole different planet. Oh, God, that was *me* on his lips, his tongue, in my mouth. That was the salty pleasure he'd drawn from me. And I *liked* it.

Suddenly, I was sitting up again, drawn straight like a string just plucked on a violin. My hands grasped at his naked arms, then felt their way down as if moving of their own accord. I wasn't under the influence of anything, but I was still caught in a trance as I unbuckled his belt, flicked open his pants, and pushed his boxers down to reveal the part of him that was responsible for every change in my life over the last five years.

Lord, he was big. Of course he was big. The man was roughly the size of an NBA point guard, and all his parts were perfectly proportional. I shouldn't have been surprised, given that I was intimately familiar with this particular part of him. Had worshipped its smooth steel shape, brought it to my lips, between my legs, felt its mastery of nearly every part of me.

Really, I should have hated him for it.

Instead, I licked my lips.

"Here." From a pocket, Xavier produced a condom, ripped it open with his teeth, then held it out to me. "Would you?"

His eyes had softened somehow, yearning, even.

I gulped and accepted the small packet. "I—ah—it's been a while."

That full mouth tipped on one side into a half smile I was beginning to recognize as fondness. "I know, babe. I still want you to."

Awkwardly, I fumbled with the packet, hurried by the throbbing want between my legs despite my nerves. Somehow, I managed to get out the bit of latex, pulled out the tip, then pressed it over the end of his cock.

"Um," I murmured. "It's—how do I—"

"Let me help."

His hands gently closed over mine, guiding the rubber over his erection, holding both our hands still over him once we were finished so he could kiss me again, this time with considerable force.

"Can I?" he murmured, poised just at my opening.

I looked down. He was so big. And I was…not. But once, he had fit there. And God, I wanted it again.

I spread my legs wider, scooted forward until I was sitting at the very edge of the counter, then took him in my hand and guided him forward. We both watched, rapt, as he slid in one slow inch at a time on a low, animal groan.

"All right?" he asked in a voice twisted with desire. "I don't want to hurt you."

A bead of sweat slid down the center of his forehead. He was working hard, if only at constraining himself.

"I'm fine." I closed my eyes, allowing my body to adjust to his size. But it *had* been a long time. This would take a second.

"Ces."

My eyes opened to find his blues focused on me with a heady mix of concern and desire.

"You're going to have to give me a bit more than that," he said.

Dazedly, I turned my face toward him. "Kiss me, Xavi."

Slowly, his mouth turned up, farther and farther, until, at last, his bright white teeth were on display. A full, glowing smile that lit up the dim room. And it was all for me.

"With fucking pleasure."

On another groan, our mouths collided. His lips massaged mine, tongue dancing through my mouth, devouring me whole like he was a starving man. Slowly, he started to move, seating himself completely before pulling out, allowing me a break before pressing slowly back in. It wasn't until I grasped for his naked ass, eager to feel its rhythm, that he really started to move. Home, home, and home again, shaking our bodies, the counter, the very earth we stood on, all without breaking the magic our mouths were making.

"Xavi," I gasped against his lips. "Oh, God. Oh *God*, I'm gonna—"

He broke away suddenly, making a mad grab for my chin and yanking it up.

"Look at me," he ordered. "Look at me when you come, Francesca. Look at me when I come for you."

And then he slid home once more on a deep, powerful thrust. I began to shake as I gripped the counter, arching back so he could see all of me quivering there just for him. I yelped as one spasm flew through me, then another, then another, until they crashed together at my core, around *him*.

"Fuck! Francesca!" he crowed as he surged forward, again and again, every muscle in his big body tensed and rigid as he came.

But through it all, I did as he asked. I looked at him while he looked at me. And I could see in his eyes every decibel of want and fear reverberating deeply through my soul. I could feel through every vibration the clash of duty and vice.

And truly, nothing had ever felt better.

23

When the house came back into focus, the sweet, musky scents of salt and man cocooned me. After Xavier had gone out of his way to show me exactly how desirable I was once more on the kitchen table and then again over the back of the couch, we landed on the soft cushions, naked together. Xavier on his back, me splayed across his chest and cradled in his big arms.

The world was quiet again. Not just outside the house, where Red Hook was a ghost town in the wee hours of the morning. For once, my mind was also still as I lay there, eyes closed while the solid thump of Xavier's heartbeat played under my temple.

We said nothing. Neither of us was much for trite words or meta-critiques to begin with, but right now, nothing seemed appropriate. No "Well, that was something," or "What did we just do?"

There was something else familiar about Xavier that I had almost forgotten. This moment after the fact, when lying together skin to skin in the dark of the night, was more of a meditation than an existence.

And so we did, measuring our breaths, content just to be in each other's arms. Until soft and muffled, Sofia's voice cut through the quiet with an unintelligible cry.

Xavier tensed, grabbing my shoulders as he clearly prepared to move.

"Relax," I said, pressing my palm flat to his chest to push myself up slightly and look at him. "She talks in her sleep. But once she's out, she could sleep through a hurricane."

He sank back into the couch cushions but didn't relax. Not

completely. He looked at the ceiling for a minute before sighing, blue eyes finding mine with the depth of unknown loss.

"There's so much I don't know," he said quietly. "How she sleeps, for instance. I followed your instructions. Read her a story. Sang a song to that bunny or whatever. Said good night."

I chuckled. "She got you to sing? She never makes me sing anymore."

He snorted. Sofia had clearly already wrapped him around her little finger, but it didn't seem to bother him at all. In fact, he seemed all the more game to make a fool out of himself just for her enjoyment. Just like he used to with me five years ago.

"But then I had to leave," he continued softly as his hand began to play up and down my back, occasionally taking pieces of my hair and combing through them. "So I don't know what happens after that."

I lay back down, chin propped on my forearm so I could still watch his face. "On her back, arms overhead like she's in a freefall. But only after I lie with her for at least thirty minutes and let her run her mouth about the day. She only goes to sleep on her own for other people, the little minx."

He didn't smile. Not quite. But his mouth quirked at the edges, reminding me just how much I wanted to see that grin more often. As frequently as possible, really. I wanted to see it every day.

Xavier remained quiet, staring at the ceiling, still lost in his thoughts as his fingers traced the divot of my spine.

"I understand now why you did it," he said after a long while.

I blinked. "Did what?"

"Kept her from me," he confirmed with a quick, dark glance down. "I would have done the same thing."

My hand paused somewhere over his sternum. "You would have?"

He nodded. "I didn't understand at first. I thought, what right does she have, keeping the girl from her own dad? And maybe I still think that a little. But I see now when I look at her, and—Jesus God, she scares the shit out of me, Ces. This feeling…" He splayed a big hand over mine, except his covered most of his chest, whereas mine covered only a fraction. He pressed both our palms down hard and took several deep breaths. "I look at her, and I can hardly breathe, I'm so scared."

I nodded. "Yeah. Parenthood does that."

"Fucking hell. It's only been a few days. What's it like after four years?"

I shrugged, then lay my cheek back onto his chest. "Weirdly, you get kind of used to it. But sometimes it's worse. I love her so much, the idea of anything happening to her now makes me feel like I honestly couldn't go on. I get why people who lose their kids fall apart. It's not natural."

He quieted again, but his hand had stopped moving. Instead, he spread his fingers and pressed his palm flat to the small of my back, as if to hold me even closer.

"You know, I'm not what you think I am."

"Oh?" I mumbled into his neck. "What do I think you are?"

"Cold. Callous. Angry."

"You're not those things?" It was news to me. "You want to tell that to the date you just scared off?"

He chuckled. It was nice to hear. "Well, not always."

"I don't really think that about you," I said as I started tracing my own fingertips up and over the broad lines of his pectoral muscle. "You've changed since I first met you, of course. But mostly…mostly I think you're just sadder, somehow."

That hand at my back tensed. "You mean pathetic?"

"No, no."

I pushed myself back up so I could look at him again. Shyly, he tucked a few loose strands of my hair behind my ear.

"Sad as in…forlorn," I clarified. "Sorrowful. Unhappy. Except when you're with Sofia. When you met her, you finally smiled, you know."

"Well, she doesn't really give you a choice."

Said smile made a slight appearance. But it faded just as quickly. I balanced on top of him, waiting for some kind of explanation. To tell me exactly what had happened in the course of five years that had made him like this.

Instead, Xavier just cleared his throat. "Anyway, yeah. I wouldn't have told me either. You were right to be careful."

I frowned. "But…but that's just it."

He looked down at me. "What?"

I swallowed. Why was this so hard to say? "I'm glad you understand. But Xavi, I was wrong to keep her a secret."

At that, he pushed himself up to a sitting position, forcing me to straddle his waist, but keeping an arm around mine so we remained close. We stared at each other for a long time, blue eyes matched to green. But there was nothing predatory in his gaze, and for the first time in a long while, I felt no shame and not the slightest bit self-conscious. Here, together with Xavier and naked in the dark, I wasn't the frazzled teacher or the exhausted mother. Not the needy sister or the five-year liar. I was forgiven. Here in Xavier's arms, I was only myself.

I had missed her.

"You've changed too," he murmured as his hands drifted down and settled on the fullest part of my backside. "You're…I don't know…riper somehow. Like a piece of fruit."

My face twisted. "I think that's a polite way of telling me I got chubby."

"God—woman, just listen, will you? Did I not just spend the last two hours showing you exactly how exquisite I think you are?"

His hands kneaded lightly on my sensitive flesh, and for a moment, I thought he was going to ignore my apology completely and start hour three as he kissed me again, lips full of promise.

But then he pulled away and shook his head hard enough that that wayward lock toppled forward onto his forehead.

"You weren't wrong," he told me. "I know who I am, Ces. And I know who I was. Fuckboy headcase. Good for a few weeks' shagging, but left you for another woman, didn't I?"

"No," I said emphatically. "If I don't get to see the worst in myself, then neither do you."

"Still."

I pressed my palms to his cheeks, stroking the lines of his strong bones with my thumbs. His eyes closed for half a second, vulnerable and wide when they opened again.

"I see you with her, Xavi," I said softly. "How gentle you are with her. How you watch her, interact with her. I see how you care for her, even after just a few days. That man isn't cold or a headcase. He's a father. Am I wrong?"

He stared up at the ceiling, lips pressed into a thin, almost white line while a muscle ticked at the corner of his jaw. He was silent long enough that I thought he wasn't going to say anything at all. But when he finally looked back at me, his blue eyes were shining, wet and bright. A tiny tear slid down one side of his face, so small I might have missed it if it hadn't caught the light that gleamed on the edge of his chiseled cheekbone.

"No," he said in a deep, rumbling whisper. "You're not wrong." He swiped the tear away, then barked at the ceiling in a vicious parody of a laugh. "Christ. I feel like my heart just got ripped out of my chest. Is this what you've felt all the time, the last four years?"

I chuckled and kissed him. "Since pretty much the second she arrived, yeah. When she's not pushing my buttons, anyway. And even then…" I shrugged. "You never stop loving your kid. Even when she drives me up the wall, I'd jump in front of a bus for her."

"I can see that." He grabbed my hand and squeezed it against his chest. "You're a good mum, Ces. She's lucky to have you. *We're* lucky to have you."

There was nothing sexual in his touch. He didn't want anything, per se—or at least not right now.

"Your family," he said. "Are they really as intense as you say? Or was that just an excuse to keep me a secret while you decided whether or not I was a decent bloke?"

I swallowed. "Some of both. I needed a reason, but they are legitimately…a lot."

I could just see the looks on my sisters' faces if Xavier ever crossed Nonna's threshold. Like vultures, all of them. They'd peck his eyes right out. And that was if Matthew didn't beat the crap out of him first.

Xavier shuddered like he was reading my thoughts.

"Do you want her to know?" I ventured.

It wasn't until then I realized that I did. It hadn't taken long, but I realized I'd only been delaying the inevitable. All the reasons had only been because of one thing: my own fear.

But here in the dark with him, I felt perfectly safe. And I knew without a doubt that Sofia would always be safe with him too. Maybe Xavier didn't understand love—yet. Or maybe he did already. Wasn't that what he had just described about Sofia?

It sounded like love to me.

"I want her to know," he said. "I do."

I stiffened. There was hesitancy there. "But?"

"But…" He shifted against me. "I've grown up my whole life having people talk about me when I wasn't there. Depending on who it was, I was either Rupert Parker's no-good bastard, or maybe Masumi Sato's son-in-rags, or else just that nasty prick who ruins other restaurants for fun."

I frowned. "I never knew you as any of those things."

He peeked down at me, a shy smile playing over his lips. "Don't think I don't love that."

There was that word again. Not in the way I wanted it, but he still used it more than he thought.

"At any rate, the rest of the world isn't you." He shook his head ruefully. "Am I a coward, not wanting anyone else to poison what she thinks of me when I haven't even had a chance to build that for myself?"

"And you think my family will do that?"

He cocked his head to one side. "You think they won't?"

I wished I could say he had nothing to worry about. My family were many things, but discreet wasn't one of them. Neither was forgiving. My sisters were expert gossips, my brother was basically a military-trained guard dog, and every one of them held a deep grudge against Xavier for his absence over the last five years. The second they knew he was back in the picture, I wouldn't be able to stop them from stalking every social media profile they could find, probably leaving him a variety of choice messages and pieces of advice shielded as threats. More importantly, however, I wouldn't be able to keep Sofia from hearing all sorts of things about her father. And most of them wouldn't be good.

"You're not wrong," I admitted quietly.

"And is there any chance of our four-year-old keeping this a secret from her aunties and her uncle while we get to know each other?"

I just looked at him.

He snorted. "What about my name? Do they know that?"

I shrugged. "Kate does. The others know Xavier Sato, if they remember it at all. But Kate won't say anything, and Mattie's in Italy. Plus, he's so damn tied up with his lady friend, he won't notice if Sof mentions you when he gets back."

Xavier nodded. "So we use Parker, tell her to call me Xavi, and keep the truth between us. Just a bit longer. A few months, maybe?" His mouth quirked again in that sad way that made me want to kiss him. "You were right about that too, I guess."

I found I couldn't argue with him. I didn't like it, but it was the truth.

So, instead, I buried my face in his neck, allowing him to wrap his big arms around me and pull me close. I wanted to sink into him, to pretend like the outside world and all its complications didn't exist. I wanted that simple peace we'd enjoyed just moments before.

There was another way to get it, I realized, as I felt him stir beneath me.

His hands tensed at my waist. I turned my lips into the crook of his neck and enjoyed the way he shivered in response.

But then he spoke again.

"We can't do this either, can we?"

I closed my eyes, willing the sudden shooting pain through the middle of my chest to ebb. Dread. That's what it was. Pure, heavy dread.

I sighed and turned my head the other way, still leaning on his shoulder, but looking toward the kitchen instead of him. "Probably not."

"It would mess with her head, wouldn't it?"

The dread tightened its grip around my heart. "Most likely."

I started to move away, but his hands slipped up my back, holding me in place.

"Not—not just yet," he said into my hair. "Just a bit longer. Please."

I relaxed back into him, and neither of us said anything more about it. We both knew what had to happen. That before the sky turned light, Xavier would have to get dressed and leave. I'd retreat to my corner at the top of the stairs, and we would both pretend like all that had passed between us was a friendly goodbye. Once again, we had to be nothing to each other but secret parents standing on opposite sides of our daughter.

But for now, we just stayed there, skin to skin in the dark while the minutes ticked by, a silent countdown until morning came. Meditating in the silence.

And in each other.

INTERLUDE II

Xavier

"Wait, wait, wait. You're saying that it's been four months of back and forth from here to New York, and that little girl still doesn't know you're her dad?"

Jagger Harrington sat in front of me with another drink in his hand, but this time at my broad marble-topped bar in London while I fixed him up with a new dish I'd been working on. Jagger was no food critic, but he was a good example of the type of person I wanted to draw at my restaurants: young, stylish, and moneyed.

"I'm giving her time," I said as I blanched needle-thin noodles in an ice bath. "I don't want to get too attached if it doesn't work out."

I pulled the noodles out to drain, then hand-tossed them with infused sesame oil.

"Mate," Jagger said evenly. "You're attached. You just named a restaurant after her. Think you might want to get around to acknowledging her too?"

I scowled. I was starting to wish I'd never told him why I'd landed on Chie as the name of my New York restaurant, due to open imminently. Chie meant wisdom in Japanese. As did Sofia, in its original Greek form.

Jagger made it sound like I was, well, my own father struggling with his illegitimate offspring, but it couldn't be further from the truth.

"She's mine," I practically growled at him. "There's never been a doubt about that. For one, she looks just like me."

I grabbed my phone and tossed it to Jagger, who took one look at the lock screen—a picture of Sofia shrieking on a swing set—and smiled.

"I think you made that same face whenever you scored at football," he said as he handed the phone back to me.

I nodded, looking at the picture once more before tucking the phone into my pocket. "I just wanted to give us time to get to know each other without all the bullshit. You know how crazy my life can be. The last thing I need is the papers getting wind of anything."

Jagger just blinked. He didn't need me to elaborate on that.

"Anyway, she and Francesca are both coming to the opening next week." I coiled the noodles onto a pair of square plates and started working on the garnishes.

"Are they really?" Jagger grinned. "Maybe I should make a trip for the big day. I wouldn't mind meeting this pearl of wisdom. And her hot mum too. Francesca, right? Sounds like a treat."

"Francesca is not a treat, and I'll thank you to keep her name out of your fucking mouth."

Most men would have run a mile at my tone, but Jagger just took a long sip of his brandy while I chopped some mizuna to cool myself down. Knife work always had a meditative effect on me.

"Calm down," he said once it was clear I was under control. "It's just banter."

"I know." I was going for light, but the words fell out of my mouth like anvils. Honestly, I was surprised they didn't crack the marble in half.

"Still hung up on her, then?"

"Absolutely not," I snapped as I swung around to the fridge and started rooting around for something else. I honestly wasn't sure what, though.

"That why you turned down an offer last night from *two* Victoria's Secret models? At the same time?" Behind me, my best friend whistled. "Shame, that."

"It has nothing to do with it. They were both idiots."

"Well, they weren't offering to give a lecture on Lord Byron."

I snorted as I returned to the counter holding a carrot and some spring onions. The idea of those overgrown giraffes talking about anything close to poetry was a laugh. Ces, though, could talk circles around just about anyone when it came to all things bookish. Somehow, she made it interesting, too.

For a second, I recalled the image of her sweet lips spread in a smile when she mentioned some random character. Usually one she was imagining as herself.

Right on cue, the other images arose—of those same lips open as she called out her orgasm. Her coke-bottle body spread across counters like a fine buffet. That peach-shaped arse, high and waiting when I bent her over the couch.

Fuck.

It had been a long four months since that night in January when the world made sense again for five fucking minutes. Francesca and I had gone back to being, well, not friends exactly. But at least cordial.

We had worked out a bit of a system. When I was in town, which was every other week or so, she allowed me to pick up Sofia after school and take her to the park or a museum or someplace. In order to avoid her brother, she'd meet us, we'd share a quick meal, and then she'd take Sofia home. Sometimes I could see her Sundays too, when Ces taught one of her aerobics classes. I don't want to mention the dirty thoughts that went through my mind when she told me *that* choice bit of information. All I needed was to see her in skin-tight leggings to threaten my self-control.

On a few occasions when her brother had been out, she'd invited me to dinner at the little brick house that was disturbingly like the flat where I'd grown up. Ces was a bit ashamed by its shabbiness, but I felt right at home.

She'd let me cook for Sofia while we made polite, empty conversation. Hello, Xavi. Goodbye, Xavi. How's the weather in London, Xavi? Have fun at the park. These noodles are great. See you next week.

Sometimes, though, if she managed to get Sofia to sleep quickly, Francesca would come back downstairs, lips curved into a suggestive smile as she accepted a second glass of wine and let me join her on the sofa. I'd asked her about what book she was reading (there was always one), and then listen as she launched into a retelling of some random novel. I should have been bored. But I was fucking transfixed.

Maybe it was the way the wine stained her lips just a bit darker. Or the way she rolled her ankle hypnotically while she spoke. Or maybe it was the curve of her smile when she remembered some forgotten passage, like the characters themselves had asked her to keep some scandalous secret.

Whatever the draw, it was in those moments that a few other choice phrases floated into my head. Things that were the opposite of nice, but somehow exactly what I wanted to say.

Do you still think about that night too?

Do you also wake up at three every morning grabbing for me in the dark?
Do you wonder if we made the wrong fucking decision?

I blinked and shook my head, forcing my focus back on julienning the carrots. I'd made this choice on my own. My absence during the first four years of her life had already fucked up my daughter enough. I wasn't going to do more by messing around with her mum. Didn't matter how tight her arse looked in those bloody yoga pants or that after I left, I usually had to take a very long, cold shower at my hotel. I had to do what was right. I owed Sofia nothing less.

I finished chopping the carrots, then moved on to the dipping sauce, taking shoyu, mirin, and a few other choice ingredients from the fridge.

"I should tell you, I'm probably going to stay on that side for a bit after the opening," I said, finally broaching the topic that I'd been putting off for weeks. "Most of the summer, probably. Maybe longer."

Jagger looked at me like I'd lost my mind. "You can't be serious."

"I can. And I am. Look, Chez Miso opened smoothly with you here. I was barely needed."

"Xav, you had to fly back four times just to tell that frog where to shove it. He bloody well doesn't listen to me. What am I supposed to do if you're gone?"

I shrugged. Jean Le Ver was a legitimate pain in the ass, but now the menu was set and things were running smoothly at Chez Miso. A Michelin star, probably two, were in the wind. It was inevitable.

"If Chie does as well as we think, it would make sense to start a New York office for the Parker Group," I said. "I can open up a few more spots there, maybe one in Boston, and another in Philadelphia. Washington. Miami. Maybe expand west eventually."

"What about Paris?" Jagger asked. "Not to mention the new Dublin pub and the bistro in Prague? Xavier, you're throwing out the entire roadmap here."

I knew why he was arguing. This wasn't nearly as easy as it sounded, and it was about to cause a massive headache for my CFO. The Parker Group was mine in name, but we had investors to answer to. A business plan to follow. One that would probably have to be tossed right out the window if we did what I was suggesting.

I just shrugged again and started grating ginger into the sauce. "Americans are rich, and they love to eat, Jag. There's a lot of people on that side of the ocean. I'd be an idiot not to have a go."

Jagger just stared at me for a long time. Then, as I'd seen him do all the other times I'd made horrifyingly rash decisions (some of which had made us both very rich men), he tossed back the rest of his drink and slammed down his empty glass. "Well, that explains it."

I looked up from the cutting board. "Explains what?"

"Why this flat looks like it's half-emptied already. You might have told me you wanted to relocate the business a bit earlier. I could have helped."

I frowned, first at the spring onions, then back at my flat. I hadn't realized it, but he did have a point. Half my shit was already piled into boxes. But that's because I'd been trying to get rid of things, not because I was moving.

Right?

"I didn't know," I said as I sprinkled the onions atop the coiled noodles, then grabbed the pièce de résistance—the melted uni sauce I'd been working on since that trip to the fish market with the girls—and dribbled it over the rest of the meal. "If I had, I would have told you."

Without waiting for him to answer, I slid the bowl across the counter and offered my friend a pair of chopsticks. As always, he didn't wait to dive into what I'd made.

"Shiiiiiit," he muttered through a mouthful of noodles. "Fuck me, that's good. What is it?"

"House-made *somen* noodles with uni, truffle-infused sesame oil, and mizuna," I said. "I made it for Sofia last weekend, and she went bonkers. Thinking I might put it on a kids' menu at the next spot. Something cute for a placemat or what."

Jagger blinked at me like I was speaking a foreign language.

"Placemat?" Jagger repeated when I told him. "Kids' menu? I'm sorry, who the fuck are you, and what have you done with my best friend?"

I smirked, then gazed out at the panoramic view of London my flat afforded. For years, this was the only place I found much solace. I'd come from nothing, maybe stepped on a few shoulders, but in the end, found myself on top of a city so many said could never be mine. I would come here at the end of every day, and the sight of London would remind me that I wasn't all the labels that were thrust upon me. I was the man *I* wanted to be.

But for the last few months, when I would enter this tower in the sky, I felt as alone as I did right after Mum died. When I had to sleep in our flat by myself, wondering if there would ever be anywhere in the world I could call home if she wasn't in it.

I'd thought I didn't need a home. I'd thought I didn't need anyone.

Now I knew it was a lie.

I wanted to be with her. Them. There was a piece of my heart living across the ocean, and she was about three feet tall with a smart mouth that could challenge the Prime Minister.

I was just about to admit it too when there was a loud knock at my front door. Jagger and I both turned toward the sound.

"Doorman?" Jagger asked.

"Must be."

I went to open the door and found a small man in a tracksuit with an enormous wood box balanced on a cart.

"Xavier Parker?" he asked.

"That's me. Did David send you up?" I wondered, thinking of the doorman.

"He did when he saw who sent me," said the man with a distinctly northern accent I wasn't particularly fond to hear. "Sign here."

I accepted the clipboard and offered my signature. The delivery man took one look at the name, then glanced back at me curiously.

"Not what I would have thought you'd have looked like, Your Grace, if you don't mind me saying so."

"I absolutely mind," I informed him. "And it's Mr. Parker, thanks."

The delivery man just blinked. "Whatever you say. Where do you want her hung, then?"

"Her?" I asked.

"What is it?" called Jagger.

The man didn't seem to care. "That wall's bare. I'll put it there."

"Put *what* there?" I demanded as he wheeled the box around me toward one of many white walls in the flat.

"Your clock."

With a loud snap, he opened the lid of the box with a crowbar. Jagger had come to stand next to me, and we both watched as the man unloaded a brown clock approximately the size of my briefcase, but completely covered in ornate carvings, its face bearing two gilded hands and a bloody great pendulum that gleamed the same gold.

"Doing a bit of redecorating?" Jagger looked doubtfully at the time-piece. It was a far cry from the modern decor around us.

"Definitely not." I glanced back at the delivery slip. Cumbria. I flipped it over. Oh, fucking hell.

"All right?" asked the man.

"Return it to the box," I ordered. "And send it back to the bastard who sent it."

"Can't do that," he said. "I think it would look quite nice here. Though your flat's a bit modern for this piece."

"Back in the fucking box," I snapped as I snatched an envelope off the top of the lid, tore it open, and began to read the letter within.

Boy—

I growled. I fucking *hated* when he called me that, and he never stopped, did he?

Since you stubbornly refuse to acknowledge any part of your distinguished lineage, I've taken the liberty of sending a piece of that heritage to you. This clock was presented as a gift from his tenants to the Duke of Kendal when he received his title in 1597. Local legend says that its maker's wife was a powerful witch who tied the wealth of the Kendal estate to its legacy. She instructed only the Duke of Kendal may wind the clock, lest the entire estate fall to ruin.

The clock has sat at Corbray Hall for nearly four years. I've been patient since your father died, but it's time to do what's right. The vultures are descending. I'm sure you know whom I mean.

You've had your fun, but it's time to come home. I've fulfilled my duty as steward, but you cannot evade your responsibilities forever. Starting with this one.

I expect your reply promptly, as well as your return, with the wound clock, to Corbray Hall before summer, when I fully expect to take a long due holiday in Scotland.

Do not disappoint.

— H. Parker

I stared at the letter for a long time, then looked back at the clock, now sitting on its box. The man was completely mad. Vultures? Really? Who was at Corbray Hall other than villagers and the house staff? He couldn't mean...

I shook my head. No, it wasn't possible, not after what had happened at the funeral. They wouldn't dare. Uncle Henry just wanted to be done with the books so he could have more time to hunt. That was all.

The delivery man had long since left, leaving me there with my letter, wondering what the fuck I was going to do with a clock and my uncle's request.

"Fuck off," I muttered, then tore up the note before tossing it on the counter.

"Who's it from?" Jagger asked, eyeing the bits of paper even as he returned to his seat and pulled his plate of noodles closer.

"No one," I said. I wasn't giving Henry Parker the time of day when I had too many more important things to do. "Now eat up. I've got a plane to New York out of Heathrow at seven, and I've still got to pack."

24

"**M**ama, *stop.*"

Sofia batted my hands out of her hair for what was probably the fifth time that morning.

I couldn't help it. I was nervous. Not just for myself, but for Matthew, who was taking a very, *very* big step today.

I'd known about it for a couple of weeks. Honestly, I'd tried to dissuade him. Bringing a woman home to attend church with his family was a big enough deal. It was basically declaring his intentions to all of us—that this was someone he wanted to be family too. Maybe someone he wanted to marry.

That might have been acceptable. Unfortunately, the one he was bringing home was already married. And every person in this family was acutely aware of it.

Three months ago, Matthew had returned from Italy a changed man. He had pretended it was nothing, that he had just had a nice break from reality. But I knew better. My brother had been depressed for more than a year, and suddenly he was prancing around Brooklyn like Gene Kelly.

Then, a few weeks back, Matthew had finally confessed that he and Nina had been seeing each other for months. I had smacked him on the head and said, "No shit, you idiot." I'd heard his phone calls late at night to the girl he called "doll." I knew whom he was rushing out to meet at ten o'clock at night and whose lipstick was smeared on his collar when he returned the next morning.

I was lucky, really, that Matthew was too preoccupied with his own love life to pay much attention to mine. Or, I should say my daughter's. Because over the past few months, Sofia had also fallen deeply in love with a man she still didn't know was her father.

Our plan had been working like gangbusters. Xavier had been back and forth between New York and London, showing up every few weeks to take Sofia to a park, a movie, children's museums, or whatever else he had come up with to spend time with her. It was always something she would talk about for days, but luckily Matthew was so distracted that he barely noticed her chatter, much less put together that "Xavi" was, in fact, my ex, Xavier Parker.

But I couldn't ignore the fact that Xavier's name was on Sof's lips every other sentence. One way or another, the cat was going to jump out of the bag. As easy and comfortable as it had been to let them get to know each other, a decision was coming. It was time to tell Sofia. And everyone else.

First, though, Matthew had news of his own. Because today, as we drove the final blocks to Nonna's for Sunday Mass a few weeks after Easter, Nina de Vries, my brother's obsession, sat primly in the front seat of Matthew's Corolla while he parked outside the old house off Arthur Avenue.

There we were, the secret keepers. Me, Sofia, Matthew, and his Upper East Side princess.

Nina de Vries was everything I wasn't. A bona fide socialite who had literally graced the covers of magazines. She was reserved, as still as a statue, someone who wore her breeding and wealth like a mask.

But when she looked at my brother, something in her icy demeanor shifted. Her eyes shone with pure, absolute love. I didn't need to ask if she would do anything for him. It was etched into every crystalline feature.

That alone was enough for me to give her a chance.

———

THE SERVICE WAS JUST STARTING as we slipped into the second row of our family's customary pews. All of my sisters were present this weekend. Not surprising, since Matthew had informed us all in a group text that he had an "announcement." For that, I had received another four texts from our sisters asking me what the hell was the big secret.

I wouldn't say. I had a newfound respect for secrets, and Nina wasn't mine to tell.

Now, as we crept into the pew behind the rest of them, Lea

predictably turned around, eyed Nina with suspicion, and hissed at Matthew. "Nice of you to show up."

"Eyes front, ladies," Matthew snapped back in a whisper. "God hates a gossip, you know."

I snorted. Lea always acted like the oldest, but Matthew had her by several years. It always gave me, one who had borne the solid brunt of her henpecking, satisfaction when Matthew put her in her place.

"Hush," was all Lea could come up with.

"Yeah, hush, Zio," Tommy, her eldest, parroted.

"Psst!"

We all sat up a little straighter at Nonna's familiar hiss. Above all, she hated when we misbehaved in church. That hiss was the one that threatened a spanking when we got home, no matter how old we were.

"Hush," Sofia whispered next to me, though she wasn't quite brave enough to admonish her cousin in the middle of church.

I smiled encouragingly. When it really came down to it, Sofia just wanted her cousins to like her, bozos or not. Unfortunately, since they were all boys except for the baby, it was harder than she would have liked.

She caught me watching her, then reached up and tugged on my sleeve so I could bend down.

"What's up, bean?" I whispered.

"Mama, can we bring Xavi to church with us sometime?"

I blinked, then glanced toward Matthew, who was busy whispering something into Nina's ear that made her smile. I looked down at my daughter, whose blue eyes shone as brightly as any stained windowpane.

"I think so," I told her. "Someday. Maybe soon."

She smiled, and the warmth of it filled my heart.

"Good," she said. "I think he'll like it."

———

THE SERMON WAS one I had heard before, a retelling of part of the book of Daniel. It started with the more famous story of Daniel and the lion's den, but switched quickly to one of my favorite parts, where the king sees a disembodied hand writing a message on his wall during a feast. Nothing like a good ghost story on a Sunday morning.

Even the kids listened, rapt, as one of the deacons read the story aloud, going through the threats that Daniel interpreted, all the king's sins, one by one. How he betrayed God. Did not heed His warning, honor His temple, forsake all other gods, only glorify the truth of the one true God.

The deacon was a good reader, and by the end, everyone in the church stood stock-straight, as if they themselves were being condemned. On one side of Matthew, Nina clasped a hand over the gold encircling her wrist, as if she were the one glorifying gold idols. On his other side, Sofia's mouth had dropped while the deacon read the message on the stone:

Mene, God has numbered your kingdom and put an end to it;
Tekel, you have been weighed on the scales and found wanting;
Peres, your kingdom has been divided and given to the Medes
    and Persians.
Then, by order of Belshazzar, they clothed Daniel in purple, with
    a chain of gold around his neck, and proclaimed him third in
    governing the kingdom.
That very night, Belshazzar, the Chaldean king, was slain.

He finished with "The word of the Lord," and everyone in the church repeated back, "Thanks be to God." I, however, sat in my seat like I was made of stone. The story wasn't about me. I wasn't worshipping idols or desecrating temples. But the message I had always gotten from passage like this wasn't necessarily about gold or jewels or temples. It was about truth. The importance of acknowledging the truth, speaking it, knowing it, honoring it.

I was ignoring the truth and had been for years. I'd hidden my daughter's identity from her and everyone else. Even now, I refused to tell my family, my friends, hardly anyone about what was really going on in my life. I was constantly living lies in the name of my daughter, but right there, it occurred to me that it wasn't out of fear for her, but for myself.

I couldn't help feeling that the writing of all my secrets was indeed on the wall, waiting to be revealed.

And when they were, would I be ready for them?

––––––

EVERYONE BEHAVED themselves through the service—mostly. The boys were predictably squirrelly as Lea and her husband, Mike, herded them up to take communion and back to sit quietly in their pew upon threat of dismemberment and loss of video games. Sofia trotted up with me and I tried not to look guilty while I drank from the chalice. I was a sinner. I had sinned for years and I was sinning now and I had absolutely no right to be up here pretending I was absolved and even allowed to take the holy Eucharist.

Sinner, sinner, sinner.

It was once the priest and the rest of the procession had formally left the church that things really went haywire. The organs were still playing when Lea whirled around in her seat, looking like the wrath of God embodied.

"What is *she* doing here?" she demanded.

At first, I wondered if she saw right through my little act.

But then I realized she was glaring at Nina, who, in turn, looked like she wanted to bolt.

Matthew immediately leaned in front of Nina, a warrior defending his maiden. It didn't matter that the enemy was his sister.

"What the hell, Lea?" he snapped.

"Matthew!" Nina's admonishment was quick.

"Sorry," he said, a bit more quietly. "But seriously, Lea, what the hell?"

"Zio!" Sofia piped up, always aware of her uncle's penchant for profanity. I had to laugh. She'd started policing Xavier too and had a solid fifty dollars saved up in a separate jar hidden under my bed from Matthew.

One more pang of guilt as I remembered yet another secret I was keeping.

Lea's kids all immediately chimed in, as eager as ever to join the fray.

"Dad, Zio said 'hell' in church, so why can't I?" asked Tommy.

"Lea, come on." Mike rubbed his face wearily, then grabbed one kid by the collar and the other by his sleeve. "Let's not do this here, huh?"

I had a feeling Lea had been gearing up for this moment with Mike behind closed doors. Sometimes I wondered if Mike enjoyed sparring with his wife. Lea had always been the type to boss people around, and he generally didn't seem to mind it. She'd been doing it since they were kids, when Mike was an apprentice mechanic in Nonno's shop and Lea helped balance the books. But right now, the guy just looked exhausted.

"Take the boys back to the house with Sofia," Lea ordered, handing their fourth baby, Lupe, to Mike. "And for God's sake, don't let Father Deflorio hear them talking like that on your way out."

Sofia's face dropped with irritation, but I shushed her with a look and nodded my head, indicating she should follow her uncle and the boys back to Nonna's.

"I told you this wasn't a good idea," I said to Matthew after they were gone. Church was never going to be the best place to introduce his married girlfriend to the family.

"Stop." His reply was curt and not to be disobeyed.

Nina, however, wasn't about to be overshadowed. Instead of allowing Matthew to shield her from the rest of us, she pushed around him until she was facing Nonna. Smart, that one. Nonna hadn't even uttered a legitimate word, but Nina knew exactly who was in charge.

"Hello, Signora Zola," she said with a polite wave. "It's nice to see you again."

Nonna, however, wasn't a pushover. Lea was louder, but she took every cue from our grandmother. And every grudge.

Sofia Zola, the elder, stopped in the middle of the church and examined the speaker as if she had only just realized Nina was there. Her dark eyes looked almost as black as her dyed hair, fixed on Nina like she was a speck of dust that needed to be cleaned up. It was an expression my sisters and I affectionately called the Look of Death. We had practiced it in the mirror since we were little. But only Nonna's original masterpiece could stop people in their tracks and impart infinite words without a single one spoken.

To her credit, Nina didn't cower or flee. She looked like she wanted to. But she didn't.

Then, instead of answering, Nonna turned to Marie and Joni, pushing lightly on Joni's back so they would start moving out of the church. The rest of the pews were nearly empty. We all filed out in a jumble. I, for one, was eager to get a little fresh air, for more than one reason.

"I love your fascinator, by the way," Kate pushed ahead of me to tell Nina. "Very Jackie O."

Nine smiled. "Thank you."

"Doesn't make it all right for you to be here, though. Not after everything you've done to my brother."

My jaw dropped. Kate was never this, well, Lea-like.

Joni and Marie immediately started giggling.

"Yo!" Matthew's voice reverberated around the church, hinting of the thunder of God.

"Maybe I should go," Nina murmured to Matthew.

"What?" He whirled back to her. "No. I asked you here. I didn't know the vultures would descend the second we showed up. In a *church*, for God's sake."

"Why?" snarled Lea. "Wasn't she married in one?"

I swallowed. Matthew had never been violent toward any of us, but at that moment, I really thought he might smack Lea for her smart mouth. He and Nina were trapped in the middle of all of us, and we were no better than harpies, ready to peck out her eyes for what? Existing?

Matthew glanced at me. I didn't know what to say. But the way my brother's shoulder fell broke my heart a little.

"I'm sorry," Nina tried again. "I don't understand. Did I do something—"

"Yes, you did something wrong," Lea mimicked her cruelly. "You took my brother for a ride. You wrapped him around that little lacy finger of yours and made him fall in love with you. And then you ruined his life. He lost his job because of you. Did you know that?"

The memory of hearing that Matthew's leave had turned into him permanently losing his job washed over me, as did my own anger. Aside from the recent bad news, I'd been living with happy Matthew for the last few months, but before that, he'd been more depressed than when he'd come back from Iraq as a broken Marine. This woman had been responsible for that and more. And she might do it again.

Matthew glared at me like he knew what I was thinking. But I only raised my chin. I wasn't going to feel sorry for loving my family.

"So, he lost his whole career, everything he cared about, not to mention you wrecked him for other women who could *actually* make him happy," Marie piped up. She was more than a little bitter about the last one. Only last year, Matthew had completely thrown over her good friend, Annalisa.

"And every time he thinks he's rid of you, somehow you come waltzing back to stick your claws into him all over again," Joni ended, for once on the same page as Marie.

They nodded at each other with satisfaction, as if to dare Matthew to argue.

"I think that covers it, don't you?" Kate asked.

"I—I—" Nina turned between each of us, landing on Matthew, eyes pleading with desperation. "Matthew, I—"

I wasn't having it. I'd felt for them in the car, but after having all her sins counted for us, my sympathy had vanished. I was with my sisters on this one.

"It's not just that," I pointed out. "He's been moping around this city for almost a year at this point, pining for a woman he can't have."

"No offense, Nina. You're fabulous and everything. But you shouldn't be here," Joni added.

"Ever," Kate finished.

Nonna, for her part, stood on the outside of our little circle, arms crossed, but watching us like she was our puppet master. Her lack of interference confirmed one thing: that she approved of every word.

Matthew looked helplessly between us, but eventually, my brother's broad shoulders drooped in defeat.

My fury vanished. And suddenly, I found myself in his place, and what was happening scared the hell out of me. Every fear I'd ever had about introducing Xavier to my family as Sofia's dad was being confirmed right here, right now. They couldn't even handle Nina, who, while cold, had been trapped in a legitimately awful marriage for years by no fault of her own. Anyone could see she was crazy about Matthew, and they were doing everything they could to move forward.

If they couldn't give her a chance, what hope did Xavier have?

"That's how you feel? Fine, then. We're going. We don't need this."

Matthew grabbed Nina's hand and shoved past me and Kate, pulling her toward the front of the church.

My sisters and I all watched, somewhat dumbfounded. Matthew was stubborn, yes. And clearly in love. But I don't think any of us really imagined he would completely abandon his family for…her.

Then again, I realized as he didn't look back, why wouldn't he? We were absolutely horrible.

I was about to rush forward to tell him so, and the look on Kate's face told me she was thinking the same, when I noticed that he and Nina had stopped again at the entrance of the church. My sisters and I crept forward, and eventually, I was able to see who they were speaking to.

Sherry Alvarez. Matthew's ex-girlfriend. The woman who had cheated on him while he was fighting in Iraq. The woman who had absolutely shattered his young heart.

If there was anyone my sisters and I hated more, I couldn't say. This one, in particular, had been wished into the bowels of hell on more than one occasion.

Kate and I led the pack, ready to jump in to protect our brother from Sherry's acrylic-nail-shaped claws. But to my surprise, Nina had beaten us to it.

"I know you're the kind of woman who cheats on the best possible man there is," she was saying as we came within earshot. "I know you're the kind of woman who lets her lover go to war and cheapens his sacrifice by opening your legs to any other man who comes your way."

"Oh, listen, now," Kate whispered in my ear.

I nodded.

Lea pushed ahead, as ready as ever to intervene. "Mattie—"

"*Hush.*" I found myself pulling on her arm.

This was Nina's fight. I wanted to see how she would fare.

"I also know you're the kind of woman who regrets it," Nina continued in a voice as crystal-clear as any of her porcelain features. "So I'll say this to you nicely the first time, but next, the gloves will *really* come off. You don't deserve him. Now, in case you've forgotten, he also has an entire family of fierce women who don't take kindly to people who hurt him."

"No, we do *not*," Joni whispered, though no one paid her any heed.

"Nor do I," Nina finished. "Like Matthew, I come from a family who will do absolutely anything to protect the people they love. And I do mean anything. I suggest you don't test me on that point."

For the first time, I saw—really saw—what Matthew saw in Nina de Vries. She was as strong as any one of us in her own refined way and was ready to defend my brother against anything.

That alone was worth giving her a real chance. And just maybe, *maybe*, made her his equal.

Sherry flipped her over-blown hair, eyes dancing between Matthew, Nina, and the rest of us behind him. Then, with a few more shuttered words, she turned and slowly made her way out of the church with all the dignity of a maimed dog.

"Oh my *God*," Lea mumbled in front of me, so low I was the only one who could hear it.

"What?" I whispered, unwilling to break the silent satisfaction while Sherry moped her way out of the church.

But Lea's eyes were fixed on something else. Something shiny that was only *just* evident through the prim lace gloves Nina had been wearing throughout the service. Now that I saw it, though, I couldn't ignore the gleaming, if modest diamond, shining through the delicate material.

"You're *engaged*?" Lea squawked, unable to keep it in anymore.

Matthew froze, then made a grab for Nina's hand. "This wasn't really the way we were planning to tell you, but yeah, Lea," he said. "I asked Nina to marry me. And she said yes."

I gaped, right along with the rest of my sisters. *What was happening?* Months he'd been back from Italy. Months he'd been whistling around the house like he was one of the freaking seven dwarves. And all the while, my brother had been engaged to be married.

And he hadn't told me.

Hurt vibrated through my entire body. I knew I was just one of many here. One of the gossips. One of the hens.

But Matthew and I lived together. We took care of each other.

Didn't we?

"Signora Zola." Nina broke the awkward standoff, turning her attention back to Nonna once more.

My grandmother stood behind us all, arms crossed firmly over her conservative wool sweater, the gold crucifix she always wore on Sundays swinging lightly across her chest. Nonna's creased face was as made up as ever, cat eye in place, cheeks rouged, mauve lipstick perfectly applied. But she was unreadable—perhaps in fear. Perhaps in fury.

"I realize it's a surprise," Nina ventured, "but I would very much appreciate the chance to…explain everything. Please."

Matthew looked more in love with her than ever. But even he managed to tear his gaze away to speak to Nonna. "Please, Nonna. Just give her a chance to say her piece. Fair's fair."

We all turned to Nonna, waiting for her to make her judgment. This was it, I realized. If she said no, it was over. Matthew would leave. He'd already made that clear. And the rest of us would be expected to treat him as if he'd never existed, at least in our grandmother's house.

My heart already felt like it was breaking. Was this what it meant to love someone your family didn't?

What if he loved your daughter too?

But then, Nonna spoke.

"Yes," she said. "I think so. We need to talk. With Matthew *and* you."

25

The house was empty when we filed in. Lea had called Mike on our way over and told him to bring the kids to their house so we could talk to Matthew and Nina adults only. I had only smarted a little. As much as I didn't like Lea making decisions about where my kid should or should not go, she was right. This wasn't a conversation for children, that was for sure.

"Thanks for ratting me out, by the way," Matthew said once we had filed around the dining room table like we were about to start massive negotiations.

Joni and Marie were at the other end, already sniping at each other as if nothing was wrong. Kate and Lea were helping Nonna in the kitchen.

I frowned. Is that what he thought? I barely knew anything about him and Nina. Honestly, I was a little pissed he hadn't said more.

"It's not like I would have wanted to talk to them myself about losing my job, Frankie."

Oh, *that's* what he meant. Okay, yeah, I'd told them the news. But what did he expect? He certainly wasn't going to say anything, and he deserved his family's support. Particularly when he had supported so many of us.

"I don't know, would you?" I replied testily. "You're about as proud as it gets, Mattie. It took you weeks to even tell me when you started taking shifts at Envy last fall."

I didn't add that he had genuinely worried me during that time, having fallen into such a deep depression, I wasn't sure he would ever come out.

Matthew just frowned intensely, ignoring Nina's confused expression next to him. "Still. How would you like it if I dropped the bomb that you ran into Xavier a few months back and didn't tell anyone, huh?"

My eyes popped open. No, no, *no*, he wouldn't.

"Xavier?" Lea said as she popped into the kitchen, followed by Kate.

The look on Kate's face told me she was eager—too eager. She was as tired as I was of holding on to the secret of Xavier's appearance.

Minutely, I shook my head, hoping she would understand.

To my relief, her expression shuttered.

"Thanks a lot," I muttered to Matthew.

"Wait, wait, wait," Joni said brightly. "Isn't Sofia's dad named Xavier?"

It took a superhuman effort not to bury my face in my palms.

"Brilliant," Marie was saying. "She really cracked it this time!"

"Shut up, Marie," Joni snapped back at her.

"It's really *none* of your business," I told all of them.

"No freaking way," Joni said at the same time Marie said, "You're joking."

"Frankie, maybe—" Kate started.

"*No*," I said, cutting off that thought at the knees.

"Who is Xavier?" I heard Nina ask on Matthew's other side. "Other than Sofia's father, I mean. I gathered that."

She honestly just sounded thankful to have a reprieve from the rabble. Here we were. Her out of one frying pan, and me flipped right into the fire.

"He charmed Frankie's socks off before leaving her high and dry with a kid on the way and no one to contact," Lea said as she entered the room with a plate of boiled and quartered artichokes. "He's the kind of man who leaves people in the lurch. Sound familiar, Nina?"

"Hey," Matthew barked even as Nina laid a hand on his arm. "For real, should we just go?"

I breathed a sigh of relief. I felt bad for Matthew now, but I wasn't really into being the object of interrogation. Particularly since I wasn't sure how well I would hold up.

Unfortunately, I had no such luck.

"Xavier was at Jane and Eric's Christmas party," Matthew informed everyone, but mostly Nina, as he turned back to her. "Tall guy. British. Black hair. Deep voice."

Every small description felt like a punch to the gut. Not just because I could see each trait like I'd drawn them myself, but because it was almost like Matthew was calling his presence here. Poof, there was the hair. Poof, now the eyes.

"No *way*," Joni said. "Holy crap, he sounds hot."

Oh, girl. You have no idea.

"He sounds like a jerk," Marie countered.

Matthew nodded. "To be honest, doll, I was more focused on finding you that night."

He grinned at Nina. But she wasn't really interested in flirting.

"You don't mean Xavier Parker, do you?" she asked.

I froze. This was just what I needed—the Ice Queen spreading her poison on the man Sofia was eventually going to call "Daddy." I didn't care how much sympathy I had for Nina de Vries. I wanted her to shut up before she ruined everything.

"Why, do you know him?" Matthew's tone was curious, but with a threatening undercurrent that he always had whenever Sofia's dad was mentioned.

"Not well, but we've met a few times," Nina said. "He lives in London, but our social circles are fairly small. He went to school with Eric."

"Who's Eric?" Joni asked Marie, who just shrugged her shoulders.

"Probably one of her schmancy friends," Lea put in.

"Shut *up*," I hissed at them both, though none of them so much as spared me a glance.

"What's his story?" Matthew was asking. "Frankie's always been a damn mute about the guy."

As I damn well would continue to be, I decided, slouching farther into my seat like I was a thirteen-year-old kid having her middle-school crush discussed like chicken dinner. The. Worst.

Nina continued, seemingly unaware of my torment. "He caused a bit of a scandal, from what I recall. He's the illegitimate son of an earl or maybe a marquess."

I jerked. *What?*

"At any rate, his father didn't have other children, and then surprised everyone by naming Xavier as his heir instead of letting the estate pass to his cousin or nephew or whatever."

At that, I sat up fully. Xavier had mentioned his father's attempted bequest, but nothing about other family members. Or a freaking peerage. The way he made it sound, he and his father only had a brief (and failed) relationship, and all his recent success was founded more on his own merits.

This, however, was a story with several other dimensions.

"Grandmother's butler, Garrett, was English," Nina continued, "and had a lot to say about the whole ordeal."

"Ooh, a butler," Joni whispered loudly.

"La-dee-da," Marie agreed, only to be smacked by Lea while Nina went on.

"It was this big to-do when a boy from East London was named presumptive heir to this title, apparently."

"South London," I murmured softly to myself, though no one else was paying attention, rapt as they were with Nina's story.

In my mind's eye, though, I could see Xavier's smirk at the correction. He would have liked that I was becoming as particular as he was about these kinds of inaccuracies.

Of course, maybe at this point, he would have started laughing now that the colossal joke he'd been making for the last few months was finally finding its punchline.

I could already imagine the headline the British tabloids were so famous for: Son of Earl Fools American Trollop.

Earl. Oh *God*.

"Then what happened?" Matthew wondered curiously.

"I honestly don't know much," Nina replied. "Just that Garrett thought he was an ungrateful, rebellious brat. Attending Dartmouth, for instance, instead of Oxford or Cambridge like everyone else in his class. That's where he met Eric, who brought him home a few times when he was at school. Nice boy. Tall, like you said. After that, I heard he went to culinary school, of all things, and started several restaurants until his father died maybe three or four years ago…"

By the time she was finished, you could have heard a pin drop in the normally cacophonous dining room. Even Nonna was silent in the doorway, holding a plate of antipasti, though she was watching me, not Nina.

And I, for one, could not move.

Died. His father had…died? Three or four *years* ago, if Nina was correct? Months I'd been seeing him, and he hadn't mentioned a word about it. Oh, he was full of sob stories about his mother and Lucy, full of vitriol toward his father, the man whom he said hated his guts.

Nothing about his death on top of everything else.

Which also meant Xavier was…an earl himself?

Or was it a marquess?

Did it even matter?

Who even *was* this man?

Suddenly, I couldn't feel the ends of my fingers or my toes. The edges of my vision seemed to blur, and my siblings' faces all moved in and out of focus.

"It isn't the same Xavier, is it?" Nina asked me in her kind, quiet way.

She was clearly shocked, though. Just like anyone else would be when they realized someone like *me* had, at least for one night, captured the fancy of blue-blooded, perfect-looking, utterly aristocratic Xavier Parker.

Or been his prey.

"Sometimes he used the name Sato," Nina said as if that explained the disparity. "His mother is half-Japanese, I believe, and that's her maiden name. Is that—it's not the same person, is it?"

Everyone turned to me, and it was clear I didn't need to say that yes, in fact, it was. I could barely breathe anyway, much less speak. Or correct her on the parts of the story I knew to be wrong. South London, not East London. His mother was gone and had been from Japan, not just half herself. That Sato wasn't her maiden name, just her name— because Xavier's parents had never been married.

But how could I correct any of those things when I knew so little about the rest? When it would mean admitting to them all that I had been secretly seeing Xavier for months now?

"Wait a second," Joni said. "Are you saying that Sofia…*our* baby Sofia…could be *royalty*?"

She sounded absolutely ecstatic. I wanted to throw an olive at her. Actually, I wanted to hurl the entire plate of prosciutto.

"She didn't say her dad's Prince William, you idiot," Marie snarked.

"Did you know, Fran?" Matthew asked, reaching across Nina to set a hand on top of mine on the table. "About this title, or whatever it is?"

"I…" I just shook my head. I didn't know what to say as all of Xavier's secrets tumbled through my mind. "I knew about his restaurants. And his mother. The rest, though…" I pulled my hands out of my brother's grasp and shoved my face into my palms, if only to escape the pity launching itself at me from all sides of the table.

I was an idiot. It all made sense now. His one and only "Season." Going to a garden party hosted by the queen of freaking England. Of *course*, Xavier was more than he let on. Of course, he was legitimate nobility. And, of course, I had never clued in. I'd been too busy falling over myself in lust and awe while he fell in love with our daughter. Too busy seeing everything through rose-colored glasses than to put on real lenses to find out who he really was.

Stupid. I was so, *so* stupid.

"I never knew," I mumbled, more to myself than to them. "I have to…can you all just give me a minute, please?"

To my utter shock, my family obeyed. The rest of the conversation passed in a daze—even the part where Matthew informed everyone he was not only engaged to Nina, but that he'd asked her when he was away in Florence. Interpreting for her. *Three months ago.*

It was just one shock, one betrayal after another today, wasn't it?

But it didn't seem to matter. I listened vaguely as they told a whole other story I hadn't known. Something about Nina's family, and a secret, and a copy and a whole bunch of crap I honestly could barely listen to until I finally looked up and realized that while I'd been having a mental breakdown, Nina had somehow managed to win over my grandmother. My sisters were all looking at her like a hero.

And I couldn't take being here one minute longer.

"Welcome to the family," Nonna was saying, even as I edged my way out the door. I couldn't stay for the pleasantries. Not now.

I walked a full five blocks from the house, ignoring the fine sunshine of the late April weather as I whipped out my phone to call Xavier.

He answered on the first ring.

"Can you read my mind?" he asked. "I was literally pulling up your number. Are you around this weekend? I'd like to see Sof, but I also want to talk something over with you."

"Is it true?" I demanded, ignoring all his questions.

"That I'm the best chef in England? Of course it's true." He was trying to joke, but uneasiness slid through his tone. "What do you mean? What is it, Ces?"

"You lied to me," I said, voice quavering under the stress. "You lied to Sofia. Matthew's—my brother's—whatever. She *told* me everything!"

"Told you what?" His voice was oddly calm. Almost stony.

"Who you really are!" I exploded. "That you're not really just estranged from your father. That he died four years ago. That you're not just a restauranteur in London, but you're a fucking *earl*, a member of the peerage, something like, I don't know, probably eighteenth in line for the throne of England!"

"Forty-seventh," Xavier muttered as if he couldn't help it. "And it's a duchy, not an earldom."

"Oh my *God*!" I paced angrily up and down the street, kicking rocks, causing a few pigeons to fly up to escape my wrath. "You haven't been flying back and forth between here and England to take care of your restaurants, have you? You've been taking care of your fucking estates. Still attending the Season or going to court or whatever else it is you stupid gentry do in your spare time!"

"What? *No*? Jesus, Ces, is that what you think of me?"

"I don't know *what* to think of you anymore. I thought we were being straight with each other, Xavi. You said there were no more secrets. You said you told me everything!"

There was a long silence on the other end of the line.

Then, "Who told you this?" His voice was subzero in temperature. "What exactly happened?"

"Nina *de Vries* happened." The name tasted sour on my tongue. I knew it wasn't her fault per se, but right now I could have quite cheerfully shot the messenger of this particular news.

"Nina de Vries. You mean Eric's cousin?"

"I mean yet another filthy rich person who apparently gets to know your secrets when your daughter and I don't." I swiped at my eyes, tears pricking their edges. No. *No*. He was not going to make me cry about this, of all things. Not again. Not ever. "You really think I'm an idiot, don't you? Stupid, simple girl from the Bronx, too out of touch, too *common* to ever discover that you're not just the estranged kid of some rich guy, but that you're *actually* a duke!"

I shrieked, only barely stopping myself from throwing the phone into oncoming traffic. I whirled around to face two men about my age striding down the street, chatting cheerfully in a mix of Spanish and English. One of them looked me up and down, and the other grinned.

"What the fuck are you looking at?" I snarled, my inner bitch coming right up to the surface.

They scurried on their way, but only after one of them gave a low, foreboding whistle.

"Francesca!" Xavier was calling through the speaker. "Francesca, come back to the fucking phone!"

"What?" I snapped.

"Can I just ask, what's really the problem here? Is it that I'm a duke, or that I wasn't one before?"

I turned toward the street, which was mostly still except for the occasional car. "Neither. It's that you lied. I could have looked you up on the internet. I'm not an idiot, Xavier. But I didn't."

"And why the fuck not?" he exploded. "Anyone else would have. If you're so bloody smart, why didn't you just find all of this out yourself instead of waiting for me to tell you, eh?"

"Because *you* should have told me!" I shrieked back. "Just like you should have told your daughter. Because I wanted to know if you really changed. But you haven't, have you? You're still the same lying, secretive, immoral *bastard* you always were. So what am I supposed to do now, Xavi? You've made us—you've made her, Sofia, fall in love with you." I hiccupped over another sob that I was determined to keep buried. "What—what am I supposed to do now?"

There was another long pause. "You're supposed to tell her I'm her dad, like was always planned. I'll tell her the rest, Ces. I won't lie to her. She's my daughter."

"She is," I admitted through a hushed sob. "But what does that make me?"

He sighed, but then there was a muffled noise while he spoke to someone else on the other end of the line. When he came back on, he was clearly moving, almost out of breath.

"I'll be there tomorrow," he said. "I'll tell you everything, Ces. Just let me explain."

I stood there on the street, listening to the sounds of my neighborhood swirling around me. For years, I'd wanted nothing more than to escape these humble streets. I'd wanted something outside of the mishmash of brick apartment buildings and ramshackle houses, where no one had nice cars or nice clothes or nice anything, but everyone knew exactly who they were and what they wanted. A good amaretto or a ride downtown. Sin on Saturday, confession on Sunday. Work, play, pray, repeat. Simple.

I'd looked down on all of it for so long. But no more.

"I don't think so," I said. "You had your chance with us, Xavi, and you blew it. I think we're done."

26

"**G**irl, six weeks left. I don't know about you, but I am counting the days. This Monday was *hard*."

I turned to smile at Jenna Reynolds, one of the other third grade teachers who had the classroom next to mine, as we exited the Monday afternoon staff meeting into the teacher's lounge. It was four thirty, and I was ready to pick up Sofia, go home, drown my sorrows in tea and chocolate, and continue to ignore Xavier's calls just like I'd been doing for the last week.

"Me too," I agreed.

"You have plans for the summer?"

I swallowed. Since Matthew's bombshell announcement, I'd been wondering the same thing. Nina was currently embroiled in a divorce, so it was safe to say they weren't getting married anytime soon. Still, I couldn't help but wonder if she was moving in or he was moving out. I had no clue what to expect for me and Sofia, and I was too afraid to ask. Matthew was still upset over what had happened this weekend. I didn't want to rock the boat.

"Probably just teach summer school and classes at the Y," I said, hoping it was true, but also sort of not. "You?"

But before Jenna could reply, my name was called across the room.

Lisa, the front office receptionist, waved at me through the window between the front office and the teacher's lounge. "These came for you just before the bell rang."

Jenna and I turned to see a massive bouquet of Easter lilies on Lisa's desk, their aroma filtering through the window into the lounge.

"Holy smokes!" Jenna squealed. "Those are gorgeous!"

I scowled. I knew exactly who they were from. And if he thought some pretty flowers were going to make up for his deception, he had another think coming.

I plucked the note from the spray and read it.

Like a ripple that chases
The slightest caress of the breeze,
Is that how you want me to follow you?

Xavi

If I knew anything about Xavier Parker, it was that his messages usually had ulterior meanings. Three short lines contained multitudes. If he was planning to follow me, it was because he had something in mind when we met. I was prepared for anything at this point. He could throw every lawyer he had my way. I wasn't budging.

"Is he cute?" Jenna asked after I was done reading.

I looked up to find her still fawning over the flowers.

"If he sent flower this big, he messed up big-time, didn't he?" she pressed.

I sighed. "I don't want to get into it."

"Oh man. He's *really* cute, isn't he?"

Across the lounge, Adam exited the conference room. When he caught sight of the flowers, he stopped, frowned, then gave a little wave before apparently deciding to come over. He hadn't requested a second date since our first disastrous one, but I could feel it coming. Especially once he realized Sofia's dad was out of the picture. Again.

"I'll tell you more tomorrow," I said to Jenna as I grabbed the flowers off the desk, eager to escape Adam's reconciliation. "Right now, I need to go."

————

AN HOUR LATER, after I had picked up Sofia and made her a quick dinner of the stupid cabbage pancake that had become her favorite food (it was *not*, she informed me, as good as Xavi's), I sat in the kitchen, staring at the note and the flowers while Sofia watched *Doc McStuffins* until the front door opened.

"Mattie?" I called. "Is that you?"

"Shower!" he called back as he jogged up the stairs. He must have been on a run.

But I wasn't to be put off. I'd been staring at these petals and Xavier's note for what seemed like forever, with no idea how to respond. I needed some brotherly advice.

I swiped the flowers off the counter, followed Matthew upstairs, and knocked on his door.

"You decent?" I called.

"Yeah, come in."

I walked in and found him stretching on the floor, face still red from exercise and dripping with sweat. His tuxedo was hanging from his closet door, pressed and ready. Shit, I'd forgotten. He had some big event he was attending with Nina tonight. He'd been talking about it since last week, but I'd been too self-absorbed to remember. Bad, bad sister. I wouldn't blame him if he kicked me out after all.

Matthew took one look at the lilies in my hands and grinned. "Aw, that's sweet, Fran, but I'm more of a red rose kind of guy, you know."

"Oh, shut up," I retorted. "I'm having a personal issue and I need your advice."

Well, it was out now.

Matthew swiveled to stretch over his opposite leg. "If you don't like him, send them back. And if you *really* don't like him, send me." He then balanced on his butt and started Russian twists. "So, who's the new guy?"

I sighed. Maybe it was time to just tell him everything. "Not new. Old. More than four years old, if you know what I mean."

Matthew paused, twisted toward me. "Xavier?"

Didn't miss a beat, my brother.

But immediately, the light in his face darkened. After last week's conversation, Matthew had asked a few times about my interactions with Xavier. I still couldn't bring myself to tell him the truth. It would break his heart that I'd been keeping secrets and hadn't asked for his help. And it would break Sofia's heart to realize not everyone thought the world of her beloved Xavi.

Rock, meet hard place.

"Lea told me to call him," I fibbed. "So I sent an email to his office."

It was a stupid lie. One that could be checked immediately. But it was the first thing I thought of at the moment.

Matthew sat up completely, slinging his arms over his knees. "Whatever happened at the Christmas party?"

I shook my head, switching my flowers from one hand to the other, bracing myself for the cross-examination. Matthew *was* a lawyer, after all. Before he got canned, he was actually a prosecutor. "We, um, talked."

"Not about Sofia, I take it?"

"More the, um, 'alone' kind of talking. And then I left. I'll spare you the details."

Well, at least that was the truth. For the most part.

Matthew made a face like he'd just bitten into a lemon. "I appreciate that. And you haven't talked to him since?"

I shrugged. "He doesn't have my number. He sent a few emails to my work address, but I didn't answer. I didn't know what to say. Until now, apparently."

Lies, lies, lies.

Why was it so damn hard to tell him the truth?

I knew why. This was my brother.

"Are you thinking you're going to tell him about Sof?"

His dark eyes, intense and green like mine, bore into me like a drill. I could feel him waiting for me to make a mistake. Say the wrong thing. Need his rescue.

It was what he had always done for me.

The thing was…I wasn't sure I wanted him to anymore.

"I don't know," I said honestly. "I barely know him, Mattie. We had a fling almost five years ago now, and he was with someone else at the time, and then…" All of it was true. So I plunged ahead with a little white lie to round it out. After all, I wasn't here for confession. I was here for advice. "Anyway, I just said it was nice to see him again. That was it. That was this morning. These arrived while you were out. Plus, this."

My complex web of lies and truth secure, I handed him Xavi's card, which he immediately opened and read aloud.

Like a ripple that chases
The slightest caress of the breeze,
Is that how you want me to follow you?

Xavi

Matthew whistled when he was done. "Not subtle, is he?"

"He didn't write it or anything," I said. "It's a famous Japanese poem. I looked it up."

Also the truth. I wasn't sure how I felt about it. Xavi wasn't much for books, but he knew I was. He knew I'd appreciate a well-placed verse more than most people. And if he had actually taken the time to track this one down…

Matthew handed me the card, then went back to doing crunches. "I don't know how I feel about reading my little sister's love letters, Fran."

"Don't be a jerk. What does it mean, though?"

"Seems pretty clear to me. He's asking what you want."

I huffed. "Which is…"

Matthew rolled over into a plank. "Do you really need me to tell you that?"

"I do when I don't know!" I cried.

Matthew wasn't usually this cagey. Most of the time, we were more than happy to give unsolicited advice about each other's lives. Now it was like he knew I was keeping things back, and he wasn't going to volunteer any clarity because of it.

"You messaged him, Frankie. Seems like you want to talk to him."

I made a face. "And say what? Hey, don't know if you remember me, but thanks for the two one-night stands, they were super fun. Oh, and by the way, I got pregnant that first night and had your baby and never told you."

I bit my lip. More lies. It had been a month, not two nights. And yeah, I was way past *that* conversation, though that didn't stop my anxious mind from reliving it.

I huffed, set the flowers on Matthew's dresser, and sat on his bed. Matthew just kept moving through another ab exercise like I wasn't there before finally pausing on his forearms again.

"It seems like he a lot more than remembers you. And he sure as shit seemed to remember you at Christmas."

"You don't want to know," I muttered at the ceiling. He really, really didn't.

"I thought you were going to have mercy on me with that."

Was it just me, or did he sound hurt? It wasn't like he ever *wanted* details about my sex life. Or maybe it was just that he knew I hadn't really had one since then.

"I can't go there again," I added. "It was bad enough back then. He was engaged, you know."

"Humph." He did know. "What about now?"

"Well, in December, he said he was single." I flopped back onto the bed and stared at the ceiling. "I wanted to tell him. But I just kept thinking of…"

I drifted off. This wasn't working. Half-truths and four-month-old versions of this story weren't getting me anywhere.

"Thinking of what?" Matthew asked from the floor.

"Mom."

It slipped out before I could stop it. But then I realized it was true.

"What about her?"

When I sat back up, Matthew was back on his heels and turned to give me his full attention. He was in the dark, but my brother still had radar for bullshit. Just like he also knew when something really mattered.

"The way she left after Dad died. I mean, it's all right that Lea and them are making peace with her. But I remember too. I remember how it feels to have your own parent walk away from you. Like you're nothing." I wrapped my arms around my shins and hugged my legs to my chest. "I think you were right, you know, staying away from her. It's why I don't let her near Sofia. I don't want her to break her heart."

"Yeah, but Sofia doesn't know Xavier," Matthew pointed out. "You don't really either."

No, I didn't, but not in the way he thought. For months, I'd believed I was actually getting to know the real Xavier again. Doing right by my kid. Preventing him from blindsiding her like our mother had done to us.

Matthew got up and came to sit next to me on the bed. This was it. He was going to force the truth out of me, like he always did. And then I wouldn't be the one trying to protect my kid. I'd be the little sister disappointing him and everyone else all over again.

Shit, shit, shit.

But Matthew said the last thing I ever thought I'd hear.

"You know, I'm wondering if we shouldn't at least *try* to say hi to Mom next time she calls."

I gawked at him. "You're kidding. *You* want to talk to Mom?"

Matthew rubbed his neck, clearly uncomfortable with the idea. "I don't know if I *want* to, per se. But if there's anything I've learned over the last year, it's that people can change. And something she did ten, twenty years ago…well, it might not be the person she is now. I'm not saying we have to invite her in, or anyone else you don't want for your own sake and Sofia's. But, you know, when it comes to Sofia's dad, maybe you can answer the door. Maybe you can talk on the porch. Have a conversation. You know what I'm saying?"

I sat there for a minute, taking in his words. My brother had nursed a grudge against our mother for more than twenty years. Essentially, since *he* had been the one to raise us alongside our grandparents. At fourteen, Mattie had grown up way more than he should've had to, watched Mom break all our hearts again and again. She'd lied, stolen, neglected us, totally forgotten us at times, all for the love of the bottle.

And here he was, turning the other cheek. Preaching forgiveness? Color me shocked.

"Yeah," I said slowly. "Yeah, I see. Something to think about anyway."

"All right. I wish I had more brotherly advice for you. But I'm tapped out, and now I have to get ready."

"Say no more." I jumped up from the bed, not wanting to be any more of a burden. But then I thought of something else. "Hey, Mattie?"

Matthew looked up. He really was handsome, I thought for the first time in a long time. Dark hair, roguish charm. I could see why so many girls liked him. I could see why Nina loved him.

"Yeah?" he asked.

I smiled. I could forgive too. At least for his sake. "You know, I thought about it and I think it's a good thing, you and Nina, after all. She loves you. Anyone can see that."

Matthew grinned. "You finally coming around, little sister?"

"I think it's good for you, too," I told him as I grabbed the flowers and walked to the door. "I see how you love her. How you talk about her daughter."

My heart squeezed when I thought about Matthew around someone else's little girl. I couldn't lie. Sometimes, it made me a little jealous. We were his family. Sofia and me.

Weren't we?

"Soon you'll have a real family to protect," I said quietly. "Not just me and the others. We're all grown. You need a family of your own. I'm glad you're getting one."

As sad as it was, I meant every word. Even though I knew it meant I'd have to patch my own little family together at last. Whatever that looked like.

Matthew's smile widened. At least I had that.

"Thanks, Fran," he said as he got up from the bed, already grabbing a towel off a hook on the wall.

"Have fun at the ball, Cinderella," I teased as I left, though the levity didn't quite reach my heart.

Because at that moment, I knew Matthew was right.

I also knew what I had to do.

27

The flowers continued through the week. Along with other choice bits of poetry, some Japanese, some English, but all of them totally pertinent to the situation. They even came directly to the house, as if Xavier knew somehow that I would have at least told Matthew something about him.

I ignored them all, still uncertain about how to deal with the new revelations about his life and family. Except now it was Friday, I'd finally agreed to see him, and Xavier was due to arrive in New York this weekend. And I had absolutely no clue what to say.

I was still trying to figure that out on my way out of school to teach my Friday dance class when I heard my name.

"Frankie! Hey!"

Dread creaked through my mind like a rusty door hinge. I turned on the foursquare court to face Adam Klein, who was pushing his way out of the school's main exit, his messenger bag slung across his body, glasses crooked over his nose, ever-present driver's cap pulled on backward in his hurry.

"Frankie," he wheezed after jogging across the playground. "Hey."

"Hey Adam," I said, checking my watch. "Can this wait? I have a class to teach at five, and—"

"It'll only take a second."

Adam stood up straight, still catching his breath, but tipped his head expectantly. Still, it wasn't without humility. Though he had tried multiple times to get my attention in the months since our date, he hadn't been *too* persistent. As if he knew I needed time to get over the fact that he had tried to force a kiss after too much wine and my kid's father had threatened to punch his lights out for it.

I sighed, waiting. "All right."

"I was wondering, ah, what you were doing this weekend. Maybe we could catch a movie or something. I feel like I owe you for last time."

I had to fight a grimace. "Adam, I don't really think that's a good idea—"

"I don't mean like that. I just never got to apologize properly for how our date ended." His brown eyes widened with earnest, unwavering, and kind. "I know I messed up. I was nervous and drank way too much that night. You're just so pretty, and I didn't know how to deal with it, and…"

He continued babbling while I looked everywhere but at him, trying to figure a way out of this conversation. Unfortunately, before I could, I caught sight of the Duke of Kendal striding around the corner, making straight for the entrance of the playground.

"Shit," I muttered.

"Huh?" Adam asked.

I turned back to him, dancing on the balls of my feet like a sprinter waiting for her gunshot. "Look, it's all right. Water under the bridge. Consider yourself forgiven. Now, I'm going to be la—"

"Well, I'd like to make it up to you," Adam rattled on, oblivious to my discomfort. "Maybe a do-over on that drink? Or just coffee if you like…"

"Francesca. Ces!"

I froze. Goddammit, he really just couldn't wait outside the school grounds, could he?

Adam frowned, looked over my shoulder, and then his expression morphed to shock. "What the hell is *he* doing here?"

"I wish I knew," I said, more to myself than to him.

"Francesca! I know you can hear me."

I sighed. "Adam, I'm really sorry. Can we talk another time?"

But now Adam wasn't paying attention to me either as a shadow fell over both of us in the exact silhouette of one Xavier Parker.

The man himself came to stand next to us, looking a far cry from gentry but still every bit his delicious, slightly dangerous self in a pair of jeans, his black leather jacket, and silver aviators covering his sapphire blues. His tattoo snaked out the top of his T-shirt, licking his neck.

"Hey, Xavier," Adam said. "We were having a conversation, if you couldn't tell."

"Do I know you?" Xavier demanded irritably. "Because you're talking to me like I do."

Adam's eyes narrowed through his thick lenses.

"Oh, for God's sake," I snapped. "Yes, you know each other. Xavi, you're just too self-absorbed to remember that you and Adam were at Eton at the same time together."

"Adam Klein?" Adam reminded him. "We had biology and calculus together. I was the ambassador's son."

Xavier blinked, completely nonplussed. "Oh right. Lizard, wasn't it?"

Adam's eyes practically bugged out of his head. It wasn't hard to imagine where the nickname had come from.

"I don't really go by *that* anymore," he said.

"Good for you, then," Xavier retorted. "Are you still trying to assault women with your lizard mouth on their doorsteps too, or is that also a thing of the past?"

"Xavi!" I hissed. "Cut it out!"

"Not that it's any of your business, but I've apologized for that behavior," Adam gritted through his teeth. "Didn't I, Frankie?"

"Her name is Francesca."

"Only to self-important jerks who barely know her."

"Barely know her? You can fuck right off, mate."

"Jesus." I shoved my way between them. "Can we not with the schoolyard antics? There are enough actual children on the property."

I placed a hand on both their chests and shoved. Hard. Adam took several steps back, but Xavier stood his ground for an extra few seconds before taking one single step backward.

"All right," I said. "Adam, let's get a drink next week, all right? Maybe at Pioneer Works after we're done here? We can talk more then and look at some art too."

Adam brightened, though he was staring at Xavier when he answered, "Sounds perfect. I'll get your latte."

"She drinks tea, you twat," Xavier snarled, though he quieted once I shot him another glare.

"A latte sounds great," I told Adam. "I'll see you then. Xavier, I have a class to teach in thirty minutes. If you want me to listen to whatever reason you showed up here, you can walk me there."

Xavier smirked at Adam like he'd won some kind of fight. "Be delighted."

I rolled my eyes. Freaking cavemen. "We good here, gentlemen?"

"Perfect," Adam gritted out.

"Perfect," Xavier replied.

But I was already on my way out of the schoolyard, no longer interested in being witness to further dogfighting.

"Francesca, hold on."

I didn't bother waiting, but Xavier caught up with me as I began the walk up Court Street to the YMCA. He had such long legs, it only took a few seconds.

"I thought you were going to let me talk," he said.

"I'm walking. You can talk if you want to."

Xavier sighed. "So it's like that? I don't even get a chance to explain myself? That's messed up, Ces."

"No, messed up is going four months not telling me you're a freaking duke! Telling me this sob story about your horrible relationship with your dad when, in fact, he passed too, didn't he?"

"Yeah, he did!" Xavier exploded. "And so what? At least it isn't four years of not telling me I have a daughter, who is very much fucking alive!"

I whirled around. "That is beside the point now, don't you think?"

He scowled. "Not really, no."

"And why is that?"

"Because to start with, I'm not a fucking duke."

I pressed my lips together. "So Nina was lying about your family?"

"I—no—" He shoved a hand through his hair. "It's complicated."

I turned back on my way. I had nothing more to say to that.

We strode another block, but Xavier remained mute, sidestepping people, poles, mailboxes, while he apparently figured out what to say.

"It started after Mum died," he said at last. "Like I told you, my dad shoved me off to boarding school rather than deal with me in person. That's where I met Harry Potter back there."

I bit back a laugh. With his brown hair and glasses, Adam did sort of resemble the famous wizard.

"So you did recognize him."

"'Course I did. But he's a prick, so I wasn't going to give him the satisfaction." He wrinkled his nose. "Honestly, Ces, I don't know what you see in him."

I blinked. "Whatever it is, it's none of your business."

Xavier grunted, clearly thinking otherwise. But rather than argue, he continued with his story. "Look, it's really no different than what I told you. My dad *was* a politicians. He was just in parliament, not a councillor. And yeah, he had a title. Not that it made a lick of difference. I didn't know him either way. When Mum was alive, he was just the stranger who paid for school, and after she was gone, he was the arsehole who shipped me off to Eton until I came of age. He refused to pay for culinary school, but I handled that by selling Mum's flat. Did a year at Dartmouth just to piss him off, but in the end, he just hated that I wouldn't do what he said. Stay quiet in my little corner of London and behave."

I nodded. I couldn't exactly imagine Xavier being quiet anywhere.

"Things changed, though, after I was done with school. I told you he had a bit of a change of heart. Got testicular cancer and realized his chances of having any other heirs was nil. His wife had a son from her first marriage, but that didn't mean a thing to him. So after his his wife left him, he asked me home."

"You must have put up quite the fight," I snarked.

I could just imagine him at that age, not much younger than when I met him. Stubborn and confrontational, just like he was now. Fewer suits, more T-shirts and jeans. Tall, of course, but maybe with the longer hair he'd had when I met him. Maybe even still past his shoulders, like Adam had described. Lankier, slightly rounder-faced with the innocence of youth.

Well, some innocence, anyway. I had a feeling Xavier had never been *that* innocent.

Xavier shrugged. "He was nice, really. Apologized for being such a wanker and blamed it on his ex-wife."

I pursed my lips. I didn't really buy that but let him continue.

"Anyway, he sort of made up for lost time. Taught me all the things a man teaches his son in that sort of life. How to ride, shoot, play polo. It helped, of course, that Lucy's family owned the neighboring estate."

"And was her dad a duke too?"

I couldn't help the tinge of bitterness. I knew it was wrong to be jealous of a dead woman, but I couldn't help it. So much of Xavier's life had been affected by one of the few people he said was a true friend. He said he didn't believe in love, but I did think he had loved her.

Xavier just took off his sunglasses and peered down at me. "No, a viscount. Why?"

I just huffed. I couldn't even make a joke about any of this, could I? Because things that seemed absolutely ridiculous to me were actually reality to him.

"Anyway, I was only twenty-three. Thought I knew everything, but the truth was, I was just a kid who missed his mum and wanted a family again, even if it was just an old man and his housekeeper. And Luce encouraged it. She said he was a good person and everyone deserves a second chance. And so, for a while, I actually enjoyed myself. He even gave me a place to start my first restaurant—a little pub in the nearby village where I could experiment all I wanted."

"Where is the village?" I wondered, trying to place him in some sort of setting. "Or the…the manor? Is that the right term?"

This was all so foreign. The Xavier I knew was an undeniably urban creature. I couldn't imagine him riding horses in the country or chasing foxes with a bunch of dogs.

He peered down at me, almost looking grateful that I was finally asking questions. "Corbray Hall. It's in Cumbria. Near the Lakes District, just northwest of Kendal."

The fondness in his voice was unmistakable.

"So, what happened with him?" I asked. "You always talked about your dad like you hated him."

"What happened was, it was all a lie," he said. "I made Corbray Hall, and his house in London, my homes for five years. Dad actually embraced my culinary work, but always close to home. He made no secret of wanting me to be his heir, and with Lucy around, it seemed plausible that someone like me could do it. And I liked it. I actually *liked* being Rupert Parker's son. I wanted him to like me too. More than like me."

He shook his head and muttered something like "idiot" under his breath.

"I don't understand," I said. "It seems like you were getting what you wanted. Why all the vitriol?"

He sighed. "It started with Lucy. I told you we stuck together that Season. I was useless in society, and she was sick a lot and not much of a looker. But her parents treated the Season like it was the nineteenth century, you know? But she couldn't even get through most of the events without feeling poorly. And she hated most of the men who ever tried to talk to her anyway. Fortune hunters, all of them."

I made a face. I hated that idea on principle. I couldn't imagine being in her shoes—no doubt wanting to be loved, but never knowing for sure if anyone could love her for anything but her money.

"You also remember, her parents gave her an ultimatum. Dad said I should help her out." Xavier's eyes narrowed, as if he wanted to go back and shout at the man. "He made it sound like it didn't matter if we didn't love each other—that would come, or maybe it wouldn't— but in the meantime, we could remain friends. Take care of each other as we grew old. Continue the way they had been. That we would stay a family." He shrugged. "I guess I believed him. So I talked to Luce, and she agreed to get engaged for our parents' sakes. She'd stay at her family's estate and run things. Help my dad when he wanted. I could keep working on my business in London. We decided that if neither of us found anyone else before we were forty, we'd get married for real."

"Sounds great for all of you," I remarked, unable to keep the sour taste from my mouth.

"Well, it was. Until I met you."

I closed my eyes briefly. The city seemed to be pulsing around us, but I couldn't hear it over the memories. The idea of Xavier, young, happy, and ambitious, traveling and looking for new inspiration. Me on the precipice of my own studies, dreams about to come true. Our hope was intoxicating. He hadn't said anything about his past back then. But of course, we were too wrapped up in each other to notice anything else.

Xavier stopped on the sidewalk, tugging me to face him. His blue eyes shone with intensity. "You changed *everything*, Ces. I honestly thought I was set up. I had my fun and my restaurants. The dad I always wanted. And then I met you, and the world shifted. I really did lo—" He cut himself off, his gaze flickering all around us. "Well, you know what happened after that. I came here, and for the first time in my whole life, I wasn't Rupert Parker's son or bastard, the heir to Kendal. I wasn't a mistake, and I wasn't rebel gentry, and I wasn't a fucking disappointment. You looked at me like I was a whole person, someone really worth knowing. And you know I thought the bloody world of you."

I swallowed. His emotions made his eyes sparkle like stars, even in the light of day. He was looking for me to confirm that I had felt the same way. That I had been equally enthralled.

Instead, I kept quiet.

"So I went home, ready to tell Lucy all about you," Xavier continued. "She would have been happy for us, Ces, I know she would have. But when I got there, she was too far gone for even a conversation, much less a wedding or anything else I promised her. Six months later, she died."

He wiped his eyes. I didn't see any tears there, but he seemed to be feeling them, gazing around like he was uncertain of where to land those deep blue pools of sadness. I couldn't help it. I had to hug him. Obviously surprised, he allowed me to wrap my arms around his waist tightly, pressing my face to his chest. I felt his hands slide tentatively down my back, keeping me in place. He didn't make any other move. Not until I did, at which point he released me with a frustrated huff.

"Thanks," he murmured.

"You seemed like you needed it."

"Yeah, well. Anyway." Xavier cleared his throat and pulled at his jacket. "Once Lucy's estate was settled, that's when I started to look at the numbers. Her family's land had largely been sold off years before we met. She had a huge fortune, but the viscount's title was already going to a distant cousin." He swallowed, fury replacing the sadness. "It was the Kendal estate that was upside down. Had been borrowing money from the Douglases for years just to get by. Half the land taxes unpaid. Farmers, whole villages left to crumble. Walking on the edge of losing everything until Dad realized I was best friends with a cash cow and decided to make it work to his advantage."

I frowned. Something wasn't adding up. "Xavi, can't it be both? Can't your dad have wanted to save his estate and loved you and Lucy at the same time? Because it kind of sounds like he did."

He just shook his head in disgust. "I confronted him about it, but he couldn't explain it. He manipulated her, just like he manipulated me. He pretended to love me, Ces. Pretended he actually *wanted* to be my father. But in reality, he was playing puppets with me and her, nudging and pushing our friendship so he could sell me off to his debtors like a fucking stud horse."

I gulped. It certainly didn't sound good. I was starting to realize why Xavier had avoided talking about his father. I understood parental betrayal too. Not much hurts worse than the person who is supposed to protect you turning out to be the one who attacks.

"So I left," Xavier said. "Told him he could shove the estate and his title and everything else up his arse. I never returned, even when he died the year after when his cancer returned too. Bit of karma, that. After all, it was Luce that kept me there, Ces. Not Rupert Parker. And now that they're both gone, I'll never go back. They can't make me be the Duke of Kendal. No one will."

His story finished just as we stopped outside of the Y. I had less than ten minutes until my class started, but now I was in no hurry to go in, mulling instead over everything I'd just heard.

There had been so much loss in Xavier's young life. First his mother, then his best friend, and last, his father. Death and betrayal. No wonder he didn't trust me with his secrets. He didn't seem to trust anyone at all, and by this point in his life, he really had no one left.

I swallowed. It was a lot. But then Xavier Parker, erstwhile Duke of Kendal, was always a lot.

"Who's there now?" I asked finally. "At Corbray Hall, I mean?"

In my head, I imagined an abandoned manor covered with ivy and crawling with wildlife. But I had a feeling that wasn't what had happened over the last four years.

"My uncle Henry stewards the estate, like I told you," Xavier said shortly. "I gave him pretty much everything but the title since I'm not allowed to pass it on. Sometimes he makes noises about me coming back, but it's a joke. It was always a joke."

He rolled his eyes, like he thought it was absurd. Honestly, it sort of was. This whole story was unbelievable.

And yet, it was true.

"Why didn't you tell us?" I asked. "If this was all in the past, it wouldn't have mattered. But you left it all out."

"To be honest, when I saw you again, I thought you knew who I was. And then, when it was clear you didn't, I just..." Xavier shrugged, obviously struggling. "It was addictive. You and Sof, you're addictive. You both looked at me, and I was only Xavi again. Even when you were mad. Even when I fucked up. I hadn't had that in years. I didn't want to lose it because of some title that doesn't mean shit."

We stared at each other for a long time, green eyes meeting blue, an ocean between us.

"Do I have to call you 'Your Grace' now?" I wondered, almost laughing at the idea. The day I'd bow to Xavier Parker was the day I'd fly over the moon.

"Fuck no," Xavier replied. "For all intents and purposes, that's my uncle in everything other than name. He runs the estate. He lives there. Kendal belongs to him."

He picked up my hands and gripped them tight in front of his chest. For a moment, I had a feeling like he was going to propose. Nonsense, of course. But there it was, nonetheless.

"To you, and anyone else who matters, I'm Xavi," he said. "Maybe, if Sofia's ready, I can be Dad too. That's all that matters to me now. That's all that will *ever* matter. Ces, please. Tell me you believe me."

"I want to...but I just...Xavi, it's a lot to take in. I need some time."

"Time?" he repeated incredulously. "*Time*? Fuck time, Francesca. You've had five years with her and the last four months to get used to me again. This bullshit—history, titles, whatever—it's just details. So what do you really need here? Get down on my knees? Pray for your forgiveness? Atone for my sins?"

I perked up. Actually, that wasn't a bad idea. "You know what? Yes."

Xavier frowned. "Yes?"

I nodded. "You want to be in her life? I think it's time to do it for real. Sofia asked for you to come to Sunday Mass. Come sit through the service, and then we can tell Sofia the truth afterward at the park or something. And then you can meet the rest of my family. You're right. It's time."

I smiled at the scenario I'd been dreading for months. If Nina's appearance was any indicator, my family was all but guaranteed to jump into battle mode the moment they met Xavier. And right now, I was sort of eager to watch him wage that particular war.

But to my surprise, Xavier straightened, looked at me directly, and nodded.

"Tell me when and where. I'll show up."

28

wo days later, I stood on the front porch of Nonna's house, bouncing slightly from foot to foot while I waited for Xavier to arrive. I dressed up even more than usual for a Sunday in my favorite green polka-dotted wrap dress that flounced around my knees and matched my eyes. The sun was shining, matching the bright yellow gerbera daisies blooming on the porch. A few blocks away, Arthur Avenue was a hub of tourists and locals alike enjoying the weather with a la fresca lunch, but I barely noticed anything other than the fact that every car that drove past for the last thirty minutes was *not* the big black Mercedes.

To put it lightly, I was a ball of nerves.

Because Xavier was late. A last-minute emergency at the restaurant had prevented him from coming to Mass. Our revised plan was to take Sofia to a park as soon as he arrived, tell her the truth about Xavier, and then take her for gelato before bringing him home to meet the rest of the family.

But the May weather cooperated a little too well, and so when another text from Xavier informed me that traffic was delaying him even more, I couldn't for the life of me come up with a reasonable excuse to keep Sofia from joining her cousins at the park without letting the cat out of the bag. And so here I was, wondering what the hell I was supposed to say to my sisters when Sofia's genetic code walked through the door without a word of warning.

Finally, a familiar Mercedes pulled up to the house and Xavier jumped out of the back and practically ran up the porch steps. Clearly, he was stressed too, if the way his hair was pulled in odd directions was any indicator. His collar was also standing up on one side, and his tie, a pretty blue thing that matched his eyes and stood out from the otherwise classic white shirt and black suit he was wearing for the occasion, was yanked loose and into a horribly tight knot.

"She's still at the park?" He looked up at the house from the third step.

"Yes," I said as I strode to meet him. "Come here. You're a mess."

He waited patiently while I straightened his tie and collar, then smoothed back his hair. Our eyes met as I pushed back that errant lock.

"Thanks," he said softly.

I pressed my lips together, resisting the urge to look at his. We hadn't been this close in months, but I hadn't forgotten that salty-sweet scent of his. The one that made me want to throw my arms around his neck and kiss him until I forgot his name.

Stop it, I told myself. *You're mad at him, remember? Focus.*

I stepped back. "Look, I know we were going to find her and tell her first, but my family already knows something's up because I've been out here for the last fifteen minutes. I guarantee at least four of Nonna's friends have already spotted us, and if you don't come in soon, the whole neighborhood will be calling to ask who Frankie is talking to on the front step."

Xavier smiled grimly, reaching up to yank at his collar before I batted his hand away. "Basically, I'm fucked either way, is what you're saying."

I shrugged. "Yes. But I wouldn't use that language around Nonna if I were you."

That just earned me an eye roll. "She has a swear jar too? Ces, I'm not here for them. I'm here for Sof. Let's just go get her. Fuck the neighbors."

Above us, the second-floor curtains twitched—a telltale sign that at least one of my sisters had already spotted who was here.

I turned back to Xavier. "Look at it this way—at least if she freaks out on us, she'll have six other shoulders to cry on. Just come in and get it over with. We'll find Sofia and get us all some gelato to numb the shock."

The thought did not seem to comfort him, but he followed me inside, nonetheless, with the posture of a pirate being led to walk the plank.

Well, it wasn't far off.

"Frankie!"

The hammering of two pairs of feet down Nonna's old creaky stairs greeted us, followed by Joni and Marie toppling into the foyer, one after the other. Ah, the spies.

"Helloooo, Mr. Blue Eyes," Joni greeted Xavier with her patented flirtatious smile. "First Mattie, then you? What is in the water in Brooklyn, huh?"

"Pleasure to meet you," Xavier said stiffly, offering a hand.

"Oh my God, that *voice*!" squealed Joni, clutching her shirt with glee. "You sound just like Tom Hiddleston! Frankie, where did you meet this one, and does he have a brother?"

"Joni, can you take it down a notch or ten?" I asked, although I was a little relieved. At least she wasn't giving him the third degree.

Marie, however, wasn't so easily distracted.

"You look familiar," she said, pushing her glasses up her nose as she peered up at Xavier. "Have we met before?"

"Er, I don't think so," Xavier said, looking slightly uncomfortable with her sudden close proximity.

"Maybe from the papers?" Marie pushed. "Or do you know the Lyons from Westchester? Carmichael and Kathleen?"

"Marie," I said, pulling her off him. "Give the man some space."

"Frankie? Are you back?" Kate wandered down the hall to see what was going on, took one look at me and Xavier, and her jaw dropped to the floor. "Holy shit," she said, then immediately pivoted and marched back to the dining room.

I sighed. "Come on."

Xavier frowned. "What just happened?"

"You've been found out," I said. "Time to come in and meet everyone else."

"I don't get it," Joni said behind me. "What secret?"

"You never do," Marie told her.

"Oh, please. Like you do?"

We entered the dining room at the back of the house, stopping near a hutch to take in the scene while Marie and Joni slipped around us to find seats at the table and avail themselves of the plate of fresh berries in the center.

Xavier paused in the doorway to take in the humble space. I found myself shrinking, just like I did when he first came to the house in Red Hook. Following his gaze, I noticed all the little things that always faded into the normalcy of the place whenever I was here—the scuffs on Nonna's Queen Anne-style table, the hand-crocheted doilies stacked on the hutch, the tiny stains on the knock-off Persian rug. Everything was neat and clean, just like Nonna, but a little shabby, as a house might be after having been lived in by three straight generations.

I frowned and forced myself to stand up straight again. Maybe this wasn't what Xavier was used to. It wasn't a manor or whatever fancy place he had in London. But it was the place I had called home for most of my life—a place that, on some level, would always be home. My grandparents had worked hard to carve out this small bit of the Bronx for themselves and share it with the six of us. I could never be less than proud of that.

When he finally turned all the way back to the dining table, Xavier found my five siblings all staring at him openly. Nonna walked into the room carrying a pitcher of iced tea, took one look at Xavier, and immediately placed the pitcher on the table so she could cross herself and mutter, "*Mammamà*" under her breath.

"Apparently, it's not just me who sees the resemblance," I murmured.

"It's—you are—" Nonna looked around me, then at Xavier, then back at me. "Where is Sofia?"

"She's at the park, Nonna," Lea said. "I guess now we know why."

I swallowed. "Yeah. Um. It's time you met Sofia's dad. Everyone, this is Xavier Parker."

I waited for a response, the immediate clamor that only my family could produce. But instead, what I got was a silence so thick you could hear the screechy brakes of the Bx17 bus four blocks away.

Holy crap. Had I done the impossible? Had I stunned the Zola family into submission?

"Excuse me."

My brother's voice broke the silence at last, and I exhaled with relief. Matthew would know what to say here to make things right. I watched, grateful, as my brother rose from the other end of the table, then strode around meaningfully to where we stood.

"Hey, mate. I'm Xavier. It's great to finally meet you." Xavier held out a hand to Matthew.

My brother looked down at it, then back up at its owner. Then he pulled back his fist and punched Xavier straight in the jaw.

"What the fuck!" Xavier exclaimed, clutching his cheek.

He had been forced a few steps back, but not much more. That alone was impressive. My brother knew how to fight dirty. In his younger days, I'd seen him lay out a man with a lot less than that sort of punch, so the fact that Xavier took it cleanly was no small feat.

Even so, I was appalled.

"Mattie!" I shouted as I jumped between them. "What the hell was that?"

Matthew stood there, shaking out his quivering hand, but still keeping his gaze lasered on Xavier. "*That* was for leaving Frankie and Sofia high and dry for the last few years, *mate*. I should give you a lot worse for being engaged to another woman while you were treating my sister like your own fuckin' play toy, but there are ladies present."

"I'd like to see you try," Xavier growled, though he was smart enough not to push Matthew further.

"Oh my *God*." Kate rolled her eyes. "Could you *be* any more nineteen fifties, Matthew? Who else's delicate sensibilities are you going to protect today?"

"I wasn't talking about *you*, Katie," he snarled over his shoulder. "I was talking about Nonna."

We all quieted. Maybe none of us could be (or wanted to be) classified as "ladies," but Nonna certainly did. And where she stood clutching the edge of the hutch, she looked awfully pale.

Matthew turned back to Xavier.

"Part of me would like nothing more than to give you the beating you deserve for what you did to my sister and my niece," he informed him. "But my grandmother likes a clean floor, and I doubt she'd appreciate it painted with your blood. So here's the deal. One wrong move—just *one*—and I'll haul your ass outside and continue this lesson for the whole neighborhood to see. We clear?"

Xavier just stared down at Matthew with a murderous blue glare, but wisely remained where he was behind me, rubbing the side of his mouth. I had a feeling that if he wanted, he'd be able to give Matthew just as good as he got, and the tic in his jaw told me he was dying to try.

But this wasn't about the two of them. There were bigger fish to fry.

"Come here," I told him. "I promise my brother will behave. Won't you?" I said sharply.

Matthew just flexed his hand. "Him first."

"I have apologies to make," Xavier said. "To all of you. I know that. But in my defense, I *did* only just learn I had a daughter about five months ago. Maybe almost six now."

Around the table, there was a collective gasp. Matthew took a step back like he was the one who'd been punched.

"Six months ago," he muttered before his eyes opened wide and turned to me. "The Christmas party. When you saw him again…that's when you told him, didn't you?"

The others' heads swiveled toward me.

I swallowed, nodded, and absorbed their incriminating stares. I had nothing to justify here. I had done what I thought was best for Sofia, yes. But I was wrong. I knew it, and I wouldn't deny it.

"And since then…" Matthew shook his head. "It's been a hell of a lot more than a couple of emails and some flowers, hasn't it?"

I flapped my hands nervously. "I—yeah. He's been coming around a bit for the last few months. He and Sofia have been getting to know each other without all the pressure of…" I drifted off with a toss of my hand.

Matthew shook his head, then flopped backward into one of the empty chairs at the table.

"If it's any consolation, I didn't know either," Joni told him as she rubbed his shoulder.

Behind her, Marie snorted.

"You're damn right, we didn't," said Lea as she got up and went to guide Nonna to a chair. Nonna just batted her away, content to remain where she was at the hutch, like a cat keeping its exit at the ready.

Matthew kept running a hand through his hair, staring at the wall like he was seeing a ghost.

"I had no idea," he said, more to himself than to anyone. "All that time—right under my nose. You—Jesus, Frankie, you never said a word. Not about him. Or that you didn't tell him. Or that he's been around…Christ."

The guilt that had been cramped in my gut for months bloomed into a full-on knot. I knew he wasn't saying anything more because of the secrets he had kept about his own personal life. But that didn't mean it was okay. We were supposed to be family. Family didn't lie like this.

"How about Sofia?" Kate wondered. "Does she know now?"

I shook my head. "Not yet. We planned to tell her today. But Xavier arrived before they got back from the park, and you know how the neighbors would gossip if he just sat there…"

Immediately, all my sisters nodded their heads. We'd all been victims of the neighborhood gossip chain from time to time.

"I'm confused," Lea said sharply. "Why haven't you told Sofia before us? Don't you think that *she*, of all people, deserves to know she has a dad?"

"Of course she does," I said. "And we were going to, until, well, she went to the park, and Xavi's here, and what else were we supposed to do? Go for a walk?"

Everyone seemed to think that would have been exactly the right thing to do.

I pouted. "Well, we didn't. And now you know. So when she gets back from the park, Xavi and I are going to take her out for gelato and tell her honestly, all right? And *none* of you are going to get in the way of that. Do you understand?"

"Oh," Lea said. "*You're* Xavi. You know, when I heard her telling the boys about her new friend Xavi the other week, I thought she meant someone from school. Not a full-grown man who looks like David Gandy."

"Oh my God, he *does*," Joni tittered, though she only received a dirty look from Marie for her efforts.

"So what now?" Matthew asked sharply, cutting through the entertainment once again. "Now you know. But you're what, a duke or earl or something on top of being a hot shot restaurant owner or whatever? You don't live here. So are you going back to England all over again? Break your kid's heart alongside my sister's this time?"

Beside me, Xavier's hands balled into fists, and he started to chew his bottom lip. The rest of him was a statue. Matthew couldn't know the effect that such an accusation would have, but I did.

What I didn't know, however, was the answer to his questions. What *would* he do once Sofia found out?

"As it happens," Xavier said through his teeth, trying to be civil the same way a lion might try to charm a mouse. "I have plans to move to New York while I expand the Parker Group in America. The first restaurant opens next week in Soho. It's called Chie. That's Japanese for wisdom."

"Sofia means wisdom too."

We all turned to Nonna, who had spoken.

"It's my name too, you see," she finished. "And my great-grand-daughter's."

Everyone pivoted immediately back to Xavier.

"I know," Xavier said, meeting my grandmother's sharp gaze straight on. "That's why I chose it. I wanted the first step in this country to remind me every day of why I'm really here. It's not for a business. It's for my daughter." He swallowed, taking on a more genial tone. "And you're all welcome to attend the grand opening, by the way. As family, of course."

He couldn't have picked a better thing to say. The entire room sprang into excitement, the invitation eliciting eager smiles and jabber from Joni and Marie, tentative nods of approval from Kate and Lea, and even a look of mild respect from Matthew.

"I just want to know one thing."

Nonna's voice shut down the commotion once again. She might have been the smallest in the room, but she was undeniably the matriarch of the Zola clan. Even Matthew would have given her the shirt off his back if she asked for it.

Nonna took a few steps forward until she was less than a foot from Xavier, forcing him to hunch slightly so she didn't have to stare so far up. "Who are you really?" she asked.

Xavier looked like he was waiting for more, and when it didn't come, glanced at me as if for answers. I just shrugged. It was a simple question. How to answer it was much more complicated.

He swallowed. "They call me a lot of things back home. Some call me duke, but only if they don't know me. Others say I'm a rude offspring, a rebel heir, or maybe just a bastard, and for a long time, I believed them." He shook each of the words away like a dog shaking water off its back, then rotated slightly so he was facing everyone, not just Nonna. "But in the last six months, I've learned who I really am. I'm that little girl's father. I'm the man responsible for showing her what's right and wrong in the world, how to be treated and how to treat others, how to respect people and how to respect herself. That's all that matters to me anymore. Not my estate or business or restaurants or anything else. Just her. Just being Sofia's dad."

"You're my dad?"

Everyone in the room froze, this time including me. At my side, Xavier's eyes grew approximately the size of Nonna's dinner plates. I, for one, couldn't feel my legs. I glanced at Kate, who only just managed to give me a weak smile as all the other heads in the room began to turn one by one, mine the last, toward where Sofia stood on the stair at the entry of the room, tiny hand tucked into Nonna's skirt while her great-grandmother stroked her hair.

Sofia, however, only had eyes for Xavier, who slowly turned and found the girl who looked so much like him. If he was conscious of the seven pairs of eyes glued to him, he showed no sign of it. His attention was focused purely on Sofia as he made his way to her, then folded his legs into a squat so that he was at her level.

"That's right," he told her solemnly. "Got a bit delayed there, but yes. I'm your daddy, sweet girl. And I always will be. I promise."

His deep voice was shaking by the time he finished, though no other part of him betrayed what I knew had to be excruciating nerves. I knew because I was feeling them myself.

Sofia's eyes found me over Xavier's shoulder. "Mama?"

Silently, I nodded. "It's true, Sof."

For a split second, I wondered if she would be angry. If she would ask versions of the same questions we'd just suffered from my siblings. Why I hadn't told her? Why I'd held onto such a secret? Why I had kept him from her for so long?

But instead, my daughter turned back to the man whose eyes matched hers, gave him a grin that was brighter than any star in the universe, and launched herself at him so hard that her tiny body managed to knock his enormous one over with the force of her embrace.

"Daddy," she whispered before burying her face in his neck. "I *knew* it. I prayed and prayed for it. I did."

"That's right," Xavier whispered. "I'm your daddy. And I—" He took a deep breath. "I love you."

No one spoke. No one dared. Sofia and Xavier rocked slowly in each other's arms, whispering tiny secrets between themselves while the rest of us witnessed a solemn, if unspoken, bond that had been months in the making. Years, really. Or maybe it had been there from the start.

"Here." Kate materialized next to me with a tissue floating in her hand.

I took it, only to realize that tears were streaming down my face, just like every other person in the room, my brother and Xavier included.

"Well, fuck," Xavier laughed through his own tears, swiping them with the back of his broad hand. "I guess we've got another reason to celebrate Friday, don't we?"

"Swear jar, Daddy," Sofia said, opening up her palm expectantly.

"Ha," Matthew said even as he dabbed with his handkerchief. "At least now I won't be the only one getting that treatment."

At the casual use of "Daddy," Xavier grinned, yanked a bill from his wallet, and popped it into her hand with a kiss to her cheek.

"No, a *real* one, Dad," Sofia said.

Xavier just rolled his eyes, and I couldn't help but giggle.

"On Friday, yes," Nonna piped up, reaching down to clasp Xavi's face between her palms. "But Katie, go get the *limoncello*. In this house, we can celebrate more than once."

29

"Will you stop fidgeting already? God, Frankie, you're worse than the kids, do you know that?"

For the fourth time that evening, I stopped pulling at the hem of my dress while I waited impatiently for the car to arrive at Chie. No, not a car. A freaking limousine.

One week after his big reveal to my family, Xavier had done more than just invite us to the opening of Chie. At seven o'clock on Friday, an enormous limo pulled up outside of Nonna's house, where he'd instructed me to get ready instead of Brooklyn. It was large enough to carry all six of us, plus Sofia, Lea's brood, Nonna, even Nina wedged next to Matthew.

We hadn't even reached the restaurant, but I was already out of my league.

We were all in our finest for the event—I had planned to wear Nonna's black dress again, but Kate shook her head and pulled out something I hadn't seen in a long time—the slinky red number I'd worn the night I found out I was pregnant.

"No way," I said. "I can't pull that off anymore."

"Frankie, you teach aerobics classes four nights a week and you do crunches like it's your religion. Your ass and abs could win awards, so just put it on and see what it does."

What it did was surprise. Once I had the dress on, every one of my sisters piled into Joni's room to ooh and ahh at the thin red silk. Even Sofia darted in with the gold and white party dress that Xavier had bought her, informed me that we *both* looked like princesses, and then

ran back out in search of her stuffed unicorn, which suddenly needed a
party dress of its own.

Now we were here—the Zola family, zooming down the West Side
Highway like a bunch of movie stars, not a middle-class family from
Belmont. Kate had styled all of us using her considerable skills and the
clothes at her disposal.

"Oh my God, could you be showing any more leg?" Marie chided
Joni, who was wearing a particularly short gold number that, yes,
showed off her dancer's legs.

"Should I have dressed like a nun instead?" Joni retorted, looking at
Marie's long black dress that, while form-fitting, was fairly
conservative.

"Can you two cut it out?" I hissed. "This is a really big deal tonight,
both for Xavi and Sofia. And all of us, really. It would be nice if you
could act older than twelve for once."

"Holy crap," Joni said, ignoring me completely as she looked over
my shoulder.

The limo came to a stop. I turned to see what had her so rapt. And
was practically blinded.

Cameras were *everywhere*, and their flashes lit up the night. The
sidewalk was lined with photographers, reporters, and what looked
like the kinds of screaming fans I'd seen on E!. I could just make out
some music playing over the hum of the crowd and a searchlight
soaring upward toward the heights of the city. Beyond that I spotted
the entrance to the restaurant itself—enormous black doors, over which
a sign written in delicate, looping script read Chie.

"What is going on?" Lea asked as she stared at the crowds. "You'd
think this was a movie premiere, not just a little restaurant launch."

Beside her, Mike looked like he wanted to hurl. The boys were too
interested in a video game to notice much of anything.

"Restaurant openings are a big deal," Kate said knowingly. "Especially in New York. And especially when it's someone like the Parker
Group. I'm guessing there are a bunch of celebrities coming too."

"I'm sure," Nina said. "All the ones I've attended usually have at
least three or four."

Lea rolled her eyes but had the good sense not to say anything rude
when she caught Matthew's eye.

"We might meet someone famous?" Joni squealed. "Oh my God, I
knew I liked your man, Frankie."

"He's not my man," I said stubbornly, even while I was feeling out
of breath.

"Mama?"

I looked down at Sofia, who was clutching her stuffed unicorn against her chest and staring at the cameras. "What's up, bean?"

"Do we have to go in there?"

I looked at the cameras, then back at Sofia. "We do. Daddy's in there waiting for us. Why, does it look scary?"

Slowly, she nodded. "Daddy's in there?" she repeated.

I nodded back. "That's right. Waiting to see you. He named this place for you, you know."

At that, she grinned. She and Xavier had shared more than one FaceTime discussion this week talking about it. "Chie. It's Japanese for Sofia."

"Well, then, we'd better see what it's all about," I said. Then I turned to everyone else. "You go on. I'm going to take her around to the back entrance."

"You're not going to walk the red carpet?" Joni demanded. "That's the best part! We might even get our pictures on *Page Six*!"

But I just shook my head. "We'll be fine. Have fun."

Sofia and I waited for everyone else to exit the limo. To my surprise, Matthew and Nina remained in the car with me, apparently wanting to keep their own presence discreet as well.

"I've done enough of those for a lifetime," Nina said kindly. "You're not missing anything, I promise."

The driver took us around to the back alley, where a door was open onto the street, leading into the kitchen of the restaurant. Feeling a little like a stowaway, I followed Matthew and Nina through the kitchen, ignoring the irritated looks of the staff until we had found our way to a pair of swinging double doors through which servers were running in and out with trays and other things balanced on their shoulders.

Then we were inside. And I couldn't believe what I saw.

Xavier had designed a dream. Chie sparkled with tiny droplet lights hanging from a black-blue ceiling, over sophisticated black tables and chairs clustered throughout the large space that seemed to tunnel into the city. A long glass-topped bar wound through the room like a starlit river, beginning near us, where a live band played music to a small crowd of dancers. The bar eventually reached the other end, where a hostess stood imperiously at the front entrance.

Every other inch of the place, however, was pink and purple. Camellias, cherry blossoms, and lilacs bloomed on nearly every inch of the walls and ceiling, as well as on the table tops and arranged in vases as tall as me. It was a color scheme borrowed directly from Sofia's bedroom.

The restaurant was jam-packed, so we grabbed the first space we found—a bar style table near the dance floor surrounded by four high stools—but only after Matthew found the others at a table and a booth on the other side of the room.

I picked up one of the paper menus sitting in the middle of the table. On the back, I spotted a small children's section decorated with a tiny drawing at the top—a flower I would have bet my life had been drawn by Sofia. Beneath it was a few simple Japanese dishes: *Somen* Sofia, *Okonomi* Sofia. They were all named after her. As I read through the ingredients, I recognized bits and pieces from some of the meals he had made her over the last few months.

This wasn't just a restaurant. It was Xavier's love letter to his daughter.

"Want something?"

I jerked and turned to find Xavier standing next to us, a shy smile on his face. Even through his nerves, however, he still projected dark confidence, several inches taller than most of the people in the room and lording over this little world he had created in an exquisitely tailored black suit with satin lapels.

"Daddy!" Sofia yelped, launching herself off her stool and into his arms without a thought for his fine clothing.

Xavier didn't seem to care either.

"What do you think, Sof?" he asked her as he bounced her lightly on his hip. "Like it?"

She looked around the restaurant with the discerning eye of a food critic. "I do," she told him. "Especially the colors. You did what I said."

"Pink and purple, just for my girl," he told her. "Did you see the menu?"

"Daddy, don't be silly. I can't read."

I held it up so they could both see it.

"That's my flower!" Sofia squealed. "And that's my name!"

"That's right," Xavier said. "And see right there? It's the dish we made. *Somen* Sofia, just for you, babe."

"With the *uni* sauce?"

"Absolutely. Just for my girl."

Sofia grinned so hard it looked like her face might break, and Xavier grinned right back, their twin smiles and sapphire eyes practically lighting up our small corner of the restaurant.

Something deep in my chest tugged. Hard.

Sofia kicked her little legs, begging to be let down. "I wanna go show the boys," she said. "They didn't believe the restaurant was mine."

She snatched the menu from me and trotted off through the crowds like she owned the place. Xavier and I watched until she had reached the booth where Lea and her family were. Then Xavier turned back to me and opened his mouth like he wanted to say something. But nothing came out.

I frowned. "You okay?"

"Fucking hell," he murmured, rubbing the side of his jaw.

"What?" I asked. "What is it?"

His eyes raked down my body, then back up to my face, looking somewhat overheated by the time he was done. "Wow. That's a, um… that's a dress, Ces."

I peered down at my dress, then back up at him with a smile. I couldn't help it. Any doubts about whether or not I could still pull off this slinky thing vanished with Xavier's heated expression. "Thanks."

"No, thank *you*." He swallowed, appearing to compose himself. "Sorry. But you should know you look, ah, bloody fantastic."

His voice creaked slightly on the last word, and my smile only grew as mentally I made a note to thank Kate again for forcing me to wear it.

"*This* is fantastic," I told him, gesturing around. "I had no idea. When you said you were opening a new Japanese restaurant, I thought it would be, I don't know, like a regular sushi bar."

Xavier just smirked. "I don't do regular, Ces. You know that."

"It's for her, isn't it?" I asked. "Not just the name. The flowers, the menu, the decor. All of it."

His smirk disappeared. Looking almost bashful, he nodded. "She's been a help."

"She loves you."

"And I her," Xavier said plainly. "She's taught me…" He shook his head. "Christ, she's taught me how stupid I was about all of it. I had no idea what love was until I met her. No fucking clue."

I chuckled. "Kids have a way of doing that."

"She's not the only one."

He looked me over once more, then curiously took my hand and turned it over and back, like he was examining a precious stone, or maybe an ingredient in the kitchen. Then, slowly, he raised it up and pressed his lips to my knuckles.

"Xavi…" I started, though his hand was already slipping around my waist. I felt myself moving closer, lost, like a magnet.

For once, though, it wasn't just lust in his eyes. There was something deeper there. Some odd longing I knew was probably echoed in my own.

It wasn't a good idea.

Was it?

"Ces—" he started.

"Xavier! Mr. Parker!"

We both turned to locate the source of the interruption—a slight man with short, bleached hair waving his hand madly at Xavier.

Xavier turned back with a lopsided smile. "Shit. That's Leonard, the manager. I'd better sort that. Get you a drink later?"

I nodded. "Sure. Take your time."

———

"You know he hasn't stopped staring at you all night?"

I turned to find Kate next to me, sipping a yuzu cocktail while she peered across the room at Xavier, who was back to holding Sofia in his arms while he spoke to someone who looked a lot like Benedict Cumberbatch.

"That's a laugh," I said. "And anyway, it doesn't matter."

"It doesn't?" Kate eyed me closely. "Are you really telling me there's been nothing between the two of you since you…you know?"

I sighed. I'd broken down and told Kate about the little one-night mistake Xavier and I had made a few months ago. Just like I'd told her that since, he'd been the perfect gentleman.

Well, almost the perfect gentleman.

I shrugged. "Nothing. Not that it's a problem. It would complicate things too much."

I also wish I believed that as much as I thought I did.

"Are you sure about that? You don't think it might make things…better?"

"Kate, please. You know what he said. How is it going to make anything better for me to go down that path again? You think it's easy, watching him with her? I already know what it was like being in love with the man before he was a wonderful father. Now…" I shook my head. "He can't love me. He said so."

We both watched Sofia giggling into her dad's shoulder while he tickled her lightly and made some sort of joke. Both of their eyes gleamed.

"That doesn't look like a man who can't love to me," Kate said. "It looks like a man who is completely besotted."

"With his daughter," I told her. "We are not the same person."

"No, you aren't. But that doesn't mean he can't love you too."

I could only shrug. I knew the score. Xavier was attracted to me, sure. But sex wasn't love. I'd already made that mistake with him. I wouldn't ever do it again.

"Well, in case you meet someone else tonight, I wanted to let you know that I'm bringing Sof home with me," Kate said. "I'll take her to Nonna's in the morning. You can take your time tomorrow. Sleep in. Or, you know, *not*."

I turned. "What? Why? I don't have any other plans after this."

"*Yet*," she added meaningfully. "You don't have any plans *yet*. Don't waste a good red dress, Frankie."

Before I could argue, she strode off into the crowd, swishing her drink and her hips, clearly satisfied with putting me in my place.

"Brat," I murmured, but didn't chase her down. To be honest, I could have used a night alone. My emotions seemed to be all over the place. I needed some time to think.

"Frankie?"

I turned around to see the last person I expected to find in a place like this.

"Adam?" I wondered. "What are you doing here?"

Adam Klein looked completely different than he did at school. Dressed in a sleek gray suit, light brown hair combed back neatly. Only his tortoise-shell glasses remained of the messy art teacher I knew. He actually looked quite dapper.

"My dad knows some people. I pulled a few strings. It's a bit much, isn't it?" He gestured around. "The flowers, I mean."

I glanced around at the walls with their vibrant pinks and purples. "I think it's nice. It's for Sofia."

Adam frowned. "Sofia? You mean your kid?"

I sighed. "I—well, yes. The owner is her dad."

Adam's brows popped up well above the rims of his glasses. "Oh, that's right. I almost forgot. You'd never know."

I frowned. "You can't see it? Most people think they look like twins."

Adam only shrugged. "Honestly, I just thought she looked beautiful, like her mom."

His sideways glance was full of meaning. But I did my best not to meet it. I knew what he was doing.

"I have an idea," he said. "What about a drink and a dance instead of coffee?"

I glanced around, spotting the rest of my sisters mingling in the crowd. Joni was cutting a rug on the dance floor, twisting back and forth between two eager partners, while Matthew and Nina were swaying slowly together in one corner, uncaring for the tempo and utterly lost but for each other. Kate was at the bar, handing her card to one rich prospective client after another. Marie sat with Nonna nearby, both of them devouring plates of Xavier's scrumptious menu with glee, while next to them Lea and Mike were busy trying to keep their kids from scaling the walls.

And of course, in the middle, still held by her father like a precious bouquet of the flowers that covered the walls, was Sofia, arms wrapped around Xavi's neck while she giggled and bounced and grinned like I'd never seen.

Xavier's bright gaze lit on me, hope in his eyes, but morphed immediately into a scowl when he spotted Adam next to me.

Shit.

I sighed. Kate was wrong. Even if I wanted to put my dress to use as she suggested, this was not the place to do it, under the watchful eyes of my family and an overeager coworker. And that was even if I was in the mood to go looking for love or lust or whatever else people did in places like this.

I turned back to Adam. "I'm sorry, but I think I'll take a rain check."

He frowned. "Why, because of *him*? You can't let him run your life, you know."

"He's not," I said a little too sharply. "I'm sorry, but I really need to go."

Sometimes there were benefits to being small. Namely, the ability to move quickly through tight spaces.

Before Adam could stop me or anyone else in my family could figure out what I was doing, I deposited my glass on the bar top and darted quickly out of the restaurant. I took deep breath after deep breath as I stepped out to the curb and held up my hand for a cab.

This was right. *They* were right. Sofia was cared for. The only thing I wanted now was to go home and sort out whatever this odd feeling was in my stomach. A cross between regret, yearning, maybe something like hurt.

Whatever it was, I didn't like it.

A good book and a cup of tea would sort me out. It had to.

30

I didn't go straight home from the restaurant. Honestly, the idea of burying myself on the couch or crawling into my little space at the top of the stairs felt more than a little pathetic, and that was exactly what I was trying to escape by leaving.

Part of me wanted to stay. Xavier had so clearly made room for everyone else important to me. I should have been thankful that he was turning out to be the kind of dedicated father I myself had never had. All my fears about him and Sofia proved to be unfounded. It was more than I could have wished for. For her, anyway.

But in a way, it sort of made me feel even worse. It was clear that he could offer Sofia so much more than I ever could. His wealth, of course, made almost anything possible. But on top of that, there was simply the fact that, like the party where we had stumbled into each other, I just didn't fit into his world. That restaurant was for her—as well it should have been. And it was for the patrons, the ones who could afford to spend hundreds of dollars on the world's most expensive fish. Or girls like Joni, who loved to flirt with the kind of men who would pay for her meal regardless. Or men like Matthew, sophisticated no matter what, but even more so with someone like Nina at his side.

Me, though. No. It was like I didn't exist.

And honestly, maybe I shouldn't.

So I went to a place I always went when I needed a bit of cheering up—a bookstore. And after treating myself to a cup of tea and some Brontë, eventually I found my way back to Red Hook.

It hadn't quite worked, though. I had wanted to dive into *Jane Eyre*

and get lost in the fantasy of Mr. Rochester along with her. Instead, I
kept coming back to the moment St. John finds her on the moor. When
she's lost, fleeing the house so far above her station, where she believed
for one fleeting moment she might belong.

Except she didn't.

The problem, I supposed, was that yet again I was faced with an
impossible circumstance and impossible choice. Story of my life.

No one expects to get pregnant out of nowhere. No one expects the
father to all but disappear. No one expects for him to show up again
and turn out to be a duke of all things like you're actually living in a
Julia Quinn novel.

Then again, no one expects the duke to be sitting on their doorstep
either.

Well, not unless you're a duchess.

Nevertheless, there he was, sitting on my front stoop, elbows
balanced on his knees, tuxedo jacket undone, neck freed from the top
buttons of his shirt, black tie dangling down his shirtfront. He looked
more than worse for wear, tired and tortured. But like a still-life painting, as beautiful as ever.

"Xavier?" I asked.

He jerked up, a few black locks dangling over his forehead. His blue
eyes shone with fury and concern.

"Jesus, Francesca. Where the fuck have you been?"

I frowned as I drew my keys from my purse. "What do you mean,
where have I been? Why aren't you at your opening?" I looked around.
"Where's Sofia?"

The question was automatic before I recalled my sister's offer.

"With Kate," Xavier confirmed. "You don't think I would have left
her there."

I swallowed guiltily. Of course, he wouldn't.

Oddly, it only made me return to that feeling of uselessness. At least
five months ago, I had parenthood over him. I knew when she was
hungry and when she was tired. I could trust that I'd never forget her
places and remember her favorite stuffed animal. My family helped,
yes, but no one could ever replace her parent.

Now, what was I good for?

"What are you doing here?" I asked.

Xavier frowned. "Ces, what do you think I've been doing? I went
out looking for you—fucking everywhere, I might add. Why haven't
you answered your phone?"

I took it out and only then realized it had run out of battery long ago.

He just shook his head. "Had the car take me to every bloody book-shop in Manhattan."

"I went to one in Brooklyn," I murmured.

Xavier did not look impressed. "Why?"

I toyed with the keys in my hand.

Xavier didn't press, but I could feel that insistent blue gaze on me anyway.

Finally, he stood, taking a few short steps toward me on the walk. "Who are you now, then? Which book is it?"

I closed my eyes. How did he always know?

"*Jane Eyre,*" I mumbled, knowing there was no way I'd get out of admitting it.

"*Jane Eyre,*" he repeated. "I've heard of it. What's that one about?"

I looked up incredulously. "You've never read *Jane Eyre*? Isn't that required for everyone on your side of the pond?"

"This might shock you, Ces, but when I was in school, I was more interested in watching football and riding motorbikes than reading old books. But I will now if it means that much to you."

The idea of Xavier curling up by a fire with one of the Brontë sisters was enough to make me laugh.

Well, almost.

"So what happens in it, then?"

I sighed. "It's the story of a young girl who comes from nothing. She's brought to the estate of a wealthy man—Mr. Rochester—to care for his ward. Against all odds, she falls in love with him, but on their wedding day, his secret comes to light—that he's married to a madwoman in the attic, and that Jane has no place as his bride. Heart-broken, she runs away."

There was more to the plot, of course. But I'd only flipped through it at the shop, skipping to the parts I'd read so many times before, though it certainly spoke to me differently today.

I looked up at him, willing my chin to stop quivering, my eyes to stop watering, my entire body to stop shaking. Could he really not see what must have been written plainly all over my face?

"'Do you think, because I am poor, obscure, plain, and little, I am soulless and heartless?'" I whispered, reciting from my favorite passage.

Sometimes only another's words will do.

Xavier blinked. "It's a quote, isn't it? You've just given me another quote."

Cheeks pinked, I nodded. "From the book, yeah."

Two large fingers slid under my chin, tipping it up so I was faced with the blue abyss of his starry eyes.

"I don't think you're any of those things."

"Even little?" I wondered.

One side of his mouth rose slightly but fell right back down again. "Maybe little. But the others? Not at all. Poor and obscure? No. Plain? Try beautiful. Soulless and heartless? Farthest from it."

I bit my lip. It was hard to believe.

"Why would you think I did? It was a restaurant opening, Ces, not a wedding. And there's no madwoman in my attic."

I closed my eyes, despite being held. The intensity there was too much. Xavier was always too much.

"I just felt...don't get me wrong, Xavi. It was beautiful. You should be so proud, and I know Sofia loved it. Just like she adores you." I sighed. I loved that she loved him. "I also know that I had no part in it. I didn't belong there." I shook my head. "I never thought I would feel that way with my family. Around my own daughter. But I can't pretend she needs me quite so much when she's with you. So I thought it would be best if I left. Let you share your victory together. You deserve to have things to share on your own with her. Just like I did for the last four years."

Xavier blinked silently for a long time as he processed my words.

I sighed. Maybe there was no point in explaining this at all. Maybe it was time I just accepted the inevitable.

"It's all right," I whispered. "I won't get between you two anymore."

Eyes prickling, my vision wet and blurry, I tried to push past him. A hand on my wrist stopped me.

"Ces."

I gasped. "Xavi, please let me pass."

He didn't, though. Instead, he pulled me back to face him. Standing on the stoop in my heels, I was still nowhere near eye to eye with him. But there wasn't so far to look either.

"Don't you understand?" he said, gripping my hand tightly. "You don't need to worry about getting between us. We need you there, Ces. We don't work without you."

"I know," I said sadly. "I'm the glue. For now. Don't worry, Xavi. I'll make sure you catch up. I'll help you remember the birthdays and the playdates and stuffed animals she likes and her favorite foods. I'll help you catch up so no matter who she's with, she'll always feel at home. But I know she has a family with you now just like she does with me. She deserves that. I won't stand in the way anymore, that's all."

I would too, even if the very idea of sharing her with someone made my skin crawl. I could see it now. Xavier would return to England, and he would go back to his life there, whatever that meant. Dazzling parties like the one he'd just thrown. Sumptuous manor in the Lakes District. The London Season or jet-setting around Europe. He'd take Sofia with him wherever he could, and I wouldn't be able to deny her, because I knew how much she loved him.

And maybe it would be fine for a while. Until, of course, he found a duchess to join them, someone who would be just as tall and beautiful and charismatic as he was.

I only hoped she would love Sofia too.

Xavier just stared at me for what seemed like hours, brow furrowed as if he was trying to decipher a recipe in a foreign language.

Then, at last, he shook his head emphatically. "No."

I blinked. "*No?*"

"That's right," he said. "No."

"But—what? What about everything you said to her at Nonna's? How you were at the restaurant?" My melancholia was quickly evaporating. "Xavi, what the hell? You said you loved her? You *told* her that!"

"I do love her," he said emphatically. "Of course I do. But Ces, you're missing something fucking important. I also love you."

My mouth dropped open in utter shock.

"Say something," he prodded.

How could I say anything when I could hardly breathe?

"Xavi," I whispered. "Don't."

Once again, the words from *Jane Eyre* floated through my mind. He couldn't really be this cruel, could he? He couldn't really believe I was so heartless it wouldn't matter.

"Why?" Xavier demanded, taking my shoulders and shaking them slightly. "Why can't I say it?"

"Because I can't take it if it's not true!" I burst out. "I barely managed to put my heart back together after you broke it before. But now…"

I closed my eyes. But now, all I could see were him and Sofia together. Everything was muddled.

"What, Ces? Don't hold back on me now."

"Now, I'd be ruined," I said softly. "I'd never recover. I'd be that girl, wandering the moor, dying slowly of a shattered heart."

"Francesca Zola." His breath was warm and sweet on my face as he clasped my cheeks and nuzzled my nose with his. "*We're* a family," he said solemnly. "You. Me. Our perfect, beautiful daughter. I adore Sofia for her own sake, yes. But, baby—Francesca—if she is the newest piece of my world, *you* are the sun we both revolve around."

I hiccupped a sob. "I can't—I can't believe that could possibly be true."

"Believe it," Xavier said and set his lips on mine. "Don't fight it. I love you, Ces. I'll say it again and again until you believe it. But you can't stop it. It's inevitable, just like us."

He kissed me again, and with every touch of his mouth, every insistent lick of his tongue, I felt my defenses crumble.

Love. Xavier Parker loved *me*.

Suddenly, I couldn't get close enough. My arms twisted around his neck, pulling him down so I could devour every bit of him. Tears were rolling down my cheeks, seasoning our kiss with their salty flavor. Love, pain, lust, desire. All of it was mixed together, and the taste was intoxicating. I felt myself lifted off the stoop, then returned to my feet only to be walked backward until my back hit the front door.

"Please," Xavier mumbled against my mouth before his lips dropped a line of kisses down my neck. "Let me in, Ces. Let me in forever."

31

S omehow, I twisted around and managed to unlock the door,
even with his enormous body pressed against me. But as soon
as the door was opened, Xavier swept me up princess-style in
what I was starting to consider his trademark move.

"Let someone carry you for once," he said as he kicked the door
shut, then turned for the stairs.

Up we went, mouths fused until, finally, I was set on my feet once
more on the floor of the landing. Xavier's palms slid up my neck to
frame my face.

"So beautiful," he murmured, eyes drifting over my nose, cheeks,
lips. "So perfect."

"I'm not perfect," I protested weakly.

His hands slid back down over my neck and shoulders, taking with
them my shawl and the thin straps of my red dress. Down they went,
over my arms, my hips, until I stood in front of him in nothing but my
underwear and shoes.

Xavier's full mouth hung slightly open, like a starving man at a
buffet.

"I don't think you could ever convince me of that," he said, then
swept me up once more and turned to lay me gently on my bed.

I watched, transfixed, as he made quick work of his shirt and jacket,
tossing them carelessly onto the chair next to us. The moonlight
streaming through my small window cast a silvery halo over his lanky
form, softening the sharp lines of his chest, arms, and shoulders. The

tattoos curving up and down his right arm glowed, but not so much as his eyes as he looked down at me.

Love. That was what I saw there. Lust, desire, yearning—that too. But all of it was wrapped in pure, unadulterated love I'd never received from anyone. Not even my family.

I reached up. "Don't leave me here alone."

"Never," he promised as he kneeled on the floor beside me. "I'll never leave you or her again."

He pressed kisses along around my waist, across the ridges of my hip bones, and lingering over the softer part of my stomach, the place that no matter how many crunches I did, no matter how many aerobics classes I taught, would never again be perfectly flat.

"I wish I could have seen her here," he said, hands cupping a nonexistent bump just under my navel.

I weaved my fingers into his hair, luxuriating in its silky softness. "I wanted you here. Xavi, I'm so sorry—"

"Shh. I know."

He rested his chin on my hip and looked up at me. For a moment, we didn't speak. I trusted he could see the regret in my eyes, know the pain I still felt over stealing that part—or any part—of her life from him, even if it's what I believed was necessary at the time. In his face, however, I only saw forgiveness and love. The knowledge that if we were to continue this path together, there could only be trust between us. And that it was time to let the past go.

I relaxed and smiled. And to my utter delight, he smiled back, shining the light of his joy over both of us before he turned his head and pressed his cheek to my stomach. Then he continued delivering kisses down my body, taking my underwear with him until I lay naked on the bed.

"I love this," he whispered as his lips feathered over my sensitive skin. "And this." Gently, his hands pushed my legs apart. "And this."

His mouth landed on my clit, locating that most sensitive part of me. I arched naturally into his touch, allowing him to slip his hands under my bottom and hold me up to his lapping tongue.

"Xavi," I gasped.

"Mmm," he hummed, sending a delicious vibration through me while he worked.

My thighs clenched around the breadth of his shoulders. His hair fell forward, tickling the insides of my thighs while his hand teased the wet entrance that was aching for him—any part of him.

His finger dipped inside, soon joined by another. Curled within me. And pressed.

I started to shake.

"Xavi, *please*," I begged, though I couldn't have said for what. "Please, I can't…"

"Yes, you can," he grumbled before nipping me lightly between his lips. "Come for me, Ces. Show me how much you want me."

Three fingers slipped inside, stretching, rubbing, offering the delicious friction that, combined with his mouth, was quickly my undoing.

My fingers threaded into his hair, and I yanked. Hard. My eyes shut tightly, and automatically, my mind searched for something, anything, to latch on to. A character. A story. Erotic or not, but anything that could help me toward that final destination.

"Focus," he ordered, then sucked hard again. "You're here, not in some fucking book."

"I know," I whimpered. "Xavi, I know."

"Then think of me, beautiful girl. It's me with my mouth on your pussy. Me worshipping your beautiful body." He punctuated every statement with a vicious swipe of his tongue, a thrust of his fingers. "Me that loves you, Francesca."

Love.

It was all I needed.

"Oh!" I cried as my orgasm overtook me. "Xavi!"

He feasted on me as if his life depended on it, tongue and hand moving in disciplined, concentrated movements designed to draw out my ecstasy. I vibrated under him as waves of pleasure pulsed through me.

It didn't get any better than this. It couldn't.

Until he showed me how.

Slowly, so slowly, I came back down to earth, only to find him watching me with a satisfied half-smile. His gaze drifted down my body, hovering between my legs. My own gaze dropped below his waist as he stood to remove his pants and boxers. His erection sprang free, solid and demanding.

I licked my lips.

"One day," he said as he found a condom from his pants pocket before dropping them back to the floor, "it will be only us. No barriers. Nothing between us. You know that, don't you?"

I could barely nod.

"Yes," I managed in a voice torn with lust. But then I swallowed, reached up and stopped him just before he rolled on the thin bit of latex. "It could start now."

Xavier froze, as if he wasn't sure I'd actually spoken. "Are you—are you sure?"

I swallowed. "I—if you're safe, then yes."

He nodded. "I—there's been no one else since you and I—and I was tested just before coming here."

I exhaled. I didn't want to think about him with anyone else. It was a small relief that we had started on somewhat of a clean slate, so to speak.

"I'm on the pill," I whispered, grasping for his hand. "And there's only been you, Xavi. You know it's only ever been you."

He shuddered as if the truth of my piety to him was too much to bear. "Christ, woman. You've no idea what that does to me."

Without a second more hesitancy, he tossed the condom aside, then pulled my legs apart so he could kneel fully between them. I wriggled under his touch, eager to feel him inside me. But he maintained my legs in a steely hold, staring between them with the look of a man who had just reached the promised land. His cock rested lightly at my aching entrance. Teasing. Provoking.

He slid inside less than an inch. "God, I could tear this body in two, Francesca. But I don't want to hurt you."

His words vaguely registered. My God, he really had no idea. I wasn't the delicate virgin he had known five years ago. I was a mother. My body had been through more than he could possibly imagine.

I grabbed his chin, reveling in the sandpaper texture of his unshaven jaw.

"Believe me," I said clearly. "You won't."

He grunted and surged forward, seating himself fully within me on a low, guttural groan. "Oh, *fuuuucckkk*."

I arched back with a gasp, spreading my legs wider to take him fully. He was so big, yes, but still utterly perfect, the shape of him fitting to every part of me with undeniable precision.

His lips found my breast, pulling the berry of my nipple into his mouth and sucking hard as he pulled out and then thrust in, harder this time, eliciting moan after moan that I couldn't muffle if I tried.

"Fuck," he breathed again against my neck. "Fucking hell, Francesca."

My fingers clawed at his broad back. "Xavi, don't stop! Take all of me, please."

"Never," he growled.

He pushed up onto his knees, then grabbed my thighs and tilted my hips up to meet him, pound for unmerciful pound. His hands gripped hard enough I knew they would leave bruises, and yet I urged him on, rocking upward, reaching overhead to grab the iron rods of my headboard, and shouting my desire into the night, sure it and he would swallow me whole.

Suddenly, he pulled out and flipped me over onto my front, hips yanked back as he drove into me with ruthless precision. He took harsh handfuls of my backside, kneading and slapping as if he were shaping me into one of his culinary masterpieces.

"Fucking hell," he barked as his thumb tickled just around the last, undiscovered part of me, only a few inches from where he currently resided.

He wanted more. I could tell he wanted more. But he was still afraid to ask for it.

"Do it," I ordered sharply, more on instinct than anything else. "I mean it, Xavi. *All* of me. I belong to you."

In response, his groan practically shook the room. His hand darted back to his mouth, and when it returned, I shivered in pleasure as his finger pressed against my delicate rosette.

He paused, pulling out so that his cock was only an inch or so inside me, throbbing at the entrance of my pussy. Then, at an excruciatingly slow pace, he pressed back in while his thumb made the same journey at my ass. Inch by delectable inch, he entered both parts of me at once. Taking me everywhere. Worshipping all of me.

The feel of that slow, purposeful penetration in not one but two places was too much to bear. Then, slipping a hand over my hip, he located my clit, essentially trapping my pelvis with the power of his fingers for a few final thrusts until, on a shout, I exploded under him.

"Xavier!" I called, clawing at my pillow, trying to escape the shocks overwhelming me, yet internally begging that they would never stop.

"Francesca!" he roared, taking a few final, utterly brutal thrusts.

We shook together on my small bed so hard I thought the entire house might crumble around us. At last, his hands left me as he fell forward, pressing me into the mattress while he emptied himself inside me.

"Francesca." This time it was a depleted moan, not a shout, directed into the crook of my shoulder, his breath warm against my neck.

For a few moments longer, we just lay together, sharing breath and sweat and the glow that remains even after the throes of ecstasy subside.

Then he pushed himself up and pulled out, gently rolling me over so I was facing him once more.

"I love you," he said as he pressed kisses to my lips, cheeks, chin, and eyes. "Do you believe it?"

Still caught in my post-coital daze, I nodded. "Yes, I believe it."

"Then the next time you want to run away into one of your books because you're scared, will you tell me so I can remind you again?" His hips pressed forward, informing me just how he intended to do that.

I smiled against his lips. "Yes, I will."

"Good," he said as he buried his face into my neck. "Because I meant what I said earlier too. I just don't work without you, Ces. I've been trying for too long. I don't like who I've become."

I sighed, wrapping my arms around his shoulders. "It goes both ways, my love."

He pressed up onto his forearms. "Do you really mean that? You've never said it. I don't want to force you, but…"

He drifted off, uncertainty playing over his strong features as his eyes darted over my face, unwilling to meet mine.

I blinked in confusion, retracing my words from earlier. Between quoting Charlotte Brontë and crying my fears, was it possible I hadn't actually told the man the truth that lay deep in my heart?

I looked back at him, begging his blue eyes to meet my own, wanting to dive into them, swim in them, and let him feel every emotion pulsing through me, emotions *he* inspired.

But for now, I had only words.

My words.

Simple and true.

So I gave them up.

"I love you," I told him honestly.

And meant it with all my heart.

32

Have you ever woken up thinking that a dream was real?

How about when you think reality might be the dream itself?

I'd had a few of those moments in my short life. When Sofia was born.

And the morning after Xavier Parker, Duke of Kendal, said he not only loved the little girl we made together, the daughter he never knew he had, but that he also loved me too. Small, inconsequential, nobody Francesca Zola.

But not to him.

The light shining in through the window above my bed seemed exceptionally bright this morning. Warmer than usual, even for a gorgeous May Saturday where I was alone without the wake-up call of my daughter or the rustle of Matthew (who seemed to have stayed with Nina last night).

But it wasn't the glow of spring or the house's quiet outside that cast the world with such a perfect hue. It was the golden aura of the man surrounding me on my tiny twin mattress.

"Xavi," I whispered, more to taste his name on my tongue than because I wanted anything.

"I'm awake." His voice was scratchy but had the warmth of a fire-place of embers.

I just hummed and pressed my face into his chest. Is this how Rapunzel felt when the prince finally found his way up to her tower?

Who knew? Or even cared?

Right now, not I.

"Who are you pretending to be now?" Xavi wondered.

I smiled but shook the character away. I wasn't trapped in an attic or a tower, or any other sort of place. I was in my own bed, in my own home, nestled with the man I loved. A man who had spent the majority of the night showing me in every way possible just how he loved me too.

Francesca Zola, this is your life.

"No one," I said honestly. "Just me."

I turned and set my chin on his chest, if only so I could look up and catch the light on the edge of his cheekbone.

He looked down. "If you tell me this can't happen again, Ces, I'm more than happy to show you all over again why it must."

I grinned against his pec. "It can't happen again."

"Minx."

"Devil."

For that, I was flipped onto my back, Xavier caging me against my little mattress. My bed frame shrieked in protest, and Xavier cringed.

"I need to get you out of this bed," he said. "It's too bloody small."

"Why are you so tall?" I wondered as he nosed his way down my neck. "Aren't Japanese people usually on the smaller side like me?"

"As it happens, the height is from the Parker side. My grandfather was apparently six foot six. But that's a gross stereotype, Ms. Zola."

"Yes, but isn't it kind of accurate?"

He chuckled. "I did bang my head in parking garages in Japan. And shower nozzles only came to my chest."

I giggled, imagining Xavier smashed inside a tiny shower.

"You laugh, but it was sort of miserable."

"And you dealt with it for two years?"

He shrugged. "I had other things to focus on at the time. And it's not like everything in New York fits either. I do miss my flat in London. I had everything designed to accommodate. The bath, the counters, the ceilings. Everything is tall enough." He sighed. "Bliss."

"Like Julia Child?"

For that, I received a flick on my shoulder.

"Ow!"

"That's what you get for being cheeky."

He tipped my chin up and delivered a kiss—also apparently retribution. What started quick, however, morphed into something slower, languid. People said a lot of things about Xavier Parker, but the man knew how to take his time and do a job right.

By the time he was done, though, another thought had entered my mind. One I couldn't quite shake.

"So, you'll go back, then?" I asked. "To London."

"I…well, I don't know," he said honestly. "I thought I'd stay here for a bit. If the restaurant does well, it would make a bit of sense to open a few more up and down the East Coast. I could make New York my base of operations."

"What about your other restaurants? Your estate? Your whole life back there?" Something told me that the history with his father and uncle wasn't finished.

"I've access to a plane, haven't I? I can run a bloody empire from anywhere."

Any further protestations were interrupted by another thorough kiss.

"Ces," he murmured.

"Mmm?"

"Shut up. I'm staying."

Relief washed through me before I could stop it. Slowly, my lips curved into a smile against his.

"You going to say something?" he mumbled.

"You told me to shut up."

Now his smile matched my own. "I'm glad you're finally listening."

After another brief but equally thorough kiss as the last, Xavier rolled me carefully into the corner of the bed, then reached his arms overhead, took hold of my headboard and gave an almighty stretch before curling up in a motion that made every bricked muscle of his abdomen stand out in high relief. I watched with overt appreciation as he stood, unabashed in his nakedness while he located his clothes.

"Stop staring," he said without even looking.

"Can't," I said. "You take up the whole room."

There was an audible snort. "Coffee? Or at least tea?"

"English breakfast, of course." I shoved out of bed and grabbed my robe off the hook on the wall. "Give me five minutes, I'll bring you a cup."

I grabbed my phone to send Kate a quick text while I jogged downstairs to make us both some tea and hopefully locate something else in the pantry that wouldn't completely earn Xavier's disgust. Before I could even put on the kettle, however, my phone chimed.

"Xavi?" I called absently, walking back up the stairs as I flipped open my messages.

"What d'you need, babe?" He popped out of the bathroom dressed only from the waist down, hair slightly wet.

"Do you take cream or sug—what the hell?"

I couldn't get out the question before my legs turned to noodles in complete and total shock.

"Ces!"

Xavier caught me just before I slumped onto the top stair.

"What the fuck just happened?" he sputtered, checking me up and down. For bruises? I wasn't sure " Are you all right?"

"I'm—this—look at this!"

I flipped my phone around to show him a text message notification from my bank containing a receipt of funds.

Xavier glanced at it, then back at me. "What's that?"

"It's from my bank. Someone just put over two hundred thousand dollars into my account!"

His big shoulders relaxed. "Oh, that," he said flippantly, almost immediately getting up when he was sure I was stable. "I was wondering if you'd noticed, or if you just didn't care."

I was having a hard time speaking. I barely even noticed that he was still only clad in boxer briefs that left absolutely nothing to the imagination.

"Xavi." I made a wild grab for his arm before he could walk away. "Did you do this?"

He shrugged. "Few days ago, yeah. Must've just gone through."

"And you didn't think to tell me about it?"

He just rolled his eyes. "Well, I owe you about five years of child support. Consider that a start, yeah?"

I gasped. "Xavi, that's more than I make in a single year. Or…four, actually!"

He nodded, unfazed. Then he frowned. Finally catching the concern on my face, he squatted down and sat next to me at the top of the stairs.

"Ces, for the last four years, you've been raising our daughter alone."

"Yes, but…that was *my* fault."

"It wasn't only your fault. And anyway, I owe you a lot more than that," he said. "Look at you. Look at where you are. I know your brother's done a lot for the two of you, but can you honestly say you want to sleep at the top of a stairwell for the rest of your life?"

He gestured behind him to the humble area where we'd just spent the night together. I followed his hand. Honestly, I sort of looked at the space in a new light, considering everything we'd just done. That said…

I swallowed. "Of—well, of course not. But—"

"Good. Because I don't fancy spending another night in your single. I love you, babe, but I couldn't feel my feet when I woke up this morning."

I giggled. "I think your shoulders take up almost the entire thing too."

"Exactly."

We both chuckled, then, but his smile faded quickly.

"I want my family in a place where we can all stay together." He tipped his head, looking for all the world like a nervous young man getting ready to ask a girl he liked to the movies. "What do you say?"

I frowned. "I…I'm not sure what you're asking here."

"It's not rocket science, Ces. If I stay in New York, will you and Sof move in with me?"

For a moment, I couldn't breathe. I had too many questions. Where exactly would he want to live? How would we handle things like rent and rooms and furniture, not to mention the absurd amount of money sitting in my bank account? Xavier clearly wanted to take care of me and Sofia, but there was something about the arrangement that made me slightly uncomfortable. I wasn't anyone's kept woman.

To his credit, he managed to wait patiently while I thought things through. His eyes, though, were large, earnest, and oceanic.

But before I could answer, his phone rang.

That earnestness transformed into a scowl as he glanced at the number and answered it.

"Jag. I'm kind of in the middle of something. You mind if I call you back?"

I watched as the levity on his face slowly drained away.

"He *what*?" Xavier's eyes shuttered, and when they opened, looked stone cold. "Right. Yeah. I'll let you know." He ended the call, then stood without looking at me and yanked on a few articles of clothing. "I've got to make another call outside. Back in a moment."

With a quick kiss to my cheek, he was gone.

I sat at the top of the stairs for a few more minutes, pondering my fate. But when he didn't immediately return, I got up and went back downstairs to finish our tea and make some toast. Xavier probably wouldn't eat it, but at least it was something to do while I tried to navigate the seismic turns my life was taking.

A bit later, Xavier came back inside, still shirtless under his tuxedo

jacket, apparently uncaring that he had just paraded half naked in front
of the entire neighborhood for the last fifteen minutes. I was sitting at
the kitchen counter having a second piece of toast with butter along
with the proper pot of tea I'd made and the two cups I'd set out quite
proudly.

"Tea?" I started but stopped when I caught a look at his pale face.
"Oh my God, Xavi, what's wrong?"

He rubbed his brow so hard I thought he might take off some skin.
"My uncle."

"Your—oh, you mean your dad's brother? The one who runs the
estate?"

He nodded shortly but didn't say anything more.

Please, I begged internally. *He's had so much loss. He doesn't need any
more.*

"It's not that," he said. "He's disappeared."

I reared. "What? How?"

In an apparent daze, he could only shrug. "Don't know. He's just…
gone. The housekeeper at Corbray Hall hasn't seen him for a week, and
no one at the London house has been able to find him either. He went
hunting in Scotland, and that was three weeks ago. Without him,
there's no one to manage the estate. The tenants, the portfolio, the
manor. All of it." He looked up, brow crinkled with tension. And fear.
"Ces, I have to go back."

And just like that, my heart broke, both for me and for my daughter.
This was a disaster of the first order. He couldn't ignore it—that was for
sure. No matter how flippant he was about his father's holdings, I
knew Xavier cared about them and his history. He wouldn't just
abandon them. Not after all they'd cost him.

But, of course, that meant a loss for us. Managing something like
this could take months, maybe longer. Sofia would have to say goodbye
to the father she'd only just gained. And I would have to give away the
man I loved for the second time in my life.

"Francesca."

I looked up, sucking in sharp breaths if only to stifle the tears that
threatened. He didn't need me to fall apart on him now. He had enough
to handle.

But *oh*, it was hard.

Xavier reached out a big hand and gently, so gently, wiped away the
tear that tracked down my cheek.

"Damn," I whispered. "Oh, damn."

"No, Ces. Listen," he said softly.

I looked up, waiting for the death blow. He was going to break my heart all over again. I just knew it. "I want you to go with me. Please. Will you and Sofia come with me to London?"

I gasped. "You—you want me to move to London?"

"That's right. Will you?"

EPILOGUE

Xavier

"You've got the plushy ducks on the bed?"

Elsie nodded but didn't look up from her phone, where she appeared to be checking things off with her stylus. "Yes, sir. All three."

"The mum, the dad, *and* the baby?"

"Right there on her pillow. First thing she'll see in her new room." Elsie finally looked up at me over the rims of her thick acrylic frames. "I'm sure she'll love them."

I sat back in my seat of the Range Rover and pressed my hands together. It had been nearly a month since Francesca had agreed to bring Sofia and spend the summer with me in the UK. She'd asked for a few days to think about it, which only gave me a minor heart attack. But a few more nights together showing her that I loved her and our daughter more than anything on the planet had, in the end, convinced her to take the leap.

What was she going to do? Choose her brother's stairwell landing over the love of her life?

Well, I hoped I was the love of her life. I knew without a doubt she was the love of mine.

Maybe that was why I felt so nervous now that I was about to pick her up from Heathrow. For the last four weeks, I'd been splitting my time between Paris and London, getting Jagger started on the next

Parker Group location while preparing my flat for its two newest residents.

Meanwhile, my uncle was still missing from Corbray Hall, a fact that neither the police nor the private investigator I'd hired had any answers to. He'd gone stag hunting near Inverness at the beginning of May and had disappeared off the face of the earth. We shared no love, but I wouldn't have wished the man dead. Particularly since he fulfilled nearly every role expected of the Duke of Kendal other than holding the title itself.

Now, that had to be me.

I shook my head. Somehow, I'd managed a few trips to Cumbria over the last few weeks. Enough to appoint a new steward and make sure the tenants were happy, nothing was burned down, and things were generally in order. So far, Freddy seemed to be doing all right. But I knew my stepbrother wasn't a long-term solution.

I shook my head. I didn't want to get sucked into the family drama right now. After five years, I was being forced to reacquaint myself again with what exactly it meant to be Rupert Parker's son, even if he wasn't around anymore. That in itself was hard enough without considering everyone else's thoughts on the matter.

And right now, I had more important things to consider.

Two more important people, to be precise. Who were arriving from JFK in about thirty minutes.

I turned to my other side and nudged Jagger in the gut. God, I was nervous.

"I told you, I have to work up the numbers on Kendal before I can tell you whether or not we can reopen the pub there," he said irritably. "It's going to take some time."

"It's not that," I said. "It's the other...you know."

I noticed Elsie stiffen. Shit. I should have waited until we were out of the car to ask.

Jagger glanced at me, then recognition dawned on his goateed face. "Right, right, right. Yeah, I picked it up. You sure you want it now, though?"

He nodded toward the front seat, where Elsie was clearly pretending not to listen.

I made a face. "Mmm. Maybe not. I want to be prepared, though. When the time's right."

Jagger nodded. "I'll slip it to you when we're out."

"Oh, please."

We both looked up to find Elsie spinning around in her seat to eye us both.

"I don't know why you bother trying to hide things from me," she informed me. "I saw the requisition form on your desk last week. So go on, then. I want to see it too."

I drooped. I really couldn't keep a secret from these two.

Elsie just pointedly looked at Jagger, who looked at me.

I shrugged. "Let's have it, then."

My best friend reached into his coat pocket and pulled out the small leather box I'd asked him to retrieve before picking me up. I took it from him, then held it out between the three of us. My stomach was in knots.

"Open it, then," Elsie prodded. "We haven't got all day."

I flipped open the top, revealing the engagement ring I'd commissioned the day after I'd come back to New York. Not a week after Francesca had agreed to follow me here.

Elsie gasped.

Jagger hummed with approval.

I just nodded, satisfied with the result.

It was a nice ring. The best, in fact. I'd toured every major antique dealer until I'd found a setting that truly felt like Francesca—a Georgian cluster ring fashioned around 1800, right when her favorite novels took place. I could just see her looking at it, thinking of its history, fancying herself one of the characters from Jane Austen's works. Elizabeth Bennett, probably. Although Fanny Price ran a close second.

Yes, I'd read both *Pride and Prejudice* and *Mansfield Park*. In fact, I'd read almost everything of Austen's while I waited for Francesca to finish the school year and pack her things. I wanted to know why the woman was so bloody obsessed.

They weren't half bad for something that old.

The stones of the ring, however, were new. They had been replaced with every pink diamond I—or at least the good men at Cartier—could track down. Forty-eight in all, clustered together like a bouquet of camellias and amounting to more than eight carats of pink stardust. It was perfect for her, and I couldn't wait to see her wear it.

If, of course, she said yes.

"You're not going to do it at the airport, are you?" Jagger asked.

I snapped the box shut and popped the ring into my jacket pocket. "Are you mad? I've had enough problems with the paparazzi without inviting them to my engagement."

The tabloids had fixated on me after news of my uncle's disappear-

ance had hit the papers. It had been a few years since I'd been of interest. Errant dukes seem to do that in England, though once I faded out
of the picture, so did their interest. But now that I was forced back into
the position, the papers seemed to follow my every move. I probably
should have sent Jagger alone to pick up Francesca and Sofia.

But I couldn't. I needed to be the one to welcome my girls. Me and
no one else.

The Range Rover pulled to a stop outside the terminal, and the three
of us got out.

"Wait at the short stay car park, Ben," I called to the driver. "Elsie
will let you know when we're ready."

Ben nodded and pulled away.

I glanced around. We were at the far end of the terminal, away from
the usual spot where the paps hung out, waiting for famous arrivals.

"There." Jagger pointed to a man slouched against one of the big
cement columns, a camera slung around his neck.

"Shit," I muttered, turning away.

"I'll talk to him," Elsie said and immediately took off down the
sidewalk. "Excuse me, sir!" she cried in her patented "old lady needs
help" voice. "Can you *please* help me locate the departures for Valencia?
I'm about to miss my flight, and I've no clue where I'm supposed
to be!"

I smirked. Elsie visited her daughter and grandson in Spain at least
once a month, and as a result, probably knew Heathrow better than
most of its employees.

The photographer looked appropriately bewildered by being
accosted by a shrieking twin of Dame Angela Lansbury.

On her cue, I followed Jagger into the terminal without being spotted. My height was always a giveaway, though right now I looked more
like someone's assistant than a CEO, dressed down in jeans, a T-shirt,
and an Arsenal hoodie to cover my tattoos. Elsie could talk the ear off
an elephant, but I'd likely be recognized again.

The ring in its box thumped against my chest with every step.

"Attention: Baggage from American Airlines Flight AAL124 from
New York will be arriving at claim four."

I turned at the announcement.

"Over there," Jagger said, pointing to the stream of passengers
appearing near the carousel just mentioned.

We walked toward them, and it was clear from their chatter that the
lot of them were Americans. Francesca's flight, no doubt about it.

"Easy." Jagger laid a hand on my shoulder. "I know you're excited to see your girl, mate, but you're bouncing around like a boxer. Calm down."

I stopped bobbing between my feet, but my gaze remained glued to the crowd. The passengers exiting customs were thinning now. Where was she? Fucking hell, this was exactly why I wanted to pay for a private plane. She wouldn't let me, of course, stubborn minx. Barely allowed me to upgrade her and Sof to first class.

And then they were there. The security doors opened, and Francesca walked through carrying what looked like a month's worth of luggage strapped across her chest, towing a booster seat in one hand and holding tightly to a bleary-eyed Sofia with the other.

She looked tired, of course. But still mind-blowingly gorgeous in a way she was never conscious of, and that only made her that much sexier. Casual as always in a pullover that fell off one shoulder and a pair of those tight yoga pants that made her arse look like it had been sculpted by Michelangelo. Hair loose and curly about her shoulders, she looked a bit like Jennifer Beals in *Flashdance*—one of my mum's favorite movies. And, as it happens, my first childhood crush.

For a half-second, I could hear Mum teasing me after I'd watched the scene where she dances to "Maniac" for the thousandth time. I saw her smile when I swore up and down it was because I liked the choreography, not the way the actress looked in those legwarmers when she was running in place.

Not for the first time, I wondered what Mum would have thought of Francesca and the granddaughter we'd made her.

My chest squeezed so hard at the thought, I thought my heart might actually stop.

So this was what it felt like to love someone so much it hurt. Two someones, really. Fuck me, I really was done for.

"That them?" Jagger's voice pulled me out of my daze.

He knew, of course. Anyone else would have known from the grin that was practically splitting my face in two.

My girls were here. Finally, they'd come home.

"Ces!" I shouted, unable to help myself.

I should have waited until she found me, of course, rather than calling any attention to myself in the crowded terminal. But instead I found myself jogging through the crowd, waving like a crazy man until Francesca and Sofia's faces found me and promptly lit up like torches.

"Daddy!"

Most men might have had a heart attack when they heard that word used for them. But now, I'd never stop loving the way it sounded. Not coming from her. Not as she shook her mother off and darted through the crowd like a flea until she had the space to spring for me with everything her tiny legs could muster.

"Hey, peanut!" I caught Sofia's flying leap into my arms, sweeping her off the ground and to my hip with ease. "You made it, did you? I've been waiting here for years."

She'd grown over the last month. I was sure of it. Still tiny like her mum, but a father knows.

"You're huge," I informed her. "What's Mummy been feeding you, eh? Super human growth juice?"

"She keeps trying to make oh-kimono-mocha," Sofia informed me with her particular pronunciation of *okonomiyaki* that I'd never for the life of me correct. "But it doesn't taste like yours, Dad."

I grinned, touched my nose to hers. "'Course it doesn't. That's because Daddy's got the magic touch."

"I'll say he does."

We turned to find Francesca standing to my left, carrying the car seat, wearing her enormous backpack, and also towing the yacht-sized suitcase behind her.

"Shit," I said. "You didn't have to do that, babe. I would've gotten it for you."

"I didn't mind."

There was no passive aggression in her tone. Instead of being upset I'd been too busy reuniting with my daughter to help with her bag, Francesca was watching the two of us with the same expression of a cat who'd just found a massive bowl of cream. Satisfaction, that's what that was. And love.

Which reminded me of another kind of satisfaction I could bring her.

I leaned down and pressed a short but extremely thorough kiss to that heart-shaped mouth. Fuck, she tasted good. Even after seven hours on the plane, she still had the flavor of tea, honey, a bit of lavender, and something that was just her. Heaven, that's what it was.

"God, I've missed you," I mumbled against her lips.

They curved into that sweet smile, and if I wasn't mistaken, those were her hands that reached around for a cheeky grab of my arse.

"Right back at you, chef," she said.

And just like that, I was half hard.

"Fuck, you little minx. What do you think you're doing?"

"Swear jar, Daddy."

We broke apart to find Sofia, still perched in my right arm, holding out her little hand expectantly. With a sigh, I fished a pound coin out of my pocket and handed it to her.

She looked at it. "That's not enough. It's a dollar for each swear."

"We don't have those in the UK, babe. That's one pound sterling—worth more than a dollar, I'll have you know."

Sofia shook her head, causing her shiny black curls to bounce around her face. "No, it's not."

I frowned. "Yes, it is."

"No, it's not. It's a coin. Dollars are paper. Everyone knows that."

I sighed and swallowed back the urge to argue. Five seconds off the plane, and she was already at it. I'd give my life in a second for this tiny creature, but she already knew how to press my buttons like no one else.

"Let's not start that again," Francesca cooed, taking Sofia from me and dropping her to the ground. "This one barely slept on the plane. Can we get out of here? She needs dinner and a nap, pronto."

"Absolutely," I said. "My car's waiting outside. Come on, girls."

I walked them toward the exit, where Jagger was waiting, soon joined by Elsie. Both of them looked excited. But also a little worried.

"Jagger. Els. This is Francesca and Sofia. Girls, these are the people who make my life work, Jagger Harrington and Elsie Bledsoe."

"Pleased to meet you," Francesca greeted each of them warmly with a kiss on the cheek. "We've heard so much."

Sofia hid behind her mother, though I could tell she was curious about both of them. She really must have been tired. Any other time, and she would have been interrogating them about their favorite Disney characters.

"Has Ben brought round the car?" I asked Elsie.

"He has, but, sir, you might want to choose another—"

"Meet us out front," I barked, unwilling to wait any longer.

"Mate," Jagger said. "You should probably—"

"Sir—"

Eager to be done with the airport, I grabbed Francesca's bags with one hand, her hand with the other, and towed her and Sofia out the door, followed by Jagger and Elsie.

We only made it about five feet.

"Xavier!"

"Your Grace!"

"Your Grace, over here!"

Flashes went off everywhere, brighter than the sun and much more invasive. It seemed Elsie's ploy hadn't worked as well as I thought.

Where there had been one photographer, now there were at least fifteen, all of them crowding the exit like flies to honey.

"Back off," I snarled, trying, and failing, to see around them to the Escalade.

The paps, however, were ruthless, forming a wall of cameras and notepads as they continued peppering me with questions.

"Your Grace, is it true your uncle is still missing?"

"Is he dead?"

"Did you kill him?"

"Who's that with you?"

"Why are you holding her hand?"

"How do you know the child?"

"Is that your love child?"

"Are you dating a single mum?"

"Mommy?" I heard Sofia wonder through a voice choked with tears. "Mommy, what's happening?"

"I don't know, baby," Francesca murmured, picking her up and cowering behind me. "Xavi, what's going on?"

I couldn't answer, only because I didn't know exactly what to say. More photographers were already arriving, and now other people were joining the fray, eager to learn what all the fuss was. The Escalade might as well have been on the other side of the world.

So I pushed myself in front of them silently and did whatever I could to shield them from the chaos, still wondering how the hell I could explain this once I had the chance.

Because how do you tell the people you love that you unwittingly just invited them to a scavenger hunt?

And what's more, they turned out to be the vultures' next meal?

―――

To Be Continued in *Then Come Lies*
Coming Fall 2022

To join my blogger/bookstagram/TikTok list, please visit **www.
nicolefrenchromance.com/bloggers**

ACKNOWLEDGMENTS

Eighteen months. That's how long it's been since I last published a book. Maybe more at this point.

I won't go into all the reasons why you've had to wait so long for this book. You know. We all know. The last two years have been utter catastrophe from one side of the planet to the other. I'm just grateful for my corner, where I've been able to take solace in this story from time to time, and for you, readers, whose patience has been so kind and who (I hope) haven't forgotten me yet. Thank you so much for reading.

Other people, of course, were instrumental in making this book happen. A massive thanks has to be extended to Patricia and Dawn, who cheered me through every chapter and waited patiently for others. Best alpha team ever. Kymberly and Lacie added much valued feedback as well—your love of these stories is utterly inspiring. Thank you as well to Michaela and Jayne, my English beta readers who made sure Xavier didn't sound like a total idiot when he talked (well, at least in the right way) and who offered much-needed comments on the basics of English society and norms. You are worth your weight in gold and more.

Thank you as well to my amazing support team: Danielle Leigh, my assistant, whose ever-present cheer and kindness is a light in these dark days; Dani Sanchez and crew at Wildfire Marketing, who never doubted I would finish even when I kept. Pushing. The. Date; Emily Hainsworth, my editor extraordinaire who will never be rid of me; and Marla Esposito, whose pinch-hitting as a proofreader made the book shine.

Lastly, to my cohort of romance authors. This community inspires me alway—a force of literature largely by women for women can never be stopped. In particular I am grateful for Jane, Crystal, and Laura for always providing honesty and kindness whenever I need it.

Made in the USA
Las Vegas, NV
19 May 2023

72277454R00185